RAVE REVIEWS FOR
THE BOOK OF LOST NAMES

"A fascinating, heartrending page-turner that, like the real-life forgers who inspired the novel, should never be forgotten. A riveting historical tale that I devoured in a single sitting."

—Kristina McMorris, *New York Times* bestselling author of *Sold on a Monday*

"Harmel brilliantly imagines the life of a young Polish-French Jewish woman during the depths of World War II. . . . This thoughtful work will touch readers with its testament to the endurance of hope."

—*Publishers Weekly* (starred review)

"Not since *The Nightingale* have I finished a book and been so choked with emotion. . . . Sweeping and magnificent."

—Fiona Davis, *New York Times* bestselling author of *The Lions of Fifth Avenue*

"A heart-stopping tale of survival and heroism centered on a female forger who risks everything to help Jewish children escape Nazi-occupied France."

—*People* (The 20 Best Books to Read This Summer, 2020)

"With exceptional skill, Kristin Harmel constructs *The Winemaker's Wife* between the past and the present, giving equal weight and importance to both. . . . Once you start reading this moving novel, you will not be able to put it down until you reach the last page."

—Armando Lucas Correa, *USA Today* bestselling
author of *The German Girl*

"The lives of several strong women intervene in a complicated historical tale of love and war. . . . This World War II novel takes a unique approach."

—*Booklist*

"Written in heart-wrenching prose, *The Winemaker's Wife* is a complex story of love, betrayal, and impossible courage. . . . I couldn't turn the pages fast enough and savored every moment at the same time."

—Anita Hughes, bestselling author of *Christmas in Paris*

THE ROOM ON RUE AMÉLIE

"Harmel writes a poignant novel based loosely on the true story of an American woman who helped on the Comet Line, which rescued hundreds of airmen and soldiers. This compelling story celebrates hope and bravery in the face of evil."

—*Booklist*

"*The Room on Rue Amélie* is a World War II story of courage against all odds and fighting for what you believe in."

—*PopSugar* (31 of the Best New Books You
Should Read This Spring, 2018)

WHEN WE MEET AGAIN

"Harmel . . . authentically weaves American history into this engaging novel. An appealing family saga that connects generations and reaffirms love."

—*Kirkus Reviews*

"Centering on a lesser-known facet of American history, *When We Meet Again* is a gripping novel of history, art, and the power of love. Kristin Harmel's work is always riveting, but her storytelling reaches new heights with a tale that is layered, complex, and satisfying to the last page."

—Michelle Gable, *New York Times* bestselling author

THE SWEETNESS OF FORGETTING

"Kristin Harmel writes with such insight and heart that her characters will stay with you long after you've finished her books."

—Emily Giffin, *New York Times* bestselling author

"Kristin Harmel . . . has a way of bringing the reader into her stories in such a powerful way that they can often forget they're reading at all. *The Sweetness of Forgetting* may just be Harmel's best book yet."

—Lisa Steinke, SheKnows Book Lounge

"Absolutely enthralling . . . Readers will remember *The Sweetness of Forgetting* long after the final page is turned."

—*Fresh Fiction*

THE
Book OF
Lost Names

KRISTIN HARMEL

G

GALLERY BOOKS

NEW YORK LONDON TORONTO SYDNEY NEW DELHI

G

Gallery Books
An Imprint of Simon & Schuster, Inc.
1230 Avenue of the Americas
New York, NY 10020

First Gallery Books trade paperback edition May 2021

GALLERY BOOKS and colophon are registered trademarks of Simon & Schuster, Inc.

For information about special discounts for bulk purchases, please contact Simon & Schuster Special Sales at 1-866-506-1949 or business@simonandschuster.com.

The Simon & Schuster Speakers Bureau can bring authors to your live event. For more information or to book an event, contact the Simon & Schuster Speakers Bureau at 1-866-248-3049 or visit our website at www.simonspeakers.com.

Interior design by Jaime Putorti

Manufactured in Canada

10

Library of Congress Cataloging-in-Publication Data is available.

ISBN 978-1-9821-3189-0
ISBN 978-1-9821-3190-6 (pbk)
ISBN 978-1-9821-3191-3 (ebook)

*To my Swan Valley sisters—Wendy, Allison, Alyson, Emily,
and Linda—who understand, as only writers and readers
truly can, that books shape destiny.*

*And to librarians and booksellers everywhere, who ensure that the
books with the power to change lives find their way into
the hands of the people who need them most.*

Chapter One

May 2005

It's a Saturday morning, and I'm midway through my shift at the Winter Park Public Library when I see it.

The book I last laid eyes on more than six decades ago.

The book I believed had vanished forever.

The book that meant everything to me.

It's staring out at me from a photograph in the *New York Times*, which someone has left open on the returns desk. The world goes silent as I reach for the newspaper, my hand trembling nearly as much as it did the last time I held the book. "It can't be," I whisper.

I gaze at the picture. A man in his seventies looks back at me, his snowy hair sparse and wispy, his eyes froglike behind bulbous glasses.

"Sixty Years After End of World War II, German Librarian Seeks to Reunite Looted Books with Rightful Owners," declares the headline, and I want to cry out to the man in the image that *I* am the rightful owner of the book he's holding, the faded leather-bound volume with the peeling bottom right corner and the gilded spine bearing the title *Epitres et Evangiles*. It belongs to me—and to Rémy, a man who died long ago, a man I vowed after the war to think of no more.

But he's been in my thoughts this week anyhow, despite my best efforts. Tomorrow, the eighth of May, the world will celebrate the sixtieth anniversary of Victory in Europe Day. It's impossible, with all the young newscasters speaking solemnly of the war as if they could conceivably understand it, not to think of Rémy, not to think of the time we spent together then, not to think of the people we saved and the way it all ended. Though my son tells me I'm blessed to have such a sharp mind in my old age, like many blessings this one is mixed.

Most days, I just long to forget.

I blink away the uninvited thoughts of Rémy and return my attention to the article. The man in the photo is Otto Kühn, a librarian from the Zentral- und Landesbibliothek in Berlin, who has made it his life's mission to return books looted by the Nazis. There are apparently more than a million such books in his library's collection alone, but the one he's holding in the photo— *my* book—is the one he says keeps him up at night.

"This religious text," Kühn has told the reporter, "is my favorite among the many mysteries that occupy our shelves. Published in Paris in 1732, it's a very rare book, but that's not what makes it extraordinary. It is unique because within it, we find an intriguing puzzle: some sort of code. To whom did it belong? What does the code mean? How did the Germans come to possess it during the war? These are the questions that haunt me."

I feel tears in my eyes, tears that have no place there. I wipe them away, angry at myself for still being so emotional after all these years. "How nice it must be," I say softly to Kühn's picture, "to be haunted by questions rather than ghosts."

"Um, Mrs. Abrams? Are you talking to that newspaper?"

I'm jolted out of the fog of my memory by the voice of Jenny Fish, the library's assistant manager. She's the type who complains about everything—and who seems to enjoy suggesting at every opportunity that since I'm eighty-six, I might want to think about retiring soon. She is always eyeing me suspiciously, as if she simply cannot believe that at my age, I'd still want to work here.

She doesn't understand what it means to love books so passionately that you would die without them, that you would simply stop breathing, stop existing. It is quite beyond me, in fact, why she became a librarian in the first place.

"Yes, Jenny, indeed I am," I reply, without looking up.

"Yes, well, you probably shouldn't be doing that in front of library guests." She says it without a trace of irony. "They might think you're senile." She does not have a sense of humor.

"Thank you, Jenny. Your advice is always so very helpful."

She nods solemnly. It is also apparently beyond her comprehension that someone who looks like me—small, white-haired, grandmotherly—is capable of sarcasm.

Today, though, I have no time for her. All I can think about is the book. The book that held so many secrets. The book that was taken from me before I could learn whether it contained the one answer I so desperately needed.

And now, a mere plane flight away, there's a man who holds the key to unlocking everything.

"Do I dare?" I murmur to the photo of Otto Kühn. I respond to my own question before doubt can creep in. "I must. I owe it to the children."

"Mrs. Abrams?" It's Jenny again, addressing me by my surname, though I've told her a thousand times to call me Eva, just as she addresses the younger librarians by their given names. But alas, I am nothing to her but an old lady. One's reward for marching through the decades is a gradual process of erasure.

"Yes, Jenny?" I finally look up at her.

"Do you need to go home?" I suspect she says it with the expectation that I'll decline. She's smirking a bit, certain that she has asserted her superiority. "Perhaps gather yourself?"

So it gives me great pleasure to look her right in the eye, smile, and say, "Yes, Jenny, thank you ever so much. I think I'll do just that."

I grab the newspaper and go.

As soon as I arrive at my house—a cozy bungalow just a five-minute walk from the library—I log on to my computer.

Yes, I have a computer. And yes, I know how to use it. My son, Ben, has a bad habit of pronouncing computer terms slowly in my presence—*in-ter-net* and *e-mail-ing*—as if the whole concept of technology might be too much for me. I suppose I can't blame him, not entirely. By the time Ben was born, the war was eight years past, and I'd left France—and the person I used to be—far behind. Ben knew me only as a librarian and housewife who sometimes stumbled over her English.

Somewhere along the way, he got the mistaken idea that I am a simple person. What would he say if he knew the truth?

It's my fault for never telling him, for failing to correct the error. But when you grow comfortable hiding within a protective shell, it's harder than one might expect to stand up and say, "Actually, folks, *this* is who I am."

Perhaps I also feared that Ben's father, my husband, Louis, would leave me if he realized I was something other than the person I wanted him to see. He left me anyhow—pancreatic cancer a decade ago—and though I've missed his companionship, I've also had the strange realization that I probably could have done without him much sooner.

I go to the website for Delta—habit, I suppose, since Louis traveled often for business and was part of the airline's frequent-flier program. The prices are exorbitant, but I have plenty stashed away in savings. It's just before noon, and there's a flight that leaves three hours from now, and another leaving at 9:35 tonight, connecting in Amsterdam tomorrow, and landing in Berlin at 3:40 p.m. I click immediately and book the latter. There is something poetic about knowing I will arrive in Berlin sixty years to the day after the Germans signed an unconditional surrender to the Allies in that very city.

A shiver runs through me, and I don't know whether it's fear or excitement.

I must pack, but before that, I'll need to call Ben. He won't understand, but perhaps it's finally time for him to learn that his mother isn't the person he always believed her to be.

Chapter Two

July 1942

The sky above the Sorbonne Library in Paris's fifth arrondissement was gray and pregnant with rain, the air heavy and thick. Eva Traube stood just outside the main doors, cursing the humidity. She knew, even without consulting a mirror, that her dark, shoulder-length hair had already doubled in volume, making her look like a mushroom. Not that it made a difference; the only thing anyone would notice was the six-pointed yellow star stitched onto the left side of her cardigan. It erased all the other parts of her that mattered—her identity as a daughter, a friend, an Anglophile working toward her doctorate in English literature.

To so many in Paris now, she was nothing but a Jew.

She shuddered, feeling a sudden chill. The sky appeared foreboding, as if it knew something she didn't. The shadows cast by the gathering clouds seemed to be the physical embodiment of the darkness that had fallen over the city itself.

Courage, her father would say, his French still rough around the edges, with the vestiges of a Polish accent. *Cheer up. The Germans can only bother us if we let them.*

But his optimism was unrealistic. The Germans were perfectly free to bother France's Jews anytime they wanted to, whether Eva and her parents acquiesced or not.

She looked skyward again, considering. She had planned to walk home in order to avoid the Métro and the new regulations—Jews were to ride only in the last, sweltering, airless car—but if the skies opened up, perhaps she'd be better off belowground.

"Ah, *mon petit rat de bibliothèque.*" A deep voice just behind Eva jarred her from her thoughts. She knew who it was before she turned, for there was only one person she knew who used "my little book rat" as a pet name for her.

"*Bonjour*, Joseph," she said stiffly. She could feel the heat creeping up her cheeks, and she was embarrassed by her attraction to him. Joseph Pelletier was one of the only other students in the English Department who wore the yellow star—though unlike her, he was only half Jewish and nonobservant. He was tall, his shoulders broad, his hair thick and dark, his eyes a pale blue. He looked like a film star, a sentiment she knew was shared by many of the girls in the department—even the Catholic ones, whose parents would never allow their daughters to be courted by a Jew. Not that Joseph seemed the type to court anyone. He was more likely to seduce you in a shadowy corner of the library and leave you swooning.

"You look awfully pensive, little one," he said, smiling at Eva as he kissed her on both cheeks in greeting. His mother had known hers since before she was born, and he had a way of making her feel as if she were still the small child she'd been when she first met him, though she was now twenty-three to his twenty-six.

"Just wondering if it will rain," she replied, inching away from him before he could notice that the physical contact was making her blush.

"Eva." The way he said her name made her heart skip. When she dared look at him again, his eyes were full of something disquieting. "I've come looking for you."

"What for?" For a split second, she hoped he would say, *To invite you to dinner.* But that was perfectly ridiculous. Where would they go, in any case? Everything was closed to people who wore the star.

He leaned in. "To warn you. There are rumors that something is brewing. A massive roundup, before Friday." His breath was warm on her ear. "They have as many as twenty thousand foreign-born Jews on the list."

"Twenty thousand? That's impossible."

"Impossible? No. My friends have very reliable sources."

"Your friends?" Their eyes locked. She'd heard about the underground, of course, people working to undermine the Nazis here in Paris. Is that what he meant? Who else would know such a thing? "How can you be so sure they're right?"

"How can you be sure they're not? As a precaution, I think it's best for you and your parents to go into hiding for the next few days."

"Into hiding?" Her father was a typewriter repairman, her mother a part-time seamstress. They barely had the means to pay for their apartment, let alone a place to lie low. "Perhaps we should check into the Ritz, then?"

"It's not a joke, Eva."

"I dislike the Germans as much as you do, Joseph, but twenty thousand people? No, I don't believe it."

"Just be careful, little one." It was at that moment that the sky opened up. Joseph was swept away with the rain, vanishing into the sea of blooming umbrellas on the fountain-flanked sidewalk leading away from the library.

Eva swore under her breath. Raindrops pelted the pavement, making it slick as oil in the late afternoon half-light, and as she dashed from the steps toward the rue des Écoles, she was drenched in an instant. She tried to pull her cardigan over her head to shield herself from the downpour, but doing so only meant that her star, as big as the palm of her hand, was now front and center.

"Dirty Jew," a man muttered as he passed, his face hidden by his umbrella.

No, Eva wouldn't be riding the Métro today. She took a deep breath and began to run toward the river, toward the soaring mass of Notre-Dame, toward home.

"How was the library today?" Eva's father sat at the head of their small table while her mother, her hair wrapped in a faded handkerchief, her stout body swathed in a threadbare cotton dress, spooned watery potato soup into his bowl, and then into Eva's. They had all gotten caught in the rain, and now their sweaters hung drying just inside the open window, the yellow stars facing them like three little soldiers all in a row, silently watching.

"It was fine." Eva waited for her mother to sit before taking a small taste of the bland meal.

"I don't know why you insist on continuing to go," Eva's mother said. She paused for a spoonful of soup and wrinkled her nose. "They'll never allow you to get your degree."

"Things will change, *Mamusia*. I know they will."

"Your generation and its optimism." Eva's mother sighed.

"Eva is right, Faiga. The Germans can't keep up these regulations forever. They make no sense." Eva's father smiled a smile they all knew was false.

"Thanks, *Tatuś*." Eva and her parents still addressed each other with Polish terms of endearment, though Eva, born in Paris, had never set foot in her parents' native country. "So how was your work today?"

Her father looked down at his soup. "Monsieur Goujon does not know how much longer he can continue paying me. We may have to . . ." His gaze flicked to Mamusia, then to Eva. "We may have to leave Paris. If I lose my job, there's no other way for me to make a living here."

Eva had known this moment was coming, but still it hit her like a punch to the gut. If they left Paris, she knew she would never return to the Sorbonne, would never complete the degree in English she had worked so hard for.

Her father's employment had been in jeopardy for a long time, since the Germans started to systematically remove Jews from French society. His reputation as the best typewriter and mimeograph repairman in Paris had saved him for the time being, though he was no longer allowed to work inside any government offices. But Monsieur Goujon, his old supervisor, had taken pity on him and was paying him for off-the-books work, most of which he did at home. In fact, there were eleven typewriters in various stages of disassembly currently lined up in the parlor, indicating a long night of work ahead.

Eva took a long breath and dug deep for some hope. "Perhaps it would be for the best if we left, Tatuś."

He blinked at her, and her mother went silent. "For the best, *słoneczko?*" Her father had always called her that, Polish for "little sun," and she wondered if he saw the bitter irony in it now, as she did. After all, what was the sun but a yellow star?

"You see, I ran into Joseph Pelletier today—"

"Oh, Joseph!" Her mother cut her off, placing her palms on her own cheeks like a smitten schoolgirl. "Such a handsome boy. Did he finally ask you for a date? I always hoped the two of you might end up together."

"No, Mamusia, nothing like that." Eva exchanged glances with her father. Fixing Eva up with a suitable young man seemed to occupy an absurd proportion of Mamusia's thoughts, as if they weren't in the middle of a war. "Actually, he sought me out to tell me something. He heard a rumor that as many as twenty thousand foreign-born Jews are to be rounded up sometime within the next few days."

Eva's mother frowned. "That's ridiculous. What on earth would they do with twenty thousand of us?"

"That's what I said." Eva glanced at her father, who still hadn't spoken. "Tatuś?"

"It's certainly a frightening thing to hear," he said after a long pause, his words slow and measured. "Though Joseph seems the type to embellish."

"Surely not. He's such a nice young man," Eva's mother said instantly.

"Faiga, he has made Eva upset, and for what? So that he can puff out his chest and show her that he's well connected? A decent fellow shouldn't feel the need to do that." Tatuś turned back to Eva. "Słoneczko, I don't want to ignore what Joseph said. And I agree there is *something* brewing. But I've heard at least a dozen rumors this month, and this is the most outrageous. Twenty thousand? It's not possible."

"Still, Tatuś, what if he's right?"

In response, he rose from the table and returned a few seconds later with a small printed tract. He handed it to Eva, who skimmed it quickly. *Take all necessary measures to hide . . . Fight the police . . . Seek to flee.* "What is this?" she whispered as she handed it to her mother.

"It was slipped under our door yesterday," her father said.

"Why didn't you tell us? It sounds like a warning, just like what Joseph said."

He shook his head slowly. "This isn't the first one, Eva. The Germans rule with fear as much as they do with their weapons. If we cower every time a false notice goes around, they will have won, won't they? They will have taken our sense of security, our sense of well-being. I won't allow that."

"At any rate, we haven't done anything wrong," Eva's mother interjected. "We're productive citizens."

"I'm not so sure that will matter in the end." Eva's father leaned over and patted Eva's hand, then touched his wife's cheek. "But we will be all right for now. So let us eat before the soup grows cold."

Eva had already lost her appetite, though, and as she pushed potatoes around in her bowl, her stomach twisted with a sense of foreboding that her father's words couldn't banish.

Later that night, after Mamusia had gone to sleep, Tatuś found Eva in the small library off the parlor, shelves piled high with all the books the two of them treasured so much. He had taught her to love reading, one of the greatest gifts a parent could give a child, and in doing so, he had opened the world to her. Most evenings, she and her father read here in companionable silence, but for now, Eva was too distracted. Instead, she sat on the couch, doodling in a notebook, a nervous habit that dated back to her childhood, when sketching the people and things around her had made her feel more at ease.

"Słoneczko," he said softly.

She looked up, her pencil pausing over a detailed drawing of the modest chandelier overhead. "I thought you were in bed, Tatuś."

"I couldn't sleep." He came to sit beside her. "There's something I need to tell you. If the Germans come for your mother and me, I want you to go see Monsieur Goujon immediately."

Eva stared at him. "You said you didn't believe Joseph."

"I don't. But terrible things are happening here all the time. I would be a fool to pretend they can't happen to us. But you, słoneczko, you should be safe. You are French. If we are taken, you need to flee before things get worse."

"Tatuś—"

"Get yourself to the free zone—and if possible, on to safety in Switzerland. Wait there for the war to end. We will come back for you."

She felt suddenly numb with grief. The free zone? The border lay many kilometers south of Paris, slicing off the half of the country the Nazis had agreed to leave to the French. Switzerland felt worlds away. "Why can't we all leave together? Now?"

"Because we would be too conspicuous, Eva. I just want you to be ready for the day you might have to go. You'll need documents that don't identify you as a Jew. Monsieur Goujon will help you."

She felt as if the breath had been knocked out of her. "You've already spoken with him?"

"Yes, and I've paid him, Eva. Everything I had in savings. He gave me his word. He has access to everything needed to make you a set of false papers. It will be enough to get you out of Paris."

She blinked back tears. "I won't go without you, Tatuś."

He reached for her hands. "You must, Eva! Promise me you will, if it comes to that."

"But—"

"I need you to give me your word. I cannot survive if I don't believe you are doing all you can to do the same."

She looked into his eyes. "I promise. But, Tatuś, we still have time, don't we? Time to find another plan that allows us to leave for the free zone together?"

"Of course, słoneczko. Of course." But his gaze slipped away. By the time he looked back, the despair in his eyes was deep, dark, and Eva knew he didn't believe his own words.

It was just past four in the morning two nights later when the first knock came. Eva had been sleeping fitfully, dreaming of fierce dragons encircling a castle, and as she lurched to the surface of consciousness, her chest seized with fear. *Joseph was right. They're here.*

She could hear her father moving through the apartment, his footsteps slow and steady. "Tatuś!" she called out as she grabbed her robe and jammed her feet into the worn leather boots she had placed beside her bed for the past year in case she needed to flee. What else would she need if the Germans had come for them? Should she pack a bag? Would there be time? Why hadn't she listened to Joseph?

"Tatuś, please!" she cried as her father's footsteps stopped. She wanted to tell him to wait, to stop time, to freeze for one last moment in the *before*, but she couldn't find the words, so instead, she lurched out of her bedroom into the parlor. She arrived just in time to see him open the door.

She clutched her robe around her, waiting for the barked order from the Germans who were surely on the other side of the threshold. But instead, she heard a female voice, and could see her father's face soften slightly as he stepped back. A second later, Madame Fontain, their neighbor from the end of the hall, followed him into the apartment, her face pinched.

"Tatuś?" Eva asked, and he turned. "It's not the Germans?"

"No, słoneczko." The lines on his face hadn't fully relaxed, and Eva knew he'd been as afraid as she'd been. "Madame Fontain's mother has fallen ill. She was wondering if you or your mother would come sit with her daughters while she takes her to *Docteur* Patenaude's apartment."

"Simone and Colette are still sleeping, so they shouldn't be any trouble," Madame Fontain said, not making eye contact. "They're only two and four."

"Yes, I know how old they are," Eva said stiffly. Just the day before, Eva had happened upon the girls in the courtyard. She had bent to say hello, and the older one, Colette, had begun to cheerfully chatter about butterflies and apples, when suddenly, Madame Fontain had appeared out of nowhere and hastily pulled both girls away. As they'd disappeared around the corner, Eva had overheard her scolding them about the danger of socializing with a Jew.

"I tried other apartments but no one else would answer the door. Please. I wouldn't ask if it wasn't necessary."

"Of course we will watch your daughters." Eva's mother had emerged from her bedroom, her nightgown already replaced by a simple cotton dress and cardigan. "That's what neighbors do. Eva will come with me. Won't you, dear?"

"Yes, Mamusia, of course." The girls' father was gone to the front, possibly dead, and they had no one else.

"Eva, get dressed, quickly." Eva's mother turned back to Madame Fontain. "Go. Don't worry. Your girls will be fine."

"Thank you," Madame Fontain said, but still, she wouldn't meet their gazes. "I'll be back as soon as I can." She pressed a key into Mamusia's hand and was gone before they could say another word.

Eva quickly threw on the dress she had worn yesterday and smoothed her hair before rejoining her parents in the parlor. "You do know Madame Fontain's feelings about Jews, don't you?" Eva couldn't resist asking.

"Half of Paris feels the same," her mother said wearily. "But if we shrink from them, if we lose our goodness, we let them erase us. We cannot do that, Eva. We cannot."

"I know." She sighed and kissed her father goodbye. "Go back to bed, Tatuś. Mamusia and I will be fine."

"Good girl," he said, kissing her cheek. "Look out for your

mother." He kissed Mamusia gently, and as they stepped out into the hall, he closed the door. It latched with a gentle click behind them.

Two hours later, with Colette and Simone still asleep in their beds and Mamusia snoring lightly beside her on the sofa in Madame Fontain's apartment, Eva had just dozed off when a banging in the hall startled her awake. The faint light of early dawn was filtering through the edges of the blackout curtains. Perhaps Madame Fontain and her mother had returned.

Eva rose from the sofa, careful not to disturb Mamusia. She crept to the door and put her eye to the peephole, expecting to see Madame Fontain fumbling with her keys. What she saw instead made her gasp and draw back in horror. Trembling, she forced herself to look again.

In the hall, three French policemen stood in front of Eva's own apartment a few doors down. The same banging sound that had awoken her came again; it was a uniformed officer pounding on her door. *No, Tatuś,* Eva screamed silently. *Don't answer!*

But the door to the apartment swung open, and her father stepped out, dressed in his best suit, his yellow star affixed perfectly to the left side. One of the policemen, the one holding a neat sheaf of papers, said something to him, but Eva couldn't quite make it out. Biting her lip so hard she could taste blood, she pressed her ear to the door.

"Where is your wife?" Eva could hear a deep voice asking. Another officer shoved his way inside the apartment, pushing Tatuś aside.

"My wife?" Tatuś sounded strangely calm.

"Faiga Traube, age forty-eight, born 1894 in Kraków, Poland." The man's voice was taut with impatience.

"Yes, of course. Well, she's out caring for the children of a sick friend."

"Where? What is the address?"

"I'm afraid I don't know."

"Well, when will she be back?"

"I'm not certain of that, either."

Eva could hear the policemen mumbling to each other. The officer who'd gone into the apartment emerged and shook his head.

"And your daughter?" The first officer spoke again, his tone angrier. "Eva Traube? Age twenty-three?"

"She's with her mother." Her father's tone was suddenly icy. "But she was born here in France. You have no need to bother her."

"She is on our list."

"Your list is wrong."

"We are never wrong."

"You think there is anything about this that is right?" her father retorted, his voice finally rising, and Eva heard a muffled thud and a sharp intake of breath. She dared look through the peephole again and saw her father clutching his nose. One of the policemen had struck him. Eva clenched her fists, her eyes prickling with tears, as she pressed her ear back against the door.

"Enough of your insolence. You will come with us now," the man said. "Or if you prefer, we will be happy to shoot you right here. One less Jew for the trains, no matter to me."

Eva stifled a gasp.

"Let me just pack a bag," her father said.

"Oh, we'll come back for your valuables, don't worry."

When Tatuś didn't reply, Eva looked back through the peephole just in time to see her father pulling their door closed behind him. He glanced once over his shoulder, in the direction of the Fontains' apartment. Did he know she was watching? That she had heard everything?

But it didn't matter. Tatuś was gone before she could blink, and a minute later, the front door of the building closed with a loud thump of finality. Eva raced to the window, pushed the blackout curtains aside, and stared down at the street, which was clogged with dark police trucks and a swarm of uniforms leading men, women, and children—some of them looking bewildered, some angry, and some crying—away from their homes. Eva recognized the Bibrowskas—the mother, Ana, the father, Max, and the children, Henri and Aline, who were just toddlers—and the Krosbergs, the elderly couple across the way who always waved to her as she left for the university in the mornings.

Eva watched, her hand to her mouth to muffle her sobs, as her father was shoved toward a truck. A hand came from the back and pulled him in. Just before he disappeared, he glanced up toward the building, and Eva pressed her palm against the cool glass. He nodded, and Eva was sure he had seen her, sure he knew that her silent wave was a promise that she would look out for Mamusia until he returned.

"Eva?" Her mother's voice sounded thick and groggy behind her in the darkened room. "What on earth are you doing?"

Eva watched the vehicles pull away before turning to her mother. "Tatuś is gone," she whispered. "The police . . ." She couldn't finish her sentence.

"*What?*" Her mother leaped from the couch and lurched toward the door. "Where? We have to go after him! Why didn't you wake me, Eva?" Her words were choked as she clawed in vain at the locks. But her hands were shaking, and Eva was there to catch her when she collapsed to the floor, sobs racking her body. "Why, Eva? Why didn't you stop them? What have you done?"

Eva felt a surge of guilt. "Mamusia," she said gently as her mother wailed in her arms. "They were also here for you. And me."

Mamusia sniffled. "That's impossible. You are French."

"I am a Jew. That is all they see."

Just then, a sharp cry came from the girls' bedroom. "*Maman? Where are you, Maman?*" It was the older daughter, Colette, her voice high and scared.

Mamusia looked up at Eva in anguish. "We have to go after your father," she whispered. She grabbed Eva's hands, her grip like a vise. "We have to save him."

"Not yet," Eva said firmly as Colette cried out for her mother again. "First, we must figure out how to save ourselves."

Chapter Three

Dawn broke an hour later, and with it, silent chaos. The
street below the Fontains' window filled with people, but
there was hardly a sound. Neighbors clustered together, whispering, none of them wearing the yellow star. The Jews of the
Marais district had vanished last night.

"We must go look for your father," Eva's mother said, hugging herself as she rocked back and forth on the Fontains' sofa.

The two little girls, still in their nightgowns, sat on the floor,
staring at her with wide eyes. Eva finally took a deep breath,
turned from the window, and crossed the room to kneel between
them. She put one arm around Colette, the other around Simone.
"We're not going anywhere," she said with forced cheer, squeezing the girls' shoulders. "Not until Madame Fontain returns."

"When is Maman coming back?" Colette whimpered. It
was clear that she could read the fear in the room, though she
couldn't understand it.

"Soon, my dear." Eva forced a smile. "There's no need to
worry."

"Then why is Madame Traube so afraid?"

Eva glanced at her mother, who was pale as an unbaked baguette. "She's not," she said in a tone firm enough to get her mother's attention. Mamusia looked up, her gaze unfocused, as Eva added, "She's simply not feeling very well. Are you, Mamusia?" Her mother still didn't respond.

Colette searched Eva's eyes for a minute, and then her face relaxed. "Shall I get her something to help her to feel better?"

"I think that's a wonderful idea, Colette. Why don't you take Simone with you?"

Colette nodded solemnly before grabbing her sister's hand and leading her toward their shared bedroom.

Eva turned to her mother as soon as the girls had disappeared. "You need to pull yourself together."

"But your father . . ."

"Is gone," Eva said firmly, though she couldn't keep the tremor out of her voice. Fear always found its way in through the cracks. "We will come up with a plan to secure his release. I promise. We can't do anything if we're arrested, too, though."

"But—"

"Please. I just need to figure out how—"

"Madame Traube?" Colette's voice interrupted their hushed conversation, and they turned to see the four-year-old standing in the doorway, wearing a paper crown and clutching a little metal tiara in her hand. She held the tiara up. "When I'm feeling blue, sometimes I like to play dress-up. If you want, you can be the princess and I can be the queen."

"Dress-up?" Mamusia looked dazed.

"It's a game where you pretend to be someone you're not." Colette frowned. "Don't you know what dress-up is, Madame Traube?"

Mamusia didn't answer, but Eva felt as if a lightbulb had gone on in her head. "Yes, of course," she murmured, her heartbeat suddenly accelerating. She thought of her father's words about Monsieur Goujon. If her father's boss had been paid to help her, surely he could do something for Mamusia, too. She and Mamusia would just have to become different people, on paper at least—a dress-up game with the highest stakes

"Mademoiselle Traube? Do you want to play, too?"

Eva knelt beside the little girl. "No, Colette, but you've just given me a wonderful idea. Look out for Madame Traube, will you?" She turned her attention to her mother and added, "If Madame Fontain returns, Mamusia, you stay right here in her apartment, no matter what she says. I'll come back as soon as I can."

"But where are you going?"

"To see someone who will help us."

In her own apartment, Eva groped her way through the darkness, thankful for the bit of daylight filtering in through the shades, enough that she could see the outlines of their furniture. She knew the rooms well enough that she could probably find her way in pitch blackness under normal circumstances, but her head was spinning, and she didn't trust herself. Nor did she trust that her neighbors wouldn't betray her if they heard her moving around inside rooms that were meant to be empty.

Had one of them reported on her family? It made some sense that the names of her parents, both of whom had emigrated from Poland in their early twenties, would be among those to be taken away to labor camps; Joseph's dire warning had been about foreign-born Jews. But who had added her name to the list? Someone who wanted her gone, too, so her family's apartment would become available? The Traubes had lived here for more than twenty years, and there was no denying that theirs was one of the nicest units in the building, twice the size of most of the other apartments. Could jealousy and greed have turned a neighbor into a traitor?

Eva pushed the dark thought away. There wasn't time to be consumed by anger. No, her only job now was to get her mother safely out of Paris. After the roundups, they couldn't walk around with the yellow stars on their chests, of course, but simply discarding them would be even more dangerous. The second they ventured out, they would be at risk of encountering a French policeman or a German soldier, and if asked for their papers, they would be immediately arrested for the crime of leaving their stars at home. No, they had to become other people entirely, and the key to that lay in the typewriters that sat, silent and hulking, in their living room.

She would bring one back to Monsieur Goujon, using it as her ticket into the prefecture. Tatuś had said that his old boss had promised to make false documents for her; she would need to persuade him to do the same for Mamusia. It was their only hope.

Eva moved silently into her parents' bedroom, where she pulled out three of her mother's best dresses, several blouses and skirts, an extra pair of shoes, and a heavy coat, though the July day was sweltering. But who knew how long they'd be gone? She placed all the items carefully into the family's beat-up leather suitcase.

In her own bedroom, she added three dresses, a pair of trousers, a skirt, a few blouses, a coat, and a pair of boots to the suitcase, then picked up her *carte d'identité*, stamped with the word JUIVE in bold capital letters. Her mother's card was even worse, for it immediately marked her as a foreign-born Jew, prohibited from travel.

She zipped up the suitcase and moved back into the living room, where she folded one of the typewriters into the carrying case, her identity card and her mother's tucked beneath it. Perhaps Monsieur Goujon would need them to help craft their false documents.

As soon as she'd closed her apartment door behind her, leaving the filled suitcase behind for the time being, she took off briskly for the stairs, grasping the handle of the typewriter case with white knuckles and keeping her head down. Venturing out without her star was a risk, but she was banking on the fact that the police were too busy arresting other Jews to pay her much mind, especially if she looked confident about where she was going. After all, why would a Jew be fleeing straight into the heart of Paris with a typewriter and a smile?

It took Eva twenty minutes to walk as casually as she could to the soaring *préfecture de police*, the city's police and administrative headquarters, situated just across the Seine on the Île de la Cité. It was where her father had worked before the first anti-Jewish statutes had come down, and it was surely where last night's raids had been orchestrated. She was walking into the belly of the beast, but there was no other way.

Holding her head high, she glanced back at the soaring twin towers of Notre-Dame, which loomed just behind her. As she opened the door to the prefecture confidently and strode inside, she wondered how the police commanders who worked here every day, the ones who were carting Jews off like yesterday's trash, could do such evil things in the shadow of God's house.

"Mademoiselle?" A voice to her left startled her as the door slammed closed. She turned and swallowed hard when she realized it was a German soldier standing there, staring at her.

"*Oui*, monsieur?" She was trembling, sweating.

But he merely looked exhausted, not suspicious. "Where are you going?" he asked, his German accent thick. As she hesitated, he looked her up and down, his eyes lingering on the swell of her breasts beneath her dress. By the time his gaze returned to her face, she knew how to play this.

With a deep breath, she flashed him her most flirtatious smile, batting her eyelashes. "I hadn't realized how handsome those uniforms are up close, all those perfect creases." His face turned red as she added quickly, "You see, I am delivering this typewriter on my father's behalf. He repairs them, but he is ill, and I'm told it's needed today."

She held her breath as the German, who couldn't have been more than eighteen or nineteen, studied her. If he asked for her identity papers or searched the typewriter case, she was done for. "Who are you going to see?"

"Monsieur Goujon, second floor."

"You know where his office is?"

"Oh yes, I've been here many times before." It was true. When she was a young teenager, long before the Germans had come, Eva had loved accompanying her father to work when classes were out. All the stamps and pens and machines fascinated her, and Monsieur Goujon had often given her a stack of paper and a pencil to occupy her while her father fiddled with the typewriters. She had loved sketching and had become good at it, good enough that Monsieur Goujon told her father that she should think of pursuing a career in art. But drawing was never her passion the way words were, and she told her father that just because one was good at something did not mean that one had to spend a lifetime doing it. Her father had chuckled and told her to count herself lucky that she had such a talent. *One day*, he said, *you will appreciate God's gifts.*

"Go ahead, then," the young German said, his shoulders sagging again with fatigue.

Eva was already moving toward the stairs. "*Merci!*" she called over her shoulder.

Her heart was still thudding after she'd scaled the second flight and opened the door to Monsieur Goujon's office without knocking. He was alone behind his desk and he looked up, his eyes round and surprised beneath bushy gray eyebrows, as she pulled the door quickly closed behind her.

"Eva Traube?" he asked, blinking at her as if certain he was seeing things. His hair had grown much whiter since she'd last seen him, and he looked a decade older than her father did, though she knew they were roughly the same age. The circles under his eyes were pronounced, and his jowls sagged as if they hadn't the energy to keep up with the rest of his face. "Why, I haven't seen you in years."

"Monsieur Goujon, forgive the intrusion."

He stood and embraced her. "I heard about the roundups, and I thought perhaps—"

"My father was arrested," she said firmly, cutting him off. "My mother and I were on their list, too, but we were fortunate enough to be out of the apartment."

The color drained from Monsieur Goujon's face and he took a step back. "Oh dear."

"We haven't much time, monsieur. Please, I need your help. My father told me he had spoken with you, arranged things. He said you would make me false papers. My mother and I need to leave Paris as soon as possible."

Monsieur Goujon's eyes went first to the typewriter case in Eva's hands and then to the door behind her. Finally, his gaze settled back on her, his lips drawn tightly together. "But what can I do? I promised him only that I would help you, not your mother."

"I can't leave her behind. I won't."

"She has an accent, Eva, and frankly, she looks like a Jew. It would be too risky. She'll surely be caught. And then if she reports me . . ."

"Surely you're not refusing to help us." Eva's panic began to harden into anger. "My father worked for you for many years, yes? He was reliable, kind."

Monsieur Goujon's forehead creased, and for a second or two he looked as if he might cry. "Eva, I want to help you, but if I were to be caught forging documents, especially for a Polish-born Jew . . ."

"You would be arrested, maybe executed. I know." Eva took a step closer and lowered her voice. "Monsieur Goujon, I know what I am asking you. But the only chance we have is escaping to the free zone, and then I can figure out a way to come back for my father."

"I—I cannot do what you're asking." He looked away. "I have a wife and child to think about, and—"

"My father trusted you. He paid you the last of what he had." He took a deep breath, but he didn't say anything.

"*Please*, monsieur." She waited until he looked at her again. "I'm begging you."

Finally, he sighed. "I will give you some blank identification cards, Eva, some blank travel permits. This is all I can do. You were always a good artist, I remember that."

"You—you want *me* to do the forgeries?" The spaces for personal details—name, place of birth, date of birth—would be easy enough to fill in, but how would she fake the rest? "But you promised my father, Monsieur Goujon!"

He ignored her protests, continuing in a voice that was barely audible. "I will try to find you some art pens in the colors of the stamps. There should be some in our supply cupboard. But you can't stay here. And if anyone finds out what you've done, I will deny any knowledge. I will say you stole the documents."

"But—" Eva began as he brushed past her, out the door of his office. She stood there, breathing hard, considering her options. Should she insist, beg for his help? She had never attempted anything like what he was suggesting.

He reappeared after a few minutes and held up a small envelope. "Here. It should be all you need. Use your real documents as a guide, and see if you can cut up some old photographs to serve as pictures for your identity cards; your current ones are probably stamped indelibly in red. I also included a canceled travel permit so you can see how they're meant to look. You and your mother will each need one to cross to the free zone. I added a blank naturalization certificate for your mother, too, to explain her accent, as well as a blank birth certificate for you. They should be easy enough to fill out."

"But I don't know how—"

"Tuck this underneath the typewriter," he continued, rolling over her objections as he grabbed the typewriter case from her and opened it on his desk. He carefully lifted the machine from its case, slid the envelope in, added a stapler, and tucked the typewriter on top, closing the latch again. He handed it to her. "Walk out like you know what you're doing. They won't stop you, and if they do, simply act offended. Most of the soldiers here are young boys simply pretending to be tough."

She tightened her grip on the handle with her right hand. "Monsieur Goujon, I am not a forger! This is all impossible."

"It is all I can do. What is it your father used to tell you? That God gave you the gift of artistic skills? Well, now is your chance to use that gift."

Her head was spinning with a thousand questions, but the one that finally escaped her lips was, "But . . . where will we go?"

He stared at her for what felt like a long time. "I have heard from my wife's cousin of a town called Aurignon, some eighty kilometers south of Vichy." His words fell swiftly. "I have heard that they are sheltering children there, helping them to get to Switzerland. Perhaps they would do the same for you and your mother."

"Aurignon?" She had never heard of it. "And it's near *Vichy*?" The spa town had become synonymous with the puppet government of Prime Minister Philippe Pétain; surely it was crawling with Nazis.

"Aurignon is a tiny town, tucked into the hills at the foot of some old volcanoes, nothing strategic about it. No reason the Germans would have any interest in it, which makes it a perfect place to hide. Now go, Eva, and don't look back. Godspeed. I have done all I can do." He turned around so quickly that she wondered if she had imagined the conversation.

"Merci, Monsieur Goujon." Ducking her head, she left his office and strode confidently down the stairs, every muscle in her body tense, a smile frozen on her face. The young German officer was still there at the bottom, and his eyes narrowed slightly as she passed.

"I thought you were dropping that typewriter off," he said, stepping in front of her.

"This is a different one that needs repair," she said without missing a beat. She batted her eyes again. "I really must go."

"Why are you in such a hurry?" His eyes were on her breasts again, shamelessly, like she was something he could have, something he had the right to possess.

She forced herself to remain calm and to widen her smile. "Lots of work to do, you see. The prefecture is busy with all the arrests of last night, I imagine."

The German nodded, but he was still frowning. "They deserved it, you know."

She felt suddenly ill. "Pardon?"

"The Jews. I know the arrests seemed cruel, but those people are a menace."

"Well," Eva said, already walking away, "I, for one, am hopeful that all the vermin who pollute our grand city will get what they deserve one day soon."

The German nodded enthusiastically. "Exactly right, mademoiselle. Listen, if you're ever interested, there's a group of us who meet most days at five o'clock at a café in the Latin Quarter called Le Petit Pont. I could buy you a drink . . ."

"What a grand invitation. Perhaps I'll join you."

He beamed at her. "That would be terrific."

She waved goodbye, her smile genuine, for she knew that with any luck, she and her mother would already be on a train bound for the south by the time the German sat down for his first beer.

Chapter Four

Twenty minutes later, Eva let herself into her family's apartment again. She would need to move quickly, before a neighbor came scavenging.

On the dresser sat a framed formal photograph of her parents on their twenty-fifth anniversary three years earlier, one of her father holding two typewriter cases and beaming, and another of her mother in Cabourg on holiday in the late thirties. There was also one of Eva on the same Côte Fleurie vacation, and one taken after she graduated *le lycée* four years earlier. She grabbed them all and removed them from their frames.

She found a pair of scissors in the parlor, beside one of the typewriters, and quickly carried it into the kitchen. Using the existing picture on her mother's identity card to measure the correct size, she carefully cut her mother's face and shoulders from the anniversary photograph, and then did the same with the images of herself, her mother, and her father from the other photographs, too.

Eva stuffed the identity cards and the six makeshift identity photos into the typewriter case and closed it again.

She took one last look at the wooden shelves that lined the walls, stacked from floor to ceiling with beautiful books, their pages full of knowledge she had eagerly absorbed over the years. Most of them had belonged to her father before her: texts on typewriter repair techniques, reference books about medicine, the solar system, chemistry, even a first edition of the English-language *The Adventures of Tom Sawyer*—one of the first novels written on a typewriter, and one of her father's most prized possessions. She had devoured them all and saved up her own money to buy more. They had been her escape, her refuge, and now they would be all that was left of her in an apartment she might never return to. "Goodbye," she whispered, wiping away a tear.

Then, with a final glance back at the only home she'd ever known, she left, grabbing the packed suitcase and the typewriter in its case before locking the door behind her.

When Eva knocked on the Fontains' door seconds later, it was Colette who answered, her eyes wide. "Where is my maman?" she asked. "She hasn't come back yet, and you said she would, Mademoiselle Traube."

"And she will, Colette," Eva said firmly as she stepped past the child and closed the door behind them. "Don't worry." After all, Madame Fontain was as Christian as they came. If an officer tried to sweep her up with the Jews, no doubt she would pray so loudly and indignantly for his soul that he'd be convinced of her allegiance to Jesus even before she produced her papers.

The problem was that Eva couldn't in good conscience leave the girls alone. She and her mother would have to wait to flee until Madame Fontain returned.

Mamusia was exactly where Eva had left her two hours earlier, curled up on the sofa, staring blankly into space. "Mamusia?" Eva said, crossing to her mother and placing a hand on her shoulder. She was trembling. "Are you all right?"

"She still doesn't want to play dress-up," Colette reported when Mamusia didn't answer.

"You know, Colette, I think she might be feeling rather ill. Dear, would you and your sister put away your dress-up things before your mother returns? You wouldn't want her getting upset."

"Yes, mademoiselle." Colette scooped up the ribbons and dresses she had strewn about and beckoned to her sister. The two of them scampered away.

Eva bent quickly beside her mother. "I have a plan, Mamusia, but you need to snap out of it. We need to get out of Paris as soon as possible. You must keep the girls occupied while I get to work. And if Madame Fontain returns, distract her while I finish."

Mamusia blinked at Eva a few times. "What is it you're doing?"

Eva leaned in. "I'm making us false papers."

"Forgery? You don't know how to do such things!"

Eva swallowed hard and tried to muster confidence she didn't feel. "I will learn. But there's not much time, so I need you to listen. You will be Sabine Fontain."

Mamusia gasped. "You are giving me Madame Fontain's name?"

Eva had been thinking about it since leaving Monsieur Goujon's office. They would need names of real people, just in case they were detained and an official decided to check their identification cards against records. "I think it's safer that way," Eva said. "The name Sabine could be Russian, too, and I think that's important. It would explain your accent. If anyone asks, you emigrated from Russia after the revolution in 1917. Of course, you married Madame Fontain's real husband, Jean-Louis Fontain, a French patriot missing in action at the front."

Her mother blinked at her. "What about you?"

"I'll be Colette Fontain."

"But the real Colette is just a child."

"By the time anyone thinks to verify a birth year, we'll be long gone."

"But how will you make these papers?" Mamusia persisted.

Eva briefly explained her visit to Monsieur Goujon and the blank documents and supplies he had given her. "I'll do the best I can," she concluded.

"There's no way this will work," Mamusia said.

"It has to, Mamusia."

In the kitchen, Eva opened the typewriter case, lifted the machine, and pulled Monsieur Goujon's envelope from beneath the keys. Inside, there were three blank identity cards, three blank travel documents, a blank naturalization certificate and birth certificate, and four pens, in navy, bright blue, red, and black. The envelope gave up perhaps its greatest prize last: adhesive stamps with images of coins on them, the only part of the documents that would have been impossible to forge with limited supplies. There was no way she could have purchased stamps at a *tabac* today without arousing suspicion.

She closed her eyes, whispered a thank-you to Monsieur Goujon, who had come through in at least a small way for her, and spread all the materials on the table in front of her alongside the real identity cards belonging to her and her mother. She took a deep breath. She could hear her father's voice in her head. *One day, you will appreciate God's gifts.*

She began with her mother's identity card. First, Eva had to convincingly forge the handwriting of a busy but efficient clerk at the prefecture. She carefully examined her mother's real card, reminded herself that her own flowing, meticulous script had no place here, and dove in. With the black pen Monsieur Goujon had given her, she filled in the blanks in short, neat block letters. *Nom: Fontain née Petrov. Prénoms: Sabine Irina. Née le: 7 août 1894. à: Moscou.*

She continued, filling in her mother's real hair color, eye color, height, and more. She gritted her teeth at the blank for *Nez*, nose, which was included to help authorities pick out Jews. She wrote *moyen*, medium, and moved on, penning a false address and a false registration number and finishing with the grand and sweeping signature of someone who spent the day putting his name to other people's lives.

She sat back for a second and studied her work. The handwriting looked very much like the one on her mother's original documents, certainly official enough to convince a stranger. Eva pulled the photograph she'd cut earlier from her parents' anniversary frame and placed it in its spot on the card. Carefully, using the stapler Monsieur Goujon had added to the typewriter case, she attached the picture and sat back to make sure the document looked authentic.

It wasn't perfect, but it would do. She affixed her own photo to a second identity card, added the adhesive stamps to both cards, and quickly filled in the blanks for the false Colette Fontain, born 1920 in Paris, with brown hair, brown eyes, and of course a medium nose. By the time she was done forging the signature of an imaginary clerk, the ink was dry enough to begin forging the documents' official stamps, the part of the process Eva was most worried about, for it required a sure but light hand and left no room for error. The marks couldn't look hand drawn, and they had to exactly match the mass-produced ones the French police and German soldiers would have seen thousands of times.

She began with her own identity card, figuring that if she made a mistake, she might be less suspicious than her foreign-born mother. The stamp on her real document was patchy and uneven, evidence that the ink pad had been running dry. There was no way to fake that kind of fading, Eva thought, but if she could mimic the exact lines of the stamp, it should appear real, if slightly too bright.

She started with carefully drawing perfect blue circles on both the top and bottom of her card, making sure that the higher one slightly overlapped her photo, and then she carefully filled in the logo of the Police Nationale. The hardest part of the stamp was the lettering, but Eva steadied herself and carefully wrote out the characters, allowing herself a few seconds to admire her handiwork when she finished. She duplicated the stamps on her mother's card, and then used the darker blue pen to forge a date stamp. On both identity cards, she blotted the ink with one of Madame Fontain's hand towels, sighing in relief as the sharp lines softened and smudged just a bit, as if they'd been placed there with real rubber stamps.

By the time she sat back to gaze at the cards, she was breathing hard, but the terror that had been a weight in her chest since she'd watched her father being hauled away had been squeezed aside by something buoyant, something that felt like a tiny bubble of hope. She had done it. The job wasn't perfect, but the cards might just pass muster if they weren't examined too closely.

The travel documents were easier; all Eva had to do was fill in the blanks—name, date and place of birth, profession, address, nationality, etc.—using the typewriter, so she quickly set that up and went to work. The only piece of art necessary on the documents was a forgery of the black stamp of the *Reich-sadler*, the heraldic Nazi eagle. Eva carefully copied the spread-winged bird sitting atop a swastika, as well as the German lettering that arced across the top of the round image. Over the eagle's body, she carefully handwrote the words *Dientstem-pel: Cachet* in what she hoped looked like stamped letters. For *Lieu de Destination*—place of destination—she hesitated and then wrote down the name of the town Monsieur Goujon had mentioned: Aurignon. My God, she wouldn't be able to find it on a map if asked; she knew nothing about the place. But she silenced her doubts and reminded herself that Monsieur Goujon wouldn't have risked helping her with the cards only to steer her wrong at the end.

The naturalization and birth certificates were the easiest of all; she simply had to vary her handwriting, making her script tall and narrow, and fill in the blanks with false details. The required stamps, one in blue and one in black, felt like child's play after the more complicated ones she'd drawn on the other documents. She was done in no time.

She was just about to start on her father's false documents—which she had saved for last in case she ran out of time—when she heard a key scratching in the front door's lock. She leapt up, stuffing all the supplies and false cards down her shirt and staining herself with blue ink in the process.

"Girls?" Madame Fontain's voice piped in from the entryway as the door closed.

"Maman!" Colette and Simone raced down the hall and threw themselves into their mother's open arms just as Eva entered the parlor.

Madame Fontain squinted at Eva and didn't take her eyes off her as she knelt and hugged the girls.

"You're still here, Mademoiselle Traube?" she asked when she finally straightened, emptying the girls from her spacious lap.

"Yes, of course," Eva replied.

But instead of thanking her, Madame Fontain frowned. "And your mother?"

"I'm here, too." Mamusia emerged from down the hall, her eyes still glassy and dazed. Two strips of her hair hung in flat plaits, where the girls had apparently been braiding it. "Is your mother all right, Madame Fontain?"

Madame Fontain sniffed. "My mother is none of your concern. And I'll thank you to leave my apartment immediately."

Mamusia blinked a few times. "I was simply being kind."

"I don't need the kindness of a Jew."

Simone was dancing around in a circle, babbling to herself, but Colette watched wide-eyed, following the exchange like she was watching a match at the Stade Roland Garros.

"You didn't have any qualms about asking for our kindness last night," Mamusia said, her voice sharp. The blank stare was gone from her eyes, replaced with pure ice.

"Yes, well, now you've put me in the position of harboring fugitives." Madame Fontain sniffed.

Mamusia opened her mouth to reply, but Eva swiftly crossed to her side and put a firm hand on her arm. "We were just going, weren't we, Mamusia?"

"How could she act as if we're unwelcome here after we've

done her a kindness?" Mamusia cried. "After we watched the police haul your father away?"

"Well, they got one of you, at least." Madame Fontain waved dismissively.

"How dare you—" Mamusia began, but Eva was already dragging her toward the door.

"Madame Traube? Mademoiselle Traube?" Colette asked, her voice tiny. "You're leaving?"

"I'm afraid we must, dear." Eva glared at Madame Fontain. "It seems we have overstayed our welcome."

"Won't you come back and play another time?" asked the girl as Eva moved past her, still pulling her mother. She grabbed the suitcase, leaving the typewriter behind. It was too unwieldy to bring along, and too conspicuous.

"Oh, I think not," Madame Fontain answered, giving Eva a smug smile. "In fact, it looks as if the Traubes are leaving forever."

And then the door closed behind them, leaving Eva, her mother, and all their worldly possessions alone in the cold, dark hallway.

"What do we do now?" Mamusia asked.

"We go to the train station."

"But—"

"Our documents aren't perfect, but they should at least get us out of Paris, God willing."

"And if they don't?"

"We have to believe," Eva said, starting toward the stairs. For all she knew, Madame Fontain was already calling the police, reporting two Jews who had slipped through the sieve. "Right now, hope is all we have."

Chapter Five

"Where are we going?" her mother asked in a small voice ten minutes later as they hurried along, heads down, Eva clutching the suitcase in one hand, Mamusia's trembling arm in the other. The day was hot, oppressive, and Eva could feel herself sweating.

"To the Gare de Lyon," Eva said as they passed the Place de Vosges, where Tatuś had once taught her to ride a bike, where he had picked her up countless times after she'd skinned her knees. Her heart ached and she pushed thoughts of him away.

"The Gare de Lyon?" her mother repeated, breathing hard as she struggled to keep up. She had unbraided the lopsided plaits the girls had given her, and now her hair hung in waves that clung to her neck.

Ordinarily, Eva would have slowed down, been more sympathetic to the fact that her mother didn't do well in heat and humidity. But the longer they were out on the streets, the more exposed they were. Paris was deserted today, and that would only make Eva and her mother more conspicuous. "We're going south."

"South?" Mamusia panted.

Eva nodded as they made a sharp turn onto the tree-lined Boulevard Beaumarchais, a street she usually found beautiful. Today, though, the soaring buildings on either side made her think of walls holding them in, funneling them toward an uncertain fate. "To a town called Aurignon."

"What on earth are you talking about? Your father is *here*, Eva. How can you be suggesting that we travel to a place I've never heard of?"

"Because he's trapped right now, Mamusia!" Eva said, frustration quickening her pace. "And the only chance we have of saving him is to save ourselves first."

"By running?" Mamusia yanked her arm from Eva's grip and spun to face her. "Like cowards?"

Eva's eyes darted around quickly. She could see a man watching them from a shop window across the way. "Mamusia, don't do this here. You're making us look suspicious."

"No, Eva, *you* are making us look suspicious!" Mamusia grabbed Eva's wrist, her nails digging in. "You with your fancy plans of fleeing, like we are spies from one of your books. You can't be suggesting that we simply abandon your father."

"Mamusia, he's gone."

"No, he's—"

"He's *gone!*" A sob rose in Eva's throat, and she choked it back as she pulled away from her mother and began walking again. After a few seconds, her mother followed. "I promise I will come back for him. But we have to go *now*."

"Eva—"

"Trust me, Mamusia. Please."

Her mother went silent then, but she kept pace, and that was all Eva could ask.

Fifteen minutes later, the station was in view. "Just act as natural as possible," Eva whispered to her mother. "We are middle-class French citizens who don't care one way or the other about what happened here last night."

"How convenient to so easily turn your back on your own people," her mother muttered.

Eva tried to ignore the words, but they pierced her heart as she went on. "We are secretaries, both of us. You are a Russian *émigrée*, and I am your daughter. My proud French father—your husband—has not returned from the front. We fear him dead."

"Yes, Eva, let's pretend your father has been killed." Mamusia sounded furious.

"Just *listen* to me, Mamusia! Our lives could depend upon it. We will buy train tickets to Clermont-Ferrand, via Vichy."

"*Vichy?*"

"I looked. It's the fastest way to Aurignon."

"What is this place?"

"Your sister, Olga, lives there," Eva said firmly. "She is ill and has begged for our help with her three children."

Mamusia simply rolled her eyes at this.

"Mamusia, this is serious. You need to remember everything I'm saying."

"But why this Aurignon? I've never heard of it."

"There are people there helping Jews escape to Switzerland."

"Switzerland? That's ridiculous. If it's near Vichy, it has to be three hundred kilometers from the Swiss border."

The thought had been bothering Eva, too, but she pushed it away. Perhaps that was what made it the perfect place to hide. "It's our only chance of escaping, Mamusia."

"So now you want us to leave France without your father?" Mamusia's tone was aggrieved, her voice rising an octave.

"No," Eva said. "I want us to find people there who will help us get him out."

By the time the 2:05 train pulled out of Gare de Lyon, chugging southeast and crossing the Marne just as it split from the Seine, Eva was breathing a bit more easily. Buying the tickets had been simpler than she'd expected; the agent had barely looked at her documents, yawning as he returned them. Eva supposed that it wasn't his responsibility to catch those who were fleeing. But the young German soldier who had come by just after Eva and her mother had boarded had glanced at their papers with disinterest, too, and handed them back without a word. Eva allowed herself to feel a bit of hope—and the teensiest bit of pride in her handiwork—as the train picked up speed, sailing into the countryside beyond the suburbs.

Then she noticed her mother crying beside her, shoulders shaking with silent sobs as she pressed her forehead to the window, and she tensed again. "Mamusia," she murmured, keeping her voice low. The train car was only half full, and most of the other passengers were absorbed in reading books or newspapers, but it was only a matter of time until someone noticed them. "Please, you must stop. You'll draw attention to us."

"What does it matter?" Mamusia hissed, whirling on Eva, her eyes flashing. "We are fooling ourselves, Eva. We won't get away."

"We have, Mamusia. Look. We're already out of Paris."

"They'll find us wherever we are. We cannot simply disappear. How will we eat? Where will we live? How will we get
ration cards? This is madness. We should have stayed. At least in
Paris, we know people."

"But people there know us, too," Eva reminded her. "And
it's impossible to predict who to trust."

Mamusia shook her head. "This is a mistake. You took ad-
vantage of my grief to persuade me."

"Mamusia, I didn't mean . . ." Eva trailed off, guilt sweeping
over her. She'd been in such a hurry to escape, to find a way out,
that it hadn't even occurred to her that staying might be safer.
Was her mother right?

As the train continued south, crossing trestle bridges over
rushing rivers and speeding past deserted farmland, Mamusia
finally fell asleep beside her, snoring lightly, but Eva was too
stirred up to relax. She had made this decision for both of them,
and it would be her fault if it resulted in their capture. Should
they have stayed in a place where friends could have helped them?
But who would have risked such a thing? They were fugitives
now, whether they liked it or not. Even Monsieur Goujon, who
had always seemed to be a decent man, had been in a hurry to
send them away.

The train stopped in Moulins for a half hour, during which two
dozen German policemen boarded to inspect papers, but they
all looked dull and weary. A young, dark-haired German with
ruddy cheeks examined Eva's and her mother's travel permits
only momentarily, his eyes already on the row behind them. Eva

released the breath she hadn't known she was holding, but she didn't truly relax until the Germans had disembarked and the train was moving again.

"So this is Free France," Mamusia murmured as the train slowed an hour later to crawl into Vichy, which, even in the late evening light, looked beautiful. Window boxes overflowed with blossoms, and palatial nineteenth-century buildings reached for the sky. They stopped in the middle of a rail yard, and Eva kept watch for Germans, but outside the window, only French officers patrolled. Then again, it was the French police who had come for Tatuś the night before; they could trust no one.

When the train began to move again, Eva gazed out the window, wondering if she could catch a glimpse of the palace that Pétain and his ministers had decamped to when they abandoned Paris, but all she could see were parks, apartments, and cafés. Night was falling by the time the train crossed the Allier River into vineyard-dotted farmland, and it was fully dark by the time they made a quick stop in Riom and began moving south again. It was just before nine o'clock when the train finally shuddered to a halt within the boxy Gare de Clermont-Ferrand.

"Now what?" Mamusia asked as they disembarked with two dozen other passengers. "Surely there won't be buses departing this late to anywhere."

Eva took a deep breath. Even after crossing into unoccupied France with false documents, this felt like the riskiest part of the journey. "Now we wait."

"Wait for what?"

"For morning to come." The station was quiet, but Eva and her mother weren't the only ones who would need to spend the night on its hard wooden benches. More than half of the other passengers who had arrived on the train were also carving out corners of the platform, laying their heads on valises and using coats as makeshift blankets, though the air was warm. "Try to sleep, Mamusia. I'll keep an eye out for trouble."

It was late afternoon the next day by the time Eva and her mother finally boarded a bus to Aurignon. The journey took an hour and a half through streets lined with old stone houses that gave way to verdant forests and farmland.

Aurignon sat surrounded by dense pines at the top of a hill, and as the bus rumbled into the town, the engine straining with the climb, Eva could just make out the shadows of a stout mountain range to the west. She pressed her forehead to the glass and stared at the fog-cloaked slopes until the bus turned a corner and came to a slow, squealing stop in a small square surrounded by short, boxy stone buildings.

"Aurignon!" the driver announced to the half-dozen people on the bus. "End of the line!"

Slowly, the passengers stood, gathering bags and shuffling toward the door. Eva and her mother exited last, and it wasn't until the bus was pulling away that Eva finally relaxed enough to gaze around and take in their new surroundings. They'd really made it.

Aurignon looked nothing like Paris, or indeed like anyplace Eva had been. When she was small, her parents had taken her on a few trips north to the Breton coast, where sea air swept the faces of wooden buildings, turning them gray as the wings of a dove. They had even ventured a handful of times an hour or so beyond Paris, where small houses dotted endless pastures threaded with streams, and the towns themselves were small, quaint, and orderly.

This town was more condensed, structures with narrow windows crowded together in a way that looked almost haphazard, as if they had started in neat rows but the earth had shrugged them off as it rose toward the sky. Stone paths meandered up the hill, and some of the roads that led away from the town square looked too narrow for even a single car. At the crest of the incline sat a small stone church with stained glass windows and a simple wooden cross above the front entrance.

The thing that stood out most to Eva was how alive the town felt, though only a handful of people hurried through the square. In Paris, since the Germans had come, people walked around clad in gray and black, heads down, as if trying to blend in with the buildings around them. Colors had leached from the landscape; in many places, the plants and flowers that had once thrived and brought the city to life had wilted and disappeared.

But here, window boxes overflowed with peppermint, chervil, and geraniums of pink, lilac, and white, while ivy crept cheerfully up the walls of stone buildings that looked as if they'd been here since long before the French Revolution. Clothes dried on lines strung across wooden balconies, and even the church overlooking the small town seemed to glow, the lights inside illuminating the colorful windows. The town square was anchored by a stone fountain featuring a bearded man with a cross in one hand and a pitcher of water in the other. Water gurgled cheerfully around the statue's feet. This was a town whose heart hadn't yet been trampled, and for a few seconds, Eva didn't know what to make of it.

"What is this place?" Mamusia whispered, and Eva exchanged tentative smiles with her mother for the first time since her father had been taken. She felt tears of gratitude prickling at the back of her eyes; for a few seconds, things felt almost normal.

Eva swallowed the lump in her throat. "It's beautiful, isn't it?"

"It reminds me of the village where I grew up." Mamusia breathed in deeply and closed her eyes. "The fresh air of the countryside. I had almost forgotten."

Eva took a deep breath, too, the faintest scents of primrose, jasmine, and pine lingering just beyond reach. When she opened her eyes, there were two little girls staring at her, each of them clasping their mothers' hands as they hurried by. She quickly gathered herself. They were out of Paris, but they weren't out of the woods; they were traveling on false documents and needed to find a place to stay before they became even more conspicuous. "Come," she said to her mother.

With Eva toting the suitcase and Mamusia hurrying along a step behind, they wove away from the square as if they knew where they were going. In truth, Eva felt more lost than ever, and while she forced herself to walk casually, she scanned the alleys for a sign for a boardinghouse. Surely there was something available close to the center of the small town.

But it took four more fruitless turns before, finally, a shingle hanging ahead announced the location of a *pension de famille*. Eva sighed in relief and surged forward, her mother following behind her.

The door was closed and locked, the curtains pulled tightly over the windows when they arrived in front of the narrow stone building a block and a half from the main square, but

Eva knocked anyhow and then knocked again, more insistently, when no one came to the door. She pounded on the door a third time and was just about to give up when it swung open, revealing a short, portly woman in a dotted housedress, glaring at them. Her gray hair was spiky and wild, and her cheeks were as round and red as tomatoes.

"Well?" the woman demanded by way of greeting, her eyes blazing as she looked back and forth from Eva to Mamusia. "Which one of you was making such a racket?"

"Um, madame, hello," Eva said uncertainly, forcing a smile as the woman turned on her, her nostrils flaring. In that instant, she looked just like a wild boar. "We—we were looking for a boardinghouse with a vacancy."

Some of the indignance seemed to drain from the woman, but she didn't budge. "And you think you can just show up here, demanding a room?"

Eva looked at the pension de famille sign and then back at the woman. "Well, this is a boardinghouse, so . . ."

The woman's lips twitched slightly, and Eva wasn't sure whether she was fighting back a laugh or a growl. "And at this hour? What kind of people arrive so late? It's nearly nightfall!"

"We just stepped off a bus after a very long journey."

"A journey? From where?"

"Paris."

The woman's eyes narrowed, and she crossed her arms. "And what is your business in Aurignon?"

"Um . . ." Eva trailed off, thrown by the rapid-fire questions. She hadn't expected the inquisition.

"We are secretaries, here to visit my sister, who lives nearby," Mamusia said calmly beside her. "But she has three children and lives in a very small apartment, so there's no space for us." Eva blinked at her and tried to cover her astonishment. It was exactly what Eva had insisted she memorize, but she would have sworn her mother wasn't listening. "Now, if you don't have a room available, we are happy to go elsewhere."

The woman stared at Mamusia before her lips twitched into a small smile, but her gaze remained suspicious. "I hear an accent, madame. You are not French."

Eva's mother didn't say anything for a few seconds, and in the silence, Eva prayed that her mother wouldn't get this detail wrong; a slipup here might make the woman summon the authorities, and then the game would be up. "My mother is—" she began.

"Russian," her mother said firmly, and Eva breathed a sigh of relief. "I left Russia in 1917 in the wake of the Russian Revolution and married here in France. My daughter, Ev—" She hesitated and corrected herself firmly. "—*Colette* was born here in France a few years later."

"Russian," the woman repeated.

"A white émigrée," Mamusia clarified with confidence.

"You and your daughter Ev-Colette." The woman smirked, but her eyes were no longer as angry.

"Just Colette," Eva said nervously.

"I see," the woman said. She stared at them, but still she didn't move. "*Prekrasnyy vecher, ne pravda li?*" she said, smiling sweetly at Mamusia.

Eva froze. The woman spoke Russian? What were the odds? But Mamusia didn't waver. "*Da,*" she said confidently.

The woman's eyes narrowed. "*Vy priexali suda so svoyey docher'yu?*"

Eva forced herself to smile politely as she glanced at her mother out of the corner of her eye.

"*Da*," Mamusia answered a bit less certainly.

"Mmmm," the woman said. "*Vy na samom dele ne russkaya, ne tak li? Vy moshennitsa?*"

This time, Mamusia looked completely lost. "*Da?*" she ventured.

Eva held her breath as the woman stared for a long time at Mamusia. "Very well, madame. You and your daughter, *just Colette*, should come inside before it's dark. We may be in Free France, but it would be a mistake to believe we're actually free." With that, she whirled on her heel and stomped heavily into the boardinghouse.

"What did she ask you?" Eva whispered to her mother.

"I have no idea," Mamusia replied softly. They exchanged wide-eyed glances and followed the woman inside, shutting the door behind them.

In the parlor, the woman was rummaging around inside a small desk when they entered. She emerged with a thin ledger bound in burgundy leather. "Here it is. The guest book." She opened it up and gestured to Eva with an upturned palm. "Come then, let me see your documents. I haven't all day."

Eva and her mother handed over identification cards and stayed silent as the woman examined them with narrowed eyes, nodded to herself, and filled in their details in her guest register. Eva didn't allow herself to exhale until the woman handed the documents back.

"Very well," the woman said, holding out her pen and turning the book around for them to sign. "Madame Fontain. Mademoiselle Fontain. I am Madame Barbier, the proprietress here.

There are few frills, but it is a safe place to stay, as long as you can pay. Speaking of which, you have money?"

Eva nodded.

"Very well. You'll be in room two, end of the hall, though there's just one bed, I'm afraid. There is a key to the front door on your dresser. How long will you be with us?"

"We don't know yet." Eva hesitated. "Are there other tenants here, too?"

Madame Barbier raised both eyebrows. "You two are the only ones foolish enough to take a mountain holiday from Paris in the middle of a war."

Eva forced a smile. "Very well. Thank you, Madame Barbier. Good night."

"Good night." Madame Barbier turned to Mamusia. "*Spokoynoy nochi.*"

"*Spokoynoy nochi,*" Mamusia replied politely, but she wasted no time in hurrying down the hall toward room two. Eva followed as Madame Barbier's gaze burned into her back.

Once alone in their room, Eva changed her traveling clothes for a nightgown and slipped wearily into bed. Exhaustion soon overtook her, and she slept soundly that night, curled up against her mother.

"Do you think she believed us?" Mamusia asked as Eva awoke the next morning, blinking into a room filled with sunshine. The light seemed clearer here, brighter than it was in Paris.

"Madame Barbier?" Eva yawned and rolled away from her

mother, finally releasing her hand. They hadn't let go all night. "She must have. She took our details and let us stay."

Mamusia nodded. "You told her we had money, Eva. What will we do when she realizes we don't?"

Eva gave her a guilty shrug. "We do."

"What?"

"I, er, liberated some francs from the kitchen drawer in Madame Fontain's apartment."

"You *what?*"

"I was looking for pens. There just happened to be some money there, too."

"Eva Traube! I did not raise you to be a thief!"

Mamusia looked so indignant that Eva had to stifle a laugh. "I know, Mamusia, and I've never stolen a thing in my life. But we needed it, and let's be honest, she would have sold us out to the authorities in an instant if she hadn't been so busy worrying about her mother."

Mamusia's expression softened a bit. "Eva, if she calls the police because she realizes we stole from her . . ."

"Mamusia, we're long gone. And what will the police do, add us to their list for a second time?"

When they emerged from their room thirty minutes later, Madame Barbier was waiting for them in the parlor, a bowl of plump red strawberries in front of her. She gestured to seats across from her, and after exchanging nervous glances, Eva and her mother sat down. My God, Eva hadn't seen a strawberry since before the war.

"Eat," she said simply, and Eva's stomach growled so loudly that Madame Barbier raised an eyebrow.

"We couldn't possibly," Eva said. "We don't have ration cards, and—"

"I grow these in my garden," Madame Barbier interrupted. "And you both look—and *sound*—famished. So have some food. I won't ask again."

Eva hesitated before nodding and reaching for a berry. She bit into it and had to stop herself from moaning with pleasure as the sweet juice filled her mouth. "Thank you," she said after she'd swallowed. She reached for another berry, already wondering what the price of these would be.

However, after Eva and her mother had polished off the bowl, Madame Barbier merely nodded. "Good," she said, standing. "There will be potato soup for dinner at seven sharp."

"But we can't—" Eva began, but Madame Barbier held up a hand to stop her.

"We can't have you going hungry. How would that look for my business?" And then she was gone, striding purposefully out of the room, the floorboards trembling beneath her.

"Well, that was kind," Mamusia said after a long pause.

Eva nodded, but she was troubled. Madame Barbier had been looking at them like specimens in a jar while they ate, and she had the feeling that her mother's attempt at Russian conversation last night had failed miserably. So what was their hostess up to? Still, they couldn't afford to turn down free food. "I think you should stay in the room today, Mamusia," she said softly. "Just let me go out for a bit on my own. I don't have an accent, so I'll attract fewer questions."

"My accent isn't that strong," Mamusia said defensively.

"Mamusia, you sound like Władysław Sikorski."

Mamusia made a face. "*Gdy słoneczko wyżej, to Sikorski bliżej.*"

Eva rolled her eyes at the popular saying exalting the Polish prime-minister-in-exile: *When the sun is higher, Sikorski is near.*

"Just stay inside, Mamusia. And keep the window unlocked in case you need to flee quickly."

"Now you want me to leap out the window?"

"I'm just being cautious, Mamusia. You must always be thinking two steps ahead."

"You speak as if I'm another Mata Hari, but look what happened to her," Mamusia muttered, though she stood and shuffled back toward their room anyhow. Eva waited until she heard the lock click before heading toward the front door of the boardinghouse.

Chapter Six

In the full light of day, Aurignon looked even more glorious, the sun pouring honeyed rays over the narrow lanes and buildings, washing the stone in a warm glow. The flowers that had colored the window boxes the previous afternoon were brighter now in the morning light, painting the town in brilliant pinks, purples, and reds. The fresh air here, more than a hundred kilometers south of the occupied zone, tasted to Eva like freedom.

But she and her mother couldn't leave France without Tatuś. He had wanted her to flee, but she couldn't, not if she had the means to free him. And she did, she was sure of it. She still had the blank identity documents Monsieur Goujon had given her, as well as her father's photographs, all sewn hastily this morning into the lining of the jacket she had packed in the suitcase. It was nearly everything she needed to craft a new identity for her father, too, to demonstrate to the authorities that his arrest had been an error. However, she had left the art pens behind in Paris—they would have been a sure sign to any inspector that she was carrying tools of forgery. She couldn't risk bringing them onto the train.

The problem was that she couldn't replicate the same sort of documents she had made for herself and her mother without the right kind of ink, and normal pens used for writing wouldn't do. She needed art pens in red, blue, and black. But Madame Barbier was already suspicious of Eva and her mother; no amount of free strawberries could convince Eva otherwise. So it would be too risky to ask her for the location of a store that sold such things. Eva would have to find one on her own.

As she walked briskly up and down the narrow lanes leading away from the town's main square like crooked spokes of a wheel, she peered into every window, hoping to find a shop that stocked art supplies. The town was so quiet that Eva could almost believe she had the streets all to herself, a feeling she could never imagine experiencing in bustling Paris. Away from the square, the town was even more beautiful, with some of the stone structures giving way to half-timbered buildings that reminded Eva of the pictures in fairy-tale books she'd read as a little girl. By the time she'd turned onto the fourth lane, she had begun to relax, lulled into a sense of peace by this idyllic town that didn't seem to know it was in the midst of a war. In fact, she was feeling so at ease that she almost didn't notice the tall, slender man at the end of the lane, dressed in a trench coat that was far too warm for the summer day, the lapels pulled up. He was walking with a slight limp, his right leg stiff.

She had seen him two streets ago, too, and now, as she turned another corner, she hurried into a doorway and held her breath, wondering if he'd follow. If he did, it was too much to be a co-incidence, for what Aurignon resident would need to wind methodically up and down the spidery lanes in the same pattern as she? If he didn't, she needed to rein in her runaway imagination.

The seconds ticked by. No trench-coat-wearing man. *Stop making everyone out to be a German boogeyman, Eva,* she chided herself. As she stepped out from the doorway, rolling her eyes at herself, she was just in time to collide with the man as he made a quick turn around the building. She gasped and stumbled backward.

"Oh, excuse me," he said quickly, his voice deep and muffled as he ducked his face further into his lapels.

Eva's heart raced. He didn't sound German, at least. He was perhaps in his mid-forties, with sandy hair, a narrow, pointed nose, and thick eyebrows. Was he a French policeman, tailing her because Madame Barbier had raised the alarm? But if he was, wouldn't he simply demand to see her papers? As her mind spun quickly through the possibilities, she decided that the best thing to do was confront him. Certainly his limp would slow him down if she needed to run. "Are you following me?" she demanded. She had hoped to sound tough, but she could hear the quiver in her voice.

"What?" the man took a step back, his lapels still covering the lower half of his face. "No, of course not. Excuse me, mademoiselle. Good day." He hurried on, limping away from her, and she watched him, wondering if he would glance back. He didn't, and when he vanished around a bend in the road, she let herself relax a bit. Perhaps she'd been wrong.

Still, the encounter had unsettled her, so she walked more quickly as she scanned the shop windows. The feeling of peace was gone, and now Aurignon seemed as sinister as anywhere else.

It took her another fifteen minutes before she found a small bookstore and *papeterie* that had a display case of ink pens near the window. She ducked in, hoping that they also stocked art pens. Inside, she closed her eyes for a second and breathed in deeply, the familiar scents of paper, leather, and binding glue transporting her back to her beloved Sorbonne library in Paris. Would she ever walk once more among its books, bask in its silence, revel in being surrounded by so many words and so much knowledge? Would Paris one day be hers again?

"Mademoiselle? May I help you?" The old woman behind the counter was peering at her with a blend of concern and suspicion when Eva opened her eyes.

"I'm sorry." Eva could feel heat rising to her cheeks. "I—I was just thinking how much I love being surrounded by books." The words had sounded strange, and Eva's blush deepened.

But the woman didn't look put off. In fact, she smiled, her doubt melting away. "Ah. I should have known. You're one of us."

"Pardon?"

"You're someone who finds herself in the pages," the woman clarified, gesturing to the shelves all around. They were stacked high and haphazardly, reminding Eva of the layout of the town itself, chaotic but beautiful yet the same. "Someone who sees her reflection in the words."

"Oh, well, I suppose I am," Eva said, and suddenly she felt peaceful. She wanted to stay here all day, but there was work to be done.

"Can I help you find something?" the woman asked, following Eva's gaze as it roamed over the shelves. "If you're in need of some guidance, I know every book in this place."

"I—I wish I could buy one," Eva said. "But I only have a bit of money, and I need to purchase some pens."

"Pens?"

Eva nodded and explained what she needed, and though the woman looked disappointed that Eva didn't want to discuss books, she went into the back of the store and returned with three art pens in black, red, and blue. "Is this what you're looking for?"

"Oh yes." Eva reached for them, but the woman withdrew, her expression more guarded now.

"What do you need them for? You're an artist?"

"Er, yes."

"And here I had you pegged as a book lover."

"I was. I mean I *am*." Eva inhaled the familiar scents again and sighed. "I—I worked for a time at a library in Paris."

"In Paris?"

Immediately, Eva realized she had made a mistake. Why was she telling the real details of her personal life to a stranger? "Well, I just—" Eva began as the woman turned to shuffle through one of the shelves behind her.

"You must miss it. My son lived there, too, before he was killed. Paris was a magical place indeed, until the Germans arrived."

"Yes. It was," Eva said softly. "And I'm sorry about your son."

"Thank you. He was a good man." The woman turned and held out a book before Eva could ask anything more, and after a moment's hesitation, Eva took it and looked at the cover. It was Guy de Maupassant's *Bel Ami*. "This one takes place in Paris," the woman said.

"Yes, I've read it," Eva said, puzzled. "It's about a man who seduces practically everyone in the city."

The woman laughed. "Indeed. When it comes to books, the saucier, the better, don't you think?" Her eyes twinkled. "In any case, I thought perhaps you might be missing your home."

"There's not much to miss about Paris these days." Again, Eva worried she'd said too much.

The woman nodded. "I imagine that must be the case, but this tells of a Paris long before the Germans got their hands on it, dear. Please, take it. Consider it a gift with the purchase of your pens."

"But—" Eva was thrown by the kindness of this stranger. "Why?"

"Because books bring us to another time and place," the woman said as she handed over Eva's pens and accepted the francs Eva gave her. "And you look as if you need that."

Eva smiled. "I don't know how to thank you, madame."

"You can thank me by staying safe, dear."

As Eva walked out of the store and headed back to the boardinghouse, she scanned the streets for any sign of the limping man with the trench coat, and wondered how the woman in the bookstore had known that Eva needed all the wishes of safety she could get.

Eva spent the rest of the day and evening working on her father's false papers and practicing her hand at drawing stamps on the pages of a newspaper she'd found sitting in the parlor of the boardinghouse. She would burn it in the morning. When Madame Barbier knocked on the door and announced brusquely that it was dinnertime in case Eva and her mother wanted some,

Eva and her mother took a brief break to silently inhale some potato soup served in the dining room. Eva fell asleep at the desk in her small room sometime after midnight, still holding the blue pen in her hand.

Something jolted Eva out of her slumber just after dawn, and she lifted her head from the desktop with a start, blinking into the dim room, which was just beginning to come alive with traces of sunlight. In the bed behind her, her mother slept soundly. On the desk where she'd been working lay the newspaper filled with false stamps, now damp with Eva's drool.

Just as she was wondering what had woken her up, there was a soft knock on the door, and Eva froze. Who could possibly be outside their room so early in the morning? Had Madame Barbier come to collect payment already?

She quickly shoved the newspaper into a desk drawer and hid the pens and her father's documents under the mattress. Her mother didn't stir. Eva knew she had to answer the door, for if it was Madame Barbier, she would be suspicious if no one responded. And who else could it be? After all, if the authorities were here, they wouldn't knock politely; they'd surely hammer at the door and break it down if it wasn't answered immediately. Reassured that there likely wasn't imminent danger lurking on the other side, Eva opened the door a crack and peered out into the dark hall.

It took a half second for her eyes to adjust to the dim lighting, and another for her to realize to her horror that it wasn't Madame Barbier there at all. It was the man who'd been following her around town, the tall, thin man with the trench coat and limp.

Eva gasped, stifled a scream, and tried to slam the door on him, but he wedged his foot into the opening at lightning speed. "Please, Mademoiselle Fontain," he said quickly. "I mean no harm."

Eva shoved the door in vain. Her heart hammered. He had called her Mademoiselle Fontain, which meant that Madame Barbier had betrayed her, for who else could have given him her false name?

"What do you want?" she demanded. He began to speak, but she cut him off. "If you take a step closer, I'll scream."

She was suddenly acutely conscious that her mother, who could sleep through anything, was still in the room behind her.

"Mademoiselle, please. There's no need for that, I promise. I'm a friend."

"Friends don't tail me through town and show up unannounced before dawn," Eva shot back.

"Actually, I waited until *after* dawn, you'll notice." There was laughter in his eyes, and Eva was struck by the fact that he looked kind, which was unexpected. Without his lapels pulled up to cover his face, she could see the rest of his features—a clean-shaven chin, a wide mouth, a childlike dimple on the right side. He looked younger than he had yesterday, not as menacing. A gold cross sparkled at his neck, just above the collar of his shirt.

"Who are you?" she demanded.

"I am *le Père* Clément," he said. "I'm the pastor of the Église Saint-Alban, just at the top of the hill."

"A priest?" she asked in disbelief. "Why is a Catholic priest following me around town?"

"I apologize, truly. I thought I was being more subtle." He looked embarrassed. "That was, er, my first time doing that."

"Doing *what?*"

He scratched the back of his head. "It's just that, you see, Madame Barbier told me about your papers."

Her whole body tensed again. "What about them? They're perfectly in order."

"Yes, actually, that's what she said, too." He hesitated. "She also said that your mother's documents identify her as a Russian émigrée. And that she certainly isn't Russian."

"Of course she is," Eva protested immediately, her face growing hot.

Père Clément looked uncomfortable. "You see, Madame Barbier was born in Russia. She actually *was* a white émigrée after the revolution. She was nearly positive that your mother is Polish, and is therefore traveling on false papers."

"Of course, you're wrong." Eva couldn't meet his eye. "So what? Are you going to report us?"

"No, no, nothing like that."

"Then what?"

"I was just hoping you might tell me where you got your documents, though I think perhaps I've answered my own question."

"What do you mean?"

"Your hands," he said, his voice softer now.

Eva looked down and realized with a jolt of horror that her fingertips were gray with smudged ink. "It's not what you think."

He took a step back. "If you want to be left alone, mademoiselle, I will honor that, but you see, I have friends with ink-stained fingers, too. Madame Barbier was very impressed with your papers, and I—well, I think perhaps you and I could assist each other."

"I don't know what you're talking about."

"You can find me in the church anytime today. I can provide you with better tools than you can find at the bookstore."

"But I—"

"The Germans don't just look for identification documents, you know. You'll need more than some drawing skills if you hope to safely move on." When she didn't answer, he smiled slightly. "I can help you. Please, consider it." He nodded and turned quickly. She watched as he strode down the hallway and disappeared around the corner. A moment later, she could hear the front door of the boardinghouse open and close, and only then did she release the breath she didn't know she'd been holding. She had to move her mother immediately. Whether Père Clément had meant what he'd said or not, the fact remained that their cover had been blown—and it had been Eva's fault.

Chapter Seven

"Wake up!" Eva nudged her mother, and as Mamusia blinked sleepily awake, Eva prodded her again, nearly shoving her onto the floor. "Come on, Mamusia. We've been found out. There's no time to waste."

"What do you mean?" Mamusia was instantly alert, scrambling for the skirt and blouse she'd worn yesterday, which lay neatly draped over the back of the chair near the window. "What's happened?"

"Madame Barbier knows our papers are false. A man came to the door this morning asking about them."

"What?" Her mother's face was white as she buttoned her shirt with trembling fingers and shimmied her skirt over her full hips. "Was he police?" She began to grab things from around the room, throwing them into the suitcase.

"No." Eva hesitated. "He was a priest."

Her mother stopped what she was doing. "A *priest?*"

"That's what he said."

"But—why did he come? Does he work with the authorities?"

"I don't think so." Eva was still mulling over whether he

was friend or foe. Certainly the fact that he'd left after issuing his invitation was a good sign, wasn't it? "Maybe I'm wrong, but I think he was saying he works with other forgers. I—I believe he might have been asking me if I could come work with him." The moment the words were out of Eva's mouth, she wondered if she had completely misunderstood the conversation. A priest leading a band of document forgers? It sounded too far-fetched to be real.

"What did he say?"

"He told me he could provide me with some help. I don't know exactly what he meant."

Her mother was staring at her with wide eyes. "Eva, he might be able to give you what you need to help locate your father and secure his release."

"It might also be a trap."

"Set by a priest?"

"There's no rule that all priests must be decent human beings."

"I don't know much about Catholicism, but I'm fairly certain that's part of the job description."

Eva shrugged. Her mother was right about one thing, though. The priest could hold the key to getting her father out of detention. And the clock was surely ticking. As long as she moved her mother, perhaps it was worth the risk of heading to the church to see if the man's offer had been genuine. "Very well," she said at last. "I'll go see him—but not until I take you somewhere safe."

"Where will I go?"

"I don't know, but you can't stay here. Not until we figure out whether Madame Barbier is on our side or not." Eva considered it for a moment, an idea forming. "I believe I'll take you to a bookshop I know." It was the only thing she could think of. The woman there had been kind, and Eva refused to believe that a person who had made a life from books could have evil in her heart.

After bringing her mother to the bookshop and telling the older woman there an unconvincing story about how Mamusia simply longed to spend some time browsing, Eva hurried toward the church, reassured that the woman had seemed to understand that Mamusia needed a place to lie low for a little while. *You can thank me by staying safe*, the woman had told her yesterday. Eva could only pray that those wishes of protection extended to her mother, too.

The town was coming alive in the midmorning warmth, though it was still the quietest place Eva had ever seen. She could count on her hands the number of people she passed as she hurried along: the butcher on the rue Pascal outside in his splattered apron, washing his front windows; a half-dozen women queued in front of the *boulangerie* on the rue de Levant, ration cards in hand, some gossiping with heads bent, others craning their necks to see what might still be available inside. Eva exchanged pleasant bonjours with a heavyset, middle-aged *fleuriste* arranging a small array of bright pink peonies in a bucket outside a corner shop as she passed, but otherwise, nervous and on guard, she kept to herself.

The Église Saint-Alban was only two blocks up the hill from the bookstore, so Eva reached it before she could fully gather

her thoughts—or talk herself out of what she was about to do. She hesitated in front of the main door, putting her palm on the iron handle, but she didn't go in, not yet. *Come, Eva,* she told herself. *You have to take a chance. You need something to convince the authorities to let Tatuś go.*

Summoning her courage, she pulled open the door and entered. Inside, the church was dimly lit and small, with a dozen long, narrow wooden pews marching toward an altar. On the raised platform was a lectern; behind it sat a small golden urn. On the back wall hovered a golden statue of Jesus, his face twisted in agony and looking toward heaven, his body nailed to a wooden cross. Candles flickered atop small pillars on the altar. There was no sign of Père Clément.

Eva shivered and slid into one of the wooden benches. She had never been in a church before, so she wasn't sure what to do. As the moments ticked by, and Père Clément still hadn't appeared, she began to feel nervous about her mother. What if this had all been some sort of a trap? What if Père Clément had followed her to the bookstore and led the police there as soon as Eva had departed? Then again, why would he do such a thing when he could have brought the authorities to her door that morning?

The front door of the church cracked open, and Eva turned, expecting to see Père Clément limping toward her down the aisle. Instead, it was a young couple around her age, the man's hat pulled low, and the woman, whose head was cloaked in a thin scarf, looking particularly skittish. Her eyes darted from side to side, and after glancing at Eva, she hurriedly crossed herself. The young man tugged her arm and led her toward a door in the back of the church marked with a small sign reading *Confessionnal.* They both disappeared inside.

Eva turned back around to look at the cross again, but something was bothering her. Didn't Catholics usually enter a confessional booth alone? It had seemed that way in books. And there was another thing. She could have sworn that when the young woman made the sign of the cross, she'd done it incorrectly. She'd once seen Jean Gabin cross himself in one of his films—she couldn't remember if it was *La Grande Illusion, La Bête Humaine,* or *Le Quai des Brumes*—and she was certain that he'd touched his head, his chest, his left shoulder, and then his right. However, the nervous-looking woman had started with her head before moving to her right shoulder, her chest, and then her left shoulder, a diamond rather than a cross.

Eva pretended to pray as she waited for the couple to emerge from the confessional. If the two of them weren't Catholics, what exactly were they doing? As the seconds ticked by, Eva looked up at the statue of Jesus, which had been sculpted in painstaking detail. He looked like a real man, his expression full of compassion and pain, and she thought about the way he'd been persecuted. She hadn't spent much time considering the life of Jesus, but even though she didn't believe that he was the Messiah, she certainly believed he'd been a good person whose life had been taken unjustly. It seemed murdering people who differed from the masses was a tale as old as time.

Just then, the squeak of hinges cut through the silence, and Eva snuck a look back to see the couple hurrying away. The man carried a handful of papers, which he stuffed down the front of his shirt just before opening the door. The sunlight poured in and quickly disappeared again, along with the couple.

Eva frowned and turned back around to Jesus. "I bet you know what's happening around here," she muttered to him, her voice low. "You see everything, don't you?"

"He does, actually. Or so I like to believe."

Eva gasped and turned to her left, where Père Clément calmly sat two meters or so away from her on the bench.

"Where did you come from?" Eva's heart was racing furiously.

"Oh, I joined you while you were watching my guests depart. You must always be aware of your surroundings. That will be one of our first lessons."

"Lessons?"

"Though I suspect you'll have some things to teach us, too," he continued. "And in answer to your question, I do like to believe that the Lord is watching over us. It makes me feel a bit more secure in the midst of all this chaos and uncertainty. I hope you'll find some comfort in that, too." Without another word, he stood and began to walk away. Eva stared after him. Was he leaving? Was that it? But then he turned and smiled at her. "Well, my dear? Are you coming?"

"Coming where?"

"You'll see." He didn't wait for an answer as he limped away. Eva hesitated for only a second before following. He unlocked a door to the right of the altar and entered without looking back. After giving the statue of Jesus one more nervous look, she went in after him.

"Welcome to our library," he said, closing the door behind her as she gaped at the space before her.

The place was like something out of a dream, a room lined with books, a meter-high stained glass mural running the length of the back wall above the shelves, casting colorful rays of light on countless leather-bound volumes crowded together and stacked on every surface. A wooden table stood in the center of the room flanked by two wooden chairs.

Enthralled, Eva reached for the shelf to her right, pulling a book out at random. It was bound in brown leather that had worn away at the corners, and the spine was etched with fading gold flowers and swirls along with the words *Epitres et Evangiles*. She ran her fingers over the cover with reverence. It had to be two hundred years old.

"That one, I think, was published in 1732," Père Clément said, reading her mind. She looked up, still holding the book, and he smiled at her and then gestured around the room. "Most of our volumes predate the French Revolution. This church has been here a very long time, and our library is one of our most treasured spaces. This is my favorite place in the world, in fact, a place I come to when I need to find solace. I thought you might enjoy it, too."

"It's magnificent," she murmured, forgetting for a moment that she was supposed to be wary. Books, wherever they were in the world, always felt like home to her. "You can come here anytime you like?" she asked. She set the book down on the table reluctantly, fingers itching to explore the other volumes on the shelves.

Père Clément chuckled. "I suppose I can."

She looked at him, and he smiled. His expression was open, relaxed, and she wondered if he was as enraptured with this place as she was. "Why did you bring me here?"

"I thought we might be able to help each other."

She could feel her guard going back up. "Help each other?"

His smile was gone now, and though the kindness remained in his eyes, she could see uncertainty there, too. He seemed to be considering his words carefully. "Do you have your papers with you? I would like to see them."

"What for?" Eva took a step back toward the closed door. Could it be that this glorious library was some sort of trap after all? A brief glimpse of perfection before the snare closed forever?

"Please, as I said before, mademoiselle, I mean you no harm." He scratched the back of his neck and seemed to be searching for the words. "Very well, I'll come right out and say it. We are in need of someone who is skilled at, er, artistic endeavors."

"Artistic endeavors?"

"Artistic endeavors that would fool even the most vigilant officer of the law. Artistic endeavors that would allow people who have done nothing wrong to move toward a life of freedom."

"I'm not sure what you're saying."

He looked uncomfortable. "Ah. Well, you see, my friends and I have amassed some supplies, but it seems the demand for our services has grown more quickly than our ability to adequately meet it. Madame Barbier is an associate of mine and suggested that your talents might be useful."

She took a deep breath. It felt as if she were about to jump off a cliff; there would be no going back. "Are you talking about forging documents?"

He went still and held her gaze. "Yes. Yes, I am, mademoiselle. Please, I'll ask again: May I take a look at your papers?"

She hesitated before pulling them from her pocket and handing them over wordlessly. As the priest studied them, his forehead creasing, she wondered if she'd made a mistake in trusting him.

Finally, he looked up. "These are quite good. Mademoiselle Fontain, is it?"

"Well, of course. That's what the identity card says."

"Indeed it does." He smiled at her. "Well, Mademoiselle Fontain, I'm very impressed. And now, I must admit, I'm even more desperate to ask for your assistance."

What if she could help others escape the way she and her mother had? But she couldn't even consider that yet, not with her father still in danger. She cleared her throat. "Well, you see, I would, but I'm otherwise occupied at the moment. My father has been falsely imprisoned." She looked him in the eye. "In Paris. There was a raid a few days ago. They arrested many Jews."

"Yes, it's an absolute tragedy. Somewhere around thirteen thousand."

So Joseph's dire prediction hadn't been so outlandish. "How do you know that?"

"As I said, I have friends. Most of the arrested are being held now in Drancy, northeast of Paris, in a large prison camp. You say your father was among them? I'm very sorry to hear that."

"Yes." Eva still wasn't entirely sure whether to trust the priest. This was the first she'd heard of the prison camp. "I would like to clear up the error, but I don't have the correct papers."

"Ah, I see. Well, Mademoiselle Fontain, I might be able to help you with that."

"Yes?" Eva held her breath.

"Of course, if you went to Drancy with a letter from the

Argentine consul explaining that your father is Argentine, the authorities would have to release him," Père Clément said casually. "The Germans have an agreement with the Argentine government, you see. They avoid imprisoning their citizens, even the Jews."

Eva opened and closed her mouth. It had never even occurred to her that she'd need papers like that. But of course it wouldn't be enough simply to show up at the gates of a prison and present identity documents, no matter how well forged they were. "And you have friends in the Argentine embassy?" she asked carefully.

"No." Père Clément held her gaze. "But I know what their documents look like. And I have many materials at my disposal. I would like to help you, mademoiselle. I'll need your help in return, though. We have other papers that need to be worked on, too."

"I see."

"Why don't you think it over?" He led her toward the door, and as he opened it, leading her back into the church, she felt adrift. For a moment, she could have imagined herself in the stacks of the library in Paris, with no greater worry than completing her English degree, but now the real world was intruding once more. "If you are interested, come to the church tonight after nightfall—but you must come alone. And I swear on my life, Mademoiselle Fontain, you and your mother can trust Madame Barbier."

"Even though she betrayed us to you?"

Père Clément walked her toward the carved front entrance and reached for the wrought iron handle. "Was it a betrayal, though? Or was she trying to save you both?"

With that question hanging in the air, he pushed the door open. The sunlight poured in, blinding Eva for a moment, and by the time she turned back around to bid the priest farewell, he had disappeared back into the depths of the church, leaving her alone with her racing thoughts.

Chapter Eight

May 2005

Ben shows up at my door thirty-five minutes after I call with the news that I'll be departing for Berlin in less than nine hours and would appreciate a ride to the airport.

"Mom, are you insane?" he asks without preamble when I open the door to find him standing on my doorstep, sweat beading on his forehead in the Florida heat. "You're just hopping on a plane to Germany and I'm supposed to act like that's normal?"

"I don't care how you act," I reply with a shrug. "I only care that you drive me to the airport. You're quite early, though, dear."

"Mom, you're being ridiculous." He steps inside and I shut the door behind him, bracing for an argument. The older he gets—well, the older *I* get—the more he believes he knows what's best for me. Our latest battle of wills, which is still ongoing, is the one in which he attempts to convince me to move into an assisted-living facility for my own good. But why should I? I'm in full control of my mental faculties; my vision and hearing are nearly as good as they were half a lifetime ago; I walk to work and am perfectly capable of driving myself to the store and to doctors' appointments. Sure, I had to give up mowing the lawn three year ago when I suffered an embarrassing episode of heatstroke, but there's a nice landscape man who takes care of things now and only charges me sixty dollars a month.

"I don't see what the problem is," I tell him, turning my back as I head toward my bedroom, where my suitcase lies open on the bed. "I need to pack, dear."

My room is lined with books, most of them stacked in precarious piles on the bowing bookshelves Louis assembled years ago. They are filled with other people's stories, and I've spent my life disappearing into them. Sometimes, when the nights are dark and silent and I'm alone, I wonder if I would have survived without the escape their pages offered me from reality. Then again, perhaps they just gave me an excuse to duck out of my own life.

"Mom," Ben says, following me into the bedroom. "Help me to understand what you're doing. Why Germany? Why now? You've never mentioned Germany before!" He sounds frantic, but also annoyed with me, perturbed that I have disrupted his day.

I pull a dove-gray wool cardigan from the bottom drawer of my bureau. Does it get chilly in Berlin this time of year? I fold it carefully and place it in my suitcase. "There are many things I've never mentioned about my past, Ben."

Ben, who's fifty-two now, was born long after I packed away the remnants of the life I once knew. In the way that children often can't conceive of their parents as independent beings with dreams and desires of their own, Ben has never really known me. He knew the pieces I chose to give to him, the body that nursed him, the voice that scolded him, the hands that soothed him. But there is so much more to me, pieces that had nothing to do with my role as his mother, pieces I never let him see.

"Fine," Ben says, raking his hand through his hair, which is still thick and dark, unlike his father's. Louis was nearly bald by his midforties, though he tried valiantly to cover the majority of his head with a combed swirl from the back. I never had the heart to tell him how silly it looked. "So let's do this, Mom: Why don't you just wait a few weeks, and I'll go with you, all right? I'll have to move a few things around, and it will be difficult, but if it's that crucial to you . . ."

"I believe we've already established that you're very busy and important," I say mildly. In this, I know I have failed him. I love him more than anyone on earth, but time has shown me that I made a mistake in letting him learn his priorities from his father while I lost myself in books. Where was I when he needed to learn about courage and faith and bravery? He's a good man—I know he is—but he cares too much about success and too little about the things we can find in our hearts, and that is never who I was.

"Mom, not this again." His tone is weary. "I know you think that caring about my job is a fault, but I happen to enjoy my work. That's not a sin."

I ignore him as I fold a charcoal-gray dress into my suitcase, followed by a lilac one. They're dresses that I bought years ago because they reminded me of the past, so it seems appropriate to bring them since that's where I'm headed tonight. "Ben," I say, "have I ever told you about my mother?"

Now he's raking both hands through his hair, and I'm reminded of a mad scientist. "What does that have to do with anything?" When I don't answer, he sighs, dropping his hands in apparent defeat. "No, Mom. Not really. I mean, I know she was French . . ."

"No, she was Polish. As was my father."

He looks confused for a second. "Right. Of course. But they moved to France when they were young, right?"

I nod. "Yes, but that's not what I mean. I've never really told you *about* her, have I? The way she used to dance in our kitchen when she thought no one was watching, the sound of her laugh? I haven't told you about the color of her eyes—Ben, they were the deepest brown, like dark chocolate—or the way she always smelled like vanilla and roses." I can feel him staring at me as I pause to draw a breath. "She used to fear being erased, like it was the worst fate in the world. And what have I done by not sharing her with you? I've been erasing her all these years, haven't I? Do you even know her name?"

"Mom." Ben's voice is flat. "You're scaring me. What's all this talk about your mother?"

"It was Faiga. Her name was Faiga." He clearly thinks I'm unraveling. I stare at him for a moment, and alongside the compassion and concern in his eyes, I also see distraction. He's thinking about all the things he has to do, about what every minute here is costing him. And so I realize that the only choice is to be honest with him. Sort of. "Ben, dear, if it will make you feel better, I will change my trip."

"Yes, Mom, that would be great. We can talk about this tonight, okay? And you can tell me all about why you suddenly need to go to a country you have no connection to."

His patronizing tone is back, which alleviates some of my guilt.

"Whatever you say, dear," I say. I step closer and pull him in for a tight hug. He erases me, just like I erased my own mother, by giving himself permission to see me as something I'm not. He looks at me and sees someone incapable of taking care of herself. But that's not who I am. "I love you, Ben," I add as he heads for the door.

"Love you, too, Mom." He flashes me a smile. "Don't do anything crazy while I'm gone, all right?"

"Sure, dear," I say. As soon as I close the door behind him, I reach for the phone and call the main number for Delta. Ten minutes later, I'm rebooked on the 3:11 flight today, leaving six hours earlier and arriving in Berlin at 10:50 tomorrow morning after a connection in New York. I didn't exactly lie to Ben, I reassure myself. I *am* changing my flight, just like I said.

And as I learned long ago, the truth is in the nuances. I call a taxi and throw some toiletries into my bag while I wait for my future to begin.

Chapter Nine

July 1942

"You must do what this priest says," Mamusia said after Eva had retrieved her from the bookstore and re-capped the story of the church meeting in their shared room at the boardinghouse. "It's for your father." On the walk home, the midday sun had made the town shimmer, the barrel clay tile roofs glowing in the light like they were on fire.

"This wouldn't just be about Tatuś, I think. Père Clément will expect something in return."

"So you will help him forge a few other documents," Mamusia said after a pause. "How long will that take? A day? Two? After that, we must go. We'll all leave for Switzerland together."

Eva nodded, but she wasn't sure it would be that easy.

At just past seven, there was a knock on their door, and when Eva cautiously answered, she found Madame Barbier standing there.

"I have dinner for you in the dining room," the older woman announced.

"You must know we don't have ration cards," Eva replied.

"In Aurignon, we look out for each other."

Eva took a deep breath. "Is that what you were doing when you told Père Clément about us?"

Madame Barbier looked away. "I was saving your life, mademoiselle, and that of your mother. Your papers were good, but you hadn't thought the whole thing through. You still haven't." She turned away before Eva could say another word.

When Eva and her mother sat down alone in the dining room a few minutes later, there was a veritable feast waiting for them. In the middle of a table set for three sat a roasted chicken on a bed of spring onions, and beside it a bowl of shimmering, crisp roasted potatoes, a bottle of red wine, and a carafe of water. Eva and her mother exchanged uncertain looks. It seemed too good to be true; Eva hadn't seen such a spread since before the war. Glancing around, Mamusia hastily whispered the Jewish blessing for bread, the hamotzi, followed by the blessing for wine, just as Madame Barbier strode into the room.

"I hope you won't mind if I join you," Madame Barbier said, settling into a chair before waiting for a reply. "There's a farmer on the edge of town whom I've done a favor for. In exchange, he provides me with some food on occasion. But I cannot eat all of this alone."

"Why are you helping us?" Eva asked as Madame Barbier sliced the chicken. Steam rose from the bird and Eva closed her eyes for a second, sighing in delight at the smell.

"Because you have been through a great deal." Madame Barbier placed a thick piece of chicken breast on Mamusia's plate and a crisp leg on Eva's. "And because I hope you will decide to stay in Aurignon for some time. The room here is yours as long as you want it. I'm told that Père Clément will be able to offer you a small salary, which will be more than enough to cover your lodging."

"Thank you," Mamusia said, smoothing a napkin over her lap, "but we won't be here for very long."

"I see." Madame Barbier didn't look at either of them as she heaped potatoes and greens onto their plates and her own. She poured a small glass of wine for each of them. "I was under the impression that your daughter had spoken with Père Clément."

Eva felt torn as Madame Barbier murmured a short prayer under her breath, crossed herself, and then cut into her own chicken leg. "We haven't made any decisions yet."

Mamusia gave her a sharp look. "Certainly, we have. You'll retrieve your father, and then we'll depart."

Madame Barbier turned to Eva, her eyes bright. "You feel this way, too? You would abandon us so soon after we help you?"

Eva's appetite was suddenly gone. "I—I don't know."

"But your father . . ." Mamusia said, her voice rising an octave.

Across the table, Madame Barbier cleared her throat. "Père Clément is a good man, madame. You can trust him. He's doing good work."

Mamusia glared at Madame Barbier. "I'm sure he is, but he has nothing to do with us."

"*Au contraire.* I believe he has everything to do with you if you hope to see your husband again," Madame Barbier replied evenly.

Mamusia snorted and pushed her chair back from the table. For a second, Eva was certain that her mother was about to storm off in righteous anger, but she seemed to reconsider, perhaps lured by the full plate of food in front of her. Instead, she scooted her chair back in, muttering angrily to herself, as Madame Barbier cut her own chicken, a pleasantly blank expression on her face.

"So, er, you live here alone?" Eva asked when the silence had grown uncomfortable.

"Yes, dear," the older woman replied. "My husband and I managed the boardinghouse together during happier times. Aurignon used to be a somewhat popular holiday destination for people who lived in Lyon, Dijon, even Paris, people who wanted to escape to the countryside during the summer. Then my husband died in 'thirty-nine, and war came."

"I'm sorry to hear about your husband," Mamusia said, finally looking up.

"And I'm sorry to hear about yours, but at least you still have hope. And you still have your daughter." Madame Barbier nodded at Eva. "My son went to fight for France just after his father passed. He did not return."

"I'm quite sorry to hear that, too," Mamusia said, glancing at Eva, who added murmured condolences.

Madame Barbier accepted the words with a brisk nod. "Well, as you can imagine, I don't have much fondness for the Germans, even if Pétain wishes to lick their bootstraps, the old fool. My France is the one my husband fought for in the Great War, and the one my son gave his life for." Suddenly, her eyes were on Eva, and they were on fire. "It is the France I hope you will choose to fight for, too, mademoiselle. Now, if you'll excuse me, I think I'm finished." She stood abruptly, pushing her chair back from the table and whisking her plate away, but not before Eva saw a tear glide down her cheek.

"We don't owe them anything," Mamusia muttered a moment later, breaking the silence Madame Barbier had left in her wake.

Eva sighed. "Of course we do. I would never have thought to forge documents from the Argentine embassy. And even if the idea had somehow occurred to me, I never would have known how to do it."

"So the priest gave you a bit of information. And Madame Barbier prepared us some food. So what?"

"It's the best we've eaten in two years, Mamusia."

Mamusia looked away. "That still doesn't mean you have to do anything you don't want to do."

"What if I want to help?"

"You don't even know what the priest is involved in."

"I know he's involved in helping people. Maybe that's something I should be doing, too."

Mamusia's jaw tightened. "What you should be doing, *moje serduszko*, my heart, is looking out for your family. Don't forget, France has turned its back on us. On *you*." She returned to her meal with a grunt, and as Eva watched her eat, her stomach swam with uncertainty.

France may have turned her back. But did that mean that Eva could do the same when lives hung in the balance?

After helping her mother clear the table and scrub the dishes in an empty kitchen, Eva washed up and left in the fading twilight to meet Père Clément.

The heavy front door to the church was unlocked, but inside, the cavernous space was dark and silent, lit by only a few candles burned down to nearly nothing. Above the altar, the statue of Jesus seemed to watch Eva, and she wasn't sure whether to feel peaceful or nervous. What had she expected, that Père Clément would be waiting here cheerfully to roll out the red carpet? She hesitated only a moment before heading for the door to the right of the pulpit, the one that led to the small library. It was unlocked.

Père Clément wasn't there, either, but the empty room had seemingly been prepared for her. Curtains were drawn over the stained glass windows, making the space feel cavelike, and three lanterns burned around the room, one on the table in the center. Eva made her way carefully inside, pulling the door closed behind her, and her eyes widened when she realized what was sitting in the middle of the workspace. There was what appeared to be an official form from the Argentine consulate, and beside it, several pieces of thick blank paper, and art pens in red, blue, black, and violet. An old typewriter, the kind her father would have immediately bent to examine with glee, waited for her just to the left of the lamp. The leather-bound book, the one with the gold-etched spine that Père Clément had said was printed in 1732, sat on the corner of the table where she'd left it that morning.

"Père Clément?" she called out cautiously, but only silence greeted her. After a few seconds, she sat down carefully in one of the two chairs facing the table and picked up the authentic letter from the Argentine consulate. The format was relatively basic, and the stamps looked easy enough to forge. She waited for another minute before grabbing one of the blank pieces of paper and feeding it into the typewriter. She would craft the letter first, modeling it on the real document, and then she'd worry about the letterhead and stamps.

She hummed absently as she typed out the words to a formal letter announcing that Leo Traube of the rue Elzévir in Paris had in fact been born in Argentina and thus was exempt from German detention. He was, she wrote, to be released immediately. When she was finished typing, she duplicated the flourished signature of the real diplomat and then set to work with the black art pen, carefully copying the consulate's letterhead.

Next came the stamps, red and blue, and she slid the old leather-bound volume of epistles and gospels across the table to hold down the paper while she worked. As she rendered the false stamps, her mind drifted as it often did when she created. She could feel the rhythm of her breath with every pen stroke, and as the stamps slowly materialized on the page, hope floated up within her. She was doing good work, and she knew it.

She was nearly done with the final stamp—a sun etched in blue—when the sound of a door opening snapped her out of her reverie. She jumped up with a gasp, clutching the false document. From the shadows between the shelves, a young man emerged, and Eva scrambled to grab the real Argentine letter, too. She stuffed it, as well as the false one, behind her into the stiff waistline of her skirt.

The man stared at her without saying anything. His hair was black, and his eyes looked green, or perhaps hazel, in the flickering lantern light. He was tan, square-jawed, with broad shoulders and a narrow waist. His expression was impassive.

"Good evening, monsieur." Eva was attempting to sound casual, innocent, but her voice cracked.

His face didn't change as he crossed his arms, his eyes never leaving hers. "What are you doing here?"

Eva flashed him a nervous, fake smile and groped around on the table. "Just a little reading," she said, holding up the leather-bound book.

"*Epitres et Evangiles*," he said, tilting his head to read the spine. "Ah yes. Nothing like a two-hundred-year-old guide to the weekly mass to titillate the senses."

Now she could feel her cheeks flaming. "Well, I'm very religious, you see. Père Clément said it was fine for me to be here."

The man still hadn't moved. "Yes, he's very supportive of religious scholars like yourself."

"Very."

He stared at her for another long beat, and though Eva wanted to look away, she couldn't. "I assume, then," he said at last, "that you are the infamous Colette Fontain."

Her heart skipped. Had Père Clément betrayed her after all? Or had it been Madame Barbier?

"You can stop looking like a rabbit in the headlights, mademoiselle," the man said without waiting for an answer. "Père Clément told me all about you."

Eva blinked at him and then looked down. "I don't know what you're talking about."

He took a step closer, and then another. He was so close now that she could feel the warmth of his breath on her forehead as she stared at her feet. "I think you do." And then his arm was around her, almost an embrace, and she screamed. So this was it? He'd come to arrest her? Then he stepped back, and for a split second, she felt a surge of relief, but it was short-lived. Her whole body went cold as she realized he was holding the papers that she had attempted to stuff down her skirt.

"I—I can explain those," she said.

"You really shouldn't scream like that," he said casually as he began to examine them. "People outside can hear you, you know. Do you really want to blow our cover?"

"Our . . . what?"

He looked up. "Our cover," he repeated slowly, as if talking to a small child. "Surely you know that we need our privacy here. Père Clément said you seemed quite bright, but if you don't understand that, he has oversold you."

Who *was* this man? Should she try to run? She began to inch quietly toward the door.

"Where on earth are you going?" He looked puzzled.

She swallowed hard and retreated to her original spot. "Nowhere." There had to be a different way. "Look, I just came across those papers, you see. They were sitting here when I arrived to read the gospels."

"The epistles, you mean."

"Yes, yes, of course."

He looked back at the documents. "Well, you've missed an accent over the *e* in the consul's signature. Otherwise, this is quite good. I'm impressed." He looked up and handed the letters back to her as she gaped at him. "There's just one problem. Your papers that say you're Colette Fontain? I understand they're quite good, and I commend you for that. But where did you get the name?"

"It's—it's my name, of course, monsieur."

He waved her words away dismissively. "It's late, mademoiselle. I'm clearly not here to harm you. I'm here to help. Identities pulled from the sky are perfectly fine in emergency situations that only involve travel. But if you plan to do anything more than boarding trains—such as, for instance, marching up to the gates of an internment camp and demanding the release of a prisoner—you'll need papers that are more convincing."

"I don't know what you—"

"The authorities check identities against official records, you see," he said, rolling right over her objections as if she hadn't spoken. "Now, there are several ways to lift real identities. False demobilization papers are a favorite of mine because they're so easy to forge, but that only works for military-aged men, and you're a woman, of course. There's not time to impose upon a real person to share her identity with you, and besides, this town is so small I'm not sure we'd find anyone who's a good match anyhow. And personally, I find it distasteful to troll the graveyards in search of names and birthdates." He seemed to be speaking almost to himself as she gaped at him. "But the *Journal Officiel*. Now, that's the ticket, mademoiselle. It has saved us more than once."

"The *Journal Officiel*?" She felt dazed as she followed his rapid-fire chain of thought. Of course she knew the newspaper, often called the *JO*, which recorded all official laws, decrees, and official declarations for the whole country, but what did that have to do with her?

"I bet you skip right over the sections for births, deaths, marriages, naturalizations, things of that nature. Am I right?" He didn't wait for a reply. "Of course I am. Who has time for such dullness? Well, I'll tell you, mademoiselle, I do. It's a veritable treasure trove of identities just waiting to be borrowed."

She blinked a few times as she finally understood what he was getting at. "You borrow real names from the *JO* for false documents."

"You *are* bright."

She glared at him. "So you're a forger, then."

He grinned. "Well, I prefer to think of myself as an artist—or sometimes simply a genius. But forger is fine if that's easier to understand. Now, I'm told you're good. Let's see, shall we?" He turned to the shelf just to her left and removed several books. Behind the shelf, there was a false wall that concealed a compartment the size of a bread box. She stared as he removed a small handful of blank papers. He set them on the table in front of her before sliding the wooden panel closed again and moving the books back to cover it. "Blank documents," he announced, nodding to the papers.

She looked down. Indeed, there were several identity cards and some loose sheets of paper. "But what—?"

He interrupted her again, his tone cheerful. "I've taken the liberty of choosing an identity for you. It can be tedious to go through the *Journal Officiel*, and, well, I hope it won't offend you if I note that you look exhausted."

Slowly, she shook her head.

"Marie Charpentier," he said simply.

"Pardon?"

"Marie Charpentier. You really should be writing this down." He waited patiently while, dazed, she picked up a pen and obediently jotted the name. "Middle name, Renée. Born the eleventh of February, 1921, in Paris. You're a secretary. And you live in Paris, at number eighteen on the rue Visconti in the sixth arrondissement. Oh, and there's a bus to Clermont-Ferrand that leaves the town square just past ten in the morning. Got it?"

She looked up at him. "But . . ."

"Good. You should be able to loosen the staples on your current photograph, and if you're as good as Père Clément says, you should be able to work with the portion of the stamp that's already printed there. Stamps are difficult, of course; there are so many in circulation, and I've only been able to engrave the most common ones, but I see you've made do. Impressive. In any case, we'll get you some better documents when you return from Paris. And one more question, Mademoiselle Charpentier—I hope you don't mind if I call you that. Have you much experience forging other documents?"

"I've—I've never done any of this before."

He frowned. "Interesting. Well, do make sure to extinguish the lanterns on the way out, would you? You wouldn't want to burn the church down."

"I—" she began, but he was already heading for the door.

"Enjoy reading the epistles!" he said cheerfully, finally cracking a small smile.

Before she could reply, he was gone, shutting the door silently, leaving her alone with her racing thoughts. She stared after him and then looked back at her forged letter. It was indeed missing an accent mark, just as he'd said.

Chapter Ten

Eva didn't sleep at all after leaving the church with her newly forged identity card identifying her as Marie Charpentier. Before dawn, while her mother slept peacefully, she carefully forged travel permits for her father and herself, so they would be able to journey to Aurignon after she freed him from Drancy. Though her stomach swam with doubt, she left to track down Père Clément before her mother awoke. But the church was empty and silent, and he was nowhere to be found. Nor was Madame Barbier around to confront. Though the dark-haired man had mentioned the ten o'clock bus, Eva had seen an eight o'clock route on the schedule posted in the town square, too. Eager to get to Paris as soon as possible, Eva left to catch it after awakening her mother and telling her what had happened in the church the night before.

"It still does not mean that you owe these people anything," her mother muttered.

"Mamusia, if they help me save Tatuś, I owe them everything."

Mamusia sighed. "Just bring him back safely, moje serduszko. I'm counting on you."

Hours later in Clermont-Ferrand, her mother's words were still running through her head as she presented her documents to a bored-looking French policeman and stepped aboard a train bound for Paris. *Just bring him back safely . . . I'm counting on you.* It felt as if the weight of the world was resting on her shoulders. As the train slowly chugged away, taking her north, deeper into a land saturated with Germans, Eva closed her eyes and placed her forehead against the cool window. "Please, God," she murmured, "look after my mother."

The first leg of the journey was uneventful, and Eva might have dozed off if not for the adrenaline coursing through her veins. Vineyards, windmills, and tiny villages raced past outside the glass, and Eva did her best to ignore the other passengers and the German soldiers who walked periodically up and down the aisles of the train.

They had just passed Saint-Germain-des-Fossés, north of Vichy, when a man cleared his throat loudly beside her seat. Eva ignored him, watching the winding water of a narrow stream as it ran past a small farm dotted with sheep, but when he said, "*Fräulein?* Your papers?" in an unmistakably German accent, she had no choice but to look up.

She found a light-haired man—a boy, really—in a German uniform scowling at her. He looked younger than she by several years, but he was standing ramrod straight, as if drawing himself up to his full height would make him appear more threatening. She wanted to tell him that the Nazi insignia on his chest made him frightening enough without help from exaggerated posture. But instead, she fought to keep her expression neutral as she handed over her false identity card and the travel permit she had fabricated just this morning.

The soldier examined them both, his eyes narrowed. When he looked back up at Eva, his expression was smug, hard. "Fräulein Charpentier," he said, his tone dripping with disdain, "what is the destination of your travel today?"

"Paris."

"For what purpose?"

Her heart thudded. Why had he picked her out to harass? Certainly her papers had passed muster earlier. She glanced quickly around the train carriage and found several people staring at her, some with sympathy, some with suspicion. She turned her attention back to the German. "Returning home."

"And where are you coming from?" The soldier's gaze had grown more suspicious.

"Aurignon."

"What was your business there?"

"I was visiting an aunt."

"I'll need to see some other documents."

"Other documents?"

"Surely you must have other papers? To prove that you are who you say you are?"

Eva just stared at him, her heart thudding. "But all I need to travel legally is my travel permit and my identification card."

The soldier's eyes were bright now, excited, and Eva felt like a wounded rabbit being circled by a hungry wolf. "And yet most citizens would carry with them something else that would prove who they are." He raised an eyebrow and added, "Unless they were traveling on false papers."

"What seems to be the problem?" A deep voice with a French accent cut in behind the soldier, and as he turned with a sneer, Eva's mouth fell open. Standing just a row away was the dark-haired young man from last night, the one who had interrupted her in the church library. She sucked in a deep breath.

"And you are . . . ?" the German asked.

"Her husband." He slid easily into the seat beside Eva, placed his palm possessively on her thigh, and kissed her cheek. "Hello, darling. I'm sorry I was gone so long. I grew enraptured by the scenery and lost track of time."

"H-hello," Eva managed to stammer.

"Her husband? Let me see your papers, then."

Eva stopped breathing. How on earth would he get out of this?

But he just smiled easily and withdrew documents from his pocket, handing them to the German.

"Rémy Charpentier," the soldier read, and this time, Eva gasped aloud, which earned her a swift jab in the ribs.

"Sorry, darling," he said cheerfully, glaring at her through a smile. "My arm slipped."

As Eva gaped at him, he pulled out a few other papers and handed them to the soldier. "Here you are. My wife's student identification papers, her library card, and a ticket she got last week for riding her bike without a headlight. She tends to lose things, so I hold on to them for her. You know how women can be."

The soldier shuffled through the papers without a frown and then handed them back. "Very well. But you shouldn't let her travel by herself again. She has quite a Jewish look to her."

"Yes, of course, thank you for your advice." The dark-haired man nodded politely at the soldier as he moved on.

Eva waited until the German was out of earshot before leaning over and hissing, "Would you kindly take your hand off my thigh?"

"What kind of a way is that to thank me for rescuing you?" The man grinned at her, but after a few seconds, he moved his hand. He was still holding Eva's papers, though.

"What are you doing here?"

"Why, traveling with you, darling," he replied loudly, pointing out the window. "Look, is that Varennes-sur-Allier we're passing now? Why, I think it is. Don't you love the way the river winds through the village? You can see it there, just beyond that field."

"You want me to discuss the landscape with you?"

"No." His voice was suddenly hushed, urgent, in her ear. "I want you to calm down and pretend to be in love with me. Or even simply acquainted with me. I just saved you, and the least you could do is trust me for the next few hours. I'll explain everything once we reach Paris. There are too many people here paying attention to us." He flashed a charming grin at an old woman staring at them from two aisles away. She snorted and went back to her knitting.

"Fine," Eva grumbled. "Now, will you give me my papers back?"

He handed her the documents she had forged, along with the ones he had used to persuade the German soldier that she was who she said she was. She glanced at them and frowned. "But these are absolutely terrible."

The young man looked offended. "I assume that what you meant to say was, 'Thank you so very much, handsome Rémy, for coming to my rescue.'"

"I—"

"Personally, I think they're quite good for a rush job."

She just looked at him.

"Oh, for goodness' sake, there's your rabbit-in-the-headlights look again." He rolled his eyes. "Now, be a sport and hold my hand, will you? Your soldier friend is coming back."

Eva glanced up and saw the German striding toward them from the other end of the train car, his menacing gaze glued on her. But before the soldier could say a word, Rémy leaned over and covered her mouth with his, his lips soft and gentle as he kissed her. Eva hesitated and glanced once more at the sneering German before closing her eyes and kissing back. The oxygen seemed to vanish around her, making her light-headed. By the time Rémy pulled away, looking amused, the German was gone, and her heart was racing. She knew the kiss had been merely a diversion, but his tenderness had knocked her off balance. "You can't just kiss me like that," she whispered.

He simply laughed and shook his head. "Sorry, what was that? Oh yes, was it, 'Thank you so very much, handsome Rémy, for coming to my rescue for the second time today'?"

"Was that all that was? You coming to my rescue?"

"Of course," Rémy said, settling back in his seat with a sigh, traces of a satisfied smirk dancing across his lips. "After all, you're my wife."

Dusk was falling as their train pulled into Paris after a dozen delays. Once, they'd heard explosions in the background, and closer to the city, there had been gunfire. Had it truly been only four days since Eva left the capital? Already, things felt darker, more foreboding.

Rémy held her hand and carried her small valise as they left the train, both of them nodding politely to the German who had harassed her earlier. He waved them on, but Eva could feel his eyes boring into her back as they walked away.

As soon as they had left the station and were walking north on rue de Lyon, Eva pulled her hand away. "Fine, now we're alone. Tell me what you're doing here."

"I'm still not sensing much appreciation from my lovely wife." He grinned at her.

"I'm serious. Were you following me?"

"If you must know, I came to deliver documents to you this morning at your boardinghouse, but you were already gone. I caught a ride to Clermont-Ferrand with the postman, hoping to find you at the train station, but you had already boarded, and I couldn't find you. So at the last moment, I bought a ticket. I was searching for you when I saw the German harassing you."

"What were you doing with identity papers that made you out to be my husband?"

He laughed. "I made them at the same time I was putting together your school identification papers."

"But *why*?"

"Just in case I needed them."

She shook her head in frustration, and as they passed a small cluster of German soldiers laughing outside a bar, he took her hand again and kissed her on the cheek as they walked. "Needed them for *what?*" she asked, pulling away again once they were out of the soldiers' earshot.

"For exactly the kind of situation we encountered today. Looks like I arrived just in time."

They were going in circles, and she was beginning to get the feeling that he was enjoying drawing out the torture. "Fine, well, thank you. And enjoy your journey back to Aurignon."

He stopped abruptly, and after a few more steps, she stopped reluctantly, too, and turned back. He was wearing the expression of a lost puppy.

"What?" she asked with a sigh.

"This is serious, Colette. You were in real danger."

"I would have been fine."

"I couldn't take the chance."

"Why not?"

He hesitated. "Because as much as I hate to admit it, you're good at what you do. And we can't afford to lose someone who's good."

"'We'?" she repeated.

He glanced around. "Père Clément. And others like him."

"Forgers."

"Shhhh," he said instantly.

"Look, I appreciate the compliment. And I'm touched that you came all this way. But I'm only here to retrieve my father, and then my parents and I will go to Switzerland."

He nodded. "I thought you might say that."

"Well, then, I'm sorry to have inconvenienced you. I suppose I'll see you back in Aurignon." She hesitated. "I understand that I owe Père Clément something for his help, all right? I'll stay on for another day or two to help before we head east, but I won't be there long."

"You really want me to leave you alone here in Paris?"

"This is my city."

He frowned. "I'm afraid it's not."

Now he was making her angry. "Of course it is. I've lived here my whole life."

He gestured to the Germans behind them and to a swastika flag flapping in the evening breeze a block ahead. "Colette, Paris isn't yours anymore. Or mine. It no longer belongs to the French. Not right now, anyhow."

She blinked at the flag and then took a hard look around. The rue de Lyon should have been bustling in the beautiful evening light, cafés and windowsills overflowing with happy people enjoying the summer air, but instead, it was nearly deserted, most of the windows around them shuttered and dark. She sighed and felt the last of the fight go out of her. "It's Eva."

"Pardon?"

"My name. It's not Colette, it's Eva. Eva Traube." The moment the words had left her lips, she wondered if she'd said too much. Certainly she wasn't supposed to tell people her real name, not here. He had saved her on the train, though; it was clear he meant her no harm.

He nodded and took her hand as they began to walk again. This time, she didn't want to pull away. "Well, Eva, it's very nice to meet you."

"And I suppose you are not really Rémy."

"Actually, I am."

She gave him a look. "You expect me to believe that you just so happen to share a last name with my false identity?"

He smiled. "No. The Charpentier surname is incorrect, of course, but I really am named Rémy."

"You used your real name on your false papers?"

He shrugged.

"Why would you go to that trouble?"

He squeezed her hand. "Because I'm of the opinion that no friendship should start out with a lie."

"But you've spent the day pretending to be my husband."

"Well, in that case, I suppose you'll have to marry me someday."

She laughed and quickly ducked her head so he couldn't see the color blooming on her cheeks. "Is that a proposal?"

"No. You'll know it when I propose." He held her gaze for a long time before breaking into a grin. "And for the record, it's Rémy Duchamp—just so you know the name you'll take after we're wed." He nudged her with a grin as they began to circle the Place de la Bastille. The July Column soared over them, the gold-winged *Génie de la Liberté* statue staring down at the city in disappointment. "Now where are we going? It's almost curfew, and we don't want to be conspicuous."

"To my family's apartment."

He stopped abruptly, forcing her to stop with him as his grip tightened on her hand. "Eva," he said softly.

"What? Let's go. You're right. We should hurry."

"Eva." He waited for her to look at him. "Your apartment? We cannot."

"It's only five minutes away."

"But you can't think—" He shook his head. "Eva, I'm sorry, but we can't go there."

She pulled away and began to walk again. "I know what

you're trying to say. That the apartment has probably been ransacked, that it will be hard for me to see it that way. I know all that, and I'm prepared for it."

"That's not what I'm concerned about, Eva."

"What, then, that the police will have their eye on the place? Certainly they have better things to do than watch the apartments of every deported Jew in Paris."

"Eva—" Rémy seemed to be searching for words. "There's a good chance the apartment won't be empty."

"Of course it will be."

"Eva, people aren't just ransacking apartments. They're moving in. They assume you won't be back."

She stared at him, openmouthed. "You think a stranger is *living* in my apartment? Already?"

"I'm almost certain."

"We only left a few days ago, though."

"Scavengers work quickly." He squeezed and released her hand. "Look, let me go in. I'll knock on your door. If the apartment is occupied, I'll tell the people I'm searching for my uncle and was given a wrong address. If it's not, then, well, I'll come get you, and we'll move right in."

She nodded, though her heart felt like it was a stone sinking in the sea of her chest. "All right. But I'm sure you're wrong."

Five wordless moments later, they were standing in the shadows outside Eva's building as the last rays of twilight danced at the horizon. The curfew would be in effect soon; there wasn't much time.

"Second floor, apartment C?" Rémy asked, his eyes full of a sympathy she hadn't asked for and didn't want.

"That's right."

"I'll be back in a few minutes, Eva. Stay out of sight in case anyone recognizes you."

She watched him go with a sinking heart, and when he returned three minutes later, she already knew.

"Who was it?" she asked dully as he put an arm around her and led her away from the place that had been home all her life. "Who was living there?"

"A woman with a face like a prune who had two young children, two girls," he said as they walked quickly north, trying to beat the setting sun. "She called the smaller one Simone."

"Madame Fontain." Somehow, Eva wasn't the least bit surprised.

"You borrowed your false name from that shrew?"

Eva sighed. "Well, she's undoubtedly a Christian, isn't she?"

It took Rémy a few minutes to reply. "If you ask me, that isn't really Christian, isn't it? To move into someone's home like that the moment they're gone? It's like dancing with glee on a grave. Though I'd wager with a sour puss like that, Madame Fontain has never danced a day in her life."

Eva couldn't help but crack a smile at the thought of Madame Fontain attempting a jig. "I'm sorry for wasting your time. I should have believed you."

Rémy shrugged. "Just remember from now on that I'm always right."

Eva gave him a look, but he was grinning. "So what now?" she asked. "Where will we go?"

"I know a place."

As Eva followed him into the falling darkness, she was suddenly too tired to think about any of it. She just wanted a place to sleep for the night where she wouldn't have to worry about the Germans taking the pieces of her away one at a time until there was nothing left of her at all.

Chapter Eleven

"A whorehouse? Really?" Eva asked thirty minutes later as they stood on a seedy side street in Pigalle, looking up at a stone building with opening hours listed on the left windowpane in both German and French. "You want me to stay here?"

"First of all, it's called a brothel, not a whorehouse." Rémy grinned at her, obviously enjoying her discomfort.

"A brothel, a bordello, a cathouse, does it matter?"

"Well, considering the fine folks here will be putting us up for the night, I would suggest being polite."

"Ah, yes, *fine folks*, the first phrase that comes to mind when I think of ladies of the night." Eva frowned up at the building. Just below the opening hours, a German phrase was printed on the window in block letters: *Jeder Soldat ist strengstens verpflichtet die frei gelieferten Praeservative zu benutzen.* "So what does that mean? That German soldiers are welcomed here with open arms? Or open legs?"

Rémy laughed. "Why, my dear, I see you have a sense of humor." He nudged her. "Actually, it means—and I quote—

'Every soldier is strictly obliged to use the free provided condoms.' Frankly, you have to respect a place that has standards."

Eva shuddered. "Let's just get this over with, shall we?"

"Whatever you say. But let's head in through the back entrance. I don't want any of the Germans thinking you're on the menu."

She made a face at him, but she followed him to the alley behind the building. He knocked three times on a nondescript door and pulled her quickly inside when it opened. Eva found herself in a dark kitchen that smelled of cigarettes, garlic, and sweat, a combination that made her stomach turn.

"Bonjour, Rémy." A woman stood cloaked in the shadows, and as she leaned in to kiss Rémy on both cheeks, Eva could see she was at least in her fifties, with deeply rouged cheeks and bright pink lipstick, her gray hair slicked back into a severe bun. "You have brought a friend." She regarded Eva with interest, and Eva averted her eyes.

"We just needed a place to stay for the night. My dear, this is Madame Grémillon. Madame Grémillon, this is Marie Charpentier."

"Not her real name, of course," the older woman said, looking Eva up and down appraisingly.

"You are as perceptive as you are beautiful, madame," Rémy replied.

"If she's in need of a bit of extra work . . ." Madame Grémillon began.

"Oh, I think we'll just be needing a room for the night, thank you very much." Rémy sounded as if he was trying hard not to laugh.

Madame Grémillon sighed. "Very well, have it your way.

I'm only trying to help. You can take Odette's room, 3G. She ran off with a German last week, the tarty little fool."

"Thanks, madame. I owe you."

The woman rolled her eyes, and after one last appraising look at Eva, she strode out of the kitchen, leaving Rémy smirking at Eva in the darkness.

When Eva awoke the next morning in an unfamiliar bed that smelled of stale calvados, it took her a few seconds to remember where she was. But then the events of the night before came tumbling back in, and she sat up quickly, taking in the room around her. Last night, it had been too dark to see anything, but now, in the light of day, she could see feathered negligees draped everywhere, a lacy brassiere hanging from the corner of the bedpost.

Rémy was already smiling at her from the dilapidated bedside chair where he'd slept. "Good morning, Sleeping Beauty."

"I see Madame Grémillon hasn't tidied up since the room's previous occupant ran off." A champagne coupe with a tattoo of red lipstick at the rim sat on the bedside table, a half-eaten piece of moldy bread beside it.

"Madame Grémillon is a lot of things," Rémy replied cheerfully, "but admittedly, a good housekeeper is not one of them."

"I suppose she's an old friend of yours, then. And she feels perfectly fine about catering to Germans, does she?"

Rémy shrugged. "I think of her rather like a modern-day

Robin Hood. She charges the Germans twice the French rate, and gives the difference to the cause."

"The cause?"

"People like us, Eva. Brothels are a good place to hear secrets, too. More than one German has blurted out something he shouldn't when he's at his most vulnerable."

"So you're telling me the women here are French spies, then? Patriotically lying on their backs for God and country?"

Rémy burst out laughing. "Perhaps so. There are plenty of people resisting in their own ways. Be careful not to underestimate anyone. Now, shall we have breakfast?"

"Oh, this charming establishment serves meals, as well, does it?"

"You don't think the women here work on empty stomachs, do you? Come, let's eat."

As Eva pulled herself hastily together, splashing some water on her face and applying lipstick from the worn nub she had in her purse, Rémy flipped through the papers she'd brought to secure her father's release. When she turned from the washbasin in the corner, he was no longer grinning like a madman. In fact, he looked troubled.

"What is it?" she asked. "Is there something wrong with the papers?"

"No, Eva, they're perfect."

"Then what's the matter?"

He didn't answer right away. "I just want you to be prepared for the fact that your father might not be there."

Eva's throat was suddenly dry. She looked away. "Well, of course he is. Where else would he be?"

"Deported already. Or . . ." Rémy trailed off.

Eva raised both hands, palms outstretched to push the words away. "That's ridiculous. We'll find him today and take him back to Aurignon with us."

Rémy nodded. "I'll be with you either way."

He held out his hand and she took it after carefully folding the papers for her father's release back into her handbag.

Downstairs, two dozen women in silk robes were lounging around a large table in the room the Germans had been filtering in and out of the night before.

"Morning, ladies," Rémy said casually as he led Eva in, tugging her behind him though she was trying her hardest to stall.

Some of the women looked up and regarded him with boredom; others didn't even pause in their conversations. Madame Grémillon hobbled in from the kitchen carrying a large serving platter and nodded in their direction. In the bright light of morning, and without a heavy coat of makeup, she looked even older. "You're just in time," she said to Eva. "My girls might screw like rabbits, dear, but they eat like horses. Get yourselves some food before it's gone."

Eva wanted to hold back on principle, but the tray floating by her contained fresh bread, glossy oranges, sausages, and large wedges of cheese. She stared, slack-jawed. "How . . . ?" she began.

"The Germans like to keep the girls happy," Madame Grémillon cackled, answering the question that had been on the tip of Eva's tongue. "Happy stomachs mean happy—"

"Oh, I'm not sure we have time for one of your anatomy lessons today, thank you," Rémy interrupted. "Sorry, Madame Grémillon, but we can't stay. We'll just grab something for the road."

The old woman grunted. "You always think you're too good to dine with us."

"Not at all, Madame Grémillon. I just have places to be." He grabbed a few hunks of bread, a wedge of cheese, and a thick sausage. "Thanks for the hospitality."

Madame Grémillon glared at him for a few seconds before turning to Eva. "How a pretty young woman like you could fall for a man with these manners is beyond me."

Eva felt her cheeks go warm. "But I'm not . . . he's not . . ."

Rémy grabbed her hand and planted a big kiss on her cheek. "What she means to say is that it's too late. She has already married me."

A few of the girls at the table looked up.

"No, I—" Eva protested.

"Come on, my darling. There's a train to catch. See you next time, ladies!" And with one hand full of food clutched to his chest and the other holding tight to Eva, Rémy dragged her from the room and out the back door of the brothel without a look back.

"I bet you think you're funny," Eva said between huge, ravenous bites of bread a few minutes later as they hurried toward the avenue Jean Jaurès in the nineteenth, where Rémy had arranged for them to meet a man he knew who had a car and would drive them to Drancy.

"Most people find themselves charmed by me eventually. Now come, are you trying to leave a trail behind us on the streets of Paris? Are we Hansel and Gretel?"

Eva looked behind her and realized that Rémy was right; as she had stuffed bread into her mouth, starving, she had left crumbs all the way down the boulevard Haussmann. She smiled slightly. "I suppose my table manners leave something to be desired. It's just that I'm so hungry."

Rémy handed her a big piece of cheese, firm and waxy, as he dropped back to keep pace with her. "Well, there's no table here, and I'm not judging you."

She wanted to tell him that she wasn't judging him, either, but of course she was. She had been since the moment they'd met. And perhaps that wasn't very fair.

It took more than an hour to travel the thirteen kilometers to Drancy, a bleak suburb on the northeastern edge of the city. The war-torn roads were littered with French policemen leaning on their police cars and smoking cigarettes, and young German soldiers laughing as they passed by in trucks. Their driver, a man Rémy introduced as Thibault Brun, had merely grunted a greeting at them when they got into his old truck. Eva and Rémy had awkwardly wedged into the passenger seat with their hips pressed together, and Brun didn't say a word the whole ride. But he seemed to know nearly every official they passed, waving at some, nodding at others. "Here we are," he muttered, pulling alongside a curb in a nondescript residential block. "I'll wait, but be back in an hour. Give me half the money now."

Wordlessly, Rémy handed the driver a wad of cash and unceremoniously shoved Eva out of the vehicle, landing beside her. Brun counted his money as they hurried away, the truck belching gazogene fumes that smelled like rotten eggs.

"You have some interesting friends," Eva muttered as they

made their way down the shadowy street, which was strangely silent in the middle of the day.

"Brun isn't a friend. He's a contact." Rémy didn't elaborate.

"Where did you get the money?"

"Does it matter?"

Eva hesitated. "No. And thank you."

Rémy nodded and put a hand under her elbow. "You might want to hold your breath."

"What are you—?" Eva didn't complete her sentence before it hit her like a punch in the face. The unmistakable scent of human waste was suddenly all around them, drifting in on an underbelly of brackish body odor and mud. She gagged and heaved, stumbling, but Rémy caught her before she went down.

"You all right?" Without waiting for an answer, he added under his breath, "Keep walking. Reacting looks suspicious."

"My God," Eva managed to say, her eyes watering as they reached the end of the block and turned the corner. "What is that?"

"Drancy, I'm afraid."

Eva looked up and nearly stopped again as the huge internment camp came into view. Flies buzzed around the outskirts, zipping in and out of tangled barbed wire. The buildings themselves were modern blocks, three long, clean-lined rectangles in the shape of a U. Six stories tall, they looked as if they'd been designed to provide housing for a few hundred families, but instead, the enormous courtyard in the middle was teeming with thousands of people, crammed in like cattle on a train, some of them crying, others screaming, still more with faces etched in wide-eyed defeat. There were soiled children, screaming babies, haggard elderly women, sobbing old men. Guard towers loomed over the crowd, and French policemen patrolled the perimeter, their expressions blank.

"This can't be right," Eva murmured as they approached the main gate.

"Of course it's not."

"I mean, this can't be where they're keeping prisoners. It's—it's not even fit for animals." Eva was having trouble breathing, but it was no longer the smell that was bothering her. It was the sense of becoming suddenly unmoored from anything that felt familiar. Certainly the arrests of the previous week had been heinous, but they'd been carried out with some small level of decorum. But this, this penning of humans awash in their own waste, was barbaric. Eva retched again, imagining Tatuś among the throngs. "Rémy, we have to get my father out now."

Rémy merely nodded. "Get your papers," he said under his breath. "And act calm, not outraged. Our lives may depend on it."

Eva couldn't imagine how she could pretend to the French police that all of this was fine. But then again, how were the guards here pretending it to themselves? There were dozens of officers walking around, more moving in the towers overhead, and none of them looked repulsed or even bothered by the atrocity. Could they all be that evil? Or had they discovered a switch within themselves that allowed them to turn off their civility? Did they go home to their wives at night and simply flip the switches back on, become human once more?

Rémy exchanged words with the officer at the gate, who shuffled through their papers and ushered them inside, pointing toward an office. As they walked, several of the prisoners, penned inside another layer of barbed wire, called out to them.

Please, you must call my son Pierre in Nice! Pierre Denis, on the rue Cluvier!

Please, will you find my husband, Marc? Marc Wiśniewski? We were separated in the Vel d'Hiv!

My baby is dead! Is my baby dead? My baby is dead!

Eva could feel tears welling in her eyes, but Rémy squeezed her hand so hard she could feel her bones crunching together, and she was reminded of his words. *Calm*, she told herself, drawing a shaky breath.

A French officer, dark-haired, stout, and in his forties, stepped from the office, hand extended, his eyes cool, his smile thin as he ushered them inside without a word. "So?" he asked, once he closed the door behind them, muffling the plaintive wails outside. The air in the room was still, hot, musty. In the dead of summer, the windows should have been open to catch a breeze, but of course opening the windows would invite in the voices of those being tortured just outside. "What brings you to our delightful establishment?"

That he could make a joke about the conditions made Eva even more furious, but there was Rémy's death grip around her fingers again, crushing her into submission. She forced a detached smile as Rémy spoke.

"I'm Rémy Charpentier, and this is my wife, Marie, who also serves as my secretary. I'm afraid there's been a mistake and one of our best workers has been imprisoned here. We've come to get him out." His tone was easy, jovial, light, and Eva marveled at his casual confidence.

"A mistake, you say?" The officer shook his head. "I doubt it."

"Of course we understand the mix-up," Rémy continued smoothly, as if the man hadn't spoken. "Our worker is, indeed, a Jew. But he's Argentine, you see."

Something in the officer's face changed. "Go on."

"Certainly you're aware of the diplomatic agreement between Germany and Argentina. The Argentine consul was quite distressed to learn that one of his citizens had been rounded up. And since he'd hate to have to raise the issue with his German counterpart . . ."

Rémy held up the forged letter bearing the Argentine seal, and the officer ripped it away from him, muttering angrily to himself as he scanned it. "Well, I'm not the one who made the mistake," he barked, looking up at them. "Leo Traube? Doesn't sound very Argentine to me."

"Who can tell these days?" Rémy shrugged dramatically. "Probably a Polack whose parents got on a ship a generation ago. Still, the Argentines aren't happy . . ."

"Let me see what I can do." The man left, slamming the door behind him and leaving Rémy and Eva alone in the stifling heat.

"Do you really think that—?" Eva began, but Rémy cut her off with a single raised hand.

"Shhh. The walls have ears."

Eva closed her mouth and turned to look out the window at the teeming crowd of people, miserable and sweating in the beating July sun. Was her father among them, being treated like livestock? She didn't realize that tears were running down her cheeks until Rémy hissed at her, "Pull yourself together. You're just the secretary." But when she looked up at him, there was no annoyance in his eyes, only pity. He quickly wiped away her tears with his thumb.

The officer returned then, carrying a leather-bound book, his expression unreadable as he slammed the door behind him. He didn't make eye contact as he flipped through the pages, finally stopping midway through and placing his finger on the page. "Leo Traube," he said, finally looking up.

"Yes, that's right," Eva said too eagerly, and Rémy gave her a gentle nudge in the ribs.

"Well, I'm afraid that the mix-up is not my problem any longer," the man said, turning the book around on his desk so it faced Eva and Rémy. He jabbed a meaty finger at line thirty-five, where the name *Leo Traube* was neatly scrawled, alongside his age, fifty-two, and the address on the rue Elzévir where Eva had lived all her life. "He's been relocated."

"Relocated?" Eva said.

The man's eyes were empty as he nodded and moved his finger. Eva leaned in. Clearly written beside the date of her father's arrest—16 July 1942—was another notation: *Convoi 7, 19 Juil.*

Eva looked up, dazed, and found the officer looking right at her. "That's two days ago. July nineteenth. What does it mean?"

"That he was on convoy number seven departing from Drancy," the officer said, his voice flat. Rémy had inched closer, the back of his hand brushing against Eva's, but her whole body was cold, too cold to be comforted by anything.

"And what is the convoy's destination?" Eva whispered.

"Auschwitz."

Eva just stared at him, the world spinning around her. She could hear Rémy saying something beside her, his tone calm, but the buzzing in her ears drowned out his words. "Auschwitz?" she asked in a whisper. She had heard of it, had heard rumors that Germans were sending Jews there and working them to death, but she hadn't believed it. Now, in an instant, she did.

The officer glanced at her. "It's a work camp west of Kraków. If your employee's parents emigrated from Poland, he should feel right at home there, yes?" The man finally smiled.

"Thank you for your time," Rémy said, already pulling Eva toward the door. Her feet felt as if they were made of lead. "Come," Rémy said to Eva in a low voice as the officer moved to open the door for them. "Not here." And then his arm was around Eva, and he was dragging her toward the exit, through the horrific cacophony of distress and decay and death that was all around them, past the agony and hopelessness of the people still trapped behind barbed wire.

It wasn't until they were safely back in Brun's truck, bumping down shredded roads toward Paris, that Eva finally began to cry, softly at first, escalating to a wail that sounded inhuman, even to her own ears.

"Shut her up, would you?" Brun asked.

"No," Rémy said, pulling her against him, offering his shoulder as comfort. "No, I won't."

When she could finally speak again, past the grief that had closed her throat, she whispered, "What will we do? How will we get him out of Auschwitz?"

Rémy's lips brushed her forehead. "I'm afraid it's impossible."

Eva closed her eyes. "So now what?"

"Now," Rémy murmured, "we pray."

As they made their way back toward Paris, horror set in, and along with it, determination. It might have been too late to save her father, but she had just seen up close what was happening to thousands of other Jews. If there was something she could do to help, she didn't have a choice.

Chapter Twelve

"What will happen to him?"

They were the first words Eva had spoken in more than two hours, the first she could muster, and she knew she had to say them aloud, though she didn't want to hear the answer. They were on a train headed south out of Paris, and Eva had been so drunk on her own misery that she'd barely noticed when a German soldier spent a tense minute examining her false identity card and travel permit as they boarded.

"It's impossible to guess," Rémy said, not looking at her.

"Try." She knew her voice sounded icy, but her coldness wasn't directed at him. It was just that her insides were frozen.

Rémy sighed. The train was nearly empty, but his eyes were constantly roving, looking for eavesdroppers or approaching soldiers. "The age they had down for him is correct? Fifty-two?"

"Yes."

"And he is healthy?"

"He's fit for his age."

"Then God willing, he should be selected for work detail."

"God willing?"

Rémy cleared his throat. "I have heard that the alternative is worse."

Eva studied her hands. Her eyes were red and raw, but she was all out of tears. "Thank you," she said after a moment.

"For what? I—I failed you."

She shook her head. "You are being honest with me. I appreciate that. And you didn't fail me, Rémy. I couldn't have done this on my own."

Rémy began to reply, one corner of his mouth quirking slightly into a grin, but then he seemed to reconsider. Instead, he looked out the window for a moment before saying, "You know, I have a father, too." He hesitated. "He died at the front two years ago."

"I'm sorry, Rémy."

He nodded.

"And your mother?" she asked when he didn't say anything.

"She died when I was a boy. So it's just me now."

Eva placed her hand on his for a few seconds before pulling it away.

"At least," Rémy said, turning to look at her, "you still have your mother."

"My mother." Eva closed her eyes. "My God. How in the world will I tell her the news?"

Tatuś was Mamusia's world, and Eva wondered if the revelation would break her.

"Try to get some rest," Rémy murmured after a while. "I'll keep an eye out."

Eva was too exhausted to protest, and so she nodded and placed her head on Rémy's shoulder. Finally, she slept, dreaming of her father on a train headed east to an unknowable fate.

✦ ✦ ✦

They passed through the checkpoint near Moulins easily, waved through by a soldier who took a perfunctory look at their documents and pointed to the other side with a yawn, and the remainder of the trip to Clermont-Ferrand was uneventful. It was long past sunset when she and Rémy got off the bus in Aurignon and approached the old stone boardinghouse. "Come to the church tomorrow. We will figure something out," Rémy said, reaching for her hand and squeezing.

"What do you mean?"

"A way to help. A way to fight the Germans. A way to protect others like your father." Before she could reply, Rémy added, "And your mother? She will be all right. You will, too." He gave her hand one last squeeze.

Eva nodded, mute. When Rémy let her go and walked away, she watched him disappear around the corner, and then, taking a deep breath, she turned and went into the boardinghouse.

Madame Barbier was in the parlor, and she looked up when Eva entered. Her brows were raised, her eyes wide as she looked questioningly at Eva. Eva shook her head slightly, and the other woman's face fell. "I'm very sorry, dear."

When Eva let herself into the room a moment later, her mother was already standing, her hands clasped in front of her as if in prayer. Her eyes flicked first to Eva and then to the empty space behind her. Eva watched as a shadow crossed her face. "Your father . . . ?" Mamusia asked.

"He—he wasn't there anymore. I'm so sorry."

The words hung in the silence. Neither of them moved.

Mamusia continued to stare behind Eva, as if Tatuś would walk in at any moment, surprising them both.

"Mamusia? Did you hear me?"

When Mamusia's eyes finally moved back to Eva's face, she looked dazed. "Where? Where did he go?"

"East." Eva took a deep breath. "To a work camp called Auschwitz. In Poland."

"But that's impossible. He was taken less than a week ago. And we live in France, Eva. This doesn't happen in France."

"I'm afraid it does." Eva could see the crush of people penned up at Drancy each time she closed her eyes.

"But we left Poland. We—we are French."

"We are Jews." Eva's voice was so soft she could hardly hear herself.

Her mother turned away and moved to the window. The blackout shade was drawn for the night, but Mamusia pulled it aside and stared out at the long shadows painting the streets of Aurignon. In minutes, the town would be black, invisible, and the light spilling from their room would be too conspicuous. Eva wanted to pull her mother back from the glass, draw the shade tight, but she couldn't move.

"Which way is east?" Mamusia asked in a whisper, and Eva followed her gaze outside. They were facing away from the disappearing sun, and the sky ahead of them had already turned to thick molasses.

"That way," Eva said with a nod, looking past the stout spire of the Église Saint-Alban, which they could just see over the building across the street.

"He won't come back," Mamusia said as she watched the light vanish. "He will die there."

"No." Eva thought of Rémy's words, and she wondered if he'd been lying. Were fifty-two-year-old men really selected for work duty, or was that left to the younger, stronger generation? Had Rémy merely been telling her what she wanted to hear? "No," she said again, no longer believing herself. "Tatuś is strong. He will return."

Mamusia shook her head, and when she finally turned from the window, her face was drained of all color, and her lips were set in a line so thin they had almost disappeared. "You promised you would bring him back to me."

An arrow of sharp guilt stabbed Eva in the heart. "I tried."

"You were too late."

Eva hung her head. "I'm so sorry."

"You failed him." There was only silence for a few seconds, and then a low, dolorous wail shattered the stillness. It was the sound of a desperate, wounded animal, but it was coming from her mother, whose face was contorted into a mask of pain.

"Mamusia!" Eva said, reaching for her, but her mother's hands went up like claws, and she snarled as she backed away from her daughter. The wail grew louder and louder until Eva was covering her ears, and Mamusia was on her knees, her eyes closed, keening now, her voice a primal song of grief that cut through Eva like a knife. "Mamusia!" Eva tried again, but her mother was in her own world.

Eva didn't hear her come in, but suddenly, Madame Barbier was there, her strong hands on Eva's shoulders. "Get up. Go sleep in the parlor," she said, her voice calm, firm. "I will take care of your mother."

"But I can't leave her!"

The wailing continued, an earsplitting, heartbreaking squall.

"You must. Give her time." Madame Barbier was already moving toward Mamusia, already wrapping strong arms around her. Mamusia's body was limp as she let herself be molded into Madame Barbier's ample chest. Still, the shrieking went on. "You did all you could, dear," Madame Barbier said over the din. "Now, get some rest. Go. I will give your mother something to help her relax."

Finally, Eva backed away from the room. She knew she wouldn't sleep, but she settled onto the couch and closed her eyes anyhow, letting the ghosts of Drancy torture her in the dark.

Eva awoke sometime early the next morning to the scent of real coffee, and as she cracked her eyes open, she thought for a moment she must be dreaming. She hadn't smelled anything like that since before the Occupation; coffee beans were just one of the many things that had disappeared from everyday life. She couldn't remember falling asleep the night before, but she felt a bit restored as she unfolded herself from the sofa and let her nose lead her into the kitchen, where Madame Barbier was humming to herself while she poured coffee into white china cups.

"Good morning," Madame Barbier said without turning. "I'm afraid there's no milk, but I have a bit of sugar if you take it."

"But . . . where in the world did you get coffee?"

"I've had some saved in the cellar for a while now, for a special occasion." Finally, she turned to face Eva, offering a cup of steaming black liquid. Eva inhaled deeply. "I thought you and your mother could use a lift this morning."

"Thank you." The words felt inadequate, and Eva stood there, awkwardly holding her cup.

"Drink, child," Madame Barbier said. "Drink, before it gets cold." She raised her own cup in a sort of toast and met Eva's gaze over the rims as they both sipped.

"I'm sorry," Eva said as she lowered her cup, the warmth flowing into her chest, the caffeine already coursing through her veins. "For last night."

"Oh, dear, you have nothing to apologize for."

"But I didn't know how to help her."

"No one could have. Not in that state."

"But you—"

"I gave her a pill. Sometimes a person just needs to sleep. I had some left from when my husband died."

Eva could see the pity in the older woman's eyes, and it seeped into her along with the caffeine as Madame Barbier patted her on the shoulder and handed her a second cup. "Here. Bring this to your mother. She should be awake by now."

Sure enough, Mamusia was sitting up in bed when Eva entered. Her hair was wild, the circles under her eyes half-moons of deep purple grief. "Mamusia?" Eva asked tentatively.

"Eva." Mamusia's tone was flat, but her eyes were alive again. She looked like herself.

"Madame Barbier made some coffee." Eva took a few steps closer and handed her mother one of the cups. Mamusia took it, inhaled deeply, and then set it on the bedside table. Eva inched closer to the bed, sitting on the edge of it. She reached out to touch her mother's arm and was wounded when Mamusia flinched. "I—I'm sorry, Mamusia. I wish I could have done more."

"You did what you could. I shouldn't have blamed you."
Mamusia looked toward the window. "I just can't imagine him
so far away. In such a terrible place." Her voice caught and she
wiped away a tear. "What will we do?"

"We will survive," Eva said. "And we will be waiting when
he comes back."

Mamusia sighed. "Your optimism. It's so much like your
father's. But look where that got him."

"Mamusia—"

"No, moje serduszko, I don't want to hear your hopeful
words now. There's nothing you can say to make this better."

Eva looked down. Her coffee was growing cold. Her stomach was a churning pit of guilt, regret, and acid. "I know."

"They are erasing us, and we are helping them." Mamusia's
voice was still flat, too flat. "He opened the door to them, didn't
he? Your father went without a fight. And look at us. We don't
even have your father's name anymore. He's been gone for less
than a week, and already we're denying him?"

"But, Mamusia, I—"

"What happens when they come for us, too? When they
take us east? Who will remember us? Who will care? Thanks to
you, not even our names will remain."

Eva could only shake her head. Was her mother right? Would
they disappear like dust, swept from the earth? How could she
stop it?

But then Rémy's voice played in her head. *Come to the church
tomorrow. We will figure something out.* Could the two of them
really do anything to help? It would mean staying here in Aurignon instead of trying to cross into Switzerland.

On the other hand, how could she simply do nothing?

Wasn't that what the people of France were doing? Wasn't that what the whole world was doing while the Jews of Europe circled the drain?

"Mamusia," she said softly, and her mother's eyes finally landed on hers. "I—I have to go."

"Go?" Mamusia blinked at her. "Go where?"

She stood. "To help save us."

"I'm not staying here, Eva. And neither are you. We're leaving as soon as we can." Mamusia frowned at her, but she didn't try to stop her. "So go to those Catholics, but at the end of today, say goodbye. You're a fool to think you can make any difference."

Eva tried not to wonder, as she walked out of the boarding-house, whether her mother knew something she didn't. Maybe it was too late to save anyone. Maybe there was nothing Eva could do. But how could she forgive herself if she didn't try?

The small library behind the church's altar was warm when Eva entered, and the first thing that hit her was the overpowering scent—a milky, salty, sharp odor that made her take a step back. Rémy was sitting at the table in the middle of the room, hunched over several papers spread out before him.

"What's that awful smell?" Eva asked, putting a hand over her mouth.

He turned to face her. There was ink streaked across his right cheek, and she had to fight the strange urge to step closer and wipe it away.

"Well, hello to you, too." He reached for a cloth beside him, wiped his hands, and stood up. "And it's lactic acid."

"Lactic acid?"

He ignored the question. "Are you all right, Eva? How did your mother take the news?"

She took a deep breath to steady herself, which only made the smell worse. She coughed, covering her mouth.

"Eh, you get used to it. But tell me, what happened with your mother?"

"She was inconsolable. She told me I was making a mistake in coming here this morning."

"And what do you think?"

"I—I don't know what to think."

"But you're here."

Eva nodded. "I'm here. For now." She inhaled again and wrinkled her nose. "Now are you going to explain why you're playing with lactic acid in a library?"

He smiled. "After my mother died, I had to move out of Paris for a little while, to my uncle's farm in Brittany. I apprenticed once a week at the dairy down the street. The farmers who sold us their cream sometimes became greedy and tried to water down their product. You know what the chemist at the dairy did to check the fat content?"

"Er, no." Eva couldn't imagine what butter and fat content had to do with anything.

"We took a small amount of each farmer's cream and dissolved methylene blue ink in it. Then we calculated how long it took for the color to disappear. You see, the lactic acid in the cream erases methylene blue."

"Okay." Eva felt completely lost now.

"Most of the real documents that come from the prefectures are signed and stamped using Waterman's blue ink. Waterman's is composed of methylene blue, which is typically impossible to erase. I imagine that's why they use it."

Finally, Eva understood. Her eyes widened as she glanced at the table behind him, which she now realized was lined with identity documents that looked as if they'd been sponged with water. "So you're using lactic acid to erase the ink? On real documents?"

"We've been doing it for months. Pretty smart, yes?"

"It's brilliant, Rémy. Surely this must take a long time, though."

"We haven't always had access to blank documents. Finally, we have a sympathetic official at the local prefecture, and he's able to funnel us some supplies. But for some people, it's still easier to simply modify their original papers."

Eva's eyes drifted to the table again. "And is this what you want me to help you with?"

"No. I mean, beyond figuring out the chemistry, nearly anyone could do the erasing. I suppose Père Clément was hoping you'd help me a bit with the reconstructing of the documents that have already dried. Since you apparently have a talent." He gestured toward the edge of the table, where a dozen or so distressed-looking documents were stacked. "Those need new names and details."

"I can do that."

"Good. I could use the help. We are behind by hundreds of documents."

"*Hundreds?*"

He frowned. "It's only me here, Eva."

"Perhaps I can come up with a way to get things done more quickly." She had been thinking, since she painstakingly forged her family's documents, that there must be a more efficient way to produce several documents at a time, since the stamps would need to be identical from paper to paper anyhow. She had an idea, but she would need to visit the bookstore again to see if it was feasible.

"Eva, I appreciate your enthusiasm, but I'm making documents as quickly as can be done."

"I'm not certain you are."

He looked insulted. "And you know this from your vast experience in forgery? You said it yourself: you're quite new at this. Eva, don't get me wrong—I appreciate your artistic ability—but this isn't some painting school. This is life and death."

"You think I don't know that?"

"I think you had some success under massive pressure, and now you think you know what you're doing. But look at what nearly happened to you on the train to Paris. There are many intricacies you don't understand yet."

She glared at him. "Then teach me."

His expression softened. He looked almost amused. "Teach you? Does that mean you plan to stay for a while?"

She wondered if she had somehow played right into his hands. "I don't know yet." She didn't wait for a reply before heading out into the church to find the priest, Rémy following right behind her. She would tell Père Clément that she'd had a thought about how to speed up their process, but that she couldn't stay forever to help. It was the best she could do, and it felt right. "In the meantime, there's no time to waste, is there?"

Chapter Thirteen

Ten minutes later, Père Clément was watching Rémy and Eva bicker about who had the better ideas for forgery, a bemused expression on his face. Eva had found him in an empty confession booth, and he had lowered the privacy screen and asked her to bring Rémy in for a quick chat.

"Colette," he said when Rémy finally took a breath after reminding them how revolutionary his own lactic acid idea had been. "You say you have an idea for how to produce documents more quickly?"

"Yes. Though I don't know if it will work."

Rémy muttered something unintelligible.

Eva gave him a look and then turned back to the priest. "And it's Eva, Père Clément. Rémy already knows my real name; you might as well, too."

He smiled. "It's a pleasure to meet you, Eva." He turned to Rémy. "Eva is good. Very good. You see it, too, I know you do. Would you have gone running after her to Paris without telling me if you didn't?"

Rémy's eyes flicked to Eva. "Well, I'm better than she is at erasing things," Rémy finally grumbled. "You can't argue with that."

"So let's see if Eva is better at creating them, and quickly," Père Clément said. "We need her."

Rémy shot another glance at Eva. "I would be happy to take her on as my assistant."

Père Clément's lips twitched at the corners. "I was rather thinking that you could be hers."

Rémy's nostrils flared, and this time, when he spoke under his breath, the words were clear—and not particularly nice. He turned and strode away, slamming the door to the confessional.

"Wait, Rémy!" Eva stood and started to go after him.

"Let him go," Père Clément said calmly.

Eva stopped and sighed. "I'm sorry," she said. "I probably should have—"

He cut her off. "No apologies. There's no room for ego in our organization, and Rémy knows that. He's good at what he does, too, but different people have different strengths, and we're all stronger when we join. You'll work together as equals, Eva, if that's all right with you."

"Yes, of course."

"Good. Now, shall we go into the library and get started? There's not a moment to lose."

He exited his side of the confessional, and Eva followed. She expected to find Rémy in the library when they entered a moment later, but he wasn't there, which made her feel a bit guilty. She watched as Père Clément moved a stack of books, revealing the same hidden cupboard Rémy had accessed a few nights earlier. Withdrawing some papers, he slid the door closed, replaced the books, and turned back to Eva. "Here," he said.

She looked at what he had given her. There were a few blank identity cards, four or five dozen blank sheets of the crisp woven paper used for birth certificates, and a handwritten list with names and dates of birth. She quickly scanned it. "But they're almost all children," she said, looking up. "Young children."

"Yes." Père Clément was watching her closely.

"Who are they?"

"They need to escape as soon as possible. Many are young enough that they won't need identity cards—just birth and baptismal certificates, ration cards to establish that they are who they're claiming to be, travel passes, things of that nature."

Eva felt breathless. "And their parents?"

"Already gone. East."

East. Their parents had been taken, just like her father, to Auschwitz, or someplace like it. "Where are the children now?" Eva scanned the list again. Most of the kids appeared to be under the age of ten, some of them mere toddlers. They had all lost their parents? It was almost unimaginable. "Who's looking out for them?"

Père Clément studied her for a few long seconds. "I can trust you, Eva?"

"Who would I tell? I'm a Jew in an unfamiliar place, traveling on false papers." When he merely raised an eyebrow, she cleared her throat and mumbled, "What I mean to say is that of course you can trust me."

He nodded. "You see, Eva, as you may have guessed, the church is part of an escape line that helps people reach Switzerland safely. We work closely with resistance groups in the occupied zone, and in the past several months, as arrests have been stepped up, they have been funneling refugees here, and to other towns like ours throughout the free zone." He took a deep breath. "In Paris last week, as you know, there were raids and arrests. Our networks helped get some children out before they could be taken with their parents, and now many of them are here, hiding in private homes, all without papers, all without their parents."

"All Jews," Eva said softly, her heart aching.

"All Jews," Père Clément echoed. "All in danger that grows each day."

"How do you get them out?" It would be too conspicuous to take a group this large across the Swiss border.

"That's where you come in. The children will be moved into Switzerland, three or four or five at a time, passed off as siblings traveling with a mother or father, but to execute that, we need convincing documents. And we need them quickly." He hesitated. "You see, there's been some word that the Germans plan to take over the free zone, too."

Eva could feel her eyes widen. "The free zone? But they made a deal with Pétain."

"And you think they will keep their word? Their promises mean nothing. And once they make their move, it will be much more difficult to leave France."

His eyes bore into hers, and she had the feeling he could read exactly what she was thinking. If the border was about to close more tightly, she needed to get her mother out, too.

"There's still time," he said, answering the question she hadn't asked. "I must beg you to stay here, Eva. The volume of refugees is only increasing."

She swallowed hard. "Very well."

"You said you had an idea for how to produce documents more quickly?"

"Yes, though I'm not sure it will work. It's an idea I had last night. Are you familiar with the hand-printing presses they use in schools? The ones that make copies of worksheets for students?"

"I believe I know the ones you mean. There's a felt roller with a sort of gel around it, yes? And then the teachers can write on the gel? How would this work? The documents need to appear handwritten."

"They will be, but the stamps won't. The stamps are the hardest part to reproduce, and the most time-consuming by far. If I can trace them onto the felt roller, and we can use the correct color ink, we can print fifty at a time. I can work on that while Rémy fills the documents in by hand."

Père Clément stared at her. "You think you can trace the seals accurately enough to be convincing?"

Eva nodded slowly. "I think so. I *hope* so."

"Eva, it's brilliant. Would you like to accompany me to the store to buy the press?"

She hesitated. "Won't we look suspicious?"

"Not if the shopkeeper is one of us." His eyes twinkled. "Madame Noirot had quite good things to say about you."

"Madame Noirot?"

"At the bookstore. You didn't think I approached you without checking around town first, did you?"

"The woman who gave me the copy of *Bel Ami*?" Eva was puzzled. "But how could she vouch for me? We only talked for a moment."

"Yes, but she saw in you a kindred spirit, and she guessed— accurately—at what you needed those art pens for. When she came to see me, she said that anyone who saw the magic in books had to be good."

"So is everyone in this town in on your forgery scheme?"

He smiled. "No. But we are a town of decent people. There are plenty of us working for the cause, and plenty more who are happy to turn a blind eye. So while you are mostly safe here, Eva, never make the mistake of letting down your guard. Now, shall we go see Madame Noirot?"

She nodded, but as she followed him out the door, a feeling of unease settled over her.

Ten minutes later, after making their way through a twisting series of deserted alleyways flanked with wooden balconies and elaborately swirled corbels, Eva trailed behind Père Clément as they entered the bookstore. The shop was empty but for Madame Noirot, who was neatening a display of notebooks near the front. She looked up and smiled as the door chimed.

"Ah, Père Clément. I was hoping you would return. And I see you've brought a friend." She smiled at Eva. "Have you had a chance to start *Bel Ami* yet, dear?"

"I'm afraid not, madame." It was, Eva realized suddenly, the longest she'd ever gone without reading, a thought that made her terribly sad. It was just another thing the Germans had succeeded in taking from her. "I've been . . . busy."

"Ah yes, so I've heard."

Eva looked at Père Clément, but he seemed to be deliberately ignoring her.

"So what brings you in today?" Madame Noirot asked. "Another book, perhaps?"

"No, madame, thank you. We were hoping you might have

a hand-printing press. The kind teachers use to duplicate worksheets for their students."

Madame Noirot's brow creased. "You need to make copies of something?"

"Actually, Eva had a very smart idea." Père Clément finally pulled his attention from the pens and came to stand beside Eva. "What better way to reproduce official stamps?" he added in a whisper.

Madame Noirot opened and closed her mouth. "But I thought you had Rémy etching stamps out of rubber."

Père Clément nodded. "But you know as well as I do how long that takes—and how many different stamps we have to duplicate. He happened to mention that to Eva on the first night they met, and upon thinking about it, Eva had an idea: to reproduce stamps using a roller like this, someone would need only to trace the real stamps with a sure hand."

Madame Noirot nodded slowly. "And to match the proper ink colors."

"Which we were hoping you could help with, too," Père Clément concluded.

Madame Noirot turned to study Eva for a few seconds, a look of awe on her face. "Why, if I didn't know better, Eva, I would think God himself had sent you to us."

Eva could feel herself blushing as Madame Noirot ducked into the back of the store, saying that she was certain she had a few of the hand-printing presses stored there and could order more of the gels if necessary. "Why did you tell her my real name?" she whispered to Père Clément.

He looked surprised. "Well, first of all, I only told her your first name, not your surname. And didn't Rémy tell you? He found you and your mother new identities in the *Journal Officiel*, and yours allows you to use the name Eva."

"But he already gave me a new identity. Marie Charpentier."

"That was just temporary. And since you used it at Drancy, and it's certainly a part of the official record by now, it's better to discard it. Besides, you need an identity you can use along with your mother, since you live together. Rémy has found the perfect family—a naturalized White Russian by way of Turkey who married a Frenchman and had a daughter named Eva in 1920. The fact that the family is Russian will allow Madame Barbier to easily claim your mother as a cousin, which will explain your presence at her boardinghouse. You'll be Eva Moreau, and your mother will be Yelena Moreau."

Eva stared at him. "Finding such a family must have taken him ages."

"I don't think he slept at all last night. He knew you were upset about your father, and he wanted to help you to feel more comfortable here. He thought it might help if you were able to use your real name."

Eva blinked back the tears she could feel in her eyes. She had misjudged him—not that she could be blamed entirely for thinking the worst of a man who was on such chummy terms with the madam of a brothel that catered to Nazis. "He's a good man, isn't he?"

"Indeed he is, Eva. Indeed he is."

Madame Noirot returned then, proudly holding up two wrapped hand-printing presses. "I found them. I'll come by later with some extra gels, but this should get you started. I have some of the special colored ink behind the counter, and I will order more."

"Not so much that it might look suspicious, though," Père Clément warned, taking the presses and ink from her after she'd placed them in a bag. He handed over some francs, which she accepted without looking at them.

Madame Noirot put her hand over her heart. "Why, Père Clément, you act as if this is my first time doing this sort of work." She winked at Eva. "Don't worry. I know quite well how to play the role of the batty old book rat. It's the best kind of cover."

Eva smiled at her, and as she and Père Clément turned to go, Madame Noirot called out once more.

"Wait. Eva?"

"Yes?"

"Thank you. Thank you for being here. You will save lives."

Eva smiled and mumbled a *merci* in return, but as she left the shop with Père Clément, she couldn't help feeling like a fraud. After all, she wasn't some savior for the cause—she would be here only long enough to help Rémy get rid of the backlog. Then she would take her mother to Switzerland to wait for Tatuś.

"Père Clément?" she began as they walked briskly back toward the church. "May I ask you something?"

"Of course, Eva," Père Clément said after pausing in their conversation to nod to the mustached butcher, who was closing his shop, and to wave to the stout florist Eva had exchanged bonjours with on the way to the church for the first time.

"Where did you get the money to pay for the supplies?"

He smiled. "We don't work alone here. In addition to funneling supplies, the underground sometime helps with funds, too. Speaking of which, if you decide to stay with us for a time, there will be some money for you. You'll be doing a job, and you should be paid."

"You don't have to—"

"It will allow you to pay your rent, buy your food." He winked at her. "Speaking of which, I'll get you some blank ration cards for your mother and yourself."

She swallowed her guilt. Leaving would be even harder now. "Can I ask you something else? You said the children whose documents I'll be forging are without their parents." She took a deep breath. "Who keeps track of their real names?"

He looked confused. "Their real names?"

"So that they may be reunited with their parents after the war."

"Oh, Eva, you must understand that their parents may not survive the war."

"I know." She shook off thoughts of her own father as her mother's words replayed in her head. *Who will remember us? Who will care?* "But there must be a way, Père Clément. What if the youngest ones can't recall where they come from by the time the war ends?"

"It's too dangerous to send them across the border with anything bearing their true identities, Eva." There was pity in his eyes. "I'm sorry."

"Could you—could you find out their names for me anyhow?"

"What good would it do, Eva?" Père Clément's tone was gentle.

"I would know who they are," she said softly. "Please. It—it's very important to me that they are not forgotten."

He studied her for a moment. "I will see what I can do. And Eva?"

"Yes, Père Clément?"

"Thank you. I think perhaps Madame Noirot was right in thinking that God sent you here."

That evening, as the light faded from the stained glass windows above the shelves of the small library, Eva was just finishing stamping a batch of documents when Rémy reappeared. Her shoulders were stiff from hunching over the desk, and her fingers ached from meticulously tracing stamps, filling in blanks, and signing papers. Her eyes were dry, her throat raw. She hadn't paused even for a sip of water since she and Père Clément returned to the church that morning.

It had taken her an hour to study and test out the rudimentary device, which she had never used before, and another to trace the first seal she would need. Once it was embossed in the gel, though, she'd been able to imprint the false stamp on twenty-one blank birth certificates in quick succession. The second stamp had taken less time, and then it had just been a matter of giving the children new names and birth dates, and signing the documents in an illegible scrawl. As she'd worked, her mind had wandered to the fate of the children's parents—and to her own father. How many of them were already doomed? She'd had to pause a few times to wipe away tears before they smeared the ink on the new papers.

"Well?" Rémy asked as he walked into the library, carrying a small bundle that smelled delicious. "I've brought you a bit of cheese and a potato. Have you finished some of the documents?" He set down the bundle, and Eva's stomach rumbled.

Eva bit back a smile. "Oh, a few."

"Out with it, then. How many?"

Eva held up the stack of documents. "Twenty-one and counting."

Rémy stared first at her, then at the papers in her hands. "In a day's time? But that's impossible."

"See for yourself." She handed him the stack and dug into the food, moaning as she bit into the potato, still hot from the oven.

Rémy ignored her as he flipped through the papers, examining the first few in wide-eyed detail and then shuffling hurriedly through the rest.

"But . . ." He looked up, his voice trailing off. "They're perfect. How did you do these so quickly?"

She was already bundling up the remainder of the cheese and half her potato; she would take them to her mother. "I'm sure I don't know. I'm just qualified to be your lowly assistant, yes?"

This time, she couldn't hide her smile as she stood, gathered her sweater, and headed for the door. She was halfway across the dark church when she heard footsteps behind her. Rémy appeared at her side and put a hand on her arm. "Wait," he said.

She turned.

"I'm—I'm sorry I said that. You're—you're clearly quite good at this, especially considering your lack of training."

"Well, you went all the way to Paris for me, didn't you? Perhaps we can call it even."

"Will you show me how to do it?" He lowered his voice. "If we can work together . . ."

"Of course." She hesitated. "On one condition."

"All right . . ."

"I want to keep a list of the children we are falsifying documents for. They belong to someone, all of them."

"Surely Père Clément has told you how dangerous it would be to record any of their real names."

"Then help me to find a way to make sure it's not," she said, catching his gaze and holding it. "We owe it to them. We owe it to their parents. Please."

"Why does it matter so much to you?"

Eva looked away and thought again of her mother's despair. *They are erasing us, and we are helping them.* "Because someone should remember. How else will they find their way home?"

Rémy opened his mouth and then closed it again. "I can't promise anything. But I will think about it."

"Thank you." She smiled at him. "And thank you for the food. Would you see to it that Père Clément receives the documents?" As she walked away, she could feel his eyes following her until she slipped into the quiet twilight.

"Where have you been?" Mamusia was pacing, her face flushed, when Eva let herself into the room. Her overcoat was on, and both suitcases were packed and lined up neatly by the door.

"Mamusia, what is this?" Eva stopped in the doorway and stared.

"I have decided we are going back to Paris," Mamusia said firmly. "Though now we will have to wait until tomorrow, of course. We've already been delayed enough."

Eva looked from her mother to the bags and back, then she

closed the door softly behind her. "Mamusia, we can't go to Paris."

"Of course we can!" her mother huffed. "I've thought long and hard about it. We need to be there when your father comes back. How else will he find us? If we are in Switzerland, he won't know. No, Paris is the only way."

"But, Mamusia," Eva said gently. "Tatuś is not coming back."

"How dare you say such a thing?" Mamusia's voice rose to a shriek. "Of course he is! His deportation was a mistake, and as soon as they realize the error—"

"Mamusia," Eva repeated, more firmly this time. "It wasn't an error."

"Your father will find a way to—"

"No." Eva cut her off. "He won't. He is gone."

"You're not saying he's dead?" her mother screeched.

"No," Eva said quickly, though in the depths of her heart, she knew it might well be true. The thought had been nibbling at the corners of her consciousness all day, a voice whispering in her ear as she diligently wrote names and birth dates that would perhaps save a few lives. "No, I'm not saying that, Mamusia. Just that he's not coming back right now."

"You don't know that! No, Eva, we are going to Paris, and that is final."

"Mamusia, Paris isn't the city we left behind. We can't even return to our own apartment."

"You're not making sense. Whyever not? It's ours!"

Eva took a deep breath. She hadn't told her about their old neighbors yet; she had hoped to spare her the pain. But it was too late for that now. "Because the Fontains have already moved in."

Mamusia looked at her blankly. "Eva, you're speaking nonsense. The Fontains have their own apartment, just down the hall."

"Ours is bigger, nicer. Madame Fontain has no doubt had her eye on it since the start of the war. And what do you think would happen if we went back and tried to claim it? You don't think she would call the police right away, have us arrested?"

"She's living in *our apartment?*" Something in Mamusia's face changed. "So we should just let that horrid woman have it? Despite the fact that we worked hard and paid for it honestly for decades? We should just roll over like the dogs she believes we are?"

"I don't like it any more than you do, but we don't have a choice."

Mamusia pressed her lips together, the skin around them going white with anger. "We always have a choice. And it seems to me that *you're* choosing to forsake what is ours—and to abandon your father."

"Mamusia, we aren't abandoning him. We're trying to survive. It's what he would want."

"How would you know?" Her mother choked out a sob. "We failed him, Eva! Can't you see that? We let them take him! *You* let them take him! You knew they were coming and you just stood there and did nothing."

Eva hung her head, accepting the blame. She should have tried harder to persuade her father to flee. She would never escape the weight of that on her conscience.

"And now what?" her mother demanded. She began pacing again, punctuating her words by jabbing the air. "Now you just want to start our lives over, pretend that Paris isn't our home?

You never even asked me if that's what I wanted!" Her words dissolved into a sob.

Eva blinked back tears. "Mamusia, our old life is gone."

Her mother frowned and studied her in silence. "Fine. So we will go to Switzerland, then. That's what your father told you to do, yes? He will meet us there when he resolves his situation."

Eva averted her eyes so her mother couldn't see the pain in them. Did Mamusia really think that Tatuś would somehow negotiate his way out of a German camp and find his way back across the continent? "Yes, we'll go, Mamusia. But there are some things I need to do here first."

Her mother stared in disbelief. "Some *things*? Forgery, you mean, just like the lies that got us out of Paris without your father."

"Mamusia—"

"Lies, Eva, they're all lies!" Spittle sprayed Eva. "And you're telling lies to yourself! How can you be so selfish? Why does it mean more to you to stay here and work with strangers instead of doing what's right for your own father?"

"Because I can still help them!" Eva shot back. "Because they are not a lost cause!"

She regretted the words the moment they were out of her mouth, but it was already too late. Mamusia's face was red, her eyes blazing, her lips set in a thin line. She barreled past Eva, knocking her aside on her way to the door.

"Where are you going?" Eva demanded as her mother strode into the hallway. Mamusia didn't answer; she just stormed away, nearly colliding with Madame Barbier, who had presumably come to see what all the yelling was about.

"I'm very sorry," Eva mumbled to Madame Barbier as she started after her mother.

Madame Barbier stepped in front of her, blocking Eva's path. "Let her go," she said. "You, dear, are trying to find your way forward, but your mother, she can only look back right now. She's in too much pain to see anything other than what she has lost."

"But—"

"Give her time," Madame Barbier said, her tone as soothing as a lullaby. "I will do what I can to help. In the meantime, you need to get some rest."

Finally, Eva nodded and turned back into the room. Her whole body ached, and her head throbbed from exhaustion, but she already knew she wouldn't sleep until her mother returned.

Chapter Fourteen

Mamusia let herself into the room at just past four in the morning, sliding into bed, and Eva finally allowed herself to drift off, comforted by the warmth of her mother's body.

When Eva awoke a few hours later, the sun was reaching filament fingers into the room along the edges of the blackout curtains. Eva turned to look at her mother, sleeping peacefully beside her, and she felt a surge of sadness. The fight had gone out of Mamusia, and without it, she looked like a little girl. Then again, perhaps in a way she still was. Mamusia had been only eighteen when she married Tatuś. Without her husband beside her, she didn't know who she was as an adult. Eva dressed in silence and left without waking her.

"Will you look after her today?" she asked Madame Barbier as she passed the older woman in the hall on the way out.

"That depends. Are you going to see Père Clément?"

Eva hesitated and nodded.

"Good. Then I will care for her," she confirmed. "Wait here for a moment." When she returned, she was carrying an apple and a wedge of cheese. Eva held up a hand to refuse, but her growling stomach gave her away, and Madame Barbier insisted with a smile. "I will save some for your mother, too. You will both need your strength."

The streets of Aurignon were quiet as Eva hurried toward the Église Saint-Alban a few moments later, clutching the food. But it wasn't a peaceful silence; the clean air was still, as if the sky was holding its breath, and there was no birdsong. Behind the church, the squat mountains in the distance looked ominous today as they cast their scattered shadows over the town.

Père Clément was sweeping the aisle, and he looked up when Eva entered. "Is your mother all right, Eva? I saw her in the town square last night. You should remind her that it's dangerous to be out after sundown. It's a small town, and in small towns, people talk."

"I'll tell her. And I think she's okay." She hesitated and added, "Just broken, I suppose."

"We all are." He smiled at her sadly. "Eva, Rémy brought me the documents last night. The work you did was incredible."

She ducked her head so he wouldn't see her blush. "Thank you. Will it help?"

"It already has. I've brought you more supplies. And as long as you're willing to stay, well, we would be very grateful for your assistance." He handed her a key. "Here. This will let you into the library. Aside from me, you and Rémy are the only ones who have these."

He walked away before she could reply. She allowed herself a small smile before heading to the tiny library.

When she let herself in, she was surprised to find Rémy already sitting at the table, hunched over something. He looked up with a smile as she pulled the door closed behind her.

"I brought an apple and some cheese if you'd like to share," she said, pulling the food from the pocket of her skirt and holding it out, a peace offering.

He eyed the small meal. "You don't need to give me any."

"I know I don't," she said. But she handed him the cheese anyhow and waited until he'd taken a small bite.

"Thank you." He passed the cheese back and waved away the apple. "As it turns out, I have something for you, too." He held up the book she'd grabbed in a panic the first night she met him, *Epitres et Evangiles*, the thick, faded guide to weekly masses from the 1700s.

She frowned as she took the book from him. "Are you poking fun at me?"

He laughed. "No, quite the opposite. Please, turn to page one."

She looked at him uncertainly. He laughed again and gestured to the book. "Go on."

Slowly she cracked it open and turned to the first page, which featured only the title of the book, a subtitle, the publisher name, and the year of publication. She gave him a look. "But what . . ."

"No, no, keep going. Numerical page one." The old paper crackled in protest as she leafed through the first eighty or so pages, marked with roman numerals, and found numerical page one. There was a tiny black star drawn over the *e* in *Le*, followed by a dot over the *v* in *l'Avent* on the same line.

Eva looked up in confusion. "You're defacing old books now?"

Rémy laughed. "For a good cause, I think. Keep going. Page two."

On the second page was a dot over the *a* in *car*, and on the third, a dot over the *t* in *perfécuteurs*, but nothing had been added to page four. On page five, there was a dot over the *r* in *alors*, but on page six, there were no marks. "I don't understand," she said, setting the book down.

"Have you ever heard of the Fibonacci sequence?" Rémy asked.

"I don't think so."

"I've always loved math. You see, the Fibonacci sequence starts with the number one, then the number one again. Add those numbers together to get two. Then add one and two together to get three. Two and three make five. Three and five make eight. And the series continues like that, adding the two previous numbers to get the following number. Do you understand?"

Eva squinted at him. "I understand the math. But I don't understand what this has to do with an old book."

He grinned. "Stay with me, Eva. Now, continue the sequence, if you will."

"Rémy . . ."

"Just trust me."

She sighed, feeling as if she were back in *l'école primaire*, being given a surprise quiz in mathematics. "Very well. One, one, two, three, five, eight, thirteen, twenty-one, thirty-four . . ." She trailed off.

Rémy was jotting down the numbers as she said them, then he handed her the paper with the numbers he'd just written. "Now, go to each of those pages and find the dot. Write down on this sheet of paper the letter beneath it."

Eva frowned, but she did what he said. On page eight, there was a dot over the *a* in *apôtre*. On page thirteen, there was a dot over *u* in *suite*.

It wasn't until the dot over the *b* in *considérable* on page twenty-one that she realized what she was writing. "Is this *my* name?"

"Very good. It's a way to keep a record of who you are, so that you're never erased."

She looked up at him in astonishment. "Rémy . . ."

"It's not foolproof, I suppose. But who will be looking in an old Catholic religious book to find the names of missing Jewish children? And who would think to decode the stars and dots this way? It should be easy enough. Each name will begin on a new page, and we'll simply add that number to each number of the series. For example, the second name will begin on page two, and then on to page three instead of two, page four instead of three, page six instead of five, page nine instead of eight, and so on. If there's already a dot on the page, well, simply proceed with a new dot, and it will just make the code that much more difficult to decipher if anyone ever tries."

Eva's head spun. "But what about the false names we're giving the children? How will we keep track of those without making the children discoverable?"

"Simple. Just start at the back of each person's sequence and encode the false names in reverse order. Let's take you, for example. The book goes to numerical page six hundred eighty-eight, so the last number that would fit in the book from your sequence would be six hundred ten. We'll start there with a triangle over the first *e*, then over the *v* on page three hundred seventy-seven, the *a* on two hundred thirty-three, and we'll start your false surname, *Moreau*, on page one hundred forty-four. So on like that until we have the whole name down, in reverse, on the very same pages we put your real name. If we run out of room in either direction—if there are more letters than there are pages—it's fine. The beginnings of names should be enough to jog our memories in those cases. You see, Eva? It's nearly perfect."

He grinned at her and she felt breathless. She looked back at the book, and then at him. "You just came up with this?"

"I was up all night. You were right, Eva. We can't erase the children who might not be able to speak for themselves. We'll keep a list of all of them."

"I—I don't know what to say."

"You could say, 'Rémy, you're a genius.' Or, 'Rémy, you're devastatingly handsome.'"

Eva laughed, surprised to feel tears in her eyes. "Yes, both of those things. And also, Rémy, you're a hero. This is remarkable. But what if Père Clément is right about the dangers of keeping the list?"

Rémy shrugged. "He is. And that's why this system will work. I'm sure of it. No one will discover the book, and if they do, the stars, dots, and triangles won't mean a thing. Besides, we'll keep it in plain sight on the shelves; who would think to look inside for anything suspicious anyhow?" He paused. "The pages will fill up fast, so we'll start with black ink, and if we run out of room in the book, we'll go back to the start and use blue." He opened the book once again to the first page and pushed it gently toward Eva. "But we'll never start another name on page one. That will only be for you." When Eva looked up at him, his expression was somber.

She met his gaze and then glanced down at the book, her cheeks warm. "I don't know how to thank you for this, Rémy."

"Yes, well, you'll owe me forever, of course." His easy grin was back.

Eva smiled and picked up the pen he'd left on the table. Wordlessly, she turned to page two and drew a tiny star over the r in *feront* and a dot over the *é* in *étoit*. On page three, she etched a dot over the *m* in *Romains* and on page four, a dot over the *y* in *il y a*. When she looked up again, Rémy was staring at her.

"You're writing my name," he said quietly.

"Yes," she replied. "Page two is only for you."

It took three days to convince Père Clément that their system of recording names would work, and he only reluctantly agreed after Eva had threatened to stop producing documents and Rémy had challenged him to take the book and try to decipher the code. The priest spent a day and a half poring over *Epitres et Evangiles*, and when he finally handed it back, he'd still been hesitant.

"You know, not all the children will arrive with names," he warned.

"Then we must do our best to discover who they really are before we erase their identities," Rémy replied immediately. "It's important."

Eva glanced at him in amazement, thankful that he was on her side.

Père Clément's brow creased. "You understand that God will always know who they are."

"Sure," Rémy said with a shrug. "But God is busy with many matters right now. Is there any harm in giving him a bit of help?"

"But if anyone gets a hold of the names . . ."

"They will not," Rémy said firmly. "Who would think to look in this boring, old religious text?"

The corners of Père Clément's mouth twitched. "You think this is boring?" He held up the book.

"You don't?" Rémy shot back with a grin.

Père Clément laughed. "I don't think I should answer that."

Rémy left a few minutes later, leaving Eva alone with Père Clément in the small, hidden library. "You know, Eva," the priest said as he placed *Epitres et Evangiles* on the table between them, "I was never trying to erase the children. I only want to save them."

"I know," she said softly. "I do, too. But someone has to prevent them from being lost."

He touched the spine of the book once more. "I'm glad you've joined us, Eva."

She thought of her mother. "I'm not sure how much longer I can stay."

"Remember that God's plan for you might be different than the plan you have for yourself."

Eva nodded. She wanted to believe that there was something in store for her, a greater design for her life, but how could any of this be God's plan? Then again, hadn't God's hand been present in steering Eva here, to Aurignon, to a church where she'd somehow found a home and a way to be useful? She wanted to ask Père Clément if he feared, as she did, that God had turned his back on them, but she wasn't sure she could bear the answer. "How did you become involved in helping people like me?" she asked instead.

He smiled. "I come from Paris, as you do. I'd been here for five years already when the war began, and I heard right away from my contacts in the occupied zone how terrible things were becoming. There's no strategic significance to Aurignon—we're in the hills, on the way to nowhere—and so I suggested to some old friends that they might hide out here."

"Hide out?"

He shrugged and gave her a small smile. "One of them had made the faux pas of striking a Nazi soldier in the Métro, and the Germans were hunting him. He was to be executed, along with his brother, who had been there at the time and did nothing to help."

"Your friend hit a Nazi? Is he a priest, too?"

Père Clément laughed. "No. An old schoolmate. Not a bad fellow, but when he and his brother got here, I reminded him that perhaps the best way to take on the enemy is not literally to his face, but beneath his nose.

"In any case, he needed to get out of France before the Germans caught up with him," the priest continued as Eva smiled. "He came with his own false papers, so all I had to do was to connect him and his brother with a *passeur* to get them across the border to Switzerland, an easy enough task. But the night before he and his brother departed, we stayed up late with a bottle of wine, and before he went to bed, he asked if I would be interested in helping more of his friends. He said that he had already vouched for me, and that if I was willing, a network he knew of might like to begin sending people south to Aurignon when the need arose. I imagined I might encounter one or two *résistants* a month, and so I agreed, grateful to be able to help the cause in some way.

"But when he got word back to Paris that I was open to helping, it was as if the floodgates had been opened. A man with a British accent came the following week and asked me many questions, and then the refugees began arriving. Résistants at first, and then Jews. Even a few pilots who had been shot down over northern France and were trying to get back home. There were others sent to develop a network here, to assess who could be trusted and who should be involved. And when the volume of people began to increase, they sent me Rémy."

"Rémy?"

Père Clément nodded. "He was part of a group in Paris, and he'd begun to make a name for himself as a forger, but there were others there who were faster and better, and well, as you know, Rémy has a bit of an issue with his pride. I think perhaps he shot off his mouth one too many times to the wrong people. But the network couldn't lose such a skilled forger, and so they reassigned him to Aurignon."

"As a punishment, you mean?" Eva asked.

"I prefer to think of it as an opportunity," Père Clément said with a smile. "As does Rémy, I hope. Whatever happened, their loss is our gain. As much as I sometimes enjoy suggesting otherwise, he's talented and dedicated. And though a whole network has developed here, Rémy remains the one person I truly trust with my life."

Eva opened her mouth to ask why, but she realized that she knew the answer to her own question. She'd only known Rémy for a short time, and already he had come to her rescue and proven himself an ally. He was brash, but she also sensed that once he had decided you were on his side, he would be fiercely loyal.

"As you said, Rémy is one of the good ones," Père Clément said. "And I think, Eva, that you are one of the good ones, too.

There's danger in being principled in the midst of a war, but I believe that it's more dangerous not to be."

"What do you mean?"

He seemed to be searching for the words. "I mean that I would rather die knowing I tried to do the right thing than live knowing I had turned my back. Do you understand?"

A shiver ran through Eva. Though he hadn't explicitly said it, she had the feeling he was asking whether she felt the same. But did she? Was this a cause worth laying her life down for? And even if it was, would she regret her choices if she found herself on the wrong end of a Nazi rifle one day? Was it a mistake to ally herself with this near-stranger, or was it where her life had always been leading? After all, what were the odds that she had landed right in the path of an escape network that needed a skilled forger?

And so she took a deep breath and glanced at the faded leatherbound book that lay before them, the one that would hold secrets and perhaps one day restore lives. "I do," she said at last. "I do, and I think that perhaps I am exactly where I am meant to be."

Chapter Fifteen

May 2005

I am exactly where I am meant to be. I had spoken those words to Père Clément more than six decades ago, and they haunt me still, drifting back in my native tongue whenever I believe, even for a moment, that I can lay the past to rest.

Sixty-three years ago, in the midst of a war, I made a choice to stay in Aurignon, a choice that would forever change my life. And now, here I am again, sitting at a gate in the Orlando International Airport, waiting for my world to alter irrevocably once more. Life turns on the decisions we make, the single moments that transform everything.

It's not too late for me to change my mind this time. I could turn around, go home. I could let the past go, let the ghosts sleep, call Ben, tell him I won't be going to Berlin. That would be the simple thing to do, and goodness knows, I've picked the easy way out more often than not in the years since I left France.

When I chose a future with Louis, boarding a boat to America, working hard to lose my French accent, trying my best to assimilate, I thought it would be relatively simple to leave the past behind. After all, hadn't I become a master of changing identities by then? Furthermore, Aurignon was an ocean away, and I could count the time since Rémy had died first in months, then in years, then in decades. It was all supposed to get easier, to eventually disappear behind me.

But it didn't. It never has. And now the time has come to reclaim at least some of what I lost.

As I wipe sudden tears away, my eyes alight on a little boy, perhaps three or four years old, who is lying on the floor, scribbling in a coloring book at the feet of a woman three seats away from me. His hair is curly and chestnut brown, just like Ben's was when he was a little boy, and when he glances up at me and smiles, my heart skips, because for a second, the years are erased, and I see my son just as he looked all those years ago. I must stare for too long, though, for the little boy's eyes widen in confusion, then in quick succession, he frowns and bursts into tears.

His mother looks up from her magazine. "Jay, sweetie, what is it?"

"That lady." He points at me. "She was looking at me funny."

I look at the mother in horror. "I'm very sorry. I didn't mean—"

"No, no, he's just upset because I wouldn't buy him candy for the flight," the mother says quickly. "Jay, honey, be polite." She smiles an apology, and I can see that she's exhausted. I remember feeling like that with Ben in his first few years, too, wondering whether I'd ever feel like myself again. But here we are, decades later, and I still have no idea what that's supposed to feel like. Who am I, anyhow? The student? The forger? The dutiful wife with no past? The tired old librarian who should see the writing on the wall and retire? Maybe I'm none of those people, or perhaps I'm all of them.

I shake off the unanswerable questions and force a smile. "He reminds me of my son." When the woman's forehead creases, I clarify, "Well, my Ben is fifty-two now, but a long time ago, he looked very much like your little boy."

"Ah." The woman nods and ruffles her son's hair. He has already returned his attention to his coloring, trading a red crayon for a turquoise one to color a cow that reminds me of one of the characters in *Click, Clack, Moo*, a picture book I've been recommending to library patrons for the past five years. There's something almost miraculous about seeing a child's eyes light up when you hand him a book that intrigues him. I've always thought that it's those children—the ones who realize that books are magic—who will have the brightest lives.

"Does he like books?" I ask abruptly. "Your son?" I find myself hoping fervently that he does.

The woman looks at me again, but her expression is more guarded now. "I read to him most nights," she says slowly. She adds, "He's too young to read himself," as if I might not realize that a preschooler likely isn't yet flying solo through chapter books.

"Of course. I'm a librarian, you see," I tell her, and her face softens a bit. "I just meant, well, it's always nice when children love books. Books change the world, I think."

The woman nods and returns to her magazine, effectively ending our conversation. I look at my watch—five minutes until we're due to board—and then out the window, where our fat-bellied jet shimmers on the tarmac in the afternoon sun. I tap my feet, jiggle my shoulders, try to shake off the nerves. I feel like a fish out of water, a fish who has no idea how to swim to the place she needs to go.

My eyes settle on little Jay again. I made so many mistakes with Ben when he was small, mistakes that can't be undone, because they formed the very core of who he is. I wish a better future for Jay, but the thing is, parents make all sorts of errors, because our ability to raise our children is always colored by the lives we've lived before they came along.

I feel a surge of guilt. I can't leave without telling my son, even if he has never really seen me for who I am. That's my fault, not his. I dig my cell phone out of my purse and dial his number. I take a deep breath, waiting as his phone rings twice and then clicks over to a recording of his voice. I frown. He has sent me to voice mail.

I waver before hanging up. It's for the best. What if he talked me out of this? What if he insisted I come home? Would I have done it? Would I have traded my past away once again, ignoring the siren song of Aurignon? I might have, and I would have regretted it forever.

A tinny voice comes over the loudspeaker. "Now boarding, Delta Flight 2634 to New York JFK from gate 76." My heart thuds as I stand. The passengers around me begin to move toward the queue, jostling to get the best position in line, but I hesitate. This is it. If I board this flight, there will be no going back. My connection time in New York is short, and I'll be too busy rushing to my Berlin gate to reconsider.

"Ma'am, do you need extra assistance with boarding?" A solicitous Delta employee appears at my shoulder, peering at me with the wide eyes of a twentysomething. "Perhaps a wheelchair to help you down the jetway?"

"No, thank you, I can take care of myself, dear," I say with artificial saccharine, though I know my annoyance is with Ben and young people everywhere, not just her. "I don't have a foot in the grave just yet."

My phone begins to vibrate just as she shrugs and walks away. I dig it out of my purse and see Ben's name illuminated on the caller ID. I hesitate, my thumb hovering over the screen. Then, before I can stop myself, I reject the call and turn the phone off.

I can't turn my back on the past any longer. And so I put one foot in front of the other and join the queue snaking toward the plane. It's time.

Chapter Sixteen

November 1942

By the time the leaves finished falling that November, the Germans and Italians had invaded the free zone, and all of France was under Axis control. Now refugees could find no more safety in the south than they had in Paris, which meant that those arriving in Aurignon had even less time to waste; they needed to get quickly across the Swiss border. And there were more of them than ever trying to make the journey, which was an increasing problem.

In August, the Swiss had closed their borders and then opened them again before finally slamming them shut—officially, anyhow—on the twenty-sixth of September. Now Switzerland would only accept elderly, pregnant, or sick refugees, as well as unaccompanied children and families with children younger than sixteen. Border controls had tightened, and to make it to Switzerland, those trying to flee had to travel through an increasingly dangerous chunk of France.

Despite the fact that Mamusia had begged her to reconsider,

Eva had decided to stay in Aurignon for at least a few months to help Père Clément, and Mamusia had grudgingly stayed with her—a decision that had inadvertently become more permanent with the closing of the Swiss border. Now, even with spotless false documents, a woman in her twenties and a woman in her forties would be hard-pressed to enter Switzerland, which meant that Eva and Mamusia were effectively trapped.

"How will we get your father out now?" Mamusia moaned sometimes at night after murmuring her nightly prayers, as they lay beside each other in the small boardinghouse bed. "What have you done, Eva?" It was enough to keep Eva endlessly treading the deep, dark waters of guilt. Still, she couldn't turn her back on the work, which became more vital by the day.

Eva and Rémy spent nearly every day together, working as fast as they could, but they couldn't keep up with the increasing demand. It wasn't just Jews who needed papers anymore, either. At least once a month, their network received a wounded pilot, usually from Britain, sometimes from Canada or the United States, who could barely speak French, and increasingly, the young people working for the Resistance found themselves in desperate need of cover identities and false papers to avoid the *service du travail obligatoire*, the STO, which required men between eighteen and fifty and unmarried women under thirty-five to be available for forced labor in Germany. For a man under twenty-five, it was relatively easy to buy a year or two by fabricating papers that listed him as under eighteen, but for the men who looked older than teenagers, it was more difficult; they had to establish a trail of papers identifying them as farmers, students, or even doctors, which exempted them from being shipped east. Women were easier; they weren't usually called up, but in case they were, they simply required invented husbands whose paperwork trails would hold up to scrutiny.

But the false papers that meant the most were the ones they crafted meticulously for the children. Their book of names was growing by the day.

"Thank you," Eva said to Rémy one day as they worked side by side on a new batch of orphans who had arrived that week in Aurignon from Paris, where fifteen hundred Jews had just been arrested. Eva was in the middle of making a birth certificate for a three-year-old girl who had been born just after Germany invaded Poland; she had never known a world without war.

He was sitting close enough to her that their elbows touched, though there was plenty of room at the table. She had found herself lately fighting the urge to move closer to him, and it seemed as if he was doing the same. They had become virtually inseparable. He was her first thought in the morning, and the last person she thought of at night as she fell asleep. Mamusia had warned her about him—*You shouldn't be spending so much time alone with a young man, and one who's not Jewish at that!*—but Eva had come to trust him more than she had trusted anyone in her life.

"Thank you for what?" Rémy asked, looking up from a batch of ration cards he was systematically erasing with lactic acid. The room was swimming in the acrid odor, but Eva hardly noticed anymore.

"For believing in me." She felt foolish the moment the words were out of her mouth.

He turned to her, so close that she could see the flecks of green in the irises of his hazel eyes. "Of course I believe in you." He looked puzzled.

"I mean about the Book of Lost Names. About why we need to record who the children are before we change their identities."

He frowned and looked at the birth certificate she was holding. It was only then that she noticed she was trembling. "The Book of Lost Names?" Rémy placed his hands gently over hers and held on until the paper stopped shaking. "Eva, the fact that it's so important to you . . ." He trailed off as he looked into her eyes. "It says so much about who you are. And I'm glad to be your partner in all this."

He took his hands away, and she exhaled, but her heart was still racing. It felt as if all the oxygen had disappeared from the room. She took a deep breath, but she sucked in a mouthful of chemicals along with the air, and it made her cough so hard that she doubled over. Rémy patted her back, and when she finally stopped and straightened up, he kept his hand there, his thumb moving in small, gentle circles along her backbone. Goose bumps prickled her skin as their eyes met again.

"Eva—" he began, his voice low and husky.

Suddenly the room felt too small, too warm, and she pulled back. She couldn't seem to look away, though, and he continued to hold her gaze. "Wh-what is it?" she stammered, her heart thudding.

He continued looking into her eyes in a way that made her feel as if he could see straight into her soul. "It's important you understand that we are not taking away the children's identities. The Nazis are doing that. We are giving them a chance to live. Never forget that."

She blinked at him. "But in changing who they are—"

"We don't change who they are." He touched her hand again,

and when he let her go, she had to stop herself from reaching for him immediately. "You and I have changed our names, too, but it doesn't change who we are in here." He touched her gently, just beneath her collarbone and above her heart, and her pulse raced. "It doesn't change how we feel."

"I'm not the same person I used to be, though," Eva said. "I've only been gone from Paris for four months, and I wonder sometimes if I would even recognize the old me." She hesitated and added, "If my father comes back, will he think I've changed too much?"

"Eva," Rémy said, holding her gaze. "You're still you. You've just found the strength inside yourself that was there from the start." He hesitated and then moved closer, so near that she could feel the heat of him. "I think you're extraordinary." He leaned in, and for a second, all she could think about was the kiss they'd shared on the train and how perfect it had felt, though it had only been for show. Then, abruptly, he pulled back and coughed. "I, um, need to get some air."

He was out the door before she could still her racing heart, and when he returned a half hour later, they worked in silence at opposite ends of the table.

That night, her mother stared at her while they ate beef offal stew with potatoes at the boardinghouse table. Madame Barbier had gone out, leaving them alone for the first time in weeks.

"I understand that you've been going to services at the church," Mamusia said, finally breaking the silence between them. "The *Catholic* church."

Eva looked up, guilt flooding through her. "Well, yes. It was Père Clément's idea." She'd been attending mass each Sunday for the past two months, to help her to blend in. Madame Barbier had proclaimed to anyone who would listen that her Russian cousin was here to grieve a lost husband, and that the cousin's daughter had taken a job cleaning the church each day for a pittance. People would begin to wonder if they didn't see her worshipping.

"He's trying to convert you, Eva, and you're blindly following along."

Eva shook her head. "Mamusia, that isn't what's happening. It's merely part of my cover. If the townspeople have any reason to think I'm Jewish, it could bring trouble to both of us."

Her mother snorted. "That priest has you brainwashed, then, just the way you are brainwashing those young children you claim to be helping."

"What are you talking about?"

"You give them Christian names, don't you, and send them on to Christian households, where they'll be told to forget who they are? And then you fall to your knees in front of a cross each Sunday and pray. I don't even know who you're becoming, Eva. Certainly you're not who I raised you to be."

Eva opened and closed her mouth. "Mamusia, it isn't like that."

"Isn't it? You don't even join me in saying the Shema anymore."

"I—I don't often make it home in time." The truth was, when Eva was young, her parents had taught her that saying the prayer before she went to sleep would protect her from the demons that came in the dark. But her father had murmured it each night of his life, and on a still July night, the demons had come anyhow.

"You're making excuses, Eva. You're a Jew, just like I am. Just like your father is. And by tossing that aside, by going to *church*, you show me clearly that you are forgetting who you are."

Tears prickled Eva's eyes, and she didn't answer right away. She wanted to protest, but what if her mother was right? She had never been observant like her parents were, but still, was she erasing herself the way she was erasing the children's names she sometimes cried over before Rémy arrived each morning? "I will never forget, Mamusia," she whispered.

But what if she already had?

By December, Aurignon was under a blanket of snow, food was scarce, and Mamusia had withdrawn even more into herself. Hanukkah had begun on the third of December, but Mamusia had refused Madame Barbier's generous offer of precious candles, saying stiffly that she would not celebrate this year without her husband. "It is a holiday of praise and thanksgiving," she said on the first night, as she and Eva lay in the darkness, beneath a mound of blankets to ward off the frigid chill. "And what do we have to be thankful for? Besides, the menorah is meant to be placed in the window to show the world that we're not ashamed. And yet here we are, hiding from all that makes us who we are. No, Eva, we will not light candles here in the dark to celebrate a miracle, not this year."

The growing bitterness in her mother frightened Eva, for it felt like the woman she had once known was disappearing. While Eva blossomed, Mamusia seemed to be hardening into stone. "Well, I for one am thankful that you and I are alive and healthy," Eva said. "I'm thankful we have each other."

"But I don't have you, do I?" Mamusia said after a long silence. "All your thoughts are with that Catholic boy lately."

Eva coughed. "Who?"

"You know exactly who I'm talking about. That Rémy. The one who makes you blush each time you say his name. The one you mention over dinner so frequently that I'm beginning to wonder if *he's* the real reason you hole up in that church all day long."

The words stung, not least of all because Eva had been trying to ignore her feelings. She was embarrassed to realize she had been bringing Rémy up so often. "Mamusia, he's merely someone I work with."

"You think I don't see it, Eva? The way you walk around like you're in possession of a precious secret? You think I don't know what a crush looks like? You should be ashamed. Your father is in prison, and you're acting like a lovesick little girl."

"Mamusia, there's nothing between Rémy and me." But the truth was, the more time they spent together, the more she felt for him. He was good and kind and decent, and he was risking his life every day for people like her. How could that be wrong? She had never been in love before, but she wondered if this is what it felt like at the beginning—a desire to soak up as much of the other person as you could, even if it meant throwing logic to the wind. Perhaps her mother was right, after all. "I—I'm sorry," she added weakly. "Mamusia?"

There was no reply. Her mother turned her back, rolling away from Eva, who stared at the ceiling, trying not to cry, until exhaustion finally overtook her.

The morning after Hanukkah ended, it was snowing when Eva arrived at the church, ducking inside and crossing herself in the entrance as she always did, just in case anyone was watching. It had become her routine to kneel in one of the pews for a minute or two before proceeding to the library, to ensure that there was no one else around. Sometimes there would be another person there, fingering rosary beads or staring at the cross on bended knee, and Eva would pretend to pray, too, until they were gone. Lately, though, Eva had found it a perfect place to talk silently to God. Was it a betrayal for a Jew to find God in a Catholic church? She wondered if somewhere out there, her father was still speaking to him, too, from behind a barbed wire fence in a desolate land.

Today the church was empty, and as Eva knelt to pray, she found herself thinking of her mother's words the night before. *All your thoughts are with that Catholic boy lately.* Was Mamusia right? Had Eva gradually abandoned her mother as the pull of Rémy grew stronger?

"Please, God, help me to do the right thing," Eva whispered before standing and heading for the library. As she made her way toward the altar, Père Clément emerged and nodded to her, his expression grave. She nodded back, a bad feeling forming in the pit of her stomach as he limped behind her into the small hidden room.

"We have a problem," he said as soon as he had pulled the door behind them.

"Is it Rémy?" she asked immediately. "Is he all right?"

"Rémy? Oh yes, he's fine, as far as I know. No, Eva, it's about some of the papers."

Eva felt the breath go out of her. "The papers?"

"Do you remember forging papers for a man named Jacques Lacroix? You kept his name, at his request, but you changed his birthdate and occupation?"

"Yes, of course." Eva had just completed documents for the man the week before. He was nearly twenty-four, but she and Rémy had decided to age him down to seventeen to avoid any risk of his being called to compulsory service, for in his clean-shaven photograph, he appeared as if he could pass. She hadn't been told what his role in the underground was, but Rémy knew him, and she'd had the sense he was someone important, someone vital to protect. Her throat constricted. "Père Clément, what did I do wrong?"

"It wasn't you," he said immediately. "Your documents would pass any spot check, but the blanks you're using—the ones we don't get from the prefecture—well, apparently the Germans have some new methods for spotting identification cards and travel permits made from the wrong kind of paper."

Eva swallowed hard. "Oh no. Monsieur Lacroix . . ."

"He's fine. Someone at the jail accepted a bribe, and Lacroix has long since disappeared. But, Eva, the authorities are beginning to understand that there is someone in the area forging documents, and forging them well. That puts you in danger, but it also puts the members of our network in peril." Père Clément paused. "One of the higher-ups in the underground in this area—a man they call Gérard Faucon—apparently has a way to help, but first, he needs to know he can trust you."

"Of course he can. Can't you vouch for me?"

"I already have, but he hardly knows me. He comes from Paris, and he's trying to implement some things that worked there. He would like to meet you in person, this morning." He looked at her expectantly.

"Yes, certainly. Is Rémy coming, too?"

"No, he's—" Père Clément stopped abruptly, cutting off whatever he had been about to say. "No."

A thread of worry wove through Eva again. "But he's all right?"

"I promise. Shall we go? I think the documents for today can wait until the afternoon."

Eva glanced around, her eyes landing on *Epitres et Evangiles*, her Book of Lost Names, which sat on a shelf, sandwiched between other religious texts so that it blended right in. The more names she added to its pages, the more reluctant she felt to leave it behind, but it was safer here than anywhere else. "Yes," she said, turning her attention back to the priest. "Let's go."

Père Clément led Eva through a winding maze of snow-caked alleys to a schoolhouse she'd never seen before, where a handful of children sat inside, bundled in sweaters and faded coats as they watched a teacher write something on a chalkboard. "Remember," Père Clément murmured as they walked around to the back of the building, snow crunching beneath their feet, "Faucon knows you only as Eva Moreau. No good comes from knowing each other's real identities."

There was a faded red door on the far side of the schoolhouse, and Père Clément knocked twice, paused, and knocked once more, then he reached into his pocket and withdrew a key. Without looking at Eva, he unlocked the door and went inside, gesturing for her to follow.

They entered what seemed to be a large, abandoned classroom at the back of the school. It was dark, but the dirty windows let a bit of light in, and as Eva's eyes adjusted, she could see desks and chairs empty, askew. It was as if the children who had once studied here had all fled in a hurry, leaving a broken trail as they left. It gave Eva a bad feeling, but not as bad as the one that swept over her when Père Clément said gently that he was planning to depart before Faucon arrived. "He wants to meet you alone," he said, glancing toward the door.

"But why?"

"I think that some of the things he wants to discuss are best kept between the fewest number of people." Père Clément's voice was suddenly stiff, and Eva realized that for some reason, Faucon was shutting the priest out.

"I'm sorry." It seemed like the wrong thing to say, but it made him smile slightly.

"My dear, you have nothing to apologize for."

"Are you sure this man can be trusted?"

"Absolutely." Père Clément didn't hesitate. "He has proven himself very skilled and useful. And don't worry, Eva, I won't go far. I'll be right outside if you need me. All right?"

She nodded, taking some comfort in the words, but as Père Clément slipped back out into the bright, icy morning, closing her once again into the darkness, she felt uneasy. The minutes ticked by, and she began to wonder whether she should leave. And why wasn't Rémy here? He was as involved in the forgeries as she was.

She was still thinking about him, her misgivings mounting, when the door opened and a man entered in a flash of frigid sunshine, the collar of a wool overcoat turned up, a cap low over his eyes. When he pulled the door closed behind him, the shadows wrapped themselves around him as he moved into the room. "Bonjour," he said, his deep voice muffled by his scarf.

"Bonjour." There was something familiar about him, something that unsettled her and made her feel as if she was somehow failing to connect the dots.

But then he unwrapped his scarf, and as he took off his hat and grinned at her, her jaw fell. "Joseph Pelletier?" she breathed.

"Well, well, if it isn't my *petit rat de bibliothèque*. How is this possible?" As he took a step forward and pulled her into a tight embrace, her mind raced. She never imagined she would cross paths again with the suave Sorbonne student, and certainly not here, not in this new life where she had become someone the old Eva would hardly have recognized.

"*You're* Gérard Faucon?"

"Indeed. And you're Eva Moreau, the master forger?"

Eva nodded, though his words made her feel like a fool. "What on earth are you doing here, Joseph?"

"Well, fighting the damned Germans, of course," he said cheerfully, finally pulling away and putting a frigid hand on her cheek. He stared at her, tilting her head slightly, as if making sure it was really her. "But who could have guessed that the talented young forger I've been hearing so much about was you all along?"

Chapter Seventeen

It took a full two minutes before the shock of seeing Joseph wore off enough for Eva to do more than stare in disbelief.

He looked more handsome than ever, his face chiseled by hunger, his shoulders broader, a single curl tumbling rakishly onto his forehead in a way that made her itch to reach out and brush it away. She shook her head at herself. They were both fighting for France, and she was letting herself succumb to the feelings of a silly child. "But . . . how are you here?"

"I could ask the same of you, Eva. How did you become involved? I have to say, I would not have expected this."

She hardly knew where to begin, so she started with the moment that everything changed. "They took my father."

"I heard. I'm very sorry."

She shrugged, trying to pretend that it was all right, that she had come to terms with it, but to her horror, she began to cry. Joseph pulled her close again, murmuring into her hair as she tried to get ahold of herself. Finally, mortified, she pulled away. "I—I don't know what came over me. I haven't cried about him in months. It's just that seeing you . . ."

"Seeing you brings the past rushing back for me, too, Eva." His voice was even deeper than she remembered, almost as if time had hardened him into something different. Was he thinking the same of her?

"How did you end up here?" she asked.

"Of course, I'm not supposed to tell you—network protocol and all that—but you're Eva Traube, for God's sake." He chuckled as if he still couldn't believe it. "You see, Eva, I was working for a similar network in Paris. Remember when I told you about the plans for the roundup in July and suggested you warn your parents?" The question was mild, but Eva felt the blame in it. He had given her the information necessary to save her father, but she had squandered it. She looked away.

"I tried, Joseph, but they didn't believe me."

"There were many people who didn't think it could possibly happen," he said immediately. "But now we know. In any case, it turned out I was quite good at staying one step ahead of the enemy." He flashed her another smile, and she was reminded that for all his charm, modesty had never been Joseph's strong suit. "When there was the need to expand a network in this part of France, one that could work with the underground in Paris, I was asked to come."

"How long have you been here?"

"Since the end of August." He paused. "And your mother, Eva? Was she taken, too, along with your father?"

Eva felt a stab of pain. "No, thank goodness. She's here with me."

He looked surprised. "Well, then, you were lucky. She is well?"

Eva thought for a moment about pouring out the story of her mother's increasing bitterness, and the way it felt like she blamed

Eva for her father's arrest. But Joseph hadn't come to hear her woes, and she knew that her problems paled in comparison to the things he likely carried on his shoulders if he was active in the underground. "I suppose she's as well as can be expected."

"You must give her my regards."

"She would love to see you. You should come to dinner tonight." Eva felt like a fool the moment the invitation had been extended. It wasn't as if she could offer him a gourmet meal. Even with her small salary from Père Clément and plenty of false ration cards at her disposal, it was nearly impossible to obtain anything decent in the middle of winter. Last night, for example, Madame Barbier had served a pot of vetch, which she'd been boiling all day. The hard grains were typically used only as animal feed, and as Eva had tried to choke down a few spoonfuls, she understood why: they tasted like dirty socks. Besides, even if Joseph happened to be a fan of stewed socks, certainly he had better things to do than come to dinner with Eva and Mamusia, more important people to spend his time with.

So she was surprised when Joseph smiled after only a brief hesitation. "You know what? I would love to. I will bring the materials with me."

"Materials?"

"The things I wanted to discuss with the forger, Eva Moreau. I still can't believe it's you." He patted her on the head, the way one might with a small child. "Give me your address, and I will be there."

"We're in Madame Barbier's boardinghouse. Do you know it?"

"I do. And remember, Eva, you can't tell anyone my real identity." He shook his head and reached out once more to touch her cheek, his hand lingering there, still ice-cold. "Who would have guessed, little Eva Traube fighting the Germans? Wonders never cease."

And then, replacing his cap and wrapping his scarf around his neck once again, he was gone, disappearing out into the sunny morning.

On the short walk back to the church, Eva didn't tell Père Clément that Joseph was a familiar face from the past; she told him only that the meeting had gone well and then gratefully accepted the comfortable silence that settled between them. He bade her goodbye at the door to the church, giving her a paternal kiss on the forehead, and Eva let herself into the small library with a million thoughts swirling through her head.

"So? You met Faucon?" Rémy's voice startled her enough that she let out a small shriek; he had been standing in the shadows near the back bookcase when she arrived, and she'd been in such a fog that she hadn't noticed him. He stepped from the darkness with a frown. "I suppose he wanted to tell you everything we were doing wrong here?"

"Actually, he was quite lovely."

"Not exactly the word I would use to describe him."

Eva blinked in surprise. "You've met him?"

"Twice now. And if he spent as much time helping the underground as he did coiffing his hair in the mirror, perhaps we would have beaten the Germans already."

"Rémy, he's not that bad." She wanted to explain that she and the man he knew as Gérard Faucon had been in school together since they were small, that he knew her mother, that she'd known his parents, that she knew he was a decent fellow, if a bit egotistical. But that would be giving away information that wasn't hers to share.

"I suppose he's all right. He just rubbed me the wrong way. So out with it, then. What did he want to criticize?"

"I don't know yet. He said he'll explain tonight."

Rémy raised an eyebrow. "Tonight?"

"Yes. He's, er, coming to dinner."

Hurt flashed across Rémy's face, and he turned away. "I see. A date, then?"

"No, no, of course not." But Eva couldn't elaborate. She swallowed hard and changed the subject. "So you say you've met him a couple of times? Why?"

Rémy's gaze was sad as he turned back to her. "I've been looking for ways to get more involved with the effort, Eva. I thought he might be able to help me."

"But you're already doing plenty. Look at all the children we've helped together."

"Don't you ever wish you were doing more, though? I feel so powerless here sometimes, especially since the Germans moved in last month." He sighed. "A few weeks ago, I asked for a meeting with Claude Gaudibert. You've heard of him?"

Eva nodded. It was the alias used by the man who was in charge of the Resistance in their area; she had heard Père Clément and Madame Noirot mention him.

"Well, he sent Faucon in his place, and apparently he wasn't too impressed with me. He asked me many questions about the work we're doing here, and he said he'd get back to me about other ways I could help. I didn't hear from him again until earlier this week. He said Gaudibert wanted to know if I might be available for some other operations."

"What sort of operations?"

Rémy's eyes moved back to hers. "He needs more couriers to help escort children across the border to Switzerland. It seems there's an immediate need, as one of the men who typically runs the route has been arrested."

"But, Rémy, that must be very dangerous. You're not really considering it, are you?" Eva could feel tears in her eyes, and she knew Rémy saw them, because he finally softened, taking a step closer and touching her cheek.

"I have to, Eva. I have to do more to help. It's what I came here today to tell you. I've already told Père Clément."

"Told him what?"

"That I leave tonight with my first group of children."

Her whole body felt suddenly cold. "To-tonight? But it's the middle of winter. Surely a crossing would be perilous."

He shook his head. "I'm told we send the children across near Geneva, without going through the Alps, so the weather doesn't pose a tremendous problem. In fact, it limits troop movement, which works in our favor."

"But, Rémy, what if something happens to you?"

"I'll be careful." He took a step closer, his breath warm on her cheek, and for a second, she thought he might kiss her. He merely brushed his lips against her forehead, though, and then quickly stepped back, as if he'd been burned. "Anyhow, enjoy your dinner with Faucon."

"Rémy, I—"

But he had already turned his back, and a few seconds later he was gone, the lock clicking behind him. Eva considered going after him, begging him to give the courier job to someone else, but why would he listen to her? He didn't owe her a thing.

How could Gaudibert so easily risk Rémy's life? If he was captured, how could their network absorb the loss of such a skilled forger? She tried to push the thoughts from her mind, to turn to the dozens of papers she needed to forge that day, but she knew she wouldn't be able to focus. Every time she blinked, she would see Rémy in her mind's eye, cold and alone in a snowstorm, a Nazi rifle to his head.

"Joseph Pelletier?" Mamusia's eyes lit up when Eva arrived home early that day to tell her they would be having an unexpected dinner guest that evening—but that they couldn't utter his real name in front of Madame Barbier. It was the happiest Eva had seen her mother look in months. "Why, it's a miracle! Do you know what he likes to eat, moje serduszko? We'll make him something special."

"Mamusia, I'm quite sure he understands the rations just like we do and would be grateful for anything we give him."

"But it's *Joseph Pelletier*! He was the handsomest boy in school, and from a good family, too. I'm sure I can impose upon Madame Barbier and her farmer friend to help us."

Eva bit her lip before she could reply.

When Joseph arrived just after dark, he had changed into a charcoal wool sweater and pressed black slacks, which made him look as if he'd wandered in from an upscale Parisian café. Mamusia fluttered around him, gushing about how handsome he looked, how wonderful it was to see him, what an honor it was to have him to dinner. Madame Barbier—who had managed to procure a precious chicken and some potatoes for the occasion—seemed overly impressed, too. She was involved enough with the underground to know the name Gérard Faucon—and to realize he was someone important in the Resistance.

"Jo—*Gérard*," Mamusia breathed, leaning forward hungrily as Madame Barbier uncorked a bottle of wine for them and then reluctantly disappeared to leave them in peace. "Isn't it extraordinary that you and Eva have reunited here so far from home?"

"Mamusia," Eva warned under her breath.

Joseph smiled, first at Mamusia and then at Eva, his gaze lingering on her. "Well, Eva herself is quite extraordinary."

Mamusia reddened and fanned herself dramatically, as if she herself had been the object of Joseph's compliment. "Oh, you're very kind, Joseph. She's quite a catch, don't you think?"

"Mamusia, please!"

Joseph smiled at Eva again, his eyes meeting hers. "Yes, I'm certain she is."

"Perhaps we could change the subject," Eva said through gritted teeth.

"Very well." Her mother sighed and plunged into a story about a party she had attended at the invitation of Joseph's parents in the summer of 1937, at their grand apartment on the rue du Renard, and how she had told her husband that it was simply the height of glamour and class. But at the mention of Tatuś, her smile faltered a bit, and she trailed off and looked toward the door as if she half expected him to enter at any moment.

"I'm very sorry to hear about your husband's deportation," Joseph said gravely, reaching to touch Mamusia's hand.

"Thank you, Joseph," Mamusia said with a sniffle. "I look forward to being reunited with him when the war ends. It's just that I miss him very much right now."

Eva swallowed hard and stared at her plate. Mamusia seemed increasingly unable to process the possibility that there might not be a joyous reunion with Tatuś in the making. "Mamusia," she said softly, but Joseph reached for Eva's hand under the table, squeezed it gently, and didn't let go.

"Madame Traube, I would be happy to inquire after him, if that would be helpful," Joseph said, and Eva watched as her mother's head jerked up.

"Inquire after my Leo?" Mamusia asked, her voice high and breathy. "You could do that?"

Joseph shrugged, as if it was nothing to obtain information from a Nazi labor camp, as if there were a correspondence secretary simply awaiting his letter in the land of death and despair. "I have many contacts," he said. "I'd be happy to see if anyone can find out where your husband is now. I'm sure he's thinking of you all the time, Madame Traube."

"Joseph, I don't think—" Eva began.

"Oh, Joseph," Mamusia cut her off, her eyes twinkling with tears as she beamed at him. "I always knew you were a wonderful boy. I've always told Eva that, haven't I, dear? You should wind up with a nice Jewish boy like Joseph, I've always said."

Eva covered her eyes with her right hand, mortified, but Joseph didn't laugh, nor did he let go of her left hand. He only squeezed tighter, and then his thumb began to stroke her palm, a motion of comfort, intimacy.

"Well, Madame Traube, I'd be very lucky to find a woman like Eva, too. You and your husband have raised a fine daughter."

Mamusia fanned herself again and tittered like a teenager before excusing herself to go see about the main course in the kitchen. As soon as she was out of earshot, Eva groaned. "I'm so sorry about my mother. She seems to think this is a date."

"And would that really be so bad?" Joseph asked, waiting until she looked up at him in surprise. "You have to admit, Eva, we would make a good pair."

Eva pulled her hand away from him and looked down, suddenly embarrassed. "Joseph, I—"

"Oh, don't look so worried, Eva," Joseph said with a laugh. "My work doesn't leave much time for romance. I was only pointing out how very lovely you are, and how different you seem to have become since I saw you last." He waited until Eva met his gaze again. "Is that so wrong to say?"

"Thank you." She felt like the shy schoolgirl she had once been, and desperate to change the subject, she asked, "Do you, by any chance, know how dangerous it is for members of the underground to escort Jewish children across the Swiss border?"

Joseph burst out laughing. "I thought we were having a moment, Eva, and you're asking me about the safety of our couriers? You're not very good at this."

She could feel her blush deepening. "I'm just worried about someone."

His smiled faded. "Ah. Your partner in forgery. Rémy, is it?"

"Yes, that's right."

"He'll be fine, Eva. He can take care of himself."

She searched his eyes. "You don't like him. Why?"

"It's just that at a time like this, I find it more comforting to be surrounded by people who are more predictable, people like you."

Eva wondered if it was only in her own head that the comment had sounded like a slight. Was Joseph here because he assumed she was the same old Eva, the docile English student who never spoke up, the inexperienced, sheltered girl who was too nervous to flirt? "I don't know. I think there's a certain value to being able to change when it's necessary. Otherwise, we'd never grow."

Joseph raised an eyebrow. "Eva, you're absolutely right. What I meant to say was that I admire your character, your stability. It's nice to know that I'll always know where I stand with you." He gave her another charming grin.

"So you think Rémy will be all right?" she persisted.

"Well, he's traveling on papers that the two of you made together, so I would imagine there's every reason to assume he'll be just fine. Which brings me, Eva, to the subject I wanted to discuss with you." He craned his neck to look down the hall, and satisfied that her mother was apparently trying to leave them alone for a bit, he turned back to Eva. "You see, the identity documents you've been making are fine. And you've been doing brilliantly with the stamps. But your supporting papers have been failing inspections lately."

Eva's eyes widened. Had there been more issues than just the one with the résistant named Lacroix? "Joseph, I'm very sorry. Was someone apprehended because of our work?"

"It doesn't matter. The problem is that the actual paper the documents are printed on needs to be more convincing."

Eva could feel herself blushing. "We—we've tried to make better paper, but it's not our specialty." She had always known, though, that it was a weak spot for them. Different documents were printed on entirely different types of paper—some closely woven, some fine, some textured, and some untextured—and she'd thought she and Rémy had done a decent job of sourcing the correct varieties. Rémy had even tinkered with making his own paper from wood pulp and water, but there hadn't been time to get it right, not with all the documents that needed to be made. There were only two of them, and never enough hours in the day.

"It's not your fault; it's the network's, for not providing you with the things you need. But that's about to change." Joseph stood and walked to the rack in the hall where his overcoat hung. He withdrew a packet as thick as a dictionary, and Eva wondered, as he returned to the dining room, how he had managed to conceal it so well. "Here," he said, handing it to her.

"What is it?"

He glanced once more down the hall. Her mother and Madame Barbier were still nowhere to be seen. "Open it. Quickly."

Eva unwound the string around the package and pulled back the brown butcher paper. Inside was a large stack of assorted papers, some thick, some as thin as blotting sheets, everything from blank ration cards to blank demobilization orders. She flipped through them and then looked back to Joseph in awe. "This is different from anything we've been able to get here. How . . . ?"

"They're made in free Algeria and parachuted in."

"Parachuted?" Eva had heard rumors of weapons being dropped by the Allies, but blank papers? "By whom?"

Joseph just smiled. "The less you know, the better. But those should last you for a while. Now, go put them somewhere safe for the night. I'll have a few people looking out for you on your way to the church tomorrow, but you should be perfectly fine as long as you conceal the package beneath your coat. The Germans know there's a forgery bureau going on beneath their noses, but they're not looking for a girl. And certainly not one as pretty as you."

She could feel herself blushing. "Thank you. I'll just go hide them in my room." She stood.

"Good." Joseph patted his belly. "Now, I'm starving. Where do you suppose your mother is with that food?"

Joseph left an hour later—full of chicken, wine, and ersatz coffee with a touch of real cream—and on the way out, he reassured Eva's mother that he would see what he could find out about Tatuś.

"So you truly believe, as I do, that he is alive and well?" Mamusia asked, clasping his hand.

"I do, Madame Traube." He kissed her on both cheeks. "We have every reason to be optimistic."

Eva pulled on an overcoat to walk Joseph outside. It was snowing, and the streets outside were dark, empty, and windswept. "Do you really think you might be able to get word about my father?"

Joseph didn't answer right away. "Certainly you are aware he must be dead, Eva."

She choked back a sob. Of course, she knew it was likely, but to hear the words delivered so matter-of-factly felt like a slap in the face. The pity in Joseph's eyes only made it worse. "Then why did you tell my mother that you believed he was alive?"

"I just wanted to give her some comfort. And I think I did." He pulled up the collar of his overcoat as a gust of snowflakes swept past them.

"False hope isn't comfort, Joseph," Eva protested.

Joseph stepped closer and stroked her cheek gently, his thumb rough and cold. "I disagree," he said softly. "We're all pretending to be something we're not, aren't we?" He leaned in and kissed her lightly on the lips, lingering there for a few seconds. As he pulled away, his eyes bore into hers. "In times like these, I think, there's no other way to live with ourselves."

Chapter Eighteen

For the next four days, Eva worked feverishly, turning out library cards, trade union cards, ration cards, demobilization certificates—all sorts of papers she hadn't been able to accurately reproduce before she'd received the papers from free Algeria. Identity cards had been easy enough because the blank documents were readily available at many stores, and baptismal and birth certificates were relatively basic once one had gotten the hang of the various stamps and seals, as well as the differences in documents between different regions. But the others were much harder, and had therefore apparently become the kinds of supporting documents the Germans were examining closely if they had reason to be suspicious.

Rémy still hadn't returned, but he and Eva had spent the past several months transforming the small church library into a workshop, complete with a guillotine-like cutter for cleanly trimming paper, an Underwood typewriter, two staplers, a dozen bottles of chemicals, correcting fluid for erasing ration cards, and a collection of meticulously blended inks that Rémy had mixed to replicate the most frequent types found on official documents. There were common rubber stamps Eva had carefully engraved, along with a dozen blank copy rollers for less prevalent document stamps that would need to be reproduced quickly, and a simple, hand-cranked device Rémy had fashioned that used dust and old pencil lead to make documents appear older. There was even an old Singer sewing machine, donated by a parishioner long ago, that Eva had realized last month could be used to cut out revenue stamps if only she replaced the narrow needle with a larger one.

Each night, all the supplies—with the exceptions of the typewriter and sewing machine—were tucked away into false-bottomed drawers or between books on the shelves, making the room look innocuous, even if it constantly smelled of chemicals.

Joseph dropped by the church on Thursday morning with a new batch of blanks that had arrived from the north by courier. Père Clément let him into the small library, startling Eva, who was accustomed to seeing only Rémy and the priest in the private space. As the priest excused himself, leaving the two of them alone, Eva couldn't help but feel that in a way he had violated her trust. But it wasn't reasonable to expect Père Clément to keep their secret room hidden from someone the Resistance network trusted so deeply, was it?

"You're doing extraordinary work here, Eva," Joseph said, gazing around in awe at all the machines, inks, and chemicals before sitting down beside her and putting his hand gently on her back. It felt intimate, and Eva found herself moving away from him. It wasn't that she minded his touch. Goodness knows there had been a time not so long ago that she had daydreamed about what it would feel like. No, it was that he was sitting in a chair that belonged to someone else.

"Thanks, but it's been quite difficult this week all by myself. Have you had any word from Rémy?"

"No, but we would have heard by now if something had gone wrong. These things take time. He'll be back." He stood and kissed her on both cheeks. "Give my best to your mother." He left, pulling the door closed behind him.

Eva was bent over the table, filling in blank ration cards, when the door opened again twenty minutes later. She turned, expecting it to be Joseph returning with something he'd forgotten to deliver earlier, but when Rémy entered instead, she leapt to her feet and threw herself into his arms.

"Oh, Rémy, you're all right!" she cried, and he hesitated before crushing her to his chest and burying his face in her hair. He didn't say a word, but she could feel his heart racing, and that was enough. He was alive, he was here, and he was in her arms. He was holding on to her as tightly as she clung to him, and that had to mean something.

When he finally pulled away, Eva stared at him, taking in the fresh scratches on his face, the gash on his neck, the yellowing bruise just beneath his left eye. "You're hurt."

He touched the bruise, as if surprised to realize it was there. "It's nothing."

"And the children?"

He smiled slightly. "There were four of them, all from Poland. The ones we created documents for last week."

"Arlette, Jeanine, Jean-Pierre, and Roland." She preferred to remember their real names rather than the false ones she had given them. They'd ranged in age from two to seven—far too young to be running for their lives.

He nodded. "Pages one hundred seven to one hundred ten in our book. They're safe and sound in Geneva."

"Oh, thank God. And you? Rémy, who did this to you?"

"I'm back, Eva, and I'm fine. The rest doesn't matter." His eyes slid away. "I was worried about you."

"But you were the one in danger."

"And yet you were the only thing on my mind." He coughed and turned away, and she was glad he couldn't see her flaming cheeks. "So," he said without looking at her, "how was your dinner with Faucon?"

The sharp edge to his voice replaced the warmth that had been there just seconds earlier, and the abrupt change shook her. "It was fine, Rémy. He'll be working with us more now, bringing us supplies."

Rémy's eyebrows shot up. "Supplies?"

Eva gestured to the table. "Much better paper than we've been able to get on our own. We need him."

Rémy looked down at the documents on the table. His jaw tightened. "Right. Faucon saves the day."

"Rémy—"

"I'm sorry." He blinked at her a few times and then sighed, his shoulders sagging. "It's—it's been a long few days. The destruction outside the larger cities . . ." He paused and shook his head. "Eva, I can't help but feel like I'm still not doing enough."

A chill ran through her. "But certainly you are. The work we're doing here is invaluable. And now that you're back, we can do so much more with these blank documents . . ."

"Eva, in a perfect world, there'd be nothing I'd like more

than to stay here with you. But being out there, traveling with those children . . . There's so much more to accomplish. And I can't do it here."

Her stomach twisted. She understood what he was saying, what it would mean, but he had to see that he was wrong. "I need you, Rémy," she said. "I mean—there's so much work to be done." Too late, she gestured to the papers on the table in front of her, but she knew he'd heard the real meaning of her words. He looked away, and when he looked back, there was so much pain in his eyes that it hurt her to see.

"I want to build you a better France, Eva," he said softly. "One where you have a home. I can't do that if I stay here."

"Promise me you'll wait before you make any decisions." She held her breath.

He held her gaze for a long time. "I promise."

That evening, over a meal of watery beef broth with thin noodles, Mamusia stared at Eva with narrowed eyes while Eva made small talk with Madame Barbier and tried not to worry about Rémy and the decisions he was making without her. After they'd cleared the table and Madame Barbier had gone upstairs, Eva stood elbow to elbow with her mother at the sink, drying dishes while Mamusia washed.

"You're throwing away a God-given opportunity, moje serduszko," Mamusia said suddenly, breaking the uneasy silence between them.

"What opportunity?"

"Joseph Pelletier, of course."

"Mamusia . . ."

"It's plain to see the young man has feelings for you. He said it himself: you're a catch. Are you so immersed in your little forgery operation that you don't see it? He's perfect for you, Eva. And surely it is fate that brought him here."

"Actually, I believe it was the Resistance," Eva muttered.

"Make all the jokes you want, but you can't run from God's will. He has delivered Joseph to your doorstep. What more do you need to see? Can you imagine how happy your father would be if he returned from Poland to find you happily married to a young Jewish man whose parents we knew?"

"I think Tatuś would be happy enough just to return and find us alive."

"Can't you for once listen to me, Eva? I know you think I don't know what I'm talking about, that I'm just an old fool. But tradition means something. Sticking together in hard times means something. Our *faith* means something, though you seem bent on abandoning it."

Eva threw down her dish towel and blinked back tears. "I'm not abandoning my faith, Mamusia!"

"You act as if you think I'm blind, Eva, but I see it, the way you still talk about that Catholic boy. I warned you, and you didn't listen."

The words, delivered coldly and with shame, felt like a slap across the face. Eva could feel her cheeks flaming, her blood surging with guilt and confusion. "Mamusia, you don't even know him. Rémy is a good man."

"There are lots of good men, Eva, but you want to waste your time with a papist? You think you're better than where you've come from, but you can't run from who you are."

"I'm not trying to!"

"Oh, Eva, you've been running since we got here."

As Eva turned to look at her, she was suddenly startled to see how thin her mother had gotten. How had she not noticed before now? Her shoulder blades were like birds' wings, her collarbone a sharp point beneath the neckline of her blouse. Eva felt a surge of concern, even through her anger and hurt

"Mamusia, I'm not running. I'm just . . . I'm feeling things I didn't expect. But nothing has happened."

Mamusia's face reddened. "So you admit it, then? You love him?"

"I didn't say that."

"Well, just remember this. Your father and I left Poland when we were young in search of a better life—for ourselves and for the child we hoped to have one day. You, Eva, were that child, born into freedom because of the sacrifices we made. If you throw that away, you are betraying us in a way you can never take back."

"Mamusia—"

But her mother was already heading for the door. "I'm disappointed in you, Eva, more disappointed than I've ever been."

Eva stood rooted to the spot and stared after her for a long time after she'd gone, her mind swirling, as she wondered why it felt as if everyone she loved seemed hell-bent on breaking her heart.

Eva was working alone the next afternoon when Père Clément appeared in the doorway of the small library. "How's the work coming?" he asked.

"The new papers are helping." Eva gestured with a sigh to the thick stack of documents she'd already made it through. "I—I wouldn't be able to do this without Rémy, you know."

"I'd like him to stay, too," Père Clément said. "But the underground may need him elsewhere. He has proven himself to be a smart courier, and he could be useful to them in other ways, too."

"He's useful here. I can't do this alone."

Père Clément sighed. "They would likely send someone in his place to do the work with you."

Eva blinked at him in disbelief. How could he think that anyone could fill Rémy's shoes? "Père Clément—" she began.

"The work you're doing here is so very important, Eva. You know that, don't you?"

She hung her head. "Yes, but I—"

"Eva," he interrupted, "can you spare an hour or so? I'd like to show you something."

She hesitated and nodded. Without another word, he led her out of the tiny library into the church, and then out the door into the afternoon sunshine.

In silence, they walked through the center of town. Icicles hung from eaves, sparkling in the clear light, and pristine snow caked the clay roofs. Père Clément nodded politely at a pair of Nazi soldiers leaning against the side of a building, and Eva averted her eyes. There had been more of them lately, their uniforms stiff, their gazes menacing. They stuck out in the small town, where newcomers—even those without German uniforms—were something to be stared at.

"Can I ask you something?" Eva said as they made their way away from the square down the quiet rue Girault.

"Anything, Eva."

"Do you think I'm . . ." She trailed off, then took a deep breath. "Do you think I'm betraying my religion? My parents?"

He looked at her in surprise, and they both paused in their conversation to wave to Monsieur Deniaud, who was standing outside his butcher shop, deep in conversation with a uniformed gendarme Eva had seen around town. Monsieur Deniaud looked distracted as he waved back, and the gendarme didn't acknowledge them.

"Eva, of course I don't think that," Père Clément said as they ducked down a dark, narrow alleyway between two stone apartment buildings. "Why do you ask?"

Eva was embarrassed to feel tears in her eyes. "My mother," was all she managed to say.

"Oh, Eva." Père Clément's eyes were sad as he looked down at her again. A mangy cat whose ribs stood in sharp relief against his patchy fur slunk out from a shadowy doorway, darting behind a snow-caked bicycle propped against a wall, and Eva felt a surge of sadness for the animal. He'd starve out here, or freeze, if someone didn't catch him first.

"Maybe she's right," Eva murmured. "I don't pray like she does, and I know I should. The traditions have always meant more to my parents than they do to me, and I think I should be ashamed of that, especially now. Especially as the Germans try to erase us."

Père Clément sighed. "Eva, there's something to be said for following the rules of a religion to a T. Goodness knows that rules like that are a big part of a priest's life. But if there's one thing I've learned since the start of the war, it's that as long as we believe, we take our faith with us, whatever we do, wherever we go, if our motives are pure." They turned onto the rue Flandin, a small residential street with a view of the snowy hillsides. "I think what matters most is what's in your heart. Do you still believe in God?"

"Of course I do." The question caught her off guard, because even in the midst of such darkness, even when she was wondering whether he was listening, she had never doubted him.

"And have you become a Catholic while working in the church?"

She gave him a sharp look. "Of course not!"

He smiled. "That's your mother's concern, isn't it? That you'll spontaneously become one of us?"

Eva hesitated. "Yes. She—she talks about Catholicism as if it were one of the worst fates that could befall a person. I'm sorry," she added hastily.

Père Clément shook his head. "Eva, she's merely frightened. And I don't blame her. You've found a way to help, to do some good, but think of how powerless she must feel, especially with your father gone. You can't fault her for worrying that she's losing you, too. And if it would help ease her mind, you could try to pray with her more often. Maybe you'll draw some comfort from that, too. But above all, remember to listen to what's in your own heart. You shouldn't be swayed by her words—or mine. Only you know what your relationship is with God, and you should never let anyone take that from you."

Eva felt a sense of peace as a comfortable silence settled between them. "Thank you, Père Clément."

"You can come to me anytime, Eva. And you can always come to God, too. The path of life is darkest when we choose to walk it alone." A moment later, Père Clément took a sharp right onto a small side street, the rue Nicolas Tury, pulling Eva along with him. He stopped abruptly outside a narrow, three-story stone house with a single slim balcony jutting over the street. He knocked once on the chipped black front door, paused, and then knocked again, three times in quick succession. There was a long pause before the door was opened by someone Eva recognized from church but had never spoken to, a matronly woman with narrowed eyes and silver hair spun into a bun, who broke into a wide smile as soon as she recognized the priest.

"Père Clément!" She stepped forward and kissed him on both cheeks, then her eyes darted to Eva and narrowed again. "To what do I owe the pleasure?"

"Madame Travere, I'd like to introduce you to Mademoiselle Moreau," Père Clément said, gesturing formally to Eva. "Mademoiselle Moreau, Madame Travere."

Madame Travere nodded at Eva, but she still looked suspicious. "And what brings Mademoiselle Moreau here today?" she asked, returning her gaze to Père Clément.

"She's one of us," Père Clément said. "And I'd like for her to meet the children."

Madame Travere went completely still for a second. "Père Clément, with all due respect, we like to limit their interactions with strangers." When she turned to Eva, her smile was cold. "I'm sure you understand."

"Madame Travere," Père Clément said. "I'm sure you're familiar with the false documents and travel passes we've been using to move the children."

"I'm not sure what you're—"

"Mademoiselle Moreau is the one making them," Père Clément said, interrupting Madame Travere's protests.

Some of the iciness faded from the woman's expression as she evaluated Eva again. "You don't say."

"It's difficult for her, I think, to be stuck in the church all day with no contact with anyone she's saving. It would help to be reminded of exactly what she's risking so much for."

The older woman opened and closed her mouth, and though her expression was still suspicious, she finally stepped aside, gesturing for Eva and the priest to enter. Eva murmured a *merci*, and Madame Travere nodded slightly.

They followed the older woman up two flights of stairs to the top floor, where a large parlor sat empty. Eva looked around in confusion. Certainly, there were no children around. But then, her lips pursed, Madame Travere picked up a broom and rapped sharply on the ceiling three times in quick succession. She paused, rapped twice more, paused again, and then struck the ceiling a final time.

"What is she doing?" Eva whispered to Père Clément, who merely smiled at her.

A few seconds later, a hidden trapdoor in the ceiling opened, and from the blackness above, a folding ladder descended. As Eva watched in awe, a boy of about ten climbed down, followed by another boy a bit younger, a girl of around thirteen, and another girl with lopsided pigtails who couldn't have been more than seven.

"They'd just finished school for the day when you knocked," Madame Travere said. "It took longer than usual to hustle them into the attic."

Eva just looked at her.

"They often hide when someone arrives at the door," Père Clément explained. "Just in case."

"And . . . they go to school?"

"Well, yes, of course," Madame Travere snapped. "You didn't think that was just a holiday for them, did you? Surely you don't expect me to let them simply sit around and *play*. Their brains would turn to soup."

"What Madame Travere is trying to say," Père Clément interjected with a smile, "is that we strive to keep life as normal for them as possible while they're here. And that means making sure they continue their studies. She tutors them here."

"The war will end someday," Madame Travere said, "and if they don't have an education, where will they be?"

The children had all glanced at Eva with mild interest when they descended from the ceiling, but they were all absorbed in their own activities now and were paying her no mind. The two boys were playing chess in the corner; the teenager was scribbling furiously in a notebook, and the younger girl had curled up in the corner of the sofa to read a book. Eva's gaze rested on her. "They're all Jewish refugees?"

Madame Travere looked away, but Père Clément nodded. "Yes. From the north."

"And what will happen to them when they get to Switzerland?"

"They're adopted," Madame Travere said, her tone clipped. "Temporarily. Until they can be reunited with their parents."

Eva thought of her own father and blinked back tears. "And if a reunion never comes?"

"There are provisions for that, too," Père Clément said. "Some will come back to France, some will stay with their new families. We will make sure all of them are cared for, though. It is the most important thing we do." He paused and added, "And you, my dear, are a big part of that."

"Now," Madame Travere said, clapping her hands once, "you've seen what there is to see. Shall we go?"

She began to walk away, but the little girl with the pigtails had looked up and locked eyes with Eva, and Eva felt herself drawn to the child. She moved across the room, ignoring Madame Travere, who was muttering something about interaction with the children being highly unusual.

"What's your name, dear?" Eva asked, bending beside the girl who still held the book open in her lap.

The little girl blinked at her. "Anne." From the way she said it, her eyes sliding away, Eva knew it was not the name she'd been born with, but rather a new identity someone had given her to get her here safely.

"It's nice to meet you, Anne. My name is Mademoiselle Moreau."

Anne studied her. "That is not your real name, though, is it, mademoiselle?"

Eva shook her head, feeling a surge of guilt. How could she lie to a child? But it was more dangerous to tell the truth. "No. It's not."

One day, when Eva had to produce false papers for the girl, she would learn who she really was. She wondered where she had come from, where she would go from here. She seemed so young to have her whole life ripped from her. "How old are you, Anne?" she asked.

"Six and a half. Nearly seven."

"And what are you reading?"

The girl glanced down at the book in her hands. "*Le Magicien d'Oz.* Do you know it? It's about a girl named Dorothée, who is carried into a strange land called Oz, where she meets a scarecrow, a tin woodman, and a cowardly lion."

Eva smiled. "I've read it. But isn't it quite a difficult book for someone so young?"

The little girl shrugged. "I know most of the words, and Madame Travere has given me a dictionary for the ones I do not. Besides, I think it doesn't matter, as long as you can understand the characters."

"It is rather fun to read about such fantastical creatures."

"I suppose, but that's not what I meant. I meant that in a way, I'm like Dorothée, aren't I? I'm on a great adventure, and one day, I'll find my way home."

Eva had to swallow the lump in her throat before replying. "I think that's a very good point."

The little girl searched Eva's eyes. "Do you know how it ends? Dorothée does get to go home, doesn't she?"

"Yes. Yes, she does."

"And her family is there waiting for her?"

Eva could only manage to nod.

"Good," Anne said. "One day, the yellow brick road will lead me home, too. I know it."

Père Clément appeared at Eva's side then, and he put an arm around her. "Eva, we really must be going. But I see you've met our resident book lover."

Anne smiled up at the priest. "Mademoiselle Moreau has read *Le Magicien d'Oz*, too, Père Clément!"

"Well, Anne, would you believe that Mademoiselle Moreau once worked in a very large library full of books? I believe she loves reading just as much as you do."

Anne looked back at Eva, her eyes wide. "One day, I hope to work in a library, too. Do you think it's possible?"

"Of course," Eva replied, her voice choked. "Libraries are very magical places."

Anne nodded solemnly and then returned her attention to the pages, already lost in the land of Oz once again. Eva watched her for a few seconds before Père Clément led her gently away.

Night had already begun to fall by the time Madame Travere shut the door firmly behind them and Eva and Père Clément began to walk away from the children's home, back toward the church. Snowflakes drifted down in silence, clinging to the eaves.

"Thank you, Père Clément," Eva said softly as they turned a corner.

"There are another sixteen houses in town, and seven farmhouses in the countryside, that are hiding children similarly. Madame Travere has been providing shelter longer than anyone else in town. She was the first to step up when children began arriving from Paris."

The four children Eva had seen today were only a minuscule fraction of the orphans whose parents had been stolen. What would become of them? Would their lives ever be normal again? Was it possible to rebuild when you'd been left with nothing? "How will we save them all?" she finally asked in a whisper.

"With courage, Eva." Père Clément's reply was instant. "And a bit of faith."

Chapter Nineteen

By the time 1943 arrived, it was hard to remember what warmer weather had felt like. Winter had settled its icy claws into Aurignon and was holding on tight, dumping sleet and snow, freezing the streets, sending icy gusts of biting wind racing down the alleys.

The only good thing about the weather was that it had scared the Germans inside. Instead of manning their posts on corners, they were ensconced in the town's only café beside a roaring fire, sipping coffee they'd brought from Germany. Sometimes, the scent of hot chocolate wafted out onto the streets, triggering in Eva a surge of anger so sharp that she was caught off guard. Who were they to enjoy all the comforts of a French winter while the children hidden in houses all around them were hungry and cold? Though the people of Aurignon were no strangers to preparing each year for a long, hard winter, the population of the town had swelled with refugees in the past year, and there simply wasn't enough food to go around.

Despite the muttered objections of Madame Travere, Eva had begun visiting the children once a week, taking great care to slip into the house only when she was entirely alone on the street, with no one to see where she was vanishing to. Aurignon was a small place, with no more than a thousand residents, and that meant that everyone had at least a vague sense of everyone else's business. The less people saw of her aside from Sunday mass, the better—especially since she could sometimes feel the stares of some of the gendarmes burning into her back as she knelt to pray. Letting them—or anyone else—see her as she approached Madame Travere's home each week could be dangerous.

There had been no new refugees arriving in the freezing cold, so the children Eva had met just after Hanukkah were still here and had mostly acclimated to their new home. They had classes each morning with Madame Travere, and the rest of the time, they entertained themselves in her parlor.

"Do you suppose my parents are still alive?" Anne asked Eva abruptly one day in February. They were sitting side by side on the sofa, Anne with a tattered copy of *Les Enfants du capitaine Grant* open in her lap. In front of them, the two older boys and the teenage girl were huddled around a record player Rémy had managed to procure, listening to a jazz album on low volume, whispering to each other. Madame Travere had pronounced the very existence of a record player in her house scandalous, but Père Clément had convinced her that it would help raise the morale of the children. *Very well*, she had grumbled. *But absolutely no dancing.*

"I think there's every reason to hope they are," Eva replied carefully after a long pause. She knew very little about Anne's life before coming to Aurignon, because the children were forbidden from talking about their pasts, but she understood from

Père Clément that Anne had come from a town outside Paris and that her parents had been taken in late October.

"You know," Anne said after a moment, "when Dorothée is in Oz, she has no idea whether her home in Kansas has been destroyed by a tornado. She is working so hard to get back to her aunt and uncle, but she has no way of knowing if they're there."

"Yes," Eva said carefully. Anne had finished the book just after the New Year, and she'd been talking about it ever since, pinning her hope to the fictional magic that had shown a little girl from a place called Kansas the way back to life.

"But they were there, Mademoiselle Moreau. They were there all along, worrying about her. And when Dorothée got home, they were a family again."

"Yes," Eva agreed again. She took a deep breath. "But, Anne, my dear girl, this is not Oz."

"I know that, Mademoiselle Moreau," Anne said instantly. "We can imagine, though, can't we?"

Eva didn't say anything, because of course the girl was right. That's what books were for, after all. They were passageways to other worlds, other realities, other lives one could imagine living. But in times like these, was it dangerous to dream unrealistic dreams?

"Mademoiselle Moreau," Anne said again after Eva had been silent too long, "I know it's sometimes hard to believe the best. Isn't it better than believing the worst, though?"

Eva blinked at her. The little girl was merely six; how could she have a thought like that? "You're absolutely right, Anne."

"I prefer to have hope anyhow," the girl concluded, patting Eva on the hand the way an adult might do to a child. "I think you should, too. Otherwise, things become too frightening, and it's hard to go on. Now, have you read this book yet? *Les Enfants du capitaine Grant?*"

Eva smiled. "By Jules Verne? Yes, I read it when I was about your age."

"Good. Then you must know that even when things seem darkest, there is hope."

Eva vaguely remembered that the titular children of the story are eventually reunited with their father after a harrowing journey around the world. "I suppose there is, Anne. I suppose there is."

That afternoon, Eva was working alone in the church library by the light of a single candle when Père Clément arrived, his expression grave. "There's a batch of papers needed urgently," he said, handing Eva a list. "By tomorrow morning, if you can."

Eva looked down. There were four names, all of which had become familiar to her in the past few months. She stopped, trembling, when she reached the last: little Anne. "I thought the couriers were planning to wait for warmer weather," she said softly, looking up.

"We've received word that the Germans are about to raid Madame Travere's home, possibly as soon as tomorrow. They suspect there are Jewish children being hidden there."

Eva felt as if her blood had turned to ice. "But how? Who could have told them?"

Père Clément's mouth was a thin line. "It could have been anyone: a jealous neighbor, a nosy passerby, a policeman looking to curry favor. Though most of the townspeople here hate the

Occupation, there are a handful who look at it as an opportunity to profit."

"How could they betray *children*, though?" Eva could feel her temper rising. "And what do the Germans want with them anyhow? What harm could they do?"

Père Clément sighed. "It seems that's not the point."

"Can I at least go say goodbye?"

"I'm afraid not. If the Germans are watching the house, we can't afford to have you associated with it right now. Besides, I think you will have much to do tonight if the papers need to be ready before dawn. Would you like me to tell your mother not to expect you home this evening?"

Eva nodded slowly and ran her finger over Anne's familiar assumed name, along with a false birthdate that made her five and a half instead of six. "Who is she really?"

Père Clément dug into his pocket and emerged with a second list, which he handed to her. This had become their norm; she would record the names of the children, their real names, and then burn the slips of paper. The real names were kept separate from the false ones, just in case anyone discovered the papers before they could be destroyed. "She is the first one."

Eva looked down. "Frania Kor," she read aloud. She looked up at Père Clément, her vision blurred by tears. "Her name is Polish. Do you know what it means?"

"No."

"*Frania* means *from France*, or *free*." Eva swallowed the lump in her throat. "She was probably born in France, like I was, and her parents thought that alone would keep her safe, give her a better life."

"But we can do it, Eva," Père Clément said. "We can do it for them, keep her safe, make sure there's a future for her after all." He hesitated. "I shouldn't have let you get so attached to her."

Eva wiped away a tear. "No, I'm glad you did. It has helped to remind me who I'm doing this work for." Besides, there was nothing Père Clément could have done to stop it. From the moment Eva first laid eyes on the little girl, she had recognized a kindred spirit, another dreamer who lost and found herself in books.

"But no good comes of giving away pieces of our heart in the midst of a war." Père Clément waited until she looked up and met his eye. "It's dangerous, Eva."

Eva knew then that he wasn't just talking about the children. She thought of Rémy, whom she'd been seeing less of lately as he became more involved in running errands for the underground. "It's more dangerous not to, I think." With a sigh, she turned to the bookshelf behind her to reach for the Book of Lost Names.

"I'll summon Rémy," Père Clément said. "You'll need his help to get through all the documents in time."

"Thank you," Eva said, and as Père Clément left, locking the door behind him, she turned to the book and opened it to page 147. On the second line, she drew a tiny black star over the *F* in *Fils*, a dot over the *r* in *parconséquent*. Here, at least, a little girl named Frania Kor would still exist, even though the world would try to erase her. If she made it to Oz, she would one day need to find her way home.

Eva had already made it through the first two sets of documents by the time Rémy swept in an hour later, his black overcoat still dusted with snow, a bag slung over his shoulder. He set the bag down in the corner and removed his cap, kneading it nervously.

"How are the papers coming?"

Eva sighed. "It's going to be a long night."

"Right. Well, how can I help?"

Eva pointed to the name of the boy she'd watched play checkers a dozen times, a ten-year-old whom she'd heard called Octave. His name, she knew now, was really Johann, which made her think his parents had come from Germany or Austria, but it was impossible to know. He was one of the older ones, someone who had a chance of carrying the secrets of his past with him, but Eva added him to the book anyhow, as she did with all the children. If he was captured or killed in the process of fleeing, at least there would be a record of his name. If a family member came looking for him one day, she'd be able to tell them at least part of what had happened, that for a time he had been embraced by a small town in the mountains.

"You've been gone a lot lately," Eva said mildly as Rémy began carefully filling in the false details on one of the certificates Joseph had delivered in November. The blanks were nearly gone now, and Eva knew she would need to seek him out soon to ask for more.

He looked away. "There are men assembling in the woods," he said slowly. "Training. Preparing."

"For what?"

"For the fight we know is coming."

"But I thought you were just working as a courier."

He turned to look at her, and in his eyes there was pain, but also steely determination. "I know Père Clément believes the only way to win this war is through peaceful resistance. I'm afraid I no longer agree."

"What are you saying?" Eva already knew the answer, though, and instantly, she was battling tears she knew she would cry later, alone.

"That someone has to take the fight to the Germans, Eva. No one is coming to save us. The British are helping, sure, but they're not here, are they? Nor are the Americans. We're on our own, and the Germans are only growing in power while we sit by and sneak around under their noses with our false papers. We have to stop them before it's too late, or we'll have no one but ourselves to blame for losing France."

"Rémy, I—"

He looked at her, but she didn't know what else to say. How could she beg him to stop when deep down, she agreed with him? And how could she explain that sparring with him as they worked side by side for seven months had made her fiercely protective of him? She'd learned his humor, the skills about which he was so confident—but also the insecurities that his occasional brashness struggled to mask. But it wasn't her right to feel that way, was it? They had made no promises, sworn no vows. And so she said nothing, and neither did he for a few minutes. "Eva, I'll be okay," he said at last. "I always have been. I always find a way to pull through, remember?"

"Rémy, I'm very frightened that might not matter at all in the end."

He didn't reply, and they worked in silence for the next several hours, Eva carefully etching the necessary stamps on the roller and Rémy dutifully filling in blanks with a clerk's practiced scrawl. She saved little Anne—Frania Kor—for last, and as she took the girl's documents from Rémy's hands and asked if she could be the one to fill in the blanks for her, she could feel a tear slipping down her left cheek. She looked away, but it was too late. Rémy had seen it, and slowly, with a gentleness that surprised her, he reached out and tenderly wiped it away with his thumb.

He paused, his index finger just beneath her chin, and when she looked up at him, his face was just inches away. The first rays of dawn were piercing the darkness outside the windows, and soon, Père Clément would be back for the papers and the children would be on their way east. But for now, time was as frozen as the icicles dangling from the eaves outside, and when Rémy leaned in to kiss her, it felt like coming home.

As he pulled her toward him, she fit exactly into the arc of his body, the softness of her curves and the solidity of his muscular chest pieces of a jigsaw puzzle she'd never realized was there. The way he kissed her made her feel, impossibly, as if he'd always known her, perhaps better than she'd known herself. His hands tangled in her hair and then roamed her body, timidly at first, shyly, and then with more confidence.

No one had ever kissed Eva like that before, like they knew her inside and out. She had been proper and reserved her whole life, set on making her parents proud, filled with guilt the few times she had necked with good Jewish boys at school, though she had never let things get any further than that. Now, as Rémy cupped her hips, lifting her onto the table where they worked, she wanted nothing more than to feel his skin against hers, to be as close to him as she could possibly be.

Then, abruptly, he stopped, pulling back quickly and leaving her there, still fully clothed, her cheeks hot, her body on fire. "I—we can't," he said, looking away from her as he hastily tucked in his shirt.

"But—" she whispered, at a loss. Had she done something wrong? Perhaps her inexperience had been obvious.

"It isn't you," he said, answering the question she hadn't asked. He still wasn't looking at her, but as she sat up and smoothed her wild hair, she had the feeling he knew she was fighting tears.

"Then what—?"

"I—I can't let another person down," he mumbled, looking at his feet.

"But, Rémy, you won't—"

"I will," he interrupted. She could hear a faint tremor in his firm voice. "I will, Eva, don't you see? I'll let you down, and then I won't be able to live with myself. I—I'm sorry. I need to go."

And then he was gone, running out the door of the small secret library as if the building was burning down. The only comfort Eva had was that before the door closed behind him, he looked back, just once, his eyes meeting hers. And in that split second, she read torture and sadness on his face. He was telling the truth, she knew; he was fleeing because he thought he would hurt her.

And perhaps it would always haunt her that instead of going after him, she stayed where she was, shame and loyalty to her mother rooting her to the spot. By the time she gathered herself and made it to the front door of the church, he was long gone. His footprints in the snow, heading in the direction of the children's home, were the only sign that he had ever been there at all.

✦ ✦ ✦

Eva didn't go home that morning; she wanted to be there to hand the new documents to Père Clément in person, and in the back of her mind, she was hoping that Rémy would change his mind and come back.

She couldn't face her mother, either, not with all the emotions swirling through her. When Rémy had kissed her, it felt like the best thing she'd ever done, the most natural thing in the world. But how could that be when he wasn't Jewish? Her mother would never forgive her, and what if Tatuś wouldn't, either? How could she betray them now? The longer she sat there on the church steps, the more confused she became. Would it be braver to follow her heart at the risk of failing her parents? Or braver to turn her back on a person she was forbidden to love so she could preserve the history being stripped from her people? Neither path seemed the right answer.

By the time Père Clément arrived an hour later and found her sitting in the cold, Rémy's footprints had vanished under a dusting of freshly fallen snow.

"What are you doing out here?" Père Clément asked as he dashed up the stairs, his face red with cold. "Is something wrong?"

"I—" How could she explain it to him without sounding like a fool? "I was just getting some air."

He didn't look convinced, but he nodded and helped her up. "Come inside, Eva, you'll catch your death of cold. Did you and Rémy complete the work?"

She turned away before Père Clément could see her blushing. "Yes, *mon* Père."

Inside, the church was warm, but as Eva led Père Clément

back toward the small library, she felt like she was still made of ice, her heart nearly as cold as her red and raw face. "My goodness, Eva," Père Clément said, looking at her with concern once they were together in the secret room. "How long were you out there? You look half frozen."

"Not long," she said vaguely. She had lost track of the minutes. She only knew it was enough time for the last traces of Rémy to be erased. "Rémy is gone."

"Yes," Père Clément said, and she realized that he had already known.

"Do you know where I can find him?" Eva hesitated. "I think there are some things I need to say to him, things I should have said last night."

Père Clément frowned. "He didn't tell you?"

"Tell me what?"

"Eva, he's escorting some of the children today."

"He's—what?"

"He said he knew how close you had gotten in the past couple of months to Madame Travere's wards, especially Anne, and he wanted to see them safely across the border."

Eva swallowed hard. "He went because of me?"

Père Clément's smile was gentle, and Eva had the sense, not for the first time, that he could see into her heart. "He went because he's a good man, trying to do the right thing."

"But he didn't tell me."

"Perhaps he didn't want to worry you."

Or maybe he had known she would try to stop him. Maybe the kiss they'd shared had been his way of saying goodbye. Is that what he'd meant when he said he couldn't let her down? Was he afraid he wouldn't come back? A shiver ran through her, colder than anything she'd felt from the weather outside. "The passage will be dangerous this time of year," she said softly.

"Yes."

"How long do you think it will take him to make it back to Aurignon?"

"Eva, I'm not sure he's coming back," he said after a moment. "I'm told the underground has other needs for his expertise."

"His expertise?"

Père Clément's eyes were filled with concern. "Before he found his way to Aurignon, he apparently worked a bit with explosives."

"*Explosives?* Rémy?"

"He has a background in chemistry."

"Of course," Eva murmured. "The lactic acid."

Père Clément nodded. "As I understand it, formulating explosives requires some experience with that sort of thing."

So Rémy would be out there somewhere, blowing things up, risking his life. Would she see him again? Suddenly, she felt as if she was sinking. "But I need him," she said weakly.

She wasn't sure whether Père Clément truly misunderstood her meaning or had chosen to save her the embarrassment of a real answer. "You'll be all right, Eva. In fact, the movement is sending another forger in his place to help you out for a while."

"Another forger?" Eva looked around the room in dismay. This had been the space she had shared with Rémy. She couldn't imagine another person here, breathing air that was supposed to be his, taking up space that wasn't meant to be filled by anyone but him.

"In fact, I'm told she's around your age."

"It's a woman?" Somehow, Eva hadn't expected this, but why not?

Père Clément nodded. "She should be here within the month."

Slowly, Eva reached for the papers she and Rémy had forged together last night, the ones that would allow the children safe access to Switzerland if all went according to plan. As she held them out to Père Clément, she mustered her courage. "May I come with you? To say goodbye to him?"

From the way he held her gaze, she had the feeling he could see just what was in her heart. "No, Eva, I'm afraid not. In fact, the children and the couriers are already outside the city. I'm sending someone with these documents now. It's too dangerous to do it any other way."

"So you won't see Rémy, either."

He took her hands in his. "I feel certain we'll both see him again soon. Remember, Eva—we must have faith."

She drew no comfort from his words, though, for she knew Catholics believed they would see each other again on the other side, once they were dead. And Père Clément had made no promises that Rémy would return to them alive. Perhaps he only meant that one day, if they all lived good lives, they would be reunited far away from here. But by then it would be too late.

Chapter Twenty

The new forger sent by the underground two weeks later was a twenty-six-year-old woman who went by the name Geneviève Marchand. Her short, wavy black bob reminded Eva instantly of the actress Marie Bell, and she had the sort of long legs and good looks that might have made her a star, too, in a different time and place. Here, though, her striking appearance only made her conspicuous, and Eva wondered how someone who looked like that was working for the Resistance, which relied largely on people capable of blending in, people like Eva herself.

She had come from an area known as the Plateau, 150 kilometers southeast of Aurignon. There, she had lived in a village where forgery was big business, and more than a thousand Jews were hidden, under the direction of a local Protestant pastor working with the Resistance. It had sounded like an exaggeration when Geneviève first mentioned it, but Père Clément had explained that the story was true. "Now that the networks are beginning to become more well organized, we are in communication with them," he'd said. "That's how they came to send Geneviève here. The man she trained under, a man named Plunne, has forged thousands of documents."

It turned out that this Plunne's methods weren't all that dissimilar from Eva's, though he was working on a much larger scale. It seemed that he had happened upon some of the same ideas for large-scale forgeries, including using the small copiers with the gel rollers to duplicate stamps. That meant that Geneviève fit right in immediately, and though Eva would never admit it aloud, she was better than Rémy had been, more fastidious, more careful. She sometimes caught small errors—slight misspellings or small discrepancies in details—before Eva did, and that alone was worth the price of her company. If her sharp eye saved even one person from an equally eagle-eyed German, she belonged here.

By the time the snow finally began to thaw, Geneviève had been working in the place that had once been Rémy's for more than a month, and Rémy still hadn't returned. Eva worried that she would start to forget him, but every morning, in those first few seconds between dreams and consciousness, she could still taste the sweet saltiness of him on her lips, could still feel the ghost of his body against hers. And then she would be awake and those sensations would be gone, and she would be reminded anew of just how alone she was.

But the longer he was gone, the more she began to wonder whether she'd been fooling herself thinking that her feelings for him could go anywhere. Even in a perfect world—a world where they weren't at war with an enemy who wanted to murder people like her—he was still a Catholic, and she was still the Jewish daughter of parents who would never approve. If the past nine months had taught her anything, it was how deeply family should be valued and respected. Maybe her mother was right, and Eva should forget about him, try to open her mind to someone more appropriate, like Joseph. The only problem was that as much as Eva could manage to talk her head into it, she couldn't persuade her heart that Rémy wasn't worth loving.

Still, he had left her, hadn't he? She knew he was out there fighting, doing good—if he was even still alive—but on the darkest nights, Eva found herself thinking he would have stayed if he'd loved her enough.

Geneviève didn't talk much, which suited Eva just fine. And though Eva grew to trust her, she never told her about the Book of Lost Names. At the beginning, she considered it more than once, for they worked together each day, and there was no doubt that Geneviève was as dedicated to the cause as Eva. But the secret was safer if shared only with Rémy and Père Clément, so the priest agreed not to mention it in front of Geneviève, and Eva only added names to the book when the other woman wasn't there.

On the first truly warm day of 1943, which wasn't until late April, long after the snow and ice had melted, Eva took off from the secret library a bit early and asked her mother if she wanted to go for a walk. In Paris, she and her mother had been *comme les deux doigts de la main*, like two fingers of a hand, two peas in a pod. They had shared everything, and Eva had been desperate to make her proud. Here, though, everything had shifted. Her mother didn't approve of what Eva was doing, and in order to live with herself, Eva had to pretend that she didn't care. But she did, and though she knew the work was important, the distance between them ate at her. Now that Rémy was gone, Eva could more clearly see the gaping hole in her life where affection and loyalty had once been.

"*You* want to walk with *me*?" her mother had asked, pausing midway through folding a blanket to stare at Eva in puzzlement. As Eva had thrown herself more into forging documents, her mother had taken over doing all the cleaning and cooking for Madame Barbier. In the summer, Madame Barbier said, there might be guests, but for now, Mamusia was doing her a service by keeping the place tidy for a small fee. Eva wondered if her mother suspected, as she did, that Madame Barbier simply felt sorry for her and was trying to keep her occupied.

"Is that really so strange, Mamusia?" Eva hadn't intended the edge in her voice, but it was there anyhow.

Mamusia resumed folding her blanket. "I was quite sure you'd forgotten about me, just as you've seemingly forgotten that you're not a Catholic."

"Don't talk like that."

"Like what? Like someone who gave up everything to give you a good life, only to be tossed aside?"

Eva took a deep breath. "Mamusia, that isn't what has happened."

Mamusia snorted, but she finally set the blanket down and turned to Eva. "Very well. We can go for a walk, I suppose. But I promised Madame Barbier I would make the stew tonight, so we must be back within the hour."

Five minutes later, they were walking away from the town center, in the opposite direction of the church and Madame Travere's home, and for the first time in weeks, Eva felt as if she could breathe. Geraniums were beginning to bud in balcony boxes, soaked by the sun, and even the German soldiers dotting the streets seemed to pay them no attention. She waved to Madame Noirot, who was neatening a display in the front window of her bookshop, and to Monsieur Deniaud, who was out of his butcher's apron today, but she avoided the gaze of the hawk-eyed gendarme, whose name she had learned was Besnard. His eyes seemed to follow her and Mamusia until they hurried around a corner.

"Madame Barbier has been good to us," Eva said, just to break the silence between them.

Mamusia gave her a look. "I do good work for her. I keep the house spotless. Don't make it sound like she pities us."

"That's not what I meant."

"Good, because Madame Barbier is lucky to have me. In any case, she doesn't pay me enough. Certainly not what the work is worth. Just like you're not being paid nearly enough for what you do. They don't value us, you know."

Eva sighed. The fact was, Père Clément had offered to give Eva a larger stipend, money that had filtered in from the underground, but Eva had asked that most of the money be sent to the children's homes instead. There was already a new batch of refugees in Aurignon, waiting for safe passage to Switzerland, and a bit of extra money would help feed them. "We don't need any more than we have," Eva reminded her mother.

"Of course we do. I'm putting money away for the future. We'll need it when we reunite in Paris with your father." Her mother was still convinced, against all the odds, that Tatuś would return home.

"Mamusia—" Eva began.

"You are your father's daughter, Eva," her mother interrupted. "And yet you seem bent on creating a life that will have no room in it for him."

"That's not true. I—I will always have room for him. For both of you."

Her mother snorted and went silent. Eva felt tears of frustration prickle behind her eyelids. "Rémy is gone, Mamusia. I just wanted you to know that."

Her mother was silent. "And yet you're still thinking of him."

"I'm trying not to."

Again, it was a long time before her mother spoke, and when she finally did, there was a warmth in her voice that Eva hadn't heard in a while. "Then perhaps you haven't forgotten who you are, after all."

The next day, Eva and Geneviève were working shoulder to shoulder at the table in the hidden library, neither bothering to make small talk as they carefully smudged the fine lines of the lettering they'd just added to a batch of ration cards to make the ink look older, more worn. When they had finished with the ink, they'd need to fold and refold the papers, too, a mechanical process that required virtually no thought but was necessary to make the papers look as if they'd been carried around in someone's pocket for quite a while.

"What were you before you came here?" Geneviève asked abruptly, the break in the silence startling Eva so much that her hand slipped, creating an ink trail across a card that would now need to be discarded. "Sorry," Geneviève said, giving Eva a small, guilty smile.

"It's all right," Eva said with a sigh, reaching for another blank card. "That one wasn't my best work anyhow."

Geneviève nodded, but she didn't say more. Eva knew she was waiting for an answer to her question.

"Do you mean to ask what my job was?" Eva ventured.

Geneviève nodded again. "You're just so good at this." She hesitated. "Plunne, you see, wanted to be a doctor, but the laws prevented him from studying medicine, so he became a typewriter repairman in Nice instead, before he and his mother were forced out. But I think he worked with the precision of a surgeon."

Eva raised her eyebrows. Not only was Geneviève's continued reverence for her old mentor a bit off-putting, but so, too, was the ease with which she shared his personal information. Of course, it had already been established that Eva was trustworthy, but they still weren't supposed to be so carelessly trading identifying details. Suppose Eva was arrested and tortured for information; now she knew where one of the more prolific forgers—someone the Nazis would surely want to capture—had come from, and what his profession had been. "You should be more careful," Eva said gently. "I shouldn't know those things about Plunne, though he sounds wonderful."

Geneviève turned pink. "It's not his real name, Eva, only his code name. In any case, I'm very sorry. I'm only making conversation."

"I know. I'm being too cautious." Geneviève's deep brown eyes were sparkling with tears, so Eva added, "And to answer your question, I was a student in English literature."

Geneviève wiped her eyes and smiled. She seemed to realize that the words had been a concession. The truth was, Eva had probably shared too much, but there were plenty of schools in Paris, which would make her much harder to track, even if someone had that information.

"And you?" Eva asked after a moment. "I only know that you come from the Plateau."

"I—" Geneviève began, but they were interrupted by the door to the secret library cracking open behind them. They both scrambled instantly to hide the ration cards under the books scattered on the table; it was Eva's reaction every time the door opened when she wasn't expecting a visitor. She and Geneviève were fish in a barrel.

But danger hadn't arrived today. Instead, it was Joseph standing there. "I'm very sorry for startling you ladies," he said, stepping all the way in and pulling the door closed behind him. "Père Clément gave me his key."

Geneviève looked quizzically at Eva as Joseph gave the dark-haired girl an appraising once-over. Eva realized they hadn't yet met, though Geneviève had become a part of Eva's day-to-day life. "Geneviève, this is . . . Gérard Faucon." It was still strange to call him by the code name, which didn't fit the Joseph she'd known in Paris. "And, um, Gérard, this is Geneviève Marchand, my new partner."

"Ah." Joseph crossed the room, picked up Geneviève's hand, and kissed it gently, gallantly. He smiled first at Eva, then at Geneviève, and Eva had to stop herself from rolling her eyes at Geneviève's reaction. The other woman had turned red and was tittering nervously and fluttering her long lashes. "I had no idea Eva's new partner was so beautiful," Joseph added with a grin. "I would have come calling sooner."

Geneviève giggled. "It's nice to meet you, Monsieur Faucon."

"And you, mademoiselle. Please, call me Gérard."

"Very well. Only if you call me Geneviève."

"It would be my honor. Now, Geneviève, I hope you'll excuse me if I borrow Eva for a moment."

"Certainly." Geneviève was still the color of a tomato.

"Very well, I'll return her in no time."

Joseph led Eva out of the library and gestured to a pew. "We won't look suspicious if anyone comes in," he said. "Just two lovers here to pray for peace."

His words rubbed her the wrong way; was there no other reason a man and a woman could be together in a church? But Joseph's eyes were dark, his expression serious, and she knew something was wrong. "What is it, Joseph?"

He waited until they were kneeling side by side, pretending to pray. "There were some arrests made in Annecy a few days ago. Your forgery partner, Rémy, was among those picked up."

Suddenly, she couldn't breathe. "What?"

"He was escorting a group of children to Switzerland. His papers did not pass muster when he was questioned."

"Joseph, is he—?" She couldn't say it.

He looked blankly at her.

"Dead?" She forced the word out. "Did they execute him?"

"No, no. They're questioning him now, along with the woman he was with."

The woman he was with. Certainly it was just another passeur, but the words made Eva's stomach twist with jealousy. She wondered fleetingly if that had been Joseph's intention. "And the children?" she managed to ask.

"They're fine. He was arrested on his way back across the border, after seeing them safely across."

"But—I thought he was working with explosives for the underground."

Joseph shrugged. "He was. He has experience crossing, though, and we needed someone who knew what he was doing. We just didn't expect that it would be his papers that would trip him up." He shrugged again, and Eva's face burned with shame.

"But how?" she asked. "How could the papers possibly not work?"

"The Nazis are getting savvier, Eva."

"Well, of course. That's why we've been using the *Journal Officiel.*" It had seemed foolproof; for months they'd been crafting unimpugnable identities.

"Sadly, he was using the identity of someone a local gendarme knew. And thus, the gendarme knew the young man had been killed in a farm accident last year."

"Oh my God," she murmured, the full weight of it crashing down on her.

"Look, Eva, I know this is a setback." Joseph put his arm around her shoulder. "But we must think of the future. I'll speak with Père Clément, too, but the two of you and Geneviève should lie low for the next several days."

She blinked at him. "Why?"

"In case Rémy gives you up."

Angry tears rushed to Eva's eyes. "He would never do that."

"Eva, they're undoubtedly torturing him. You never know what someone will do under that kind of duress."

She felt ill. "But I *know* him."

"Eva." He waited until she looked at him. "It's impossible to ever really know anyone. Can you even say you know yourself?"

She held his gaze. "Of course."

He gave her a sad smile. "Can you *really*, though? After all, you're not the same girl you were in Paris, are you? People change, Eva." He stood. "I'm sure you're right about Rémy, but better safe than sorry."

He left before she could protest further, and after he was gone, she felt like a traitor for not defending Rémy more strongly.

She was still sitting in the pew a half hour later, her whole body numb, when Père Clément entered through the back of the church and sat beside her. "You spoke with Faucon?"

She nodded, and when she turned to look at the priest, she was surprised to find tears falling from her eyes again. "Rémy would never betray us, Père Clément."

"I think you're right, Eva—but Faucon is right, too. You and Geneviève should leave immediately and stay away for a few days, just in case." His eyes were full of sympathy.

"I can't," she said after a long pause, and he nodded, like he'd already known this. "I have to find a way to save him. If it was the papers we made together that got him into trouble, I owe it to him to get him out of it."

"Eva, none of this is your fault."

"I know." And she did. But if there was a way to get Rémy out of Nazi hands, she would find it. "I'll go talk to Geneviève and tell her to leave for a while. You, too, Father. You should be careful."

Père Clément shook his head. "This is my home, Eva." He gestured to the silent Jesus on the cross and smiled. "I'm with him, no matter what happens."

Eva nodded. She understood this, too. When you loved someone, you didn't abandon him. That meant more now than ever before.

Chapter Twenty-One

When Eva returned to the secret library, Geneviève was hunched over the table, working on a replacement identity for a young Resistance fighter.

"Geneviève," Eva said softly, and the other woman looked up with a smile that fell from her face as soon as she saw Eva's grave expression.

"What is it?"

"You need to go now."

"Pardon?"

"There's—there's a possibility we'll be compromised. Faucon wants us to stay away for a few days, until we can be sure we're safe."

Geneviève looked confused. "But there's too much to do, and another batch of children due to leave early next week."

"I can do it myself. I don't want you in danger."

"What has happened?" she asked, her tone softening as she studied Eva's face.

Eva hung her head. "Rémy, the man who was here before you—he was arrested."

Geneviève didn't say anything, and Eva didn't hear her get up, but all of a sudden, her arms were around Eva as she pulled her toward her in a tight hug. Startled, Eva stiffened before hugging back, then she pulled away and wiped her tears.

"He means a lot to you," Geneviève said.

"Yes." It was all Eva could manage.

"How did he—?"

As Eva briefly recounted the story about Rémy's papers not matching up to official records, something in Geneviève's expression shifted. "What is it?" Eva asked, stopping in midsentence. "Do you think they've already killed him?"

"No, no, not that," Geneviève said, and that's when Eva noticed that the other woman's eyes were sparkling with something that looked like hope. "You say his identity came from the *Journal Officiel*? And you two chose a French farmer a gendarme happened to know?"

Eva nodded miserably.

"But what if we come up with a way to explain why he had the young man's identity? What if we make him a naturalized citizen from a country that is allied with Germany, and he could sheepishly explain that he was carrying false identity cards because he was afraid his French neighbors would reject him if they knew? At worst, he might have to serve a week or two in jail for presenting false papers, but they would discard him as an idiot, not execute him as a traitor—especially if he's an ally of Germany. We would just need to find a record of someone naturalized many years ago, as a child, to explain Rémy's lack of an accent."

Eva's heart began to thud. "They would demand to know where he got the false papers."

"So he'll give him the name of a forger in Paris who has already been executed. Laurent Boulanger, for instance. Or Marius Augustin."

Eva stared at her. "Do you think it could work?"

"If we can find the right identity, one that matches up with everything and is entirely ironclad." Geneviève was already moving toward the door. "Look, why don't you leave it to me to find exactly the right name, and you can get started on the documents in the queue. I'll be back as soon as I can."

"Why are you helping me, Geneviève?" Eva couldn't resist asking. "It might be dangerous."

"I don't run from danger, Eva, or I wouldn't be here."

"Thank you," Eva whispered, but Geneviève merely accepted the words with a shrug, and then she was gone, leaving Eva in the silence of an empty library that would never feel right until Rémy was home. But Geneviève was a new ally, too, and there was something to be said for finding people to trust in the dark.

Unable to close her eyes without thinking of the ways the Nazis might be torturing Rémy, Eva worked all afternoon and all night. By morning, when Geneviève appeared toting a cloth bag, Eva had finished all the identity papers and supporting documents for the next round of escaping children, and she had added them to the Book of Lost Names.

"Have you been here all night?" Geneviève asked, setting the bag down on the table and looking around at the neat stacks.

"I couldn't sleep."

"Well done." Geneviève pulled a few newspapers from the bag. "I hope you'll have energy to work on one more set of papers. I found someone perfect for your Rémy—a young man, aged twenty-seven, who was naturalized twenty years ago after arriving from Austria, and who shows up again in a marriage record from August 1942, so you'll have two things to produce that can be checked against official records. I pored over every issue of the *Journal Officiel* in Père Clément's office that is dated after that, and there was no death notice, so I think we could reasonably assume he's still alive. Here are the two journals in which he appears."

Eva took the gazettes, one of which was slightly yellowed, and shook her head in astonishment. "I don't even know what to say."

"There's no need, Eva. We're all in this together. Now, how can I help?"

Quickly, but painstakingly, Eva set about creating false documents identifying Rémy as one Andras Konig, born the twelfth of May, 1915, who had emigrated to France from the first Austrian Republic with his parents and was naturalized in October 1922. He was a farmer, thus explaining why he hadn't been called to obligatory service, and, in accordance with an issue of the *Journal Officiel* from August, she had him married in the Ain department to a French girl who'd been born Marie Travers in 1920. She still had several of Rémy's photographs, tucked away with several photographs of her, in case they needed to make identity documents quickly, so it was easy to affix one to the new identity document and cover it with the requisite stamps. A ticket for bicycling without a light in Servas, and a library card from Bourg-en-Bresse made the cover complete.

By the time Père Clément came to check on them at noon, Eva was nearly done. "How close are you to completing the documents?" he asked as he pulled the heavy door closed behind him.

"I'm almost finished."

"Excellent. When you're done, I'll take them."

Eva's smile fell. "Take them where?"

"I plan to go fetch Rémy myself."

"Père Clément—"

He held up a hand to stop her. "I prayed about it all night, Eva. It's the right thing. I'll go as myself—a parish priest concerned about one of his congregants—and I'll be able to persuade them that he's simply ashamed of his Austrian past, and a bit simple, too. I'll apologize for his terrible error in judgment in using false papers, and I'll give them my word it will never happen again."

"If they've already made him confess . . ." Eva could barely get the words out.

"I agree with what you said earlier, Eva, and I feel certain that hasn't happened. Is there a risk? Yes. But I've spent the war so far safe inside this church while men like Rémy and Faucon are out there risking their lives each day. It's time I do some of the same."

"I'll come with you," Eva said.

He shook his head firmly. "That would only complicate things and make it all more dangerous. Besides, if something goes wrong, we can't afford to lose you, too."

She didn't like it, but she knew he was right. "I—I don't know how to thank you."

"I'm the one in your debt, Eva," Père Clément said. He wrapped his hands around hers and squeezed once, comfortingly, before letting go.

✦ ✦ ✦

Three days later, Eva was working in the library by herself when the door opened. "Rémy?" she cried, jumping to her feet.

But it was only Père Clément, wearing a somber expression, and suddenly, Eva's heart was in her throat. "Père Clément, is he . . . ?"

"He's fine," Père Clément said quickly. "Rémy did a wonderful job of playing along. In fact, by some miracle, he even knew a few words of Austro-Bavarian, apparently enough to fool the gendarmes. Thank God he wasn't in German custody yet."

Relief swept over Eva, but it was still tempered by fear. She glanced behind Père Clément again. "Then where is he?"

Père Clément crossed the room and took Eva's hands. "He's not coming back right now."

"But—"

"He's all right, Eva, but he's needed farther to the north. I'm not sure why Gaudibert and Faucon had rearranged things so Rémy would be traveling so frequently across the border, but the underground needs him for his explosives expertise. He won't be making any more trips as a courier, though, now that he's on the authorities' radar. He is, as they say, *grillé.*"

"Did they . . . hurt him?"

"They roughed him up a bit, but that was it. Apparently they thought he was just smuggling black market cigarettes for profit. No idea that he was working against them. Their misunderstanding likely saved his life."

Eva exhaled. "And he's safe?"

"For now. But what he's doing is dangerous. If the Germans

catch him sabotaging them, he'll be executed immediately. Eva, you have to understand that the odds aren't in his favor."

"They aren't in mine, either. Yet I'm still here."

He gave her a small smile. "I suppose all we can do now is to pray for him—and to do our best here to support the work, as we always do."

"Père Clément?" Eva asked after a moment. "Did he ask about me?"

"Of course he did."

"And?"

Père Clément held her gaze. "He wanted to make sure you were all right, that you were safe."

"That was all? There was no message?"

"I'm afraid not, Eva."

It wasn't until Père Clément left that she allowed the tears to come. She tried to push them away, to tell herself that certainly today's news had been good: Rémy was alive. He was mostly unharmed, and he wouldn't be making any more border crossings.

But he wouldn't be coming back to her. And now she'd have no way of knowing whether he was safe. At least the false papers for Andras Konig would give him an extra layer of protection, but she knew they'd be worthless if he was caught doing something criminal—or if something went wrong and he blew himself up. Père Clément was right, all she could do was pray.

And so she turned to the stack of *Journal Officiel* newspapers and began to flip through, looking for identities she could steal for others like Rémy who were standing on the front lines of a battle the Germans wouldn't see coming.

✦ ✦ ✦

In the next week, Eva went to the boardinghouse to sleep beside her mother only three times; the other nights, she spent holed up in the church, poring over the gazettes, forging papers, and sneaking in a few hours of sleep where she could find them. There were ration cards to be printed, identities to create, children to protect, Resistance fighters to hide. The work never seemed to let up, and to her credit, though she left before sundown, Geneviève worked as hard as Eva did during the day and brought a certain lightness to the somber library.

On the Thursday night after Père Clément returned with the news about Rémy, Eva finally allowed herself to leave early. She found her mother sitting at the window in the parlor, gazing out with a blank expression.

"Mamusia, are you all right?" she asked, bending beside her.

Her mother didn't even turn to look at her. "I'm just wondering where your father is right now."

Eva squeezed her eyes shut and then opened them again. "Mamusia—" she began gently.

"Do you know what we were doing thirty years ago today?" she interrupted.

"No, Mamusia."

"We were getting married. He wore a borrowed suit, and I wore white, and I thought all my dreams had come true. We thought we would have such a wonderful life together. A *long* life. And now, look where we are. He's somewhere to the east, probably worrying about me, and I'm here, all alone."

"Oh, Mamusia." Eva had forgotten the date. "Happy anniversary. I'm so sorry I didn't say anything. You're wrong about being alone, though. I'm here."

"You are in your own world, Eva, and there's no room for me in it."

Eva wanted to tell her that there was no room for anyone, but that wouldn't be true; there had been a space for Rémy, and now that corner stood cold and dark. "Mamusia, I will always be here. I'm sorry I haven't made you feel that way."

Mamusia sighed. "An apology won't return your father to me." She walked away, and a few seconds later, Eva heard the door to their room slam.

Madame Barbier emerged from the kitchen, drying her hands on a towel. "Everything all right?"

"I—I can't seem to do anything but let my mother down."

"Dear, your mother is just exhausted, tired of hoping, tired of waiting." Madame Barbier crossed the room and put a hand on Eva's shoulder. "We all are. This war, it has gone on too long. And all she can see is that the people who matter most—you and your father—have been taken from her."

"Taken? I'm right here."

"It doesn't feel that way to her, though that's not your fault."

"But she's my family."

"And in the midst of a war like this, you realize that family is more than just blood. I'm your family now, and so is Père Clément. So are all the children you've helped save, and the men and women who can continue to fight for France because you've protected them."

"That doesn't fix things with my mother."

"One day she will understand that you did what you were born to do."

Eva looked at her. "With my father gone, though . . ." She couldn't complete the sentence.

"Dear girl, don't you see?" Madame Barbier gave her a small smile. "Without people like you, France will fall to the wolves. The only way to save your mother is to save France. And that is just what you are doing."

After Madame Barbier returned to the kitchen, Eva knocked on the locked door to the room she shared with her mother, but there was no answer.

"Mamusia, please open up," Eva called through the wood. "I love you. I'm not trying to hurt you."

"Go away." Her mother's reply was muffled but the words were unmistakable.

"Mamusia . . ."

"Please, Eva. I just—I want to be alone."

Eva considered staying, trying to wear her mother down with apologies for any hurt she was causing, but Madame Barbier was right. If France fell, she and her mother would eventually be deported, simply because of the Jewish blood that coursed through their veins. Eva had to stop that from happening, and the only way to do so was to get back to work.

The streets were empty and no one bothered her as she made her way back to the church. Inside the main room, candles burned on the altar, and Eva bent to pray. It no longer mattered to her that the man with the kind, sad eyes hanging on the cross wasn't supposed to mean anything to her. She knew now that they were all on the same side. She prayed for her mother and father; she prayed for Rémy; and she prayed for the strength to do the right thing, whatever that might be.

By the time she slipped into the hidden library and lit the

lantern a half hour later, she felt a peace she hadn't felt in ages. Maybe it was Madame Barbier's words about saving France, or perhaps God was listening to her prayers after all and steering her in the right direction. She sat down to work, and perhaps because a weight had been lifted, the ink flowed more steadily, and the work went quickly. By midnight, she had completed three new sets of papers for the newest children to arrive in Aurignon.

It was too far past curfew to return to the boardinghouse now, and though Eva's hands ached, her mind was still racing. She stood to stretch, and after pacing for a few minutes, she decided to head out into the church to say another prayer; it had calmed her earlier, and she knew she needed all the comfort she could get.

She had just cracked open the door from the secret library when she heard voices in the church. Her heart thudding, she melted back into the shadows. Who could be here this late at night? It was too dangerous now, though, to pull the door to the library closed. She was fairly confident, as the conversation continued, that no one had heard her emerge, but she might not be so lucky if she tried to retreat. She stayed stock-still and tried to breathe as shallowly as possible.

The voices—both male—were coming from across the church, and it took a minute for it to register that one of them belonged to Père Clément. She relaxed slightly; he had every right to be here, even if the timing was odd. The man with him could easily be another member of the Resistance or even a troubled parishioner who had come to seek God.

Just as she was breathing more normally, though, the man spoke again, and she stifled a gasp. The man's accent was unmistakably German. Heart thudding, she crept forward, careful not to make a sound. *There must be a logical explanation.*

But when she finally peered over the edge of a pew near the library and saw Père Clément on the other side of the church, her blood ran cold. The person with him was a man around her age with gold, wavy hair and ruddy cheeks.

And he was wearing a Nazi uniform.

Eva put a hand over her mouth and retreated into the shadows. She couldn't make a sound; if the men heard her, she'd be finished. *Unless this meeting is innocent,* she reminded herself. *The German could have sought Père Clément out because he needed religious counsel. Perhaps I'm jumping to conclusions.*

But as she strained to make out the conversation, her last shreds of optimism vanished.

"They'll be moving on the thirteenth," the German was saying in a low voice, his words just barely distinguishable.

"That's sooner than planned." Père Clément's voice was clearer.

"Yes. That's why I've come. I need names."

"And then what?"

"We're expecting Schröder or Krause to make an appearance early in the week."

"So that's it, then."

"For now. You have the list?"

"Here it is."

"I'll do what I can."

She heard rustling, and a few seconds later, footsteps. She scooted back a few more inches, trying to make herself invisible against the wall, but the sounds were retreating, moving toward the back of the church. She held her breath again until she'd heard the main door open and close. Père Clément must have exited with the German, for there were no returning footsteps. Heart pounding, Eva waited another two minutes before ducking back into the library and pulling the door quickly closed behind her. If Père Clément found her, she would act as if she'd been here all along.

Her hands shook as she sat down at the small table. Was Père Clément betraying them? Was he trading information with a Nazi? She replayed the conversation in her head and again heard the friendly tone between the two and the priest's easy familiarity with the German names the soldier had mentioned. And clearly, he had handed over some kind of list. But what could this mean? Was Père Clément playing some sort of long game she didn't understand? Or was she getting it all wrong?

Just then, there was a noise at the library door, and she gasped. As the door cracked open, she threw her arms and head down on the table and pretended that she'd fallen asleep in the middle of her work. Though she was still trembling, she forced herself to take long, slow breaths. As she felt a presence over her, she even faked a light snore, hoping that it would mask the fact that her hands were still shaking uncontrollably.

"Eva?" Père Clément spoke softly. "Eva, are you awake?"

Eva squeezed her eyes closed and prayed he would go away. He lingered there for a few more seconds before sighing and muttering something unintelligible, then she could hear footsteps retreating and the library door opening. She cracked open an eye just in time to see Père Clément, still in his priestly robe, disappearing back into the church as quietly as he'd come. He pulled the door closed behind him, leaving her in total darkness.

Chapter Twenty-Two

E va didn't dare stir or leave the library until dawn broke, and as she waited, exhaustion finally forced her into a strange half slumber filled with nightmares of monsters dressed as men.

When she finally let herself out just past eight in the morning, there was no sign of Père Clément, but she didn't breathe easily until she had returned to the boardinghouse. Her mother was still in her nightgown and robe, taking her morning ersatz coffee in the parlor, and she looked up wearily as soon as Eva entered. "Night after night, I worry sick about you," she said by way of greeting. "But I suppose that doesn't matter to you, does it?"

Eva's head pounded. "Mamusia, I can't do this right now. I have to go find Joseph."

Her mother brightened immediately. "Joseph? How lovely. Why don't you invite him to dinner again? He's handsome, he's young, he's single . . ."

"Please stop."

"Don't dismiss me so easily, Eva. He's a good man—a good *family* man. Do you know he's been coming by to check on me once a week?"

Eva stopped and stared at her. "He's been doing what?"

Mamusia's chest puffed out with pride. "He says I remind him of his own mother. He stays and prays with me, Eva, which is more than you do. You could learn something from him, you know. He'd be a wonderful son-in-law."

"Mamusia, enough!"

"It's just that you should think of him, Eva. You should be with someone like us."

"Yes, well, isn't that what the Nazis say, too, when they encourage their young people to band together against those who are different?" Eva knew she'd gone too far, but she couldn't help it. Her mother lived in a world of black and white, and Eva knew that neither of those colors existed, not really; it was all a spectrum of gray.

Mamusia's eyes narrowed. "It's easy to dismiss me. But Joseph is someone you can trust. How can you turn your back on that?"

Eva sighed. "Please, Mamusia, you must stop trying to matchmake for me."

Her mother frowned, but she didn't say another word when Eva emerged from the bedroom ten minutes later after having changed clothes and splashed some water on her face. She merely waved goodbye with a small, encouraging smile, clearly hoping that Eva would take her advice.

Eva wasn't sure where to find Joseph, though, and it wasn't as if she could ask Père Clément. Nor could she go around town asking for Faucon. But, she realized, Madame Travere might have a way to reach him in case of emergency, and certainly she could be trusted. She'd been putting her life on the line for more than a year simply to save innocent children.

She knocked on the door of the children's home twenty

minutes later, and the silver-haired caregiver appeared almost instantly, cracking the door only a sliver as she peered out suspiciously. "What is it?" she snapped.

"It's me, Eva Moreau." Using her alias with people she trusted still felt disingenuous, even after all this time. Then again, if last night had shown her anything, it was that no one could be trusted at all.

Madame Travere pursed her lips, considering, and then she opened the door more widely to allow Eva in. "This is quite unusual, Mademoiselle Moreau. I've had no notice that you were coming."

"I'm very sorry, madame. This is—an unusual situation. I need to reach Gérard Faucon, and I was wondering whether you might help me."

Madame Travere didn't say anything as she led Eva up the two flights of stairs into the parlor, where five young children, who ranged in age from around three to about eight, were playing quietly. After the raids in February, in which the authorities had turned up nothing, Madame Travere and the others had waited only two weeks before beginning to take in children again. There was no other way; there weren't enough places to put them, not enough people to entrust them to. A wave of sadness swept over Eva as she watched them.

"Mademoiselle Moreau," Madame Travere said, and as Eva turned to her, she realized the older woman had been watching her closely as she stared at the children. Her expression had softened a bit, and Eva had the strange sense she had passed some sort of test she hadn't known she'd been taking. "I understand that there are quite a few young ladies in town who would like to get in touch with Faucon, but—"

"What? No, that's not what I—" Eva stopped and shook her head, embarrassed. "I need to speak to him urgently, and I don't know how to find him."

Madame Travere stared at her for another unsettlingly long moment before accepting this with a nod. "Why haven't you asked Père Clément?"

Eva swallowed hard. Though the conversation she had overheard had seemed damning, what if it wasn't? She didn't want to be spreading doubt about the priest until she knew for sure. She owed him at least that. "I—I didn't see Père Clément this morning, so I came to you instead. Please, it's very important."

Madame Travere pursed her lips and seemed to be considering the request. "You've done a good job with the children's papers," she said at last. "You've risked a lot to help us. Why?"

Eva was thrown by the abruptness of the question, but she considered it anyhow. "Because none of these children deserve what's happening to them. Helping them makes me feel like I can bring some light to the world, even in the midst of all the darkness."

"I feel the same." Madame Travere nodded slowly. "Very well, Mademoiselle Moreau. You can ask after Faucon at the farm on the northern edge of town, the one with the blue barn and the red roses. The owners are friends of the underground. I understand it's where Faucon stays when he's in the area. Just head north on the rue de Chibottes and you'll eventually come upon it on the hillside. It's where the résistants, the ones who want to go into the forests to help, have been gathering for months now."

Eva shook her head. Every day there was something new to learn about this town and the secrets swirling around it. "Thank you, Madame Travere."

"Thank *you*, Mademoiselle Moreau," she replied, looking Eva in the eye. "And whatever this is about, please stay safe. We need you."

It took Eva forty-five minutes to walk to the farm on a road that turned to dirt at the edge of town. No one passed her going in either direction, and as the rows of hillside crops finally came into view, Eva understood why this would make a good place to hide.

The farm's land was dotted with several buildings, including a large stone house, a blue barn lined with red rosebushes, and several smaller, agricultural-looking buildings. A few men were working quietly among the rows, and they looked up as she approached. She gave a pleasant wave and felt their eyes burning into her as she walked up and knocked on the door of the main house.

It was answered by a woman around Eva's age, with long, dark hair and big, brown eyes. Her tanned skin was flawless, her cheeks flushed. Her brow creased in confusion when she saw Eva standing there. "And who are you?" she asked immediately.

"Um, I'm Eva Moreau," Eva said haltingly, caught off guard by the brusque greeting. She was still panting a bit from her walk.

The woman's eyes were hard as she looked Eva up and down. "So? What are you doing here? We have no grain to sell to the public. No eggs, either. You'll just have to wait in the queues like everyone else."

"I'm not here for grain or eggs, madame." She took a deep breath. "I'm looking for Faucon."

The woman took a small step back, her expression growing even colder. "Falcons? I'm afraid we have no birds here this time of year. Perhaps your bird-watching would be more successful elsewhere."

"No, I'm—"

"Thank you for stopping by." And with that, the door was slammed in Eva's face. She stood blinking at it before knocking again, but there was no answer.

Finally, Eva turned and headed toward the fields, intending to ask the men who'd been working there if they knew where to find Faucon, but they were gone, too. It was as if the entire farm was suddenly deserted, a ghost town.

Eva walked over to the barn and peeked inside, but it was dark and silent, a tractor and a few pieces of agricultural equipment standing guard over bales of hay. "Hello?" Eva called, but the only reply was her own echo.

Defeated, she finally left and began to walk back toward town, her shoulders slumped. Now what? Perhaps she could leave word with Madame Travere that she needed to speak with Faucon. But how long would it take for the message to reach him? In the meantime, Eva would have to continue reporting to the church as if nothing was wrong, for to do otherwise would only raise suspicion.

She was just passing Madame Travere's house when a movement in the shadows across the street to the right caught her eye. Was there someone there? She squinted into the darkness, waiting for a person to emerge.

When no one came out onto the street, she convinced herself that her imagination was simply playing tricks on her. But as she hurried along, there was another flash of movement, and she turned just in time to see a uniformed German duck onto the street from one of the alleys, his head turned away.

Relax, she told herself. *You see Germans every day.*

Then the German glanced her way, and as their eyes met for a fleeting second, she recognized him. Her blood ran cold. It was the man she had seen talking to Père Clément in the church, she was almost certain. Was he following her? But that was crazy, wasn't it? She was certain he hadn't seen her last night, but Père Clément had. What if he'd told the German that she might have overheard their clandestine conversation?

She quickened her pace, her muscles tensed to flee if necessary, but after a few seconds, the German turned down another alleyway. She was practically running now, but as she turned onto the broader rue Valadon leading to the town square, the German was nowhere to be seen. Had she imagined that he was tailing her? Perhaps he hadn't even been the same man she'd seen the night before; it had been dark in the church.

Her gut told her she'd been right, though. Something was amiss. She changed directions and headed for one of the only other people in town she trusted.

The bookstore seemed empty when Eva entered a few minutes later, but the chimes on the door alerted Madame Noirot, who came rushing out with a smile on her face that fell the moment she saw Eva's expression.

"My dear?" she asked, crossing to Eva quickly and placing both palms on her cheeks. "What is it? You look as if you've seen a ghost."

For a second, Eva faltered. What was she doing here? After all, Père Clément was close to Madame Noirot; what if she was in on the betrayal, too? Then Eva gazed around at all the beautiful books, and she looked back into the wide, concerned eyes of the woman who'd been the first to make her feel welcome here, and she felt something inside of her break. If Madame Noirot had ill intentions, too, nothing made sense anymore. She needed to trust someone, and Madame Noirot seemed like her best bet. "I—I was in the church last night and overheard Père Clément talking to a German soldier."

Madame Noirot blinked a few times and let her hands fall from Eva's face. "Well? What were they saying?"

"Something about some Germans who were expected to arrive soon. And a list. I think Père Clément gave him a list of some sort. It—it seemed quite suspicious."

"There must be an explanation."

"What if there isn't?"

Madame Noirot's knuckles were white as she squeezed Eva's hands. "Eva, don't do anything foolish. Père Clément has done nothing but help you, and I've seen him risk his life to help others, too. We owe him the benefit of the doubt."

Eva hung her head. "I know." It was why she hadn't said anything to Madame Travere. But she was terrified. "I've been trying to find Faucon. He'll know what to do."

"And you're so sure you can trust him?"

Eva nodded. They had history—and he'd already done so much to help the cause. "Yes, I am."

"Still, I think you should speak to Père Clément first. Once you've spoken to Faucon, it's out of your hands, isn't it? And sometimes, the underground reacts before they have all the facts. They're running scared, too, you know, and fear doesn't always make for clear heads."

Eva nodded slowly. Madame Noirot was right. Still, she was

terrified. What if talking to Père Clément was, in effect, signing her own death warrant? "If something happens to me . . ."

"I will find Faucon and tell him. And I will look out for your mother. But, dear, I don't think you have anything to fear."

"I hope you're right," Eva said softly. "In any case, I know it's something I must do." After all, she was already living on borrowed time. Every moment that had passed since the July roundup in Paris had been one she shouldn't have had. And it had been Père Clément who had given her life here a purpose. There was nothing to do but walk into the fire and hope she wasn't burned alive.

"Good luck, my dear," Madame Noirot said. "I will be praying for you."

Eva left the bookshop deep in thought. She needed to confront Père Clément right away, before she lost her courage. The only thing to do was to head for the church to find him. At least in the middle of the day, it would be more perilous for him to do her harm if her instincts were wrong. Whom was she kidding, though? If he was allied with the Germans, she was already doomed. That thought, strangely, made her feel better, for if that was the case, there was nothing to lose.

"Eva!" A whisper from the shadows stopped her abruptly as she hurried toward the church. She looked in the direction of the voice, but there was no one there.

"Eva!" the voice came again, and then Père Clément stepped from the alley to her right, a hat pulled low over his face.

Her heart stopped. True, she had been on her way to speak with him, but she wasn't ready yet. She didn't have her thoughts in order, nor did she have an escape plan. Her eyes darted from side to side, and she forced a smile to buy time. "Père Clément, what are you doing here?"

"I could ask you the same, Eva." He stepped from the shadows, frowning. "I usually find you in the church library this time of day."

"I—I had some things I needed to do."

He stared at her, long and hard. "You overheard me in the church last night, didn't you?"

Eva could feel her cheeks growing warm. "I—I don't know what you mean."

As he studied her face intently, she couldn't help realizing that beneath his weariness, his eyes looked sad. "Have you told anyone yet?"

She hesitated. "No." If he was going to hurt her, he would also go after anyone else who knew.

"You were looking for Faucon, weren't you?"

She bowed her head. "Yes."

"I'm very glad I found you first. Please, Eva, I'd like you to come with me. There's something I'd like to show you."

She looked up and met his gaze. "I . . ."

He blinked a few times. "Eva, I swear to God that I intend you no harm." When she still didn't move, he took a step closer. "Eva, you know me. I would never betray the vows of my faith—and I would never hurt you. It's important to me that you understand what you saw last night."

She took a deep breath. "But I saw you with a Nazi. I saw you give him a list."

"Yes." He extended his hand to her. "Please, Eva. I need you to trust me."

She hesitated before reaching out and letting him grab her hand. He was right; she couldn't imagine him going against God. And if he was going to offer an explanation, she needed to hear it.

He led her down the shadowy alley in silence. As they wove through side streets, farther and farther from the town square, she asked, "Where are we going?"

"You'll see." He took a sharp right onto the rue de Levant and then into the doorway of the Boulangerie de Levant, the town's bakery. This late in the morning, the ration queues were gone, and the shelves and cases were picked clean. Eva recognized the stout, gray-haired woman in a white apron behind the counter. Though Eva had never come here for bread, leaving the shopping to Madame Barbier, she had grown accustomed to exchanging bonjours with the bakery owner, Madame Trintignant, as she passed by on her way home from the church once or twice a week.

The older woman looked up with a smile as they entered. "Ah, Père Clément," she said, glancing once at Eva and then back at the priest. "The bread is rising in the back."

"Merci, madame." Père Clément stepped forward and kissed the woman on both cheeks. "Eva, I'd like to introduce you to Madame Trintignant. Madame, this is Mademoiselle Moreau."

"Of course. I've seen you around town. It's a pleasure to finally meet you," Madame Trintignant said, her gaze sharp and appraising behind her polite smile. She looked back at the priest and added, "I'll lock the front door and keep an eye out."

"Merci." Père Clément took Eva's trembling hand again and

led her behind the counter and through a door with an ease that suggested he'd been here many times before. They emerged into a kitchen, humid and warm from the ovens. Dozens of loaves—probably padded with potato, oats, buckwheat, or even wood shavings to deal with the wheat shortage—cooled on the counter, and the yeasty scent of baking bread enveloped them. Eva's stomach growled; she couldn't remember the last time she'd eaten.

"Père Clément, what—?" Eva began, but she stopped short when a man in a perfectly pressed German uniform emerged from a back doorway that appeared to lead to a storage area. She sucked in a sharp breath; she recognized him immediately. It was the German she'd seen last night with Père Clément in the church, the one she thought she'd spotted following her earlier. She yelped and turned to run, but Père Clément moved to block her way.

He caught her gently by the wrists. "Eva, please. This is Erich. He's a friend."

Eva stopped struggling and turned to stare at the German, who was looking back at her with wide, unblinking eyes. He was younger than she'd thought—perhaps only a year or two older than she was. His wavy hair looked blonder under the lights of the kitchen, too, and his eyes were a deep blue. She might have considered him handsome under other circumstances. "But he's a Nazi."

Something shifted in the German's expression. "I promise, I'm on your side." His accent was thick, coating the words like buttermilk.

She narrowed her eyes at him. "How can that be? You fight for Germany!"

"I wear the German uniform," he corrected gently. "I'd like to think I fight for freedom, though."

Eva looked to Père Clément in astonishment. How could he trust anything this man was saying?

"Eva, he's the one who has been tipping us off about the raids at the children's home," Père Clément explained gently, his eyes never leaving Eva's. "His warnings have helped us save dozens."

She turned to look at the German, who didn't look so threatening and imposing now. "Why are you helping us?"

"Because what my country is doing is wrong. It's one thing for the führer to try to expand our territory. But the things we're being ordered to do—to children, to Jews, to the elderly—they are barbaric." He looked at Père Clément and then back at Eva. "I am not perfect. I am trying to be a good man, though, a good Catholic. It's why I sought Père Clément out. I can't ignore my conscience any longer."

"If they discover that you're helping us . . ."

"Yes, I would be executed immediately."

Eva stared at him for a long time before turning to Père Clément. "Faucon doesn't know?"

"No."

"Why?" After all, he was high up in the Resistance, and she thought Père Clément trusted him.

"The fewer people who know, the better," Père Clément said. "Erich came to me last year, and I've kept his identity a secret since then."

"So why tell me now?"

"Because you saw us. And because I trust you, Eva. I need you to trust me, too. There will likely come a day when Erich needs papers to escape, and I need you to be ready."

Eva turned back to Erich. Up close, even in his chilling uniform, he didn't look like a terrifying monster. He was just a man—and he was a man Père Clément trusted. "In February, were you the one who warned us about the raids on a few of the children's homes?"

"Yes."

Eva thought of little Frania Kor, who dreamed of finding a way out of Oz. Because of this German, the little girl had made it to Switzerland, where she would have a chance to survive. "If Père Clément trusts you, then I suppose I can try to, as well."

Erich smiled and extended his hand. "Well, then, shall we start again? I'm Erich."

She took a deep breath. It felt like the earth was shifting beneath her. "Eva. It's a pleasure to meet you."

Chapter Twenty-Three

E va didn't see Erich for the next few weeks, but somehow, knowing he was there, knowing he was feeding information to the priest, brought her some comfort, though the idea of a German ally was still taking some getting used to. It was a reminder that it didn't matter where someone had come from; virtue could live within everyone. Knowing that Erich was apparently standing up for goodness at the peril of his own life made Eva want to be braver, too.

By June, the flowers were all in splendid bloom, and the flood of children had picked up again, thanks to the Germans' increased fervor in rooting out Jews wherever they were hiding. There were more adults now than ever pouring into the forests and hills around Aurignon, too, because of the increasing demands of the Germans for forced labor. In January, the Germans had tried to press another quarter million Frenchmen into service, leading to a French law passed in February, requiring men born between 1920 and 1922 to go to work for the führer. In April, another 120,000 men were called up. The result was that a rising number of men were fed up with the invaders and were finally ready to fight. The armed résistants hiding in the forest swelled from hundreds to thousands, maybe even tens of thousands across France. It was impossible to know, because the *maquisards*, the fighters who made up the armed *Maquis* groups, specialized in staying hidden, able to move at a moment's notice. And increasingly, they were confronting the Germans with violence. Rémy still hadn't returned, and Eva worried more with each passing day that with his explosives expertise, he was on the front line of whatever dangerous things were going on. Père Clément had heard mentions of him here and there—that he had played a role in bombing a train track near Tresnay, that he'd been in on a weapons raid of a police station in Riom—but Eva felt very removed from the news. Still, it was a deep comfort to hear each time that he was still alive.

Eva and Geneviève were working late one sunny morning on a batch of papers for a hundred new labor service dodgers when Père Clément appeared at the library door, followed by Joseph. Both women looked up, and Geneviève jumped to her feet.

"Gérard!" she exclaimed, moving toward him with pink cheeks, but he didn't even look at her. His eyes were on Eva, who stood slowly.

"What is it?" she asked.

"The group you've been crafting documents for, they have to move quickly. I need whatever you can provide, immediately," he said.

"What's happened?"

"The Germans are getting too close. They need to move deeper into the forest before they're found, and I want to help them, but the leaders there don't trust me yet. They're from a different region of France, and they don't know me well. If I brought them documents . . ."

"You want to use our documents as a way in?" Eva asked.

He frowned. "Eva, I'm trying to save their lives. Please, help me to do that."

She glanced at Père Clément. He nodded slightly. "We're not close to being done yet, Gérard," she said. "I'm sorry."

He looked at the mess of documents covering the table. "Well, what have you completed? Identity cards?"

"Only a few dozen. Although most of the ration cards are finished."

Joseph waved his hand dismissively. "Ration cards won't do them much good in the middle of nowhere. But at least it's something. Here, give me what you have."

Something made Eva hesitate. "That's not the arrangement we have with the maquisards. They send a courier."

Joseph took a step closer and gently cupped Eva's chin in his hand. "Eva, you trust me, don't you?"

She looked into his eyes and saw at once the young man who'd stood on the steps of the Sorbonne Library eleven months ago and warned her to save her family. Guilt surged through her, as well as remorse for doubting him, then and now. "Of course I do."

"I'm doing this to protect the fellows out there. Do you understand that? Rémy might be among them." He was still touching her chin, still staring into her eyes, and Eva knew he could see the pain there. "If you trust me with these documents, I promise I'll do everything I can to locate him. But, Eva, if the Germans get there before I do . . ." They both knew the sentence didn't need to be completed.

"Gérard, perhaps I can help," Geneviève spoke up beside Eva. She was staring at the two of them with concern. "Let me come with you."

"It's better if I go alone."

"But if something happens to you . . ."

"It won't." He turned back to Eva. "There's no time to waste, Eva. What'll it be?"

Eva exchanged looks once more with Père Clément, who nodded. If Rémy was out there in the forest, and the Germans had the maquisards in their sights, there was no other choice. She had to do what she could to save them. Quickly, she shuffled the completed ration cards and documents into a stack and thrust them at Joseph. "Promise me that if you see Rémy, you'll tell him I'm thinking of him."

Joseph frowned. "Eva, he cannot come back. He's needed out there."

"Please, just promise me."

He hesitated before nodding. "I'll deliver your message." And then he was gone with the documents they'd toiled over, the ones with the false names and real faces of the men hidden in the trees, waiting to fight. And though Eva trusted Joseph with her life, though she knew he had tried to save her once and would do it again, she couldn't help but feel a tiny tingle of doubt. If he wasn't cautious enough, if he crossed paths with the wrong person on his journey, he could be handing a hit list over to the Germans instead of delivering salvation to the Resistance fighters. And she would have had a hand in it.

"You did the right thing," Père Clément said, watching Eva closely.

"Did I?" she asked.

"We have to take all the opportunities we can to preserve life," he said.

"But what if someone is following him? What if he leads them right to them?"

"It's a chance we have to take, I think."

"Don't you ever wonder if this is all for nothing? What if all we're doing is prolonging the inevitable? What if we're playing right into their hands?"

"None of it is in vain as long as one life is saved, and you've already saved hundreds." He smiled gently. "As for the rest, Eva, you have to trust in God and wait for him to send you a sign. I have often found that in my darkest hour, he is there."

But as Père Clément turned to go, Eva didn't feel much better. In fact, she felt like the net around Aurignon was being cinched tighter by the day. If the Germans had an idea where the maquisards were hiding in the forest, and if they'd been tipped off more than once about the refugee children, who was to say they didn't know about her, too? She shivered as she sat back down to work.

"Is there something between you and Gérard?" Geneviève asked a few seconds later. In her troubled train of thought, Eva had almost forgotten the other woman was there. Now, as she looked up, it took her a second to remind herself that Gérard was the given name Joseph was using. No one around town referred to him as anything but Faucon.

"No, of course not," Eva said. From the stricken look on Geneviève's face, and the heat still evident on her cheeks, Eva suddenly realized what was happening. "Geneviève, is there something between *you* and Gérard?"

Geneviève looked down, and after a few seconds, she nodded.

"Yes, but I think he has feelings for you. He speaks to you with a special kind of warmth," Geneviève mumbled. "And when we're alone, he talks of you often."

"Geneviève, I've known him for a long time. We're old friends, nothing more."

"He seems so concerned about you . . ."

"Geneviève, there's nothing there. I promise. You and Gérard are involved?"

The other woman's blush deepened to scarlet. "We've had a few dates."

"Dates?" It wasn't that Eva was envious. It was just that she couldn't imagine when the other woman—or Joseph—found the time. "When?"

"We—we meet late at night sometimes. There's a loft in the barn on the property where he stays. It's very private; the family uses it only for storage. I know it doesn't seem like much, but it's actually quite romantic."

Eva just shook her head. She supposed she should be glad that one of them was finding happiness in the midst of the darkness, but somehow it just drove home the fact that Rémy was so far away.

"You're not upset with me, are you?" Geneviève asked when Eva didn't say anything. "I—I wanted to tell you, but Gérard asked me to keep it a secret."

"No, it's fine. I'm glad for you." Eva forced a smile.

"Good." Geneviève didn't look convinced. "It's nice to have someone to rely on in times like these."

"Well, it's good you have each other."

"No, Eva, I meant you." Geneviève waited for her to look up. "I meant it is nice to have *you* to rely on."

This time, Eva's smile was real. "I feel the same way, Geneviève. I'm very glad you're here."

They worked in silence for hours, and later that afternoon, when Geneviève asked if she could take a break, Eva nodded. "Are you going to see Faucon?"

She blushed and looked away. "I want to be at the place where we rendezvous, just in case. I don't know how long it will take him to get to the forest and back, but if he is able to return home, he might need comfort."

"He's lucky to have you, Geneviève. Please, be safe."

With a murmured *merci*, Geneviève left, and Eva turned back to her stack of ration cards with a sigh.

By the end of the week, Joseph had returned with good news: he had reached the maquisards in time, and though the leader still didn't seem to entirely trust him, he had accepted the documents with gratitude and agreed to move.

But Rémy hadn't been there, Joseph told Eva, and he didn't know where he'd gone. It had been nearly four months since Eva had seen him last, and she wondered if he was still thinking of her, or if he had settled in another town somewhere, perhaps even found another woman to help fight the Germans, a Catholic woman, one who wouldn't push him away because of religion and family loyalty. If she had lost him, she had only herself to blame.

You have to trust in God and wait for him to send you a sign. Père Clément's words had continued to ring in her ears, but she had begun to wonder whether God would even have the time to give someone like her a second thought. There were much more important things to be worrying about than a woman who had realized too late that she loved a man who might never know how she felt, might never come back.

Five weeks later, Eva was alone in the secret room finishing up the identity papers of eight children due to be moved across the Swiss border the next day. As she flipped to page 233 in the book to start a record for the 231st child they'd helped, her heart skipped. There was a dot on the page—over an *à* halfway down—that she was sure she hadn't put there herself. And she knew the page was part of her own sequence—*one, one, two, three, five, eight, thirteen, twenty-one, thirty-four, fifty-five, eighty-nine, one hundred forty-four, two hundred thirty-three*—numbers so familiar she could recite them in her sleep.

She stared, her hand frozen on the page. The dots that spelled *Traube* had ended on page thirty-four, and though there were dots that made up letters of a few children's names, and a triangle from her own backward sequence, those marks ended in the first paragraph. Who would have added an additional dot on this page? Was it an error? A drip of ink she hadn't noticed? Or had Rémy left her another message in the book without her realizing? Hands shaking, she flipped back to the first page and found a second star that was brand-new. The first one—over the *e* in *Le*—and the dot over the *v* in *l'Avent* were familiar, but the star over the *J* in *Jean* several lines down was not, nor was the dot just beside it over the *e* in the same word.

Quickly, her pulse racing, she flipped to page two and found a new dot over the *r* in *car*, and another new dot over the *e* in *de* on the second line of the next page. She turned to the pages in the sequence she now knew by heart, all the way to page 610, and by the time she had jotted down the letter under each new dot, the message was clear.

Je reviendrai à toi. I will return to you.

She stared at it through eyes blurred with tears. Rémy had left word for her after all, a promise, a vow to come back.

It was just the kind of sign Père Clément had urged her to look for. And now, as it sat in front of her in crisp black and white, she believed. She looked heavenward, closed her eyes, and murmured, "Thank you, God. Thank you for the sign. And please, please bring him back to me."

Chapter Twenty-Four

May 2005

My flight lands in Berlin just past eleven in the morning. I should be exhausted—it's only five in the morning back home in Florida, and I slept fitfully on the plane—but being in Europe for the first time in decades does something strange to me. I feel young again, and as I stare out the window at airport vehicles that are boxier and stouter than the ones in the States, I can't help murmuring a line from a movie I haven't thought of in years: "I've a feeling we're not in Kansas anymore."

The words remind me of a little girl who was six the last time I saw her, the child whose real name—*Frania Kor*—I recorded on page 147 in the Book of Lost Names. I wonder if she ever made it back to France, if her parents made it home, if she ever got to see the film based on the book she loved so much. Not knowing which of the children survived, or found their families again, has been a source of heartbreak for sixty years, and now my tears spill over. I retrieve a handkerchief from my bag to wipe my wet cheeks.

The woman in the seat beside me, who didn't speak at all during the flight despite my attempt to exchange pleasantries, gives me a strange look and inches away, as if my grief might be contagious.

As we exit the plane into Berlin's bustling airport, I'm swept along by a crowd. All around me, people speak to each other in German, and I have to remind myself that Hitler is long dead. Evil doesn't live here anymore; this is just a place, and the people around me are just people. And isn't that the moral of the story anyhow? You can't judge a person by their language or their place of origin—though it seems that each new generation insists upon learning that lesson for itself. I think fleetingly of Erich, whose face I've tried desperately to both forget and remember over the years, and my eyes cloud with unexpected tears. I stumble, and the man who catches me is young and blond with piercing blue eyes.

He says something in German, and despite myself, despite the fact that the war has been over for sixty years, I flinch, my heart hammering. He looks startled and moves away as soon as I'm steady on my feet.

"*Danke!*" I call after him, but it's too late; he's already gone.

After a blissfully short stop at passport control, and another at a currency exchange window, I queue in the taxi line and step into a waiting cab a few moments later. The driver asks something in German, and again, I have to swallow a thick feeling of unease.

"I'm sorry, but I don't speak German," I tell him as I pull the door closed behind me.

"Ah, English."

"Yes."

"I was asking where your luggage is." His accent is thick, but I'm relieved that we can communicate. He's perhaps a decade younger than I am, and he has a comb-over that reminds me of my late husband, Louis.

"I brought only this overnight bag." I gesture to the tote on the seat beside me. "I'm not staying long."

"Am I taking you to your hotel, then?"

"Actually, I'm going to a library, the Zentral- und Landes-bibliothek." I pull a scrap of paper from my purse and read the address aloud.

He nods and glances at me in the rearview mirror after he has pulled away from the curb. "And what brings you to Berlin?"

I consider the question. "I suppose you could say it is to see an old friend."

Berlin is modern and bustling, more beautiful than I had imagined it to be. I know it was shattered in the waning days of the war, just as France was, and I marvel at the rejuvenation around me. One would never know that six decades ago, the city was rubble. I wonder how Aurignon looks now, whether it, too, was rebuilt, whether any of the old scars remain. And what of Père Clément's church? Does it still stand?

By the time the cab pulls up in front of the library thirty minutes later, I'm emotionally spent. But the siren song of the Book of Lost Names is getting stronger, and I'm powerless to stop the memories from rolling in like waves.

"Enjoy your visit with your friend," the driver says cheerfully after I've handed him a few crisp bills and he has helped me out of the back seat. As the cab pulls away, I finally turn to face the library, my heart thudding.

It's enormous and lined with hundreds of identical windows, and even though this building is modern, angular, there's something about it that reminds me of the Mazarine Library in Paris. I try to push from my mind the number of times I stood waiting on those steps, waiting for a future that never came. But of course forgetting is impossible. The memories are all around me. Slowly, I ascend to the front door and pull it open.

Inside, I breathe deeply as my eyes adjust to the dim lighting. It's incredible how familiar the place feels, though I've never been here. Once you've fallen in love with books, their presence can make you feel at home anywhere, even in places where you shouldn't belong. I walk up to the desk at the end of the long entry hall, and the young woman seated there looks up with a smile.

"*Guten Tag, gnädige Frau,*" she says. "*Kann ich Ihnen helfen?*"

I shake my head. "I'm sorry, but do you speak English?"

Her forehead creases. "My English, it is not so good."

"*Français?*" I ask, though it's been ages since I spoke my native tongue. "Um, *französisch?*"

Her face lights up. "*Oui,*" she says. "*Je parle un peu français. Puis-je vous aider?*"

How strange, I think, to be speaking French in Germany, a country that not so long ago tried to wipe my people from the map. I tell her in French that I'm here to see Otto Kühn, and I'm surprised to hear the tremor in my own voice.

"*Certainement.*" She reaches for her phone and asks me if she can tell him who is here to see him.

I take a deep breath. It feels suddenly as if everything has been leading to this moment. *"Je suis . . ."* I hesitate, because it doesn't matter who I am. It matters what I am here to do. So instead I tell her simply that I'm here for the book.

She tilts her head to the side. *"Le livre, madame?"*

"Oui." The world seems to stop spinning. "I'm here," I tell her in French, "for the Book of Lost Names."

Chapter Twenty-Five

January 1944

B y January 1944, darkness had fallen on Aurignon, and Rémy still hadn't returned. The winter was cold, one of the coldest Eva could remember, and rations were in short supply. Germany was suffering losses now, with the Allies heavily bombing Berlin and the Red Army entering Poland, pushing the Germans back from the east. The worse the situation became for them, the more they seemed to take their anger out on the French. Here, in the mountains of southeast central France, there was never enough fuel, never enough heat, never enough food. Even the farmer who had supplied Madame Barbier had vanished, meaning that the days of occasional roast chicken feasts at the boardinghouse were long gone, too. Most of the people Eva knew in the underground gave up a portion of their rations each month to keep the residents of the children's homes nourished for the eventual journey they would take across the mountains, and that meant that they all seemed to be withering to skin and bones. Eva looked in the mirror sometimes and hardly recognized the sharp lines of her own narrowing face.

In early December, just before Hanukkah had begun, the French police had arrested Joseph with a pocketful of forged ration cards and turned him over to the Germans, but somehow—perhaps because Père Clément had gone to Vichy to plead with the German high command—he had been released. The Germans, Joseph said when he returned to Aurignon sporting a broken arm set in plaster, hadn't realized he was involved with the Resistance; he'd been arrested because they thought he was selling false ration cards on the black market. He had managed to play into their mistake, which had earned him a two-week jail sentence and an admonition that should he be caught again, the punishment would be much more severe. "Imagine what would have happened if they'd realized I was a Jew," he said one night over dinner with Eva and Mamusia, his smile not reaching his eyes.

But there was joy in the darkness, too. Geneviève and Joseph had gotten more serious after his close call with the Germans—though as far as Eva knew, he hadn't yet told her his real name. Still, a name was just words, something Eva had learned all too well. They seemed genuinely to love each other, and on the nights Joseph was in Aurignon, Geneviève always left the secret library early with stars in her eyes to spend the night with him in the loft of the old barn, under piles of woolen blankets.

"Do you think he'll ask me to marry him someday?" she asked Eva shyly one day. "I dream sometimes of walking toward him down a path that's white with blossoming cherry trees, carrying a bouquet of lilies. The dream always ends before I reach him, but I wake up feeling that it's possible. Maybe when the war ends, he will propose."

"Maybe," Eva agreed with a smile, but she wondered if Geneviève was deceiving herself. It felt as if the war would never be over, but what if the tide was turning? Germany had seemingly lost the Battle of the Atlantic, and was being beaten back from both east and west, according to the forbidden BBC radio broadcasts she, Mamusia, and Madame Barbier sometimes listened to at the boardinghouse. Was it possible that France could be saved after all? That Rémy might come back to her? Eva allowed herself to dream sometimes of a future that had him in it—and of a future in which her father returned from Auschwitz, too. But she knew that she was deluding herself imagining that Tatuś had survived this long—and she wondered if her thoughts of a life with Rémy were equally unrealistic.

On the last Saturday of the month, Eva and Geneviève were working in the afternoon on a batch of papers for the Maquis group in the forests near Aurignon, who were growing in strength and number faster than their little forgery bureau could keep up with. There were more children than ever before, too, nearly forty of them concealed in different homes around town, most hailing from Paris, all of them stuck here until the weather warmed up enough to make an Alps crossing. Eva hadn't yet started on their papers because there was plenty of time before they'd need to leave.

"Do you ever think of the life you had before the war?" Geneviève asked quietly, breaking the silence between them. She was working on an identity card for a young, dark-haired man, and when she looked up at Eva, she looked haunted.

"Sometimes," Eva said after a pause. "It's painful, though, isn't it? To think of what we once had."

"And what could have been." Geneviève touched the man's picture gently. "This one looks so much like my brother."

"I didn't know you had a brother."

"A twin." Her smile was soft and sad. "Jean-Luc. We drove each other crazy, but he was my best friend, too. He was called up to the army and died in May 1940 at the front. He never had a chance."

"I'm so sorry, Geneviève."

"Everything crumbled after that. My mother was inconsolable. My father began to drink. We all drifted further and further apart, though we lived under the same roof. We were barely speaking by the time I came home one day and found my mother dead on the kitchen floor. Stress, the doctor said, or maybe a broken heart. My father was gone a month after that, a stroke."

Eva put her hand over her mouth. "Geneviève, I didn't know. I'm terribly sorry."

She waved away the sympathy. "Sometimes, when I'm tempted to step away from the work we're doing, to just go somewhere and live an ordinary, simple life, I think of them— Jean-Luc, my mother, my father—and I know I can't stop. If the Germans hadn't arrived, Eva, my brother would be home tending our farm alongside our father, and my mother would be in the kitchen baking bread and worrying about when I would give her grandchildren. Maybe I would even have children already, and I'd be putting them to sleep at night singing 'Au Clair de la Lune,' just like she sang to me every night when I was a little girl. The Germans have already taken so much from so many people. We have to save those we can—because we couldn't save the people we loved."

It was the most Geneviève had ever said about her reasons for being here, and Eva was moved. She had never known that the other woman had suffered losses similar to her own. "I couldn't save my father, either," she admitted. "He was taken by the Germans."

"I know," Geneviève said. When Eva looked at her, she added, "Gérard mentioned it. But you didn't fail to save him, Eva. There's nothing you could have done."

Eva shrugged, though she was a bit bothered by Joseph sharing her tragedy with Geneviève so easily. "If I had tried harder to persuade him to go underground . . . If my eyes had been more open . . ."

"I feel the same about the past. We can't blame ourselves, though. We can only take the responsibility of preventing the same things from happening to others."

"Do you think we're making any difference?" Eva asked after a long pause. "Sometimes, it's still hard to feel as if we're part of any meaningful resistance. There are days when I forget there's a whole world outside these walls."

A day later, though, everything changed. Eva was cleaning up the tiny library to head home for the evening—hiding the stamps and inks, concealing the blank and forged documents in a hollowed-out dictionary, sliding the Book of Lost Names into its unassuming spot on the shelf—when Père Clément appeared at the door, his face pale.

"Is Geneviève with you?" he asked.

"No, she's already gone for the night. Is everything all right, Père Clément?"

"I'm afraid not, Eva. Come with me."

In silence, she followed him through the empty church to his small office behind the altar. As he ushered her inside, she saw Erich waiting for her in a chair with a grave expression.

"Is it—?" she asked, and then instantly stopped. She had been about to ask about Rémy, but she didn't know whether Erich knew about him yet, and she certainly didn't want to give Rémy away to a German, even if Erich had proven himself an ally. Besides, the question had been foolish. Would she even be notified if anything happened to him? Perhaps it was ridiculous that nearly a year after she'd seen him last, he still occupied such a large portion of her thoughts, her heart. But she thought of him constantly, worried about him, wondered on the darkest nights whether she would even know if he'd died. She knew instantly, as she looked back at Père Clément, that he'd understood exactly what she'd been about to say.

"No, Eva, our old friend is fine, as far as I know," Père Clément said quickly, gesturing to the chair beside Erich. "Please, join us." She sat, her unease growing, as the priest took a seat behind his desk.

"Eva, we're worried," the German said immediately. As was the case the last time she'd seen him, he was out of uniform, and but for his accent, he could easily have been one of them, a friend, a neighbor. "I believe my superiors are very close to infiltrating your network."

"What? Why do you think that?"

"They have some names—not yours, not Père Clément's, as far as I know—but I believe arrests are imminent." Erich and Père Clément exchanged looks. "I don't know who's talking, Eva, but the children are in danger."

"The children? Which ones?"

"All of them." The words sat between the three of them, stark and frightening, before Erich continued. "They now have the addresses of all sixteen homes in town where children are being held, and the seven farms in the countryside. Raids could begin as early as the day after tomorrow. They have *names*, Eva. Names of the children, names of the people helping them. That's why we have to move them, as soon as possible. I think it's over, Eva."

Eva's head spun as she stared at him. "Over?"

"All of it. Somehow, your cell has been compromised."

She turned to look at Père Clément in disbelief—surely Erich was wrong. But the priest was nodding gravely. "What will we do?" she asked.

"I need you to start on documents for the children and their keepers immediately."

"Of course." Eva paused, dazed. "Geneviève and I have been working only on the maquisards for the past two weeks. We haven't completed papers for any of the children." Then she put a hand over her mouth. "My God, Geneviève. Someone must warn her. If we've been compromised . . ."

"I'll go," Père Clément said.

"What about my mother?"

"There's no reason to think anyone knows about her. As soon as I can locate Faucon, I'll ask him to send someone to look out for her. We need you here, though, Eva. There's no time to waste."

Eva nodded, her heart racing. "And then what? What do we do after we get the documents done?"

"I think it's time for us to disperse. So work on any supporting papers you and your mother might need, too. She'll finally get her wish to head for Switzerland."

"And you?"

Père Clément's eyes were sad, his smile grim. "I'll stay here and do what I can. It's in God's hands now."

Geneviève never showed up at the church, and Père Clément returned briefly to tell Eva that he couldn't find her; she wasn't in her apartment, though it was past curfew. When Père Clément mentioned that he hadn't located Faucon, either, Eva breathed a bit easier; certainly the two were together. Yes, Geneviève's absence would leave Eva to do all the work that night, but if they were all to flee Aurignon tomorrow, it was good that Geneviève was getting one last night of sleep.

In the morning, though, Geneviève still hadn't arrived at the secret library, and Eva began to worry. She'd been up all night and was nearly finished with the documents, but she could have used help with the finishing touches and to ensure that there were no errors.

Surely Geneviève had been told by now of the impending storm; Joseph would have been notified as soon as possible. Perhaps they had already fled together, but Eva couldn't imagine Geneviève leaving without a word, without at least a visit to the library to ensure that Eva didn't need her. Still, perhaps Joseph had insisted. Perhaps he had promised to check on Eva later in the day once he had Geneviève settled safely.

But Joseph never came, either, and by the time the ink was dry and she had given each of the identity cards a final once-over, Eva's stomach was in knots. She hurried through the empty church to Père Clément's office and found him pacing, looking just as worried as she felt. He looked up when she entered and attempted a smile, but it didn't erase the sadness in his eyes.

"I'm so sorry, Eva," he said before she had a chance to say a word. "I got you involved in all of this in the first place."

"Please, don't apologize. This past year and a half has meant the world to me. I'm certain this is exactly where I was meant to be."

"But the danger . . ."

"I knew from the start that there would be risks."

He studied her for a long time before sighing. "Eva, there is one more thing I must ask of you."

"Anything." The way he was looking at her tied the knots in her belly even tighter.

"I'm afraid the network needs another person to escort children to the border. Your name has been suggested."

She stared at him. "You want *me* to go? But I've never made the crossing before."

"I know. They'll pair you with someone experienced. They're short one woman. Men traveling alone with groups of children look like passeurs, Eva. Couples traveling with children look like parents. I'd prefer to ask Geneviève, but she's gone already. Gérard has promised me that he'll come for your mother himself and make sure she gets to Switzerland safely."

Eva's mind spun. "You found Gérard? Geneviève is gone?"

"He assured me she was taken care of."

Eva shook her head. It wounded her a bit that Geneviève had left without saying goodbye, but Eva was glad that the other woman was safe, at least. "And he will bring my mother?"

"Yes. She will meet you in Geneva in just a few days. The two of you will remain there."

"But you need me here, Père Clément."

He smiled sadly. "As Erich said, the cell is blown. It's very likely that the Germans already know exactly who you are. They won't rest until they find you. And you'd be tortured and executed, Eva."

"Perhaps I could go elsewhere, start another forgery operation . . ."

"Please. Take this opportunity to get out. If we need another forger, we will send for you. You've already done so much, though. I would never forgive myself if the Nazis found you."

"And you? You still plan to stay?"

He nodded. "My place is here, at the church."

"But if they have your name . . ."

"Whatever happens is God's will."

They stared at each other for a long moment. "Will I see you again?"

He reached for her hands, and this time when he smiled, his eyes were bright and clear. "I feel certain we will meet again, Eva. After the war. And in the meantime, I will pray for you."

"And I for you." Before she could cry, she reached into the deep pocket of her faded wool dress and handed the stack of children's documents to Père Clément.

He accepted them with a nod. "You'll need to make a new set of papers for yourself; you'll be Lucie Besson, wife of André Besson, a textile trader doing business in Switzerland. He has already been given his papers."

"Made by another forgery bureau?"

Père Clément hesitated before nodding. "You should make another set for your mother, too, just in case her identity has been compromised."

Eva closed her eyes. How would she live with herself if she had put her mother in danger? "You don't think . . ."

"We're just trying to be cautious, Eva. I feel certain that your mother will be fine."

Eva relaxed a bit. "Père Clément, before I leave, I need to go see her."

He sighed. "I know. Just be careful that you're not followed. I'll need you back here before one o'clock. You'll be meeting your 'husband' tonight in Lyon."

"So you're leaving me." Mamusia didn't turn around when Eva entered the room they shared twenty minutes later, but even so, Eva could feel her mother's scowl, the anger rolling from her. "Madame Barbier has already explained everything. You're abandoning me here."

"Mamusia, it's what you've wanted! We're finally leaving. We're going to Switzerland."

"*You're* going to Switzerland."

"Joseph will see to it that you're brought there safely, too, once preparations have been made. But there are some children who need to go right now, before the Germans find them."

"And they are more important than your mother?" Mamusia finally turned, her eyes blazing. Eva hardly recognized the woman before her, the woman trembling with anger, the woman whose decision to hold on to a past that would never return had made her into something cold and unfamiliar. "More important than your own blood? I suppose you'll forget me as easily as you've forgotten your father."

"Mamusia, I haven't forgotten him!" Eva swiped at her tears. "This is bigger than us. This is about saving innocent lives. Doesn't that matter to you?"

Mamusia set her jaw, but Eva could see the doubt in her eyes now, the sag of her shoulders. "What matters is that you'd rather be a part of this false family you've let yourself believe in. Your father would be so ashamed."

Eva released her mother's arms and took a step back. "Do you really believe that? You don't think Tatuś would be proud that I'm trying to do the right thing?"

"He would have wanted you to be the person he raised you to be." Mamusia turned her back and waved her hand dismissively. "So go, Eva. Run off to Switzerland with your papist friends and leave me here. Let's be honest, shall we? You've already disappeared."

Eva stared at her mother's turned back in dismay. She longed to stay, to make her mother see her point now, but there wasn't time. They would see each other in Switzerland again in less than a week, and she would explain everything, over and over if she had to. In fact, since her role in the underground would be done then, she would have nothing but time on her hands to make her mother see the truth. "Mamusia," she said softly.

It took a whole minute for Mamusia to turn, and when she did, some of the anger on her face had been replaced with sadness. As the two women stared at each other, Eva understood that while she had sought solace by finding a purpose, her mother had found comfort by wrapping herself in indignation. It was her armor, her new identity.

"I love you, Mamusia." Eva took a step forward and hugged her mother, who was stiff and unmoving at first, but who finally sighed and wrapped her arms around Eva, too. "Joseph will take care of you. I'll see you in Switzerland in a few days, and then it will just be me and you."

"Is that a promise?"

"You have my word, Mamusia."

Mamusia pulled away. "Then be safe, moje serduszko." She hesitated and added, "I love you, too."

And then Eva had no choice but to turn and leave her mother behind. As she walked out of the boardinghouse after a brief exchange of hugs and good-luck wishes with Madame Barbier, she felt the tears streaming down her face, and she didn't bother to wipe them away.

Chapter Twenty-Six

It took Eva an hour to put together a new set of papers for Lucie Besson, false wife of a man she had never met. As she waited for the ink to dry, she got down on her knees and prayed for her mother, for Père Clément, and for Geneviève. She added a prayer for her father, too, though it seemed likely that his fate was already written. And finally, she asked God for the strength and courage to lead the children across the mountain to safety.

When she stopped by Père Clément's office to receive her instructions and to say goodbye, he pulled her immediately into a tight hug. She was reminded of the way her father used to embrace her after the war had started, to remind her that as long as they had each other, she would be safe. While it was reassuring to hear the pounding of the priest's heart, and to know he'd be praying fervently for her, she knew it wouldn't be enough. No man on earth could promise you more time, better luck, safer passage. Only God could do that.

"Here," she said as she pulled away. She held out the key to the secret library, the one she had kept on a string around her neck, just to the right of her heart, since he had first given it to her. It hurt her to part with it, but she wouldn't need it anymore.

Père Clément shook his head and gently lifted the key from her hand. He slipped the string back around her neck and smiled. "Keep it, Eva, as a reminder that you're welcome here as soon as the war ends. There will always be a home for you in Aurignon."

She bowed her head, blinking back tears. "Thank you, mon Père."

"Now, you're to take the bus to Clermont-Ferrand, and from there, the three o'clock train to Lyon, via Vichy. You'll meet your husband, André Besson, and children—your sons, Georges, Maurice, and Didier, and your daughter, Jacqueline— at the Lyon train station for the remainder of the journey. The children will be traveling with false documents that should pass basic inspection, but they'll need better ones, so when you meet them, you will give them the documents you've made already and your husband will go outside to destroy the ones the children have arrived with. There's a train that leaves Lyon for Annecy at midnight. The children will be able to sleep on the train, and your husband will explain the rest to you. You'll cross into Switzerland near Geneva."

"How will I know the man I'm supposed to meet?"

"Just wait outside the side entrance, to the left of the main door, and you will see him approach with the children."

Eva nodded, her heart thudding. There was so much that could go wrong. "Mon Père, I'm frightened."

"I am, too, but the greatest deeds in life require us to rise above our fear. Think of Moses; when God called to him from the burning bush and told him that he must save his people from slavery, he was frightened, too. He questioned God, just as you might be doing now. 'Who am I that I should go to Pharaoh and bring the Israelites out of Egypt?' he asked. But God promised to be with him, and so he went, for it was his destiny. God will be with you, too, Eva, whatever happens. Just have faith."

"Thank you." There was a sudden lump in her throat. "Truly. Thank you for everything."

"Eva, it has been a gift knowing you." As he looked down at her, there were tears in his eyes, and this, from the stoic priest, touched Eva more than anything else. "You are brave and strong and courageous, and I know you will go on to live a long, happy life."

She smiled at him. "I wish I believed you, Père Clément. And I wish the same for you."

"Until we meet again, Eva."

"Until we meet again."

Père Clément pressed train tickets into her hand and a palm to her cheek before turning back to the Bible lying open on his desk. As she turned to go, she heard him clear his throat a few times, and she knew that just as she was, he was trying not to let emotion overtake him. There was still work to be done, and the success of their mission depended upon everyone acting as if their worlds weren't being blown apart.

Eva's train pulled into Lyon just past six thirty, and as she stepped onto the platform, carrying the small hand valise she had hastily packed, a feeling of dread swept over her. She was farther east now than she'd ever been. It was closer to freedom, certainly, but it was also closer to Germany. Was she fleeing to the embrace of safety? Or walking straight into danger? Either way, it was too late to turn back. There were children relying on her.

By six fifty, she was standing just to the left of the main entrance, waiting for the children and the man she would escape to Switzerland with. As she tried to appear nonchalant and unworried, she fretted about the meeting. Would anyone be convinced that she was married to this man she'd never met? That she was the mother to children she had never seen? She recited their names in her head over and over. *My husband, André. My children, Georges, Maurice, Didier, and Jacqueline.* She could almost imagine the children, since she had created their identity documents herself: The little girl, born in 1939, was really named Eliane. The boys were Joel, Raoul, and Daniel, born in 1935, 1936, and 1940. Their false papers were tucked safely into the lining of her coat, halfway up the sleeve in a sewn-in, hidden pocket. What of the man, though? Who was he? She knew nothing of him but his false name.

Seven o'clock came and went, and by seven fifteen, Eva was feeling conspicuous—and worried. Where were they? Had a German official been unconvinced by their temporary papers? Night had fallen thick and dark on Lyon, and as she peered out at the blackness, she wondered what she was supposed to do if they didn't arrive. If she returned here the following day she would look suspicious. And surely she shouldn't proceed to Annecy without them.

It was nearly seven thirty when she saw a dark-haired boy emerge from the station, then another; they appeared to be the right ages for the children traveling as seven-year-old Maurice and eight-year-old Georges. A few seconds later, a boy of about three appeared behind them; if she was right about who they were, he must be Didier. She started forward, hoping that her smile looked motherly rather than relieved, but she stopped short as she saw the final child—the girl traveling as four-year-old Jacqueline—emerge, clutching the hand of a man.

The man's face was turned away as he surveyed the small crowd outside the station, but Eva recognized him instantly. The curve of his shoulders, the tapering of his waist, even his confident gait were nearly as familiar to her as her own. She stopped breathing for a few seconds, and as he turned and looked at her, his eyes widened, and time seemed to slow. It was Rémy, alive and healthy and here. And all at once, Eva believed in miracles once again.

His eyes never left hers as he approached, and though she knew she was supposed to be bending to casually greet the children with hugs and kisses, she couldn't look away.

"It's you," he said softly when finally he was at her side.

"It's you," she breathed, and then his lips were on hers, and he was kissing her in a way that made her forget the world around them for a few precious seconds. It was just the two of them until suddenly, a gasp from the little girl holding Rémy's hand jolted them out of the moment.

"What is it, Jacqueline?" Rémy asked, and the second his lips were no longer on Eva's, he was already too far away. "Are you all right, dear? Your maman and I are right here."

As he bent to the little girl, Eva's heart lurched, for it was a fleeting glimpse of a future she hadn't dared imagine, a future in which she and Rémy were Maman and Papa to a little girl like Jacqueline, or a little boy like Didier. Just as quickly, she reminded herself of her own mother's words that morning: *You'd rather be a part of this false family you've let yourself believe in.* She swallowed her guilt and followed the little girl's eyes to the uniformed German soldier who had just stepped out of the station for a smoke.

"Remember, Jacqueline," Rémy said, smoothly, gently, his tone betraying none of the trepidation he must have felt. "There's no need to fear the men in uniform. They're our friends."

Just a few feet away, the soldier struggled to light a match in the icy breeze. With an easy smile, Rémy let go of the little girl, who instantly clutched Eva's hand, and he crossed to the soldier, pulling a book of matches from his overcoat pocket. He struck one and cupped his hand around it while the soldier lit his cigarette.

The German, blond with a baby face, nodded at Rémy and then at Eva. "*Danke,*" he said, hastily adding, "Or, er, *merci,*" with an apologetic smile.

Rémy stepped back and slung an arm around Eva's shoulder, as if he'd done it a thousand times before. "*De rien,*" he said.

The soldier moved on, and Eva exhaled. "You are the one who made them their false papers?" she whispered to Rémy, nodding to the children.

"Yes, but mine were never as good as yours." She could feel his smile against her cheek as she whispered into his ear. "I admit it now. So I am glad you are here with your documents." He paused and added, "Well, actually, I am simply glad you are here."

"I am, too," she whispered, and when he turned back to her, his lips brushed hers again, and she wished that they could stay in the moment forever. But she knew they had to move inside, to get the children off the street, to feed them and calm them before the overnight ride ahead. "Come, my loves," she said, turning from Rémy to smile at the children. "Let's go find a seat, shall we?"

"I'll be right there to join you," Rémy said softly. "I must get rid of the children's papers first."

"How will you do that?"

His familiar smile warmed her heart. "There's nearly always a small fire burning inside the stationmaster's office, which the guards use to warm themselves. They leave the office unoccupied—and unlocked—most of the time. It should take just a moment to donate a bit of extra fuel."

Five minutes later, Rémy found them near track two, and the makeshift family huddled together, trying to get warm. The night was icy, and outside the office, the station provided no heat, so when they spoke, their words lingered in the air, puffs of white in the darkness. "What are you doing here?" Eva whispered once the children were sharing the loaf of bread and hunk of cheese Rémy produced from a coat pocket.

"I could ask the same of you." His breath was warm on her ear, and she longed to lean into him, to close her eyes, to pretend that they were two lovers on their way somewhere. But she had to keep a lookout for German soldiers or suspicious French gendarmes.

"Our cell was blown," she murmured, and as he nodded, she realized that of course he'd already known. "Père Clément asked me to help escort some children—and then to remain in Switzerland." Even saying the words felt wrong, like she was abandoning her post, discarding the cause she had worked so hard for.

Relief swept across Rémy's features and he pulled her closer. "Thank God. They finally listened to me."

"You were the one who suggested I go? But, Rémy, I belong here. In France. Working."

"No, you belong somewhere safe." When he turned to her, there were tears in his eyes, and she had to stop herself from leaning in to kiss him. "You deserve to grow old and have children and grandchildren and a happy life. That won't happen if you stay."

"What about you?"

He hesitated. "I have to remain here, Eva. But I can't do the things I need to do until I know you're safe."

"Don't you see, Rémy? I feel the same. I can't just walk away now."

"You must. You live in plain sight, Eva. Things for me are different. I live in the woods with other people finding ways to undermine the Germans."

"I could live there, too," she said in a small voice. "Surely they'll still need false documents . . ."

He touched her face. "We move every few days, and we're ready to run at a moment's notice. There would be no way to keep you and your supplies out there with us. Besides, Eva, the fight is changing. It's no longer about peaceful resistance, smuggling people out. We're taking the battle right to the Germans now."

"Rémy—"

"Once these children are out safely, the next phase begins for us." He hesitated, and in a voice even lower than a whisper, he added, "We've amassed weapons, Eva. False papers won't matter anymore."

She covered her mouth. "It will be so dangerous."

"It's the only way. It's about saving France now, maybe even the world. If we can turn the Germans back, reverse the tide, we can preserve humanity."

She shook her head. "But the Allied army is coming, isn't it? Père Clément says—"

"The Germans *know* they're coming," Rémy said, interrupting her. "They don't know we're ready to fight, too. We'll weaken them first, attack them where it hurts. And when the Allies finally arrive, the Germans won't know what to do." When he pulled away from her, his eyes were alight, and she realized he was actually looking forward to the opportunity to fight.

"Please," she whispered. "Please stay in Switzerland with me. What if you lose your life, Rémy?"

He turned away. "If I die for France, it won't be a life lost. It will be a country saved. My only regret will be that it will cost me the chance for a future with you."

A sob rose in Eva's throat, and she managed to stifle it just as a uniformed French gendarme approached.

"Papers," he barked, and Eva flashed him what she hoped was a pleasant smile as she extracted her false documents, and those of the children, from her handbag, where she had slipped them moments earlier after removing them from her sleeve. Rémy handed his papers over, too, and the policeman scrutinized them with a frown, flipping from one set to the next.

"Everything should be in order," Rémy said after a long minute had passed and the man still hadn't spoken. Beside her, Eva could feel little Jacqueline trembling.

"Perhaps," the man in uniform said, looking up at Rémy with a hard stare. He made no move to return their papers. "But you see, this is a popular route for smugglers."

"Smugglers?" Rémy's laugh of disbelief was convincing. "Sir, we are just traveling with our children. You suspect them of smuggling what? Money? Guns?"

Eva bit back a gasp; was Rémy provoking the man on purpose?

The man glanced from Rémy to the children, his gaze finally settling on Eva. "As I'm sure you know, *people are being* smuggled. How do I know these children are yours?"

"How could you suggest such a thing?" Eva feigned indignation. "I birthed them all myself. We are simply going to visit my mother, who lives in Annecy. We will return in two days' time."

He looked hard at her and then turned to the oldest boy with a smirk. "You, there. Georges, is it? These are your parents? What are their names, then?"

The boy's face turned red, and he gaped at the officer. Eva was just about to cut in, to blurt out their false names, but she was beaten to the punch by four-year-old Jacqueline.

"My maman is Lucie Besson, and my papa is André Besson," she said calmly, her eyes wide. "You see them just here. And who are you? My parents told me that German officers aren't frightening, that they are our friends, but you, you are not a German."

The man gaped at her and then turned to Rémy. "You told your daughter here that she should trust the Germans?"

Rémy shrugged while Eva tried not to exhale audibly. The man had called Jacqueline their daughter, which meant he believed them.

"Well," the gendarme said. "So then you are not smugglers, I see. You are merely fools."

He thrust the papers at them and walked away, shaking his head. Rémy and Eva waited until he was out of sight around the corner before bending simultaneously to the little girl. "How did you know to say that?" Eva asked. "You saved us."

The girl smiled. "I had two older brothers who taught me that when telling a fib, to widen your eyes to sell the act." Then her smile faltered, and as she hung her head, she added in a whisper, "They were taken with my real maman and papa."

Eva embraced the girl, wishing she could take away the pain that had already been inflicted. But it was too late. Loss would forever be etched on the child like a tattoo; it might fade over time, but it would never be erased.

Just before midnight, the train to Annecy pulled into the station, and with their heads down, Rémy and Eva led their new "family" aboard. They had spent the past few hours watching over the children as they slept and whispering to each other about the things that had happened over their time apart. Eva wanted to savor every moment, but after the children were settled into seats and the train had pulled into the darkness of the French countryside, exhaustion tugged at her. She hadn't slept in two days, and here, with Rémy at her side, she felt safer than she'd felt in months.

"Get some rest," he whispered as the children dozed nearby. "I'll keep the first watch, and I'll wake you if anyone comes to check our papers."

She stifled a yawn. "You must be very tired, too."

He touched her cheek gently. "Eva, it will be a gift to watch you sleep."

And so she dozed on his shoulder for a few hours, and after a German policeman gave their documents a bored, cursory check, she insisted on Rémy taking a turn. He leaned into her, and she stroked his hair, marveling at the miracle that had brought them back together. But how long would it be until they were separated again?

At just past six in the morning, Eva roused Rémy, and together they woke the children. The train pulled into the small station in Annecy at six thirty, and they quickly made their way down a narrow lane outside the station doors to a Protestant church nearby. It was a boxy brick building with a large cross out front. Inside, the pews were made of dark, smooth wood, and a simple metal cross shone down from above the altar.

"Stay here with the children," Rémy whispered to Eva. "If anyone enters, pretend you're praying. The pastor here is named Chapal. He'll vouch for you."

"Where are you going?"

"To see a priest."

Eva blinked at him. "A priest?"

"Here in Annecy, the Protestants and Catholics work together to get people like us out. The priest will tell me whether the driver of this morning's bus to Collonges-sous-Salève is a friend or a foe. If he's not one of us, we stay here for the night. If he is, be ready to move."

"You've done this many times." She was seeing a whole new side to Rémy.

Rémy nodded. "Though never with someone I care so much

about. Everything must be perfect." He was gone before she could reply.

The children sat silently beside her, the two older boys staring at the cross, Georges tapping a rapid rhythm on his knee, and Jacqueline twirling tangles in her hair. Eva could feel the unease rolling from them in waves. "It's going to be all right," she said in a low voice, leaning toward them. "He'll be back soon. He knows what to do."

"How do you know?" the second oldest, Maurice, asked.

"I just do. He's done this before. I trust him with my life."

"Is he really your husband?" asked Jacqueline.

There was suddenly a lump in her throat so hard she couldn't speak for a second. "No. No, he's not. But we must pretend."

"He's not pretending, though," said Georges. "He really loves you. You can tell."

Eva blinked at him. "We have known each other for a long time."

"Nah, it is more than that. He looks at you when you're not watching him. It is exactly the way Herbert Marshall stares at Claudette Colbert in *Zaza*."

Eva could feel herself blushing. "And what exactly are you doing watching an American film about a love affair?"

She meant to tease him, but the boy looked instantly crestfallen. "My papa used to love films. He took me with him whenever he could afford the movie theater near our apartment in Paris." He hesitated and added in a voice so low it was barely audible, "Papa isn't here anymore. No more movies."

"I'm so sorry." It was all Eva could think to say.

The boy sniffled and then flashed a smile that was clearly false. "And anyhow, you look at him the way Claudette Colbert looks at Herbert Marshall, too. You're Zaza and he's Du-fresne."

Eva had just opened her mouth to reply when the door to the church opened and Rémy appeared, backlit by daylight. "Come." He beckoned to Eva and the children. "The bus leaves early today. There's no time to lose."

Chapter Twenty-Seven

Forty-five minutes later, Rémy held Eva's hand as he helped her and the children onto a rickety bus headed toward Geneva. From the way Rémy and the driver nodded to each other, Eva understood that they were already acquainted.

As the bus rolled north, Eva could feel Rémy's eyes on her as she gazed out the right window at the glistening, soaring Alps. Though she'd spent the past year and a half in Aurignon, with mountains in the distance, there was nothing quite like being in their shadow; they seemed to stretch straight up, their snow-dusted peaks like something out a fairy tale. If Eva hadn't been terrified about their journey and worried about the children, the view would have taken her breath away.

They stopped in Épagny, Allonzier-la-Caille, Cruseilles, Copponex, Beaumont, Neydens, and Archamps before finally pulling into Collonges-sous-Salève, where the driver stopped abruptly at the top of a hill rather than in the city center. Rémy beckoned to Eva, and as they disembarked with the children, the driver nodded once more before pulling away. "Here we are," Rémy said cheerfully, loud enough to be overheard, though there appeared to be no one else out and about in the frigid weather. "Your mother's town. Let's go see her friend, the priest, before we visit with her, shall we?"

"Another priest?" Eva murmured as they began trudging through freshly fallen, ankle-deep snow toward a small stone cottage at the end of the lane. Smoke snaked skyward from the slightly tilted brick chimney.

"God's hand is everywhere," Rémy replied, his voice soft, and he gave the children another encouraging smile as they approached the house.

The door opened before they got there, revealing a short, portly man in a long, dark priest's robe. He was bald, his complexion ruddy, his eyes clear and blue. "Come in, come in," he said, gesturing urgently toward them. "Before someone sees."

Rémy and Eva hustled the children inside, and the man closed the door behind them with a thud.

"Eva, this is le Père Bouyssonie. Père Bouyssonie, this is Eva."

The priest's eyebrows shot up. "Ah. Eva. I have heard much about you." Eva glanced at Rémy, who was suddenly studying the floor intently. The priest chuckled. "And these, I assume, are the four children in your care?"

Eva nodded. "Yes. Georges, Maurice, Jacqueline, and Didier."

The priest bent until he was at eye level with the little girl. He looked at each of them, one by one. "It is wonderful to meet you. I want to remind you that God knows who you are. He always has and always will. He sees your hearts, even in the darkness."

The three boys looked perplexed, but the little girl was nodding like she understood exactly what he meant.

"Thanks, as always, for having us, Père Bouyssonie," Rémy said. "Is everything looking good for the crossing?"

"Yes, yes. Let's get your little family to the attic, shall we? Then I can brief you on today's movements from the border guards." He smiled at Eva. "I'm sorry that our accommodations aren't more comfortable, but the attic is a quiet and safe place to rest for the day. And best of all, there's a little window that allows you to look out to the north. You can see Switzerland not five hundred meters from here, just across the barbed wire fence."

He led them up a rickety, pull-down ladder to a small space overhead that had already been stocked with blankets and pillows. A pitcher of water rested on a small table beside several glasses, a loaf of bread, and a small jar of preserves. "It's not much," Père Bouyssonie said with an apologetic shrug. "With any luck, though, you won't be here for long." He gestured to the window. "Look, Eva. Just beyond the trees."

Eva moved to the window, and her breath caught in her throat. Just beyond the priest's yard, across a broad field, a barbed wire fence stretched as far as the eye could see. On the Swiss side, tall, slender skeletons of poplar trees reached for the winter sky, and beyond them, Swiss Army sentries with long, heavy wool coats and thick black boots walked along the border, rifles slung over their shoulders. She could feel Rémy's breath on her cheek as he crouched beside her.

"That's freedom, Eva," he whispered. "So close you can taste it."

As she turned to search his familiar green-flecked hazel eyes, she felt dazed. "But the barbed wire . . . The guards . . ."

"Don't worry." He put his arm around her shoulders and squeezed gently. "There's a way in. We'll go tonight just past nine, as long as the guards are on a normal patrol. In the meantime, you and the children should get some rest."

"What about you?"

He smiled slightly. "I slept enough on the train." He leaned in and added in a whisper, "I knew I was safe with you beside me."

"Come," the priest said, giving Eva a gentle smile as he beckoned to Rémy. "There's much to be done." To Eva he said, "See if you and the children can eat a bit and sleep. You'll need your energy. We'll be back after nightfall."

Rémy kissed Eva on the cheek and then followed the priest down the ladder, which was then pushed back into the attic floor, leaving the Eva and her four charges in darkness lit only by the small window to freedom.

"Will we be all right?" asked Jacqueline, coming to sit beside Eva.

"Yes, I feel sure of it." And for the first time since leaving Aurignon, Eva realized she believed it. Refuge was within sight, and God willing, she'd be able to help give these children a life, a future. But what about her? What about Rémy? How could she let him go back into the fight so soon after she'd found him again? She shook the questions away and put an arm around the little girl. "Come, let's have a bit to eat, shall we?"

The children murmured excitedly to each other while they ate their bread and preserves, and they took turns peeking out the window at Switzerland. After the small meal, Eva kept watch while the children snuggled under the blankets and fell asleep. Lulled by the silence and the warmth, she eventually drifted off, too. She awoke with a start sometime later to find Rémy beside her, gazing at her with tears in his eyes. He quickly looked away.

"How long have you been there?" Eva asked. Darkness had fallen outside, and the only illumination in the attic was from the faint moonlight spilling in through the window. Around them, the children were still asleep, one of the boys snoring lightly.

"Not long," Rémy said, his voice husky.

"What were you thinking about?"

He didn't answer right away. "You," he said at last. "Us. The past. The future."

But Rémy would need to stay alive if they were to have any sort of future together. He knew that as well as she did, so she bit her tongue before she could remind him. "Where do you want to go after the war?" she asked instead.

"Eva, I'll go wherever you are." His voice caught on the last word, and he cleared his throat. "Enough of that. It's time to move. The patrols on this side of the border are working at regular intervals, so the crossing should be smooth."

"Rémy—" Eva began. There was so much to say. She wanted to tell him she loved him, that she couldn't imagine a life without him, but somehow the words wouldn't come.

"It's all right," he said after a moment. He leaned in and kissed her lightly on the lips. "I know, Eva. I—I feel it, too."

"What if I never see you again?"

"You will, Eva. I promise."

There were footsteps on the ladder then, and Père Bouys-sonie's head appeared behind them. "It's time," he said. "Let's get the children ready."

Eva nodded and forced herself to pull away from Rémy. The feelings she'd been nursing for months, the things she didn't have the courage to say, had no place here, not in this moment.

She had only one job, and that was to see to it that four young, innocent lives were saved. And as Père Clément might have reminded her, the rest was in God's hands.

Twenty minutes later, the children were awake and bundled back into their fraying woolen coats. Père Bouyssonie hunched in the attic facing the little group while Rémy sat beside Eva, his fingers laced with hers.

"I'll be praying for you," the priest said, looking at each of the children one by one, and then at Eva and Rémy. "You must be brave, and you must believe that God is watching you. I've seen many people make this crossing into Switzerland, and I know you'll make it safely, too." He glanced once more at Eva and added, "God will be with you. Always."

Eva nodded, and Rémy squeezed her hand, and then they were in motion, heading down the ladder into the main room of the priest's cottage. They took turns warming themselves by the stone fireplace while Rémy quickly briefed them.

"The Germans patrol the border here, but their routine is predictable, and there are gaps in it," he said quickly, his eyes on Eva most of the time. "There are two patrols, going in opposite directions, along the road about two hundred meters from the front door. The only way to avoid them is to move to the road after the first German patrol has passed and to wait out the second; otherwise, there's not enough time before the first patrol comes back around again. Père Bouyssonie will walk down to the road, and as soon as the first patrol has gone by, he'll run back and give us the sign. Together, we'll head for the road and wait in a ditch beyond until the second patrol has passed. Then you'll all need to follow me as quickly as possible. All right?"

Eva and the children nodded their assent as Rémy continued. "Once we're over the border, run toward the first Swiss soldier you see. They will bring you to safety. But be absolutely sure that the soldier is Swiss, not German. The easiest way to tell is that the Swiss overcoats are a much darker gray, and their helmets look a bit like turtles. The Germans wear higher boots. If you see a German soldier, with big black boots to his knees, run in the other direction, as fast as you can. Do you understand?"

One by one, the children nodded, and finally, Rémy's eyes rested on Eva. "Once you're in Switzerland, you must stay there until the war is over. You will be safe there. You won't need to be frightened anymore." The words were for all of them, but Eva heard them as an admonishment intended for her. She would be a fool, he was saying, to leave the warm embrace of neutrality to return to France. "I will come find you as soon as I can," he said, and this time, there was no doubt that the words were for Eva. She swallowed hard and nodded. Still, though, she couldn't bring herself to imagine that in just a few minutes, they'd be parting once more, that she might never see him again.

"I'm off, then," the priest said. "Be waiting for my sign. Good luck to all of you. May God bless you." And then he was gone, leaving the children alone with Rémy and Eva. The fire crackled in the space where their words should have been, and after a few minutes, Rémy beckoned to the children. "Come," he said. "We will wait just outside Père Bouyssonie's door. Be ready to run when he gives us the sign."

"I'm frightened," whispered Jacqueline.

Rémy bent to her, his tone firm. "We will be right here.

We will keep you safe until you cross the border. Once you're in Switzerland, you're already free. You'll each be running with just one other child to reduce the chance of exposure, and your mother here will follow behind. Go to the first Swiss guard you see, and tell him you need help."

The girl nodded, and while she didn't look entirely reassured, she allowed Eva to take her hand and lead her out the door with the others. Once they were on the priest's front step, they were engulfed in thick darkness, and the icy air bit at their faces, though the wind, at least, had subsided.

"I can't see a thing," Eva whispered to Rémy, and he reached for her free hand.

"Your eyes will adjust," he murmured. "Until then, remember, I'm right here."

He was right; by the time the priest appeared at the top of the lane and gave them a wave, Eva could make out shapes in the blackness, and as they started toward the border at a jog, slow enough that the children could all keep up, a few lights up ahead, just past the barbed wire, lit the way.

They passed the priest, who didn't say a word as they slipped past him, and when they reached the paved road, Rémy whispered, "Get down in that ditch. You'll hear soldiers passing in just a moment. Hold your breath. I'll tell you when it's safe to go."

Heart hammering, Eva did as he said, helping the children flatten themselves against the cold earth in a shallow trench that lay just beside the road. When the little girl began to whimper, Eva soothed her by holding her close. The girl's soft crying subsided just as the thud of boots on the gravel and snow sounded nearby.

The six of them lay still and soundless as the footsteps approached, loud and heavy in the still night. There was the sound of laughter, a few words in German, and then more laughter as the sound of the soldiers faded in the other direction. Finally, the night was silent again, and Rémy whispered, "It is time."

Together, he and Eva helped the children up. "Quietly, now," Rémy reminded them, and they set off toward the barbed wire, moving as silently as they could. When they reached the fence, just a few inches of metal separated them from Switzerland, but suddenly, Eva realized she couldn't see a way across.

"How . . . ?" she asked, but Rémy was already a few steps ahead of them, confidently lifting the fence high enough that each of them could crawl beneath.

"We cut it long ago," he explained in a whisper. "It's a miracle they haven't noticed yet." And then, to the children, he added, "Go. Be safe and free."

The oldest boy, Georges, was the first to wriggle across the border. As Didier started to cross, Eva watched in awe as Georges helped him beneath the wire, picked him up, and began to run. The third boy, Maurice, crossed, too, and then waited until Jacqueline had squirmed through. "I've got her," he whispered to Eva and Rémy. "Thank you for everything." And then the two of them were off, two tiny figures in a black night, running toward the faraway lights of a Swiss village.

"It's time for you to go, too," Rémy said, squeezing Eva's hand tightly. "Quickly, before the children attract German attention on our side of the border."

Eva turned to him. A moment earlier, she had been ready to follow the children, despite the feeling of crushing loss that had begun to sweep through her. Now she knew as clearly as she knew her own heart that she wouldn't be going to Switzerland tonight. "I cannot."

"Eva, you must." Rémy's face was just inches from hers, his eyes dark and urgent in the deep night. "This is your chance."

"I know." And then, slowly, softly, she kissed him, and when he didn't pull away, she knew he understood. She couldn't leave, and he couldn't let her, even if they both knew it was the right thing for her to go.

"Are you certain?" Rémy asked when Eva finally pulled away, breathless.

"Yes."

"Then we must move now. I stay in a safe house on the edge of town before returning to the woods around Aurignon."

"You don't go back to the priest's house?"

"It's too dangerous. Come on." He grabbed her hand, and after one last look into Switzerland, where she prayed the children would find their way to safety, she followed, back into the darkness of France.

The safe house was a tiny stone cottage on the edge of the town, a brisk, fifteen-minute walk from the place where the sliced barbed wire had provided a chance at life. As they hurried along in silence, Rémy clasping her hand tightly, Eva allowed the weight of that to settle upon her. Tonight had shown her the future that all her forgery work had made possible.

Rémy used a key to open the door to the safe house, which was dark and cold inside. The moment he had closed the door, thrusting them into blackness, he pulled her toward him. Without another second's hesitation, his lips were on hers, and his hands were on her face, and then tangled in her hair, and then making their way down the curves of her body. "You shouldn't have stayed," he said between hungry kisses. "You shouldn't be here."

"But—"

"I'm so glad you did, Eva," Rémy said, his lips barely leaving hers as he pulled her back. "I love you."

It was the first time he had said those words to her, and it broke her heart wide open. "I love you, too," she murmured.

His hands were cold as he cupped her face, then ran both thumbs gently down to the hollow beneath her neck. She shivered as his lips found hers again.

"You're freezing," he said, pulling away. "Let me build a fire."

"I don't want to let you go," she protested.

"But I want to look into your eyes, Eva. Let me make us some light. I promise, I'm not going anywhere. There should be some food in the kitchen. Père Bouyssonie usually arranges for something."

Eva didn't want to leave Rémy's side, but he was right; it was frigid, and she could barely see him in the dark. She took her boots off and headed for the kitchen in search of something to eat while Rémy rearranged logs in the stone fireplace. On the counter beside a one-burner stove sat a bottle of red wine, a hunk of bread, and a large wedge of cheese, along with a handwritten note. *God is with you*, it said, and gazing at the relatively large feast before her, she understood that Père Bouyssonie had known, even before she did, that she would likely return with Rémy tonight. The note, she hoped, was his blessing.

She returned to the main room and found Rémy prodding a burgeoning fire, his coat slung over the back of a chair. He turned and smiled as she held up the bottle of wine in one hand, the bread and cheese in the other. "Père Bouyssonie is looking out for us, I see," he said.

"You don't think he'd frown upon us spending the night together?" Eva asked. The man was, after all, a priest.

"I think he understands what love looks like," Rémy answered. He put down the iron stoker and crossed to her, taking the wine and the food and setting them down on the small wooden table in the corner. Then, as the fire began to crackle and warm the room, he slipped her coat from her shoulders and gently tugged her dress over her head, leaving her standing before him in her underclothes. He pulled back to stare at her for a second, his eyes shimmering, before he pressed his lips to hers again. This time, his kiss was full of need, and she responded, tugging at his belt, unbuttoning his shirt.

They made love quickly, urgently, the sharp pain of her first time erased immediately in a flood of sensation—the feel of Rémy's skin against hers, the scent of wood smoke in the air, the heat of their breath in the cold. Then, bundled in blankets and huddled by the fire, they drank the bottle of wine and ravenously attacked the food before making love once more. This time, Rémy's kisses were slower, deeper, and they took their time exploring each other's bodies. When it was over, she lay sweaty and smiling against his bare chest, and he kissed the top of her head. "You must go tomorrow, Eva," he murmured. "You must cross into Switzerland. I can't stand the thought of anything happening to you."

"Can't I stay with you?" she asked, sighing as he stroked her hair, his fingers weaving through the tangles they'd made.

"You know you can't, sweet Eva. But after the war, I'll come for you."

"How will you find me?"

He was silent for a long time, but his hands never stopped moving, and that was a comfort. "Name a place that's special to you."

She closed her eyes and breathed in the scent of him, musk and salt and pine. "There's a library in Paris called the Mazarine," she said. "And when I was a little girl, my father used to bring me there once a week. He repaired the typewriters at many of the libraries before he got a job working at the prefecture of police, but the Mazarine was always my favorite. I would sit on the steps waiting for him, my head in the clouds, dreaming of princes and princesses and faraway kingdoms." She laughed softly. "You know, I used to imagine that I'd get married one day to a prince, right there on the library's steps."

"The Mazarine?" Rémy repeated.

"Yes, it's part of the Palais de l'Institut de France, on the Left Bank."

Rémy chuckled and kissed the top of her head. "I know. I used to play on the steps there when I was a little boy. My mother and I would walk across the Pont des Arts, and she would leave me outside while she went in to read. 'Don't leave the steps, Rémy,' she would tell me. 'There are bad people in this world.' And so I would stay right there, pretending that I was a knight fighting off enemies coming to steal the books."

Eva sat up and looked at him in disbelief. "Do you think we might have seen each other there?"

"It's possible. I was there on and off for years, until my mother died the summer I turned twelve. I never went back."

"And when my father got the job at the prefecture of police, I stopped going, too." She shook her head and settled back against his chest. Was it possible that the prince she had dreamed of so often as a little girl had been right there all along? The coincidence felt extraordinary—fate rather than chance. She sighed in contentment. "I'm very sorry you lost your mother when you were so young, Rémy. I've never heard you speak of her."

"I used to think that memories were less painful when you held them close. I think perhaps that isn't true, though. Now I think pain loses its power when we share it."

Tears in her eyes, Eva nodded. "You can always share with me."

"I know that now." Rémy kissed the top of her head again. "One day, when the war is over, shall we go there again? To the Mazarine?"

She smiled into his chest. "Paris will be Paris again, and no one will stare because I'm a Jew. We'll just be two people meeting on the steps of a library."

When quiet descended once more, Eva's eyelids began to grow heavy. She was almost asleep when Rémy broke the silence. "You said you used to dream of getting married there."

"It sounds silly now, I know."

"No, it doesn't." Rémy waited until Eva looked up at him. "What if we did that?"

"Did what?"

"Got married. On the steps of the Mazarine Library."

"Rémy, I—" She couldn't finish her sentence, though. She closed her eyes, her heart breaking. She wanted to marry him, more than she wanted almost anything else in the world. But how could she do that to Mamusia, a woman who had lost everything, a woman who might never forgive what she would see as Eva turning her back on Judaism? She couldn't say no, though, for how could she let her mother's judgment eclipse her own? It was a terrible idea to live a life dictated by someone else's prejudices. There was no right answer.

When she opened her eyes again, she could see Rémy watching her, and she knew from the expression on his face that he had read her mind. "Your mother," he said softly. "She would never approve."

"It shouldn't matter." Eva wiped away a tear that had slid down her cheek.

"Of course it should," he said gently. He kissed her forehead. "Family means everything, and right now, your family is broken."

"She'll understand one day. She's just so angry right now, angry and frightened. And she misses my father so much . . ."

"Who can blame her?" Rémy began to stroke Eva's hair. "She fears that if you love someone different from you, someone who doesn't belong to your faith, it means losing you, too."

"But it doesn't. She'll never lose me. I'll make sure of it. The way you and I found each other, Rémy, this must be God's plan."

"Then we must trust in him to bring us together again." He took a deep breath. "It doesn't matter how much I love you. I can't ask you to spend your life with me until your mother understands."

"But, Rémy . . ."

"If we're meant to be together, there will always be time. But I can't cost you the last of your family. I love you too much to do that."

"I love you, too." Eva could feel her tears falling now, soaking Rémy's chest in the darkness. "I'm so sorry, Rémy. I'm sorry I'm not stronger."

"Eva, you're the strongest person I know—strong enough that even now, you're doing the right thing, though it may break your heart."

She knew, even as she accepted his words, that she would regret this moment for the rest of her life. "I'll talk to her as soon as she reaches Switzerland. I'll make her see. It's just that I cannot make her accusations true by abandoning her. I can't become the person she fears I am. I would never forgive myself for hurting her that way."

Rémy cupped her chin gently and looked into her eyes. "Darling, I know."

"You'll still come back for me? After the war?"

"Of course I will. I'll meet you on the steps of the Mazarine, and then the rest of our lives can begin."

"*Ani l'dodi v'Dodi li,*" she whispered.

"What does that mean?"

"It's Hebrew for 'I am my beloved's, and my beloved is mine.' It's from Shir Hashirim, the Song of Songs. It's—it's something people say when they marry, to promise each other forever."

Rémy smiled at her. "Then in that case, *Ani l'dodi v'Dodi li.*" He leaned forward and kissed her, so gently it felt like he was already gone.

And though her stomach swam with uncertainty and the heat of the fire was fading, leaving the house darker, colder, Eva finally drifted off, the exhaustion of the past several days—and the joy of reuniting with Rémy—finally taking their toll. He stroked her hair until she fell asleep.

Chapter Twenty-Eight

Eva dreamed of standing on the steps of the Mazarine Library in a white dress, searching for a groom who never came. She awoke with a start, tears streaming down her face, and it took a few seconds to remember that she wasn't in Paris, that she hadn't been abandoned at the altar, and that Rémy was right there with her.

But as she blinked into the early morning light filtering through the edges of the small cottage's blackout shades, she realized that the room was cold, the fire was out, and Rémy was gone.

She jumped up, heart hammering, but he wasn't in the kitchen, and the washroom was empty, too. She threw open the door into the icy morning, hoping that he had just stepped out for some fresh air, but the garden was empty, and there were no footsteps in the freshly fallen snow. That meant that he'd left hours ago, long enough that the last traces of him had disappeared.

Eva shut the door. Numb, she backed into the small house. It was then that she noticed a piece of paper on the small wooden table she'd slept beside last night. It was a letter, addressed to her, and as she picked it up and began to read, her last shred of hope vanished.

Dearest Eva,

Being here with you has made me believe that miracles are possible, and I will treasure our night together until I see you again. I only hope that one day, things will be different for us.

You must go to Switzerland tonight, my love. It's the only way for you to live, and you must live, Eva. You must go on. I will tell Père Bouyssonie to expect you; you should return to the presbytery after nightfall, and he will help you across.

Eva, please know that I love you, and that I will love you for the rest of my life.

I am my beloved's, and my beloved is mine.

Rémy

Eva read the letter twice, tears streaming down her face. Rémy had gone out into the cold night knowing that she wasn't strong enough to promise him forever, and that cut her to the core. It was her fault, and she knew she had done the wrong thing. After all, her mother had viewed the situation through a scope narrowed by anger and loss. Why had Eva let that define her life? Her future?

And what if Rémy never returned? What if he didn't survive the coming months? What if Eva herself perished? She would never be able to right the wrong, to tell him that her answer could only be yes, to tell him that she loved him with all her soul.

Suddenly, though, Eva had a thought. Certainly the bus back to Annecy didn't run this early in the morning. That meant that Rémy was still somewhere in town, didn't it? Perhaps there was still time to find him, to rectify her mistake, to tell him that nothing mattered but him, that she would marry him and find a way to make her mother understand.

She was pulling on her coat and heading out the door before she could stop herself, although as she trudged through the freshly fallen snow toward the priest's home, doubt set in. Would appearing at the priest's home in broad daylight create a problem for him? She stopped suddenly and considered, but it took her only a few seconds to begin moving again. She had to get to Rémy.

Smoke snaked from the chimney of the priest's home, and the lights were on, which indicated he was awake already. Could Rémy be there, too? Eva said a quick prayer, took a deep breath, and knocked.

When Père Bouyssonie answered the door a minute later, he looked surprised to see Eva. He blinked at her a few times before taking her by the arm and pulling her in without a word, hastily closing the door behind her.

"You shouldn't have come until nightfall," he said, but his tone was gentle, not angry.

"I'm so sorry. I need to see Rémy."

"I'm sorry, my dear, but he's already gone."

"He was here this morning?"

The priest nodded. "He left before dawn with a member of the underground who was driving back to Lyon."

Eva's heart sank. It was too late. There would be no way to find him once he was reabsorbed into the dense forests outside

Aurignon. Her eyes filled, and she wiped her tears away, but not before the priest saw them. He pulled her into a hug, and she sobbed on his shoulder for a few seconds before gathering herself and pulling away.

"I'm sorry," she said. "I—I shouldn't have come."

"I'm glad you did, Eva." It was then that she realized that his expression was grave. "I'm afraid I have some news. It came in an hour after Rémy departed."

"News?"

He sighed. "Come with me." He led Eva toward the attic ladder, which was already down, and pointed upward. "We have a visitor." He motioned her toward the ladder and followed her up into the space above.

It took Eva's eyes a few seconds to adjust to the darkness, but as soon as she could see, she gasped. There in the corner was Madame Trintignant, the baker from Aurignon, her hair disheveled, her blouse ripped at the sleeve, her eyes bloodshot. "Madame?" Eva said. "What on earth are you doing here? What's happened?"

"Oh, Eva!" Madame Trintignant leaned in to hug her awkwardly. "It's all over in Aurignon."

"What?"

"The arrests . . ." She broke down sobbing but quickly gathered herself. "The Germans came. They arrested so many of us. Madame Barbier. Madame Travere. Madame Noirot. Everyone."

A chill ran through Eva. "What about Père Clément?"

Madame Trintignant shook her head. "He was fine when I left. He was the one who told me how to get here, who insisted that I had to flee immediately." She hesitated, her gaze sliding away. "They have your mother, Eva."

"My mother? No, no, that's impossible. She has nothing to do with this."

A single tear fell from the baker's eye. "The Germans were looking for you, and when your mother wouldn't tell them where you'd gone, they took her instead."

"No, no, no. Is she . . . ?" Eva couldn't finish the sentence.

"She was alive when I left," Madame Trintignant said quickly. "Though they took her to the prison in Clutier, I think. I'm afraid they know her real identity."

Eva's blood ran cold. "How?"

Madame Trintignant merely shook her head.

The priest leaned in to put a comforting hand on Eva's shoulder. "I will pray for her, Eva. We all will."

"But . . ." Eva's head was spinning. "I—I have to go back."

Madame Trintignant and Père Bouyssonie exchanged glances. "You cannot," Madame Trintignant said firmly. "They know who you are now. They're looking for you. They will execute you, Eva."

"I can't just abandon my mother."

"Leave it to the underground," Père Bouyssonie said. "They'll do what they can."

But Eva knew the fighters hidden in the forest would have bigger things to worry about than saving an imprisoned middle-aged woman who had no value to them. She had to go now, or her mother would die. Eva bit back a sob. "No," she said when she could breathe again. "I have to make things right."

"What has happened to your mother isn't your fault."

"Of course it is! If I had never become involved in any of this, she and I would have been safe in Switzerland a year and a half ago."

"If you return now, you'll surely be killed," Madame Trintignant said softly. "Do you want to play right into their hands?"

Eva stared at her, her heart racing with fear. The baker was right, but what choice was there? She could never forgive herself if she simply left her mother to be murdered because of choices she herself had made. When her father was taken, there wasn't anything she could do. But Mamusia's life could be saved if Eva returned. "I have to go," she said softly, her mind already made up as she turned to the priest.

He hesitated before nodding in resignation. "Then you should hurry. The bus to Annemasse leaves in thirty minutes."

"Thank you, Père Bouyssonie."

"Don't thank me. I fear I am sending you to your death." He sighed. "May God be with you, Eva. You'll be in my prayers."

It was late the next morning before Eva arrived back in Aurignon after taking a train from Annemasse to Lyon, spending a sleepless night shivering in the station, then taking another train to Clermont-Ferrand and a bus to town. She went straight to the church and found Père Clément standing in front of the altar, the pews around him broken and splintered. He turned as she entered, and his eyes widened.

"You're supposed to be in Switzerland!" he said, moving toward her, his eyes wild. His robe was askew, his face bruised. "My God, Eva, what are you doing here? It's not safe. Don't you know?"

"My mother," she managed to choke out, and all at once, his face softened, and he took the final steps toward her, pulling her into an embrace as she collapsed into him. "What happened, Père Clément?" she asked through sobs. "Where is she? I have to help her."

"Come, my dear," he said, pulling away from her and glancing around. "It's not safe here. They haven't arrested me yet, but I fear it's only because they are hoping you'll return and I'll lead them to you."

Eva wiped her tears away. "They destroyed the church . . ."

"It's not destroyed, Eva. A church always stands as long as God remains. Don't forget that. Now quickly, go out the back and to the schoolhouse where you first met with Faucon. Do you remember?"

"Yes."

"I will be along soon. Beware—they might have someone following you."

But as Eva crept out the back door, the morning was quiet, and there were no footsteps crunching in the snow behind her. She took a roundabout route, just in case, but by the time she turned the final corner to the schoolhouse, she was certain she was alone.

The building was cold and dark, long emptied of its children and their teachers. At some point since Eva had seen it last, the place had been ransacked, desks tipped over, books pulled from their shelves, pages ripped out and sent flying into piles that now lurked in the dim corners, purposeless. There was something eerie, otherworldly about the place. The shades were drawn, but sunlight snuck through jagged rips and tears, casting moving shadows each time the wind howled outside. One of the windows was broken, and gusts of biting air swept through.

Eva crouched in the corner closest to the chalkboard, her back to the wall, feeling like a sitting duck. As the minutes ticked by, her concern mounted. Had Père Clément been followed? Arrested? Were the Germans coming for her now? Had she been a fool to come to him, when doing so could only have increased the danger for both of them?

Then the schoolroom door cracked open, and in a burst of snow and sunlight, Père Clément appeared, quickly pulling the door closed behind him. "Eva," he whispered. "I'm here."

She stood and emerged from the shadows. "Père Clément. I was so worried."

As they stood together in the shivering light, he took her hand. "We don't have much time, Eva. You must leave Aurignon before they realize you're back."

"I cannot. Not without my mother."

"Eva, I'm so sorry, but chances are they've already killed her."

Eva shook her head. "No. No, I don't believe it."

"Eva—"

"What happened, Père Clément?" she interrupted. "How did things go so wrong?"

"Someone within our inner circle betrayed us, Eva. It's the only possibility. The Germans knew nearly everyone in town who was involved."

"Could it have been Erich?"

"I wondered that at first, too, but I was his only point of contact, and I was very careful with what I shared." He took a deep breath. "Eva, Claude Gaudibert was arrested and tortured by the Germans. I'm certain Erich didn't know about him, had never met him, so he couldn't have been the one to give him up."

If the Germans had gotten to the Resistance leader, they must have had inside information, for only a handful of people would have known his identity or where to find him. "Is Gaudibert dead?"

The priest nodded sadly. "They strung his body up just outside town, a warning to the rest of us."

Eva swallowed hard. "Where is Erich now?"

"Almost certainly dead, too." Père Clément looked miserable. "If the Germans knew where to find Gaudibert, it isn't a stretch to believe they also knew about Erich passing us information."

"And Faucon? Have they captured Faucon?"

"As far as I know, he's still out there."

"Then I'll go find him. He'll know what to do about my mother."

"No." Père Clément's reply was instant, firm. "Even if he could be located, you could lead the Germans right to him. It would destroy what's left of the circuit, Eva. Please, you cannot."

"I know. I just feel so helpless." She hung her head. "How will I ever forgive myself if the decisions I've made cost my mother her life?"

"Eva, the decisions you made *saved* your mother's life. You cannot look back, only forward. And right now, they are searching for *you*, Eva. If you stay, you will die."

"But if I leave, I will never be able to live with myself." She took a deep breath and squared her shoulders, looking him in the eye. "I can't abandon my mother. I must do what I can to save her."

He stared at her for a long time before sighing. "I know. I was hoping that you would change your mind, but I know. And

I think I have a plan. You go into hiding, somewhere safe. And I negotiate with the Germans on your behalf. I will tell them that if they let your mother go, you will turn yourself in."

"Won't they just arrest and torture you to find out where I am?"

"It's a chance I'm willing to take."

"Even if they let my mother go for now, won't they just re-arrest her once they have me, too?"

"There are a few people I trust in Lyon who haven't been picked up yet. Madame Trintignant made it safely to the border, didn't she? Your mother will, too. And just to increase the odds in our favor, I will try to get a message to the maquisards that we need a distraction to guarantee her safe passage."

"And then I'll turn myself in, once I know she's safe?"

"No, Eva, of course not. You'll run for your life. You'll return to Switzerland, and you'll grow old and tell people of the things that happened here."

"But if I run, they'll kill you."

"These men still think they know God. They have fooled themselves into believing they are doing his will. I have to believe that even a Nazi would have second thoughts about killing a Catholic priest in cold blood."

Her mind spun as she stared at him. She couldn't ask the priest to trade his life for hers, or even for her mother's. The trouble her mother was in was her fault—and that meant she had to be the one to save her.

"No, Père Clément. Thank you, but no. I will find another way."

"There may not be another way."

"Wasn't it you who told me that God opens doors we don't

even know are there? I have to trust that with courage and faith, anything is possible."

The priest smiled sadly. "I'm afraid that sometimes, Eva, that isn't enough."

"It's all I have. Thank you for everything. For offering to risk your life for mine. For saving me in the first place. For giving me a purpose, a home. But now it's my turn to stand up for what's right. And you should go, before it's too late. Go to Switzerland. Live. My mother and I will meet you there when we can."

She could see in his eyes that he knew Eva would never make it there, that she would die for her mother's freedom. "I'm not leaving, Eva," Père Clément said. "My place always has been—and always will be—in Aurignon. God has not abandoned me, and I will not abandon him. And I will do what I can for your mother, because I cannot turn my back on an innocent life any more than you can. It is my decision, not yours. Now go, Eva. Go, before the Germans catch up with us here."

Eva held him tight before letting go. She knew it would be the last time she would see the priest who had helped redeem her. As she slipped into the cold and windy morning a moment later, she prayed that God would be with her long enough to let her save one last life.

Chapter Twenty-Nine

E va knew, four hours later, as she walked through Clutier toward the small local prison the Germans had appropriated, that she was walking into the mouth of the lion and would probably be eaten alive. There was no other choice, though. Her only hope was that the Germans keeping watch there didn't know her, and would be fooled by the way she had swathed herself in an extra layer of bulky clothes, making herself look ten pounds heavier. She had hastily produced documents identifying herself as a forty-nine-year-old widow whose husband had perished heroically at Verdun a generation before, and though it still felt like a foolhardy plan, she hoped that the Germans she encountered would buy the ruse, if only for a few minutes. That was all she needed to see if her mother was still alive.

Please, God, she prayed silently as she hobbled toward the jail, her shoulders rounded, dragging her right leg and leaning on a cane. *Please help me to save my mother. Whatever happens to me, it is your will.* The closer she got, the more convinced she became that if she died today, it would be all right. She had always believed that after death, souls lived on, although in Judaism, the explanation wasn't as clear-cut as it was in the Christian faith. But if she was right, if there was some sort of Garden of Eden waiting for her after she died, she would see Tatuś again, wouldn't she? And one day, hopefully many, many years from now, Rémy might be there, too, on the other side. It was her belief that in the afterlife, you could see straight into each other's souls, and then, at last, Rémy would know how she felt, and how much she regretted letting him walk away.

If she lived, though, she had to get word to him that her answer was yes, had always been yes, would always be yes. After what had happened here, her mother would have to understand that in the face of such evil, the division between Christians and Jews meant nothing. All that mattered was that Rémy was a good person—and that time was too precious to waste. *If you let me survive*, she said to God as she turned the final corner onto the rue de Gravenot, *I promise, I will do all I can to make things right with Rémy, too. I must fix all my mistakes before it's too late.*

And then the jail was ahead of her, dark and threatening even in the early afternoon light. Or perhaps it was just a trick of the shadows, cloaking the bricks in cruelty and despair.

Bracing herself, Eva entered through the front door, her heart thudding as she dragged her leg behind her. A scarf covered the lower half of her face, and a hat shaded the rest. As she approached the desk, she was startled to see that the guard on duty was not German, as she had assumed he would be. He was instead a French gendarme, shuffling through papers, his eyes red-rimmed with exhaustion, his mouth set in a straight line beneath a narrow mustache.

He looked up as she approached, and in that moment, she hated him with a hot fury that surprised her. He wasn't someone born to the other side. He was a Frenchman, who had once sworn to protect his own people. But he had ignored that promise, and had chosen to side with the invaders, likely in a bid to secure himself a position of power when the war ended. The Germans would pay for what they had done one day, Eva felt sure, but there was a special place in hell for the French men and women who had sold their brothers and sisters to the enemy.

The gendarme looked up, his eyes vacant as he gave her a cursory glance. "Madame?"

Eva took a deep breath, gathering her courage, and then slumped further into her chest. "I am here to see Yelena Moreau," she said, keeping her voice low and wobbling, like a sad woman beaten down by life.

"And what is your business with Madame Moreau?" the gendarme asked, interest finally sparking in his eyes as he looked up. "Not that that is her real name anyhow, the dirty Jew." He peered at Eva with narrowed eyes, but she kept her chin tucked and her hat pulled low as she fought to keep the anger from flashing across her face. When he leaned in to try to see her better, she unleashed a violent, hacking cough, not bothering to cover her mouth. He shrank back, sneering in disgust.

"I've been sent by the church," she wheezed, and then before the gendarme could ask which church, or why, she coughed again, long and hard, spewing as much spittle as she could in his general direction. He looked repulsed, and as he scooted his chair even farther away from her, she knew she had assessed him correctly; he would be far more interested in avoiding an apparent case of tuberculosis than he would be in carrying out the mandates of the Germans.

"Yes, well, it's too late," he said, returning to his paperwork.

"Too late?" Eva managed to keep her tone even.

"That's what I said."

"She's been moved, then?" But why would they have sent her mother east if they had planned to use her as bait?

"Moved?" The gendarme looked almost amused as he snorted. "No, madame, she's been executed. Just this morning." He held up the index finger and thumb of his right hand and mimicked the firing of a handgun.

The world went still. Eva wobbled on her feet, the breath knocked out of her. She tried to swallow, but her mouth was dry as dust. This time, when she doubled over coughing, it wasn't playacting, it was pure grief. "No," she said, gathering herself. "No, no. That's impossible. She did nothing wrong."

The man's expression wavered between suspicion and indifference for a second before settling once again on the former. "I hear she had a daughter who was helping the underground. Wouldn't give her up." He leaned forward slightly and tried to see Eva's face, but she ducked her head to hide her tears. "You wouldn't know anything about that, would you? About the daughter?"

"Of course not." Eva managed to keep her tone indignant, though her voice shook. "You're certain you don't have her confused with someone else?" Perhaps her whole world wasn't dissolving into ash as he stared at her, oblivious.

"Saw it with my own eyes." The man leaned back in his chair again, looking satisfied, and in that moment, Eva had never hated another human being more. *Dead.* It felt impossible.

"I see."

The man wasn't done. Like an animal sensing fresh blood, he was suddenly animated, interested. "You know the worst part of it?"

"I can't imagine." Eva could taste bile in her throat, bitter, surging. She needed to vomit, and for a split second, she imagined unloading the contents of her stomach onto the gendarme's spotless uniform. But she couldn't risk turning his revulsion into anger.

"She was still defending the daughter as she died!" He guffawed, like he was sharing a joke with a friend rather than breaking the heart of an enemy. "The German who gave the order asked if she had any last words, and she said some nonsense about how she was proud to be the mother of someone so brave." The man shook his head and snorted. "Old fool. It's all the daughter's fault."

"Yes, it is. There's not a doubt in my mind." Eva tucked her chin as much as she could now, trying to hide the tears streaming down her face as her heart splintered. She would never forgive herself. "And the woman arrested with her? Madame Barbier?"

The gendarme shrugged. "Dead, too. What do you expect? She was helping the underground. She should have known better."

"I see." Eva could hear her voice turning hoarse with grief, but the gendarme didn't seem to notice. "Well, I must be returning to the church. I'll say a prayer for Madame Moreau and Madame Barbier, but there are other parishioners who need our help, too."

"Of course," the man said. "But perhaps you should talk to your church about not supporting traitors, yes?"

"I feel certain, monsieur," Eva replied, her voice shaking, "that traitors will get what they deserve when they come face-to-face with God."

The man nodded in satisfaction, and Eva added one last hacking, spitting cough to ensure that he didn't follow her. She threw up in the skeletal bushes just outside the prison, expelling everything in her stomach, her tears melting the ice as they fell.

There was nothing left for Eva to lose.

The Germans had taken her father and now her mother, and Eva knew she had only herself to blame. *She was proud to be the mother of someone so brave*, the gendarme had said, but Eva wasn't brave. She was terrified; she had been all along. She'd been fooling herself to think that she could swallow her fear and make a difference. The only change she had brought about was the loss of the woman who had given her life. Hadn't Tatuś's last words to her been about taking care of her mother? Instead, Eva had thrown her to the wolves.

Eva had failed her father back in Paris, and now she had failed her mother, too. Her parents were gone, and it was all her fault. She had hurt Rémy, too, by letting him leave believing that she didn't want to marry him. Who knew what would happen to him out there in the cold, dangerous forests before she could correct things? And it had all been for naught; her mother had still died believing that Eva was betraying her faith.

On a cold winter's day a year earlier, when Rémy had told her he wanted to do more to fight back, Eva hadn't really understood. Weren't they already resisting with their forgery? *Someone has to take the fight to the Germans, Eva*, he had said. *No one is coming to save us.* His words had frightened her, but that was before she had lost her mother. It was before her life had imploded because of her own mistakes.

It was before the Germans had taken everything.

It didn't matter if she lived, and that's why she decided to head for the farmhouse where she knew Joseph sometimes stayed. She would be careful that no one followed her, but she had to do something. She had to take the fight to the monsters who had stolen her family from her. She had spent the war passively helping people, but that was no longer enough. She wanted blood, and she would get down on her knees to beg Joseph to help her if she had to. He could vouch for her, send her to the fighters in the forest, tell them that she would do anything they asked.

The bus ride back to Aurignon and the long walk toward the outskirts of town did nothing to heal the gaping wound in Eva's heart, and by the time she walked up the road to the farmhouse, her boots crunching over eight inches of snow, she was even angrier than she had been when she left the jail. She had taken a roundabout route here, weaving through town, ducking into an abandoned storefront to shed her extra layer of clothing and her cane, and wrapping her scarf more tightly as a shield against the wind, which grew more vicious as she left the shelter of Aurignon's small town square. She looked once more over her shoulder as she approached the front door of the main house, but she was well and truly alone.

She knocked on the door, but there was no answer, even when she called out. The door was locked tight, and when she crept around back and peered in the one window whose curtain hadn't been pulled tight, the inside of the house looked dark, abandoned. A cobweb glistened just inside the pane.

It appeared the farmers who lived here were gone, perhaps arrested by the Germans, too. But was Joseph still camped out in the barn, as he had been before? It seemed unlikely, but she knew nowhere else to go. Panic coursing through her, Eva trudged through the snow to the lopsided old building. Inside, it smelled like musty hay and stale milk. "Hello?" Eva called out, just in case Joseph had heard her approach and was hiding. "It's me! Eva! Please, I need your help!"

Something stirred overhead, and Eva looked up. "Joseph?" she called out. "Please! Are you here?"

Her question was greeted with silence, and at last, she felt her shoulders slump in defeat. The noise she had heard had probably been a mouse or another lucky creature who had found refuge here from the harsh winter when the humans had fled. "Please?" she called out once more, but she already knew her plea was in vain. Joseph was long gone, and with him, any hope that she could join the armed resistance.

Eva turned to go, tears coursing down her face once again. Everything felt hopeless, impossible.

But then, just as she was about to walk out the door of the barn into the frigid afternoon, she heard a whisper behind her.

She turned, staring into the darkness. Had she imagined it? Was she so desperate that she was hearing things?

"Eva." There it was again, weak but undeniable. The voice was coming from the loft above her head. Someone was there.

"Joseph?" she called out as she hastily ascended the narrow ladder against the back wall. The second she emerged into the haystacks above, though, she had to stifle a scream. Several bales of hay were splashed with crimson, and there were dark stains on the wooden floor. The loft smelled of iron, and in the corner lay Geneviève, slumped awkwardly to the right, her faded blue cotton dress soaked with blood. There was a hole, dark and gaping, where her stomach should have been.

"Oh my God, Geneviève!" Eva cried out, moving quickly to her side and smoothing her blood-matted dark hair back from her pale face.

"Eva," Geneviève whispered. Her eyelashes fluttered; she was barely conscious. She stared at Eva without focusing. "Is it really you?"

"Yes, Geneviève! What in the world happened?"

Geneviève coughed, and a few drops of blood bubbled from the side of her mouth. "Gérard," she whispered.

Eva looked around. "He went for help?"

"No, Eva." She coughed again, blood trickling down her chin. "It was him."

"What?"

"He—he killed me."

Surely Geneviève was talking nonsense. "No, Geneviève. You're still alive."

Geneviève's laugh was weak and bitter. "I'm dying, Eva."

"I'll get help."

"It's too late." She coughed again and spit up another mouthful of blood. "Gérard is the traitor, Eva. The one who betrayed all of us."

Eva was shaking now. "No. No, no, no. That's impossible. I've known him for years. He would never . . ." She trailed off. "No," she added in a whisper.

"He—he told me that when the Germans arrested him in December, they offered to pay him if he'd become an informer."

"But he's a Jew!"

She sputtered, blood gurgling. "You weren't supposed to leave so early, he said. He promised you to them; he promised he would bring them the Jew who was behind all the forged documents in the region. He didn't believe I didn't know where you'd gone."

Eva's blood ran cold. "He did this to you because of *me*?"

"It's not your fault." Geneviève groped for Eva's hand, her eyelids fluttering again. "It's mine." She took a trembling breath, and Eva could hear a rattle in her lungs. "I—I trusted the wrong person."

"I trusted him, too."

"You have to go. Before he comes back."

"I can't leave you."

"For me, it's over." Geneviève's voice was getting weaker. "Make him pay for what he's done."

"But . . ."

"Eva. Go."

Eva wavered. She put a hand on Geneviève's midsection and felt only blood, hot and pooling. Joseph had shot her and left her to die a slow, terrible death, all alone. But she wouldn't be alone. Eva could do that for her, at least. "I won't leave you, my friend. I'm here."

Geneviève was too weak to argue. So while she fell in and out of consciousness, Eva held her hand and softly crooned "Au Clair de la Lune," the lullaby Geneviève's mother had comforted Geneviève with when she was just a little girl. "*Ma chandelle est morte,*" Eva sang, "*Je n'ai plus de feu. Ouvre-moi ta porte pour l'amour de Dieu.*" My candle is dead. I have no light left. Open your door for me, for the love of God.

As Geneviève slipped away, Eva sang the song again, turning the last words of the verse into a prayer. "Open your door for her, please, dear God." And then Geneviève was gone, her suffering over. Eva stood, her hands coated in her friend's blood, and headed for the ladder, one more innocent death on her conscience, one more reason to fight burning deep in her soul.

The only place Eva could think to go was back to the church. She was still reeling from the betrayal, which had knocked her sideways with confusion and guilt. How could Joseph have turned against them? Against *her*? Obviously, she had never really known him at all, the charmer with the dark good looks and a heart of stone. Fury churned within her—at Joseph and at herself. How had she been so blind, so quick to believe in him just because she'd known him in her previous life?

She had to warn Père Clément. But how would she stop Joseph if he was already here? He had a gun, and Eva had only . . . what? Her righteous anger? Her crippling grief? Still, it would have to be enough. She had failed her mother and Geneviève. She couldn't fail the kindly priest, too.

She stopped only long enough to wash as much of Geneviève's blood from her hands and face as she could, and then she grabbed Geneviève's bicycle and set off toward town. She had to walk it through the snowdrifts until she reached the main road, which had been cleared. She climbed on and rode the rest of the way as the sun sunk toward the horizon and the wind froze her tears.

The church was dark and silent, though the front door was unlocked. *This is God's house*, Père Clément had once told her. *The doors will never be closed to a soul seeking God's peace.* It wasn't peace Eva was seeking today, though.

She checked Père Clément's office, the confessional, and the secret library, but the church was deserted. A quick check of his small apartment behind the church came up empty, too; the doors were closed and locked, the windows dark. Eva retreated back to the library, though she knew as long as she remained there, she was a sitting duck. Joseph knew about it—and about Père Clément's key to the room—and sooner or later, he might come looking.

But there was something she had to do.

In silence, she lit a few lanterns and pulled the Book of Lost Names from its innocuous place on the shelf. It was the one thing Joseph wouldn't be able to take from her; she thanked God she had shared the secret only with Père Clément and Rémy.

She stared at the book for a moment as she held it in her hands. The brown leather was even more worn than it had been when she first held it, the spine more creased, two slight faded spots on the back of the book now and one on the front from her own fingertips, from the number of times she had held it without fully removing the chemicals and ink from her fingers first. She was only the latest person to put her mark on it, though. How many Catholic worshippers had held this book in their hands over the past two centuries before it found its way to her? It had existed before the French Revolution, before Napoleon had been born, before Louis XVI and Marie Antoinette had lost their heads in the name of liberty, before Eva's parents had come to France believing that doing so would give them a life of freedom and opportunity. And here it was, in the hands of a proud Jew, in the back of a church where God had seen evil and treachery unfold.

Eva blinked back tears and opened the book to page two, Rémy's page. She knew exactly what she wanted to tell him, what she should have said in that cottage on the edge of France just a few days earlier. On the first line, her hand trembling, she marked a tiny star over the *é* in *étoit*, then a dot over the *p* in *prions*. On the next page, she added another dot over the *o* in *recevoir*, and on page four, a dot over the *u* in *leurs*. She continued like that on Rémy's pages—six, nine, fourteen, twenty-two, thirty-five, and so on—until she had said what she wanted to say: *Épouse-moi. Je t'aime.*

She closed the book after drawing a dot over the first *m* on page 611; there weren't enough pages left for the final *e*, but it would be enough to piece together the message: *Marry me. I love you.* As she slid it back into place, she let her hand linger on its spine, just for a second. Would Rémy find it? Would he know she loved him? Or would the book mean nothing in the end?

Just then, there was a noise at the door, and she jerked her hand away from the bookshelf. It was too late, she realized, too late for everything. As Joseph moved into the room, clutching a handgun, Eva shrank back against the wall. She had nothing to defend herself with, nothing but books. She groped behind her, and closed her hand around the spine of a heavy Bible. He would shoot her, she knew, but she didn't want to go without a fight.

"Joseph," she murmured.

His face twisted as he moved into the space she had once shared with Rémy. "Eva, you're even more foolish than I thought. You came back? To the one place you knew I could find you?"

She took a deep, trembling breath. "I had to." Even if she died here today, which she almost certainly would, Rémy would know she had loved him.

"You know, I've never understood you, Eva Traube, even in Paris, with your wide eyes and your nose buried in books like the world outside the pages didn't matter. You were always an odd bird, weren't you? And you think I didn't see the way you looked at me? Just like all the others. I could have had you if I wanted, anytime."

She ignored him. "What have you done, Joseph? To Geneviève? To my mother?"

There were tears in his brilliant blue eyes, just for an instant, as he looked away. "I didn't want to hurt them, Eva. It got away from me."

"*What* did? How could you do any of this, you bastard?"

When he turned back, the tears were gone, replaced by a look of steely resolve that sent a chill down her spine. "I had no choice. The Germans knew I was part of the underground. They were going to execute me, so I offered them a deal."

"It was *your* idea to work for the Germans?"

"You would have done the same to save yourself."

"No, Joseph, I wouldn't have. Not in a million years."

He narrowed his eyes. "They wouldn't have offered you the chance anyhow. You're a Jew."

"You are, too!"

He shook his head, the traces of a smug smile playing across his lips. "My father was Catholic. My mother was only half Jewish. The Germans said I was lucky; one more drop of Jewish blood, and I would have been doomed."

"You're doomed anyhow, Joseph. You really think there's a place for you in Germany if they win the war? They'll never be able to see past your Jewish blood. And if France wins instead, well, they execute traitors."

"You think I haven't thought things through? The Germans have promised to pay me, enough so that I can disappear after the war and live my life." His expression hardened. "Besides, there won't be anyone left to tell them what I've done, Eva."

She swallowed hard. "So you're going to kill me, too, then. Just like you killed my mother."

His face fell. "I didn't mean for that to happen. I cared about your mother, Eva, I did. She was always kind to me. She was just in the wrong place at the wrong time. They were there for Madame Barbier, and after they arrested your mother, too, they asked me if I knew her. I was going to deny it, but she begged me to help her. She even used my real name, the old fool! After that, I couldn't deny that I knew who she was, especially because it was obvious by then that she was your mother. And she refused to tell the Germans what she knew, Eva. They might have sent her east rather than executing her if she'd told them where you'd gone. It's her own fault."

"None of this was her fault." Eva choked back the lump in her throat. "And Geneviève?"

He flexed his jaw. "If things were different, maybe we would have had a chance. But I needed to know where you were. You're my ticket to a new life, Eva. I gave them Gaudibert already. You're the second half of the bargain. If I turn you over to the Germans, give them the Jew behind the largest forgery operation in the area, I get to live. You can see my dilemma, yes? Geneviève had information, and she refused to give it to me. I only meant to threaten her, Eva, but she was selfish. I told her that giving you up was the only thing that could save my life, and she wouldn't do it."

"So you shot her in the stomach and left her to die?"

"It truly is a shame that things had to end that way."

"You're a monster."

He looked away. "I knew you wouldn't understand. How could you? You Jews don't have a future in France, but I do. Surely you see that."

She could feel the fury inside of her surging hot and strong. She reminded herself to remain calm. "So what happens now, Joseph?"

"You tell me everything about what you've been doing here the past year. I know where you're getting the papers, of course— and I've told the Germans all about the Algerian drops from the Allies—but how are your documents themselves so convincing? I've been trying to get the information from Gaudibert and Père Clément for months now, but they're both too careful, too tight-lipped. Even under torture, Gaudibert wouldn't give your secrets up! How are you and Rémy erasing information? How are you duplicating stamps so perfectly and so quickly, even when the Germans change their methods and their inks? What are the other networks you're working with? Who are your contacts? The Germans need to know so that they can crack down on all the forgery bureaus like yours across France. If I bring that information to them, they'll let me leave Aurignon, start a new life."

"You're a fool to believe they'll keep that promise, Joseph. They'll kill you."

He shook his head. "You don't know anything about it. So what'll it be? Trust me, it will be easier if you give the information to me."

"Why would I tell you a thing, you treacherous bastard?"

"Because if you don't, I'll bring you to the Germans, and they'll beat it out of you. They'll torture you until you're pleading for mercy, until you're begging for a bullet to your brain. I'm an old friend, Eva. I would rather see you go in peace. Help me, and I'll help you."

"Like you helped Geneviève?"

Something flickered across Joseph's face for an instant, something that looked almost like regret. Then as quickly as it had appeared, it was gone. "I told you, she could have saved herself. I could have taken her with me. But she didn't love me enough. She's to blame."

"*She's* to blame?" Anger bubbled up within Eva, and before she could reconsider, she pulled the heavy Bible from the shelf behind her and flung it at him with all her might. He raised his hand to ward off the blow, but his surprise made him fire his weapon. The bullet tore through the air above Eva's right shoulder, close enough that she could feel it pass. When Joseph straightened again, there was a small ribbon of blood above his right brow, and he was sneering. At least she had succeeded in wounding him, even if it was the last thing she'd do.

"Oh, Eva, you will regret that," he growled.

She squared her shoulders and thought of her mother, of her father, of Rémy, of all that she had lost because of this war. "I have more regrets than you will ever know. But hurting you will never be one of them."

He raised his gun again. "Tell me about the forgeries, Eva, or I'll torture you myself. I'd relish the opportunity, you pathetic cow. You'll give up your precious Rémy and everyone else."

"I'd sooner die, Joseph."

"Oh, you will die, Eva. It's just a matter of how much it will hurt. If you don't start talking, I'll put a bullet here, in your leg. You'll bleed to death slowly, and it will be excruciating. I'll make sure of it."

"You'll pay for this, for everything you've done." She spat at him.

His face darkened, fury burning in the eyes she had once thought were beautiful. "I don't want to do this, Eva, but you've left me no choice. You have ten seconds to make up your mind—and I'm only giving you that time because of our long-standing friendship, you see—but if you're still being this obstinate by the time I finish, I'm afraid I'll have no choice but to pull the trigger. Understand? Ten, nine, eight . . ."

"Go to hell, Joseph." As he counted down the seconds, she closed her eyes and began to pray—not to survive, for she knew there was no longer a chance of that.

". . . seven, six, five . . ."

Instead, Eva prayed that she would have the strength and fortitude to breathe her last before she betrayed anyone. No one else could die because of her; she couldn't bear it.

". . . four, three, two . . ." As Joseph reached the end of his countdown, Eva braced herself for the horrific pain she knew would come, the agony that would be only the beginning.

When the shot went off, it sounded like an explosion. It reverberated in the room, and her ears rang with the force of it. It took her a split second to realize, though, that she felt nothing. Had he missed? Her eyes flew open, and her jaw fell.

There on the ground before her lay Joseph on his belly, his head twisted to the side, his eyes open and unseeing, his mouth agape, an oozing bullet wound in the back of his head.

Above him, smoke still drifting from the pistol in his hand, stood Erich, in full Nazi uniform, his eyes on Eva. "You must go, Eva," he said. "Go now. They're coming for you."

She began to tremble as she stared at him in shock and disbelief. "How . . . ?"

"Joseph betrayed me, too. My superiors know I was helping the underground. A friend told me, and I slipped away before they could arrest me. I came here to warn Père Clément. I couldn't find him, but I heard Joseph's voice, and then a moment ago, the gunshot."

"You saved me."

He smiled sadly. "At least I have done one thing I can feel good about when I meet my maker."

"What do you mean, Erich? Come with me, quickly. We can run together."

"It's too late for me. Not for you. Go, Eva. Run for your life. Don't worry, I'll distract them for a few minutes, at least. It's the only chance you'll have."

"Erich—"

"Before I came to Père Clément to confess, there were things I did, Eva, things that can never be forgiven. I have come to terms with what eternity will hold for me. Knowing my last act was to save you, though, would give me some peace in the end. Please, let my life be worth at least that."

Suddenly, she understood what he was saying. "Erich, no!" She reached for him, but he backed away, shaking his head.

There were voices outside the church then, raised voices, barking orders in German. "Live a good life, Eva," Erich whispered, and then, without hesitation, he closed his eyes, put the gun to his head, and pulled the trigger.

Eva stifled a scream as he fell to the floor, but in an instant, she understood what she had to do. Erich had created chaos that would allow her to escape. And so just before the Nazis entered the church, she dashed out of the secret library and dove beneath a pew, holding her breath as a dozen black boots stormed past her toward the bodies of Erich and Joseph. She waited until they were all inside the little room, exclaiming to each other in disbelief, before wriggling out and making her way quickly and silently toward the back door of the church. She glanced at Jesus on the altar once more and said a quick prayer for Erich's soul before hurrying out into the icy night.

And then, just as Erich had urged her to do, she moved into the darkness, running for her life.

Chapter Thirty

Sixteen months later
June 1945

The light on the Boulevard Raspail in Paris was fading on a warm June afternoon as Eva made her way for what felt like the hundredth time to the Hôtel Lutetia, the soaring, snow-white art nouveau masterpiece in Saint-Germain-des-Prés that had once been a haven for writers and artists. The war had turned it into something different, a headquarters for the spies and torture specialists of the German Abwehr, but Paris had been freed ten months earlier, and in April, the grand hotel had taken on yet another new life as a repatriation center for refugees from the German concentration camps.

Eva had made it back to Paris from Switzerland in the fall of 1944, two months after the liberation of the city, and she had wandered the streets, hoping to meet someone she'd known in her previous life, someone who could tell her what had become of her father. But there was no one. Nothing. A family of French strangers was living in her old apartment, and none of her old neighbors had remained. She began going to the Mazarine Library each day to wait on its steps in hopes that Rémy would come for her, but as the days passed and the months grew colder, she began to admit to herself that he likely hadn't survived the war. Almost no one had.

Monsieur Goujon, her father's old boss, had helped her to find part-time work repairing typewriters, just as her father had once done, and that allowed her to pay the rent on a tiny studio apartment in the seventh arrondissement. She hadn't been able to bring herself to return to Aurignon yet, though she knew she would someday, when she was stronger and train travel through the war-shredded country had been restored. She had to know if Père Clément had survived, whether Madame Noirot, Madame Travere, and Madame Trintignant had made it through the war. She knew in her heart that the answer was probably no, but she couldn't bear to face the reality yet. As long as she waited in Paris, she could imagine them all alive and well. Besides, she had said she would meet Rémy here. Leaving, even for a few days, would be like admitting he was gone for good.

In the spring, tattered and emaciated Jews who had spent the war in the concentration camps to the east had begun to return. Those who had lost family members peered into the faces of these walking skeletons, struggling to find the people they were so sure they'd never see again. Sometimes, there were joyous reunions. Mostly, though, the survivors returned to find that everyone they loved had perished and that their reward for enduring hell was a renewed sense of loss and despair.

When the Hôtel Lutetia began processing refugees, there was some hope. The Red Cross set up there, and they kept careful lists of the former prisoners and those who were seeking them. Everyone who survived was given food, a temporary place to stay, two thousand francs, and a coupon for a new suit. Eva had posted a precious photograph of her father, and each day, she turned up holding a sign with his name on it, hoping that someone would be able to give her an answer about his fate. She knew he was dead; she could feel it in her bones. But she needed someone to say the words so she could officially close that chapter of her life. Hope was a dangerous thief, stealing her todays for a tomorrow that would never come.

Hundreds of people streamed through the front doors of the hotel each day, and Eva peered into all their faces, grew numb to their chorus of tears and the scent of the blood dried into their prison-striped clothes. She couldn't stop coming, though, not without an answer.

And then, on the fourth of June, she finally got one. She was wearily searching the eyes of the incoming refugees when someone said her name in a voice she recognized, but only barely. Her heart skipped, and when she turned, she was staring into the face of a man who couldn't have weighed more than fifty kilos. His cheeks looked sunken and carved out of bone; his hair had gone gray, and his beard was patchy. But she recognized him instantly. "Tatuś?" she whispered, too afraid to touch him for fear that he was an illusion, that he would dissipate before her eyes.

"Is it really you, słoneczko?" he asked, his voice a raspy echo of what it had once been.

She could only nod, and when he pulled her into his arms, his body felt fragile and unfamiliar, but the strength of his love felt like coming home. She sobbed into his shoulder, and he into hers. When they finally pulled away, she found the father she had once known in his wise, brown eyes.

"And your mother?" he asked her. "Where is your mother?"

"Oh, Tatuś." She began to cry again. "She died. In the early winter of 1944."

His eyes filled. "I felt it, you know. I will mourn her, Eva, but I will forever thank God that you survived."

"I'm—I'm so sorry, Tatuś. I wish she had been the one to live, not me."

"Oh, słoneczko, God has a plan for you. For all of us." Tatuś wiped her tears away. "We must always keep moving forward."

It took Eva a week to tell Tatuś what had happened to her mother, and when he cried and told her it was not her fault, she couldn't bring herself to believe him, even when he insisted that Mamusia must have been so proud of her. "All she wanted for you was a happy life," Tatuś said. "She would be so glad that you survived."

"Tatuś, I brought her only disappointment."

"That's not true, Eva."

"It is."

He was quiet as she told him the story of Rémy, of how she had fallen in love with him despite her mother's objections, how Mamusia had been furious about it and about so many of the other choices Eva had made. "I failed her, Tatuś," she concluded miserably. "If I had listened, maybe she would still be alive."

"If you had listened, słoneczko, you'd be dead, too, for you would have followed her advice right into Joseph Pelletier's arms." His expression was grave. "Just because she was your mother didn't mean she was right."

"But if I had honored her . . ."

"You *do* honor her—and me—every day by being the kind of person we raised you to be."

Eva covered her face with her hands, and Tatuś gently rubbed her back.

"This Rémy, do you still love him?" he asked after a moment.

"I'm certain he's dead by now, Tatuś."

"That's what you thought about me, too, isn't it? And here I am." He paused. "You know, your mother's parents did not want her to marry me."

Eva looked up. "They didn't?"

He smiled. "They thought I was too poor, that I could never give her a good life. They wanted her to marry a man named Szymon Lozinski, the son of a doctor. This Lozinski was a cruel man, though, and marrying him would have broken your mother's heart. I like to think that for the years I had with her, I made her happy."

"You did, Tatuś. You did."

He smiled. "My point is that every parent wants what is best for his or her child. But we are all guilty of seeing things through the lens of our own lives. We forget sometimes that it is your life to live."

"What about Rémy's religion, though? Mamusia always said that to love him would be to betray the Jewish faith, especially at a time when we are being wiped from the earth."

"You are betraying nothing if you follow your heart," Tatuś said firmly. "Deep down, you know that, too."

When she didn't say anything, he leaned in and whispered in her ear, "Go, Eva. Go back to Aurignon and see if anyone there knows what became of him. It is the only way you'll have peace—and we all deserve that."

"Will you come with me, Tatuś?"

"No, Eva, I cannot." He shivered. "I can't imagine being on another train. But you go. I will be here waiting for you when you return."

When Eva got off the bus a week later in Aurignon, it looked just as it had that summer day in 1942 when she and her mother had first arrived. The flowers were in bloom, their perfume coloring the air, and the streets were alive with honeyed sunlight and the scent of pine. Eva closed her eyes for a minute and breathed in, trying to imagine Mamusia standing beside her, but it was no use. Her mother was dust in the wind, long gone.

The Église Saint-Alban looked just as she remembered it, though it had gotten a fresh coat of paint since she had last been there, and the trees outside had grown, arching over the entrance like a canopy of welcome. The sun trickled in as Eva approached the front door.

Inside, the church was silent, but the familiar statue of Jesus on the cross was just where she remembered. "Hello there," she whispered, and it felt like greeting an old friend. The pews had been restored, the church repainted and refurbished, as if all the things that had happened here had been merely a bad dream.

She checked the confessional in the back, and the office behind the altar, but she was alone. She took a deep breath and approached the door to the secret library. She still had her key, but when she inserted it into the lock, it didn't open. She tried again, jiggling the key, but it didn't work. Her heart sank.

"Eva?" The voice came from behind her and she whirled around, relief washing over her. It was Père Clément, and he was staring at her as if he was dreaming. "Is it really you?" he asked.

She felt as if she, too, was seeing a ghost. He was a shell of the man he'd once been, thirty pounds lighter, his sandy hair turned gray, his frock hanging loosely from a skeletal frame. But he was here and alive, and she had to stop herself from collapsing under the weight of her relief. "Père Clément," she whispered.

"Eva, it *is* you." He came forward and pulled her into a hug. "I was sure you were dead."

"I feared the same of you." She breathed in the familiar scent of him, frankincense and pine. There was something else now, too, an edge of smoke, of having come through a fire. "What happened to you?"

He pulled away and gave her a small smile. "I spent some time as a guest of Germany in Poland."

"I'm so sorry."

He waved the words away. "But I've managed to return, and that is what matters. The church closed when I was gone, so I was glad to be able to repair it and open its doors once again. And what about you, Eva? You made it to Switzerland?"

She nodded and briefly told him about her return to Paris and her reunion with her father. Then, because she couldn't bear to wait any longer, she asked him the question that had been burning a hole in her heart since that cold winter night in the shadow of Switzerland's freedom. "And Rémy, Père Clément? What happened to him?"

From the shadow that crossed Père Clément's face and the pain that filled his eyes, she knew the answer before he said it. "Oh, Eva, you don't know." He reached for her hand. "I'm so sorry, my dear. He didn't make it."

She had known it was true, for if he had lived, he would have come for her. But she hadn't realized until that moment that she'd still been holding on to so much impossible hope. Her whole body went cold, and in what felt like slow motion, she collapsed to her knees, her limbs suddenly as limp as rags. She could feel the blood rushing through her veins, the tears prickling at the backs of her eyes, the air suspended in her choked lungs, the aching hole in her heart where the possibility of a future had once been. "No," she finally whispered, and then she was drinking the air in desperate gulps, unable to control the tremors that shook her whole body as Père Clément knelt beside her and stroked her back while she sobbed into her hands. "What happened?" she asked when she could finally breathe again. "What happened to him?"

"He came back to Aurignon," Père Clément said slowly. "I caught glimpses of him twice near the town square, but both times, he pretended not to know me. I later learned he was following a gendarme named Besnard, a man who used to worship here, a man whose children I baptized."

Eva blinked. "I remember him." He was the gendarme who used to stare at her, whose gaze made her uneasy, though she had tried to convince herself it was only her imagination.

Père Clément nodded and drew a deep breath. "As it turns out, Besnard had been betraying his fellow officers, the ones who were sympathetic to the French, and reporting them to the German command. He was closing in on the families of some of the maquisards. Rémy had been sent to capture him before he could do more harm."

Eva could hardly breathe. "What happened?"

"Someone tipped Besnard off, and he was heavily armed when Rémy came for him. From what I understand, there was a fight outside the same barn where Geneviève died, and both men perished."

Eva began to cry. "When?"

"The first week of June 1944."

It was four months after she had fled. If she had waited longer, would she have seen Rémy once more? Could she have persuaded him not to walk into a trap? To stay with her after all? They were questions she knew would haunt her forever. "Was he . . . was he buried here?"

Père Clément shook his head. "The maquisards took care of their own, Eva. They came for his body before it could be desecrated by the Germans. I'm so sorry." He hesitated and added, "I said funeral rites for him anyhow."

"That would have meant a great deal to him, I think." For a moment, she was silent, imagining a world without Rémy in it. It was astonishing that the sun had continued to shine, that the earth had continued to turn, as if nothing had changed. The truth that he had been gone for more than a year now seemed impossible.

"I'm very sorry, Eva. I know how much you loved him."

"If I had said I would marry him—"

"Don't do that," Père Clément said, cutting her off. "The end would have been the same, my child. He still would have fought. He felt it was his duty. He died a hero of France."

"A hero of France," she repeated in a murmur. "And what of the others? Madame Noirot? Madame Travere?"

"Both sent east. Neither returned."

"And Madame Trintignant? Did she survive, at least?"

He sighed. "I'm afraid she was caught at the border when she tried to escape into Switzerland. She died in prison."

Eva shook her head. The scope of loss was almost unimaginable. She thought of Rémy, standing outside the blue barn, knowing he might be walking right into his own death. Had he died knowing she loved him? Or had he died thinking that her answer to him would always be no? "Père Clément? Did Rémy return to the secret library before he died? Did he look in the Book of Lost Names?"

Something changed in the priest's face. "Eva, I'm afraid I don't know."

"Can you unlock the door for me? I need to see the book." Suddenly it felt like the most urgent thing in the world. Had Rémy read her message? Had he left one of his own? "Please, mon Père."

But the priest didn't move, though the sorrow on his face deepened. "Eva, the library was looted by the Nazis right around the time Rémy lost his life. It was clear the war was lost, and they were fleeing, but they wanted to take whatever they could with them back to Germany. There were several private homes ransacked, as well, along with Madame Noirot's bookstore, but our secret library suffered the greatest losses, perhaps because they perceived our collection of old religious texts to be very valuable."

"Did they take our book? The Book of Lost Names?" she whispered.

He nodded slowly.

Tears filled her eyes again. It was another staggering blow. Now, not only would she never see Rémy again, but she would never know if he'd died realizing that she wanted to marry him. Nor would she have a record of the hundreds of children whose names were changed, the ones whose pasts she wanted so desperately to preserve. The loss of the book felt like a death of hope. "May I have a few moments alone in the library?" she asked.

"I changed the lock and closed it tight when I returned to Aurignon," Père Clément said. "It's been too painful to go inside. It made me think of you and Geneviève and Rémy and all the things we accomplished here—but also all the things we lost."

Eva bowed her head. "That's why I need to say goodbye."

Père Clément nodded and led her toward the familiar room. He withdrew a key from beneath his robe, unlocked the door, and opened it for her. "I'll be just outside," he said, squeezing her shoulder. "Stay as long as you like."

It took a few seconds for Eva's eyes to adjust to the dim lighting; she hadn't thought to ask Père Clément for a lantern. Still, sunlight spilled in narrow ribbons from the stained glass windows overhead, just as it always had, and Eva found a bit of comfort in the familiar glow.

But that was the only thing that felt the same about the room. The table where she had once worked was gone, as were the chairs that had anchored it. The shelves were nearly bare, with only a hundred or so books remaining from the thousands that had once lined the room. A fine layer of dust made everything look haunted, and as Eva ran her hands over the remaining volumes, sadness swept through her.

The Germans had taken everything of any conceivable value, leaving only newer-looking volumes behind. There were some church missals that had been printed in the 1920s, some newer Bibles, and a collection of scholarly texts with spines too ragged to be of any use to anyone. They seemed lonely on the shelves by themselves, devoid of the brothers and sisters they'd spent years with, and Eva felt a surge of grief for them that she knew was illogical.

She ran her hands over the books, saying what she knew was a final goodbye to these old friends that rested in a place she knew she'd never see again. But as she neared the end of a row of familiar Bibles, she stopped abruptly, her fingertips on the tattered spine of a volume that didn't belong there.

She pulled it out and stared at the cover. It was an English-language edition of *The Adventures of Tom Sawyer*, a book she had once mentioned to Rémy as they worked side by side, two months after she'd arrived in Aurignon. He had asked about her father, and she had told him about all the books that had once lined his beautiful library at home. *Did you know*, she had asked him, *that* The Adventures of Tom Sawyer *was among the first novels written on a typewriter? It was one of my father's favorite things. We had a copy, but I had to leave it behind. Is it strange that it's one of the things I miss most from home?*

Slowly, she opened the front cover of the book, and her breath caught in her throat. There, on the title page, in Rémy's scratchy handwriting, was a note.

For E: I found this in Paris. One day I'll buy you a better copy. R
4 June 1944

She read the message once, twice, three times, searching for a meaning, a code, but the words were just words, one final gesture of kindness from a man who'd been thinking of her before he died. But had he left her a message in the Book of Lost Names, too? Or had he been in a hurry, stopping only long enough to drop off this gift? And why had he left it here if he'd known she had already fled to Switzerland? Was it because he knew she would come back if she lived through the war?

Hours later on a train bound for Paris, after she had said goodbye to Père Clément for the last time, she was leafing absently through the Twain book, Rémy's last gift to her, when she stopped abruptly on a passage in chapter seventeen. There was a mark—a tiny dot—above the first letter of the first word, which is what had caught her eye, for it reminded her instantly of the markings they'd left in the Book of Lost Names.

First one and then another pair of eyes followed the minister's, and then almost with one impulse the congregation rose and stared while the three dead boys came marching up the aisle, Tom in the lead, Joe next, and Huck, a ruin of drooping rags, sneaking sheepishly in the rear! They had been hid in the unused gallery listening to their own funeral sermon!

Eva stared at the page, her heart pounding. In the story, Tom and his friends fake their own deaths, a plotline Eva had forgotten about entirely, since it had been a decade and a half since she'd last read the book. Was it crazy to wonder whether Rémy had meant to leave her a message, a subtle sign that he planned to do the same if things went wrong? Was he trying to tell her that he might still be out there, that she shouldn't give up on him?

Then again, if he was alive, he would have come for her by now. He would have met her on the steps of the Mazarine

Library, as he'd once promised to. At the very least, he would have returned to Aurignon to see Père Clément. No, it was impossible, wasn't it? The speck of ink over the first word in the passage could just as easily have been an errant smudge of dirt or a meaningless mark from the pen of a stranger years before. Maybe it wasn't a sign at all.

Still, hope was a dangerous thing. It grew like a field of wildflowers within Eva, blossoming in all the spaces that had been filled with darkness and despair, until she began to believe with all her heart in the possibility that Rémy might have lived through the war after all. And so she returned to the Mazarine Library, where she waited each day in vain for her prince, reading and rereading the Twain passage and praying for a miracle.

It was a year later, in June 1946, that her father lay on his deathbed and begged her to stop dreaming of a reunion that would never come.

"Please, Eva," he said between gasps of air. He was dying a slow and terrible death, his lungs deteriorating from a cancer that had crept in to take what the Germans had left behind. "You must let go of your sadness, of your hope for your Rémy, or you will never have a life of your own."

"How can I give up on him?"

"Oh, my dear Eva, he's gone." Tatuś coughed again, long and hard. "And that book he left for you is just a book. You're holding on to a ghost. That isn't what I want for you. It's not what your mother would have wanted. And I never knew him, Eva, but Rémy wouldn't have wanted that, either."

"But what if—?"

"Eva, please. You must promise me that you will come back to life."

She held his hands in hers, and as he passed from this world to the next, she leaned down and kissed him on the forehead, her teardrops falling like rain. "I promise, Tatuś."

And then she was alone in the world, as alone as she'd ever been. She buried him, and with him the hope that impossible dreams can come true. She visited the Mazarine Library just once more, on a sunny afternoon that autumn, and when she stopped at Les Deux Magots on a whim for a coffee on the way home, she found herself in an animated conversation with a book-loving Jewish tourist from America who had come to Paris to follow in the footsteps of Ernest Hemingway.

Before she could second-guess herself, Eva had offered to show the man—who introduced himself as Louis Abrams—around her city, and by the end of the second day with him, she realized she was enjoying herself. It was wonderful to practice her English, and being around someone else who respected the written word as much as she did was exhilarating.

He kissed her for the first time between the shelves of the Sainte-Geneviève Library, where she had taken a job. On the fourth day, just before he was scheduled to leave, he dropped to one knee in the Jardin des Tuileries and asked her to come to the United States with him, to be his wife. "I know we don't know each other very well, yet," he said. "But I will try for the rest of my life to make you happy."

She saw in him a man who would be her friend, a companion with the same interests who could appreciate her love of books. And in his offer of marriage, she saw the chance for a fresh start. Tatuś was right, Rémy wasn't coming back. Eva knew that she would never find peace here in France, where the shadows of all she had lost still loomed so large. And so she said yes, and a month later found herself on a ship to America bound for a new life.

And as the years went by, she did grow to love Louis, though never the way she had once loved Rémy. Some chapters must be finished, though, some books closed. And when, years later, she had a son, she knew her transformation was complete. Her child saw her only as a ghost of the person she had once been. Her family had no idea she had been a fighter for France, a forger who had saved hundreds of lives, a woman who had once loved with her whole heart.

It was better that way, she told herself. The past was in the past. But never once, in all those years, did she love Rémy any less than she had on the day she saw him last. Nor did she stop wondering about the fate of the Book of Lost Names—or whether Rémy had seen her message within its pages before he died.

Chapter Thirty-One

May 2005

The German librarian, Otto Kühn, looks just as he did in the photograph that accompanied the *New York Times* article. I like him instantly; his eyes are kind, his English nearly perfect.

"I'm so very sorry for the things the Germans did, the things we took," he says once I have introduced myself and he's leading me through the library toward his office. "And I wish to apologize profusely for the theft of this book that meant so much to you."

I want to race ahead of him, to grab the book, to open it to the page that has been mine since 1942, but I force myself to breathe, to slow down. I'll have my answer soon enough, and it might just break my heart. "Sir," I reply, "we are only responsible for the things we do—or fail to do—ourselves. You owe me no apology."

"Still," he says, "it was all a tragedy. There are so many books, Mrs. Abrams, millions of them. I won't live long enough to find their owners. And, of course, so many of the people whose books were taken have been dead for years. In so many cases, it's too late." He opens the door to his office, and suddenly my heart is racing, because there, on the center of his cluttered desk, is my book. I would know it anywhere. My heart is in my throat, making it hard to breathe, hard to speak.

"It's real," I whisper. "It's really here after all these years. The Book of Lost Names."

"Ah, yes, Nicola—our receptionist—mentioned that you had called it that." He crosses behind his desk and picks up the book. "Why? And what is the meaning of the code inside? I'm very eager to know."

I gather myself. "And I will tell you. But please, Herr Kühn, may I look at the book first? I've waited a very long time for this."

"Of course, of course, ma'am. I'm so sorry." He hands the book to me, and for a few seconds, the world seems to freeze, and I simply stare at it, feeling its warm, rich leather beneath my fingertips.

I run my thumb down the familiar gilded spine and touch the worn spot in the bottom right corner of the cover, and suddenly, the memories rush back in. I can feel Rémy's hand brushing mine over this very cover on the day I met him. I can hear his voice whispering in my ear, an echo from a long-vanished chapter. It's been more than sixty years since I last saw this book—since I last saw Rémy—but the past feels like it is here again, here in this room with me, and I choke up. Without meaning to, I raise the book to my lips and kiss it. I look up and see Kühn watching me. "I'm sorry," I say.

"Please, don't apologize. These are the moments I live for. Reuniting a book with its rightful owner can be magical."

I nod, and then slowly, carefully, my heart leaping with hope I thought I'd buried forever, I open the book and turn to the first page. *My* page. The one with the star over the *e* and the dot over the *v*, the star over the *J* and the dot over the *e. Eva Traube. I will return to you.* I stare at the unadorned words, despair sweeping over me.

There is no third star. No new message from Rémy.

I flip to the second page, Rémy's page, just in case, but it looks just as it did the last time I saw it. A star over the first *r*, a dot over the first *é*. And a star and a dot for the first two letters of *Épouse-moi.*

Marry me. I love you, I wrote in code a lifetime ago, hoping that Rémy would read the message, but now I know he didn't, and as I close the book and press it to my chest, I'm shaking. The love of my life went to his grave without knowing how I felt. It is something I can never fix, never repair, and it makes me feel suddenly as if all the things I've done in my life since then have been meaningless.

"Mrs. Abrams?" Kühn's voice breaks through my grief, and I look up to see him regarding me with concern. "Are you all right? Do you need some water, perhaps?"

I wipe away my tears, tears I have no right to cry. "No, I'm sorry. I'm fine." I shake my head, trying to rid myself of the ghosts that are suddenly here with me. It is 2005, not 1944, and I owe this kind man some answers. It's the least I can do. "Now, about that code."

He leans forward eagerly. "Yes, but take your time, ma'am. Whenever you're ready."

I draw a deep breath. "The stars and the dots are the lost names, the names of the children too young to remember, the names we had to erase so they could survive. I hoped that one day, when the war ended, I could help them to reclaim who they'd once been. But we aren't defined by the names we carry or the religion we practice, or the nation whose flag flies over our heads. I know that now. We're defined by who we are in our hearts, who we choose to be on this earth."

He listens in silence, his eyes wide, as I tell him about how I learned to be a forger, how I met Rémy and Père Clément, how we worked so hard to help people escape from the tightening clutches of the Nazis. I explain Rémy's idea of using the Fibonacci sequence to encode names so we could make sure that the war's youngest victims were never forgotten.

I tell him that after the war, years after I'd moved to America, my husband told me one day about an organization called Yad Vashem that had been founded in Jerusalem, the first Israeli memorial to victims of the Holocaust. Its title, Hebrew for *memorial and a name*, made me think of the names I'd lost along with the book, and slowly over the next few months, while Louis slept soundly beside me, I lay awake at night and made a mental list of the ones I could remember. There were over a hundred. When I finally contacted the people at Yad Vashem in the spring of 1956 with the real and false names I had been able to pull from the depths of my memory, they promised me they would try to find the children who had made it to Switzerland, in hopes that some of them might rediscover where they'd come from.

"And did they?" Kühn asks. "Did they find any of the children?"

I sigh. "I don't know. I refused to tell them my name or give them my contact information. They wanted to recognize me for what I had done, but I didn't want that. I was never a hero. I was just a young woman trying to do the right thing. In the end, though, I got it all wrong."

Kühn studies me for a minute, and when he finally speaks, his tone is gentle. "Mrs. Abrams, a very wise woman once told me that we are only responsible for the things we do—or fail to do—ourselves." That earns him a small smile, and he smiles back before going on. "And it seems to me that you spent the war trying to help innocent people."

"But I lost the people I loved most." I hesitate and whisper, "I got my mother killed. And Rémy died, too, Herr Kühn. It doesn't matter how many people I helped if I couldn't do right by them."

"You're not the one who wronged them, Mrs. Abrams."

I'm crying now, blubbering like an old fool, and then Kühn is comforting me by pulling me to his chest, and it feels just like being held—and forgiven—by Père Clément all those years ago. When I finally pull away and look up at him, he holds my gaze.

"Do you know what else this very wise person told me?" he asks. "She said that we're defined by who we are in our hearts, who we choose to be on this earth. And I believe, Mrs. Abrams, that you chose to be a hero, even if you don't see it that way." He holds out the book and says, "It's yours if you want it, ma'am, after the requisite paperwork, of course, but if you don't mind, I'd love to keep it for a few days to make a list of the names. Maybe I can help with the ones you couldn't remember all those years ago. Wouldn't that be a gift, to be able to reunite some lost children with their pasts? In fact, why don't you stay and help me?"

I look at the book and then back at Kühn. "My son is probably worrying about me. I—I left without telling him."

"So call him. Explain that you have some unfinished business to attend to."

"But . . . he knows nothing of the person I used to be."

"Then isn't it time you tell him? Maybe the first identity to recover should be your own."

I stare at the book. It holds the most important message I ever sent, though I sent it too late. And isn't that the story of my life when it comes to the people I love? I was too late when I tried to rescue my father from Drancy. Too late when I returned to Aurignon for my mother. I don't want to be too late with my son, too.

I look up at Kühn. "Might I borrow your phone?"

He beams at me. "I thought you'd never ask, Mrs. Abrams. Just hit two for an outside line, then zero-zero-one to call America."

I pick up the receiver, punch in the numbers, and then dial my son's cell phone number. I listen to it ring once, twice, and then he answers.

"Ben?" I begin.

"Mom? Where are you? I've been so worried."

"There's no need to worry about me." I exchange smiles with Kühn once more and then close my eyes, trying to see Rémy's face in my mind. "Ben, sweetheart, it's time I tell you who I really am."

Chapter Thirty-Two

N ight has fallen by the time Kühn and I make it through the first six dozen coded names in the book. After getting off the phone with an incredulous Ben, I had offered to stay, for after all, I erased these names years ago; it's only fair that I be the one to help restore them.

"Do you have a place to stay, Mrs. Abrams?" Kühn asks, leaning back in his chair. "I think we should have a bit of a rest and start fresh tomorrow. There's a hotel just down the street that sometimes hosts the library's guests; I can make a call to arrange a room for you, if you'd like."

I want to keep going, but these names have already waited more than sixty years, and I suppose they can wait another day. Frankly, I'm exhausted. "That sounds lovely, Herr Kühn. Thank you."

As he picks up the phone to call the hotel, I flip to page 308, the last page on which I drew a star. This page belongs to the girl we called Jacqueline, the little one Rémy and I helped across the Swiss border on that cold winter night so long ago, the night we made love, the night he offered me forever, the night I said no. Her real name was Eliane Meisel. I wonder what happened to her, whether her parents lived, whether she found her way home.

I've just closed my eyes, trying to see her sweet little face in my mind through the fog of time, when suddenly, Kühn and I are interrupted by a voice in the doorway. "*Entschuldigung*," says a woman's voice, and my eyes snap open. A middle-aged security guard hovers there uncertainly.

"*Guten Abend*, Mila." Kühn sets the phone down and turns to the guard. "*Wie kann ich dir behilflich sein?*"

She glances at me and then rattles off a few sentences in rapid German to Kühn, nodding once to the Book of Lost Names. I try to decipher what she's saying, but I can't follow it. Kühn replies to her quickly, then stands and turns to me as she leaves.

"What is it?" I ask.

"That was our night security guard, Mila. She says that there's a man outside the library saying the book is his, that he just flew in from the States and can't wait another minute to see it."

"My book?" I pick it up and clutch it to my chest defensively. "Well, that's impossible."

"We've had a few of these, I'm afraid," Kühn says, shaking his head. "Collectors, trying to claim books for their collections. It figures that this one would come at night, when he thinks he can strong-arm us."

"Should we call the police?"

Kühn smiles. "Mila is tougher than she looks, and so am I. For that matter, I suspect you are, too. I think we will be just fine. Let me go get rid of him. I'll be back in a moment."

"I'll come with you. If there's someone trying to steal my book, I want to look him in the eye."

He hesitates, then nods. "Let's lock the book away, shall we?"

I wait while he secures it inside his desk drawer, and as I follow him out into the darkened main room of the library, I realize I already miss it, miss the warmth of it in my hands. It still feels like a part of me, even all these years later.

Mila is standing by the front door. "He's just out there," she says as we walk up beside her. "Come on."

Kühn and I follow her outside, where a white-haired man in a light trench coat stands several steps away, his back to us as he looks out over the city.

"Herr?" Mila asks, her tone firm and steely, and the man turns slowly, the hint of a polite smile on his face.

But then his smile falls and his jaw goes slack as his eyes meet mine, and I'm as frozen as he is. I'm aware of Kühn saying something beside me, but his words sound very distant, because suddenly, the years are falling away, and I'm walking toward the man, my head spinning. I'm seeing a ghost, and though my brain tells me it's impossible, my heart knows it isn't.

"You got the library wrong, Eva," the man says in French, his voice cracking with emotion.

There are tears in my eyes now, for it's a voice I was sure I would never hear again. "*Rémy?* How can it be?"

He smiles, and then he's walking toward me, too, and there are tears streaming down his face. "We were supposed to meet on the steps of the Mazarine, Eva," he says, taking my hands in his. They're rough with age now, but somehow they fit around mine in just the same way they did a lifetime ago.

"I waited for you there," I murmur. "I waited a long time."

"I thought you were dead," he says. "I went back to Aurignon at the end of 1947. Père Clément had passed away, but a few people in the Resistance who knew who you were told me you'd been killed during the war."

I close my eyes. In the aftermath of the war, chaos, confusion, and misunderstanding had reigned. "I was told you were dead, too."

"I confronted a traitor—a gendarme named Besnard, if you remember him—and I was gravely wounded in 'forty-four. I was evacuated to England. I was in the hospital for a very long time, and then, because of a diplomatic snafu, it was 1947 before I was cleared to return to the Continent. I went to the Mazarine, Eva, for months, just in case you were alive. But you never came."

"I waited there for two years," I whisper. "I convinced myself that you were trying to leave me a message in *The Adventures of Tom Sawyer*. It's what kept me holding on."

His eyebrows go up. "You found the book? It *was* a message, Eva—I intended to fake my death if things went wrong with Besnard. I just didn't count on being laid up in the hospital, and then tangled in visa paperwork, for so long."

I wipe my cheeks, but my tears are still falling. "I thought I was crazy. I finally convinced myself I was wrong, that I was holding on to a ghost. I left for America at the end of 1946."

"America? Where?"

"Florida."

"Well, imagine that. I've lived in New Mexico since 1951." He smiles. "It turned out that Los Alamos had a place for a chemist like me after I completed my degree in England."

I shake my head in disbelief. "But what are you doing *here*, Rémy?"

"I saw the book in the *New York Times* article. I came right away." He takes a deep breath, never breaking eye contact. "I came back for the book sixty years ago, Eva, before I confronted Besnard, the day I left you the Twain book. You were gone already—I assumed you were on your way safely to Switzerland—and I was praying that you'd left me one last message. But the Nazis had already looted the library. I realized I would never know."

I stare at him. This feels like a dream, but it's not. Otto Kühn is on the steps behind me, silently watching this fairy tale unfold, and Mila has retreated to the shadows. We're in Berlin, the very heartland of our old enemy, and we've found each other again, despite the impossible odds. "I did, Rémy. I left you a message."

"You did?" He holds my gaze, his eyes warm, familiar. "What was it, my Eva?"

My Eva. After all these years, I am still his, and he is still mine. "*Épouse-moi. Je t'aime.* That's what I wrote. I—I love you, Rémy. I always have."

"I love you, too, Eva. And if the offer is still open, my answer is yes." And then he closes the final inches between us, and his lips are on mine, and I'm twenty-five again, my whole life ahead of me rather than behind, all the chapters still unwritten.

Author's Note

While researching my previous novel, *The Winemaker's Wife*, which is set in the Champagne region of France during World War II, I came across a few mentions of the important role that forgers played in the Resistance. It was something I hadn't considered before, but as I read about champagne caves and the smuggling of arms, in the back of my mind lingered images of the brave people who used their artistic ability and scientific ingenuity to produce convincing documents that allowed innocent people to survive.

By the time I finished writing *The Winemaker's Wife*, my curiosity was fully piqued, but I still wondered whether writing about forgers could be the basis for a book. Then I read *Adolfo Kaminsky: A Forger's Life* by Sarah Kaminsky and *A Good Place to Hide: How One French Community Saved Thousands of Lives During World War II* by Peter Grose—two excellent nonfiction books that explore forgery during the war—and I knew I was onto something. There was so much more to the life of a World War II forger than I had imagined.

But it still felt like something was missing—that is, until my agent, Holly Root, emailed me a *New York Times* article about the Nazi looting of books—and the fact that most major German libraries are still full of books stolen in the waning days of World War II. As I read the article, penned by art writer Milton Esterow, the final piece of the puzzle clicked into place: I could write a novel about forgery, framed by a story about a looted book that meant everything to someone. It would allow me to dive deep into the research about both forgery techniques and the fascinating history of Nazi looting and share that with you, all wrapped up in a story about love, loss, courage, and the highest stakes.

This is my fifth book about World War II, and one of my favorite things about writing about the war is that I'm able to dig deep into subjects many of us may not be familiar with. In my 2012 novel, *The Sweetness of Forgetting*, for example, part of the story revolves around Muslims helping to save Jews in Paris after the German invasion, something that many readers had never heard about. *When We Meet Again*, my novel published in 2015, talks about the more than four hundred thousand German POWs in the United States in the 1940s, a piece of our history that has slipped away with the passage of time. And in 2019, in *The Winemaker's Wife*, I wrote about the resistance that occurred beneath the earth and among the twisted vines of the picturesque Champagne region. I'm always thrilled when people tell me they've read one of my books and learned about something they'd had no idea about before. Being able to share fascinating historical facts while (hopefully) entertaining you at the same time is so very rewarding.

And that brings me to *The Book of Lost Names*. Otto Kühn, the German librarian in the story, is fictional, but the work he's doing is based in reality. In Berlin's Central and Regional Library, for example, researchers estimate that nearly a third of the 3.5 million books were stolen by the Nazis, according to the *New York Times*. Researchers such as Sebastian Finsterwalder—a real-life Otto Kühn—and Patricia Kennedy Grimsted of the Ukrainian Research Institute at Harvard University are working tirelessly to reunite looted books with their owners, but it's an uphill battle, especially now that the war is more than seventy-five years behind us. Sadly, very few of the people who owned and cherished those books are still alive today.

Incidentally, if you're interested in finding out more about looted books and the search for their rightful owners, pick up *The Book Thieves: The Nazi Looting of Europe's Libraries and the Race to Return a Literary Inheritance* by Anders Rydell, which was also very helpful in my research.

In my novel, librarian Eva travels to Berlin to reunite with the eighteenth-century tome that was stolen from her decades earlier. This story is the framework for a tale in the past that is based, in part, on the real-life stories of forgers such as Adolfo Kaminsky and Oscar Rosowsky, both of whom were young Jewish men who stumbled into forgery out of necessity—much like a young Eva does in *The Book of Lost Names*—and consequently saved thousands of innocent lives in the process. Kaminsky narrowly escaped deportation and became one of the primary document forgers for the Resistance in Paris, ultimately helping to save an estimated fourteen thousand people, though he was just a teenager at the time. Oscar Rosowsky, whose story Peter Grose tells in *A Good Place to Hide*, was just eighteen years old in 1942 when he was forced to flee his home, and by a stroke of good fortune, wound up in Le Chambon-sur-Lignon, a tiny village in the mountains of France that hid thousands of people wanted by the Nazis, including many children whose parents had been deported. Much like Eva, Rosowsky began by forging identity documents for himself and his mother—but when he found himself among like-minded people, he began to develop new forging methods that were quicker and more efficient. By war's end, he had helped rescue more than thirty-five hundred Jews.

Lest you think that all forgers were male, there were plenty of women working in forgery bureaus, too, including Mireille Philip, Jacqueline Decourdemanche, and Gabrielle Barraud in the area of Le Chambon-sur-Lignon, and Suzie and Herta Schidlof, sisters who worked in Kaminsky's Paris lab.

Many of the details that appear in *The Book of Lost Names* are based on real methods of forgery during World War II. Rosowsky, for example, often used the *Journal Officiel* to search for suitable false identities. Kaminsky, who had a chemistry background, like Rémy does in this book, stumbled upon the secret for erasing Waterman's blue ink with lactic acid. It was Gabrielle Barraud who came up with the idea for using a hand printing press to mass-produce official stamps. Rosowsky even makes a covert appearance in *The Book of Lost Names*; when Geneviève arrives in Aurignon, she mentions having worked for a man named Plunne in an area called the Plateau. Jean-Claude Plunne was, in fact, Rosowsky's alias; Geneviève is talking about working for him.

During the writing of this novel, my desk was piled high with real-life examples of the kinds of documents Eva, Rémy, and Geneviève would have relied upon and forged. I have dozens of tattered copies of the *Journal Officiel* from 1944; like the forgers in the book, I even plucked a few character names from the pages of the newspaper. I have an old French baptismal certificate from June 1940, complete with official stamps, and a German-issued *Ausweis laissez-passer* travel permit stamped in Paris in December 1940. Perhaps most important, I have the real-life, leather-bound *Epitres et Evangiles*, printed in 1732, upon which the titular Book of Lost Names is actually based. As Eva and Rémy encoded names and messages within its pages, I was using the real pages of the real book as a guide.

As an amusing side note, I was a big math buff as a child; in fact, I used to lie in bed at night and try to puzzle out unsolvable math problems. I dreamed of being famous for being the first kid to solve equations that the world's most prominent mathematicians couldn't figure out. (Admittedly, I had strange aspirations! Don't worry; a few years later, I had much more normal fantasies about marrying Donnie Wahlberg and one day being a pop star.) It was during that phase of math obsession that I learned about the Fibonacci sequence, and I fell asleep each night trying to add the numbers in my head. When I had the idea of using the sequence as part of the code in *The Book of Lost Names*, I was tickled; all those nights of lying in bed and running numbers in my head hadn't been a waste after all!

These are just a few of the real-world elements that came together to inspire *The Book of Lost Names*. If you're interested in learning more about France in the first half of the 1940s, I'd heartily recommend the aforementioned Kaminsky and Grose books. Caroline Moorehead has also written a fascinating book about Le Chambon-sur-Lignon called *Village of Secrets: Defying the Nazis in Vichy France*. I relied on some of my old favorites— including *Jews in France During World War II* (Renée Poznanski),

Résistance: Memoirs of Occupied France (Agnès Humbert), and *The Journal of Hélène Berr* to round out some of my research, too. And, of course, I lived for a time in Paris and have traveled back to France countless times for research. The town of Aurignon is fictional, but it's based on several similar towns in the area south of Vichy.

I hope you've discovered something new in *The Book of Lost Names*—and that you're reminded that you don't need money or weapons or a big platform to change the world. Sometimes, something as simple as a pen and a bit of imagination can alter the course of history.

Thanks for coming along with me on this journey—and for being a person who finds something special in books. As Eva says in *The Book of Lost Names*, those "who realize that books are magic . . . will have the brightest lives." I wish you the very brightest days ahead.

Acknowledgments

O h my goodness, what a whirlwind of a year! All I do is write the words—my incredible agent, Holly Root; my magnificent editor, Abby Zidle; my amazing publicists Michelle Podberezniak (Gallery) and Kristin Dwyer (Leo PR); and my literary miracle worker Kathie Bennett (and her husband, Roy Bennett) are the ones who do the real magic. I'm forever indebted to all of you for your friendship and your hard work on my behalf. It's a joy to be surrounded by people whom I genuinely adore so enormously. Though I don't say it often enough, please know how much I appreciate all of you. I'm truly very lucky.

To my foreign rights agent, Heather Baror-Shapiro: You are such an absolute treat to work with, and I'm so grateful to you for all you have done. Thanks, especially, for your continued guidance this year—and the great new home at Welbeck. Dana Spector, you continue to be an astonishing rock star of film rights. I'm also very glad to work with marketing specialist Danielle Noe, who is as lovely as she is talented. And to Scott Moore and Andy Cohen: We are going to make a movie together one of these days—I know it! Thanks, too, to Susan McBeth and Robin Hoklotubbe, two women who run amazing events that bring authors and readers together.

To Jen Bergstrom: I couldn't be prouder to be a Gallery Books author. It has been such an honor to be part of the Gallery family since 2012, and I am forever grateful for the way you've helped me grow as an author during that time. You run a wonderful ship, and I'm just happy to be aboard. Thank you so much for all your support and kindness. Thank you, also, to the rest of my Gallery team, including Jen Long, Sara Quaranta, Molly Gregory, Sally Marvin, Anabel Jimenez, Eliza Hanson, Lisa Litwack, Chelsea McGuckin, Nancy Tonik, Sara Waber, Ali Lacavaro, Wendy Sheanin and the rest of the incredible Simon & Schuster sales team, and, of course, Carolyn Reidy. And thanks as well to my awesome team at S&S Canada, including Catherine Whiteside, Greg Tilney, Felicia Quon, Shara Alexa, Kevin Hanson, and Nita Pronovost.

A special thank-you to a handful of people who helped out with the research for this book, including researcher and author Renée Poznanski, French translator Vincent, Polish translator Agrazneld, Russian translator Michael, German translator Jens, and of course my dear old friend Marcin Pachcinski, who swept in with Polish terms of endearment exactly when I needed them.

I mention in the dedication that this book is partially in honor of booksellers and librarians everywhere. I can't say enough about how much I've been impacted by the magic of bookstores and libraries. Books can change lives, but it is the people who love them, who dedicate their lives to them, who make the real difference. If books can't find their way to the readers who need them, who will be touched by them, who will be transformed by them, they lose their power. So thank you from the bottom of my heart to anyone who works in a bookstore or a library—and especially to those of you who have been courageous and adventurous enough to become bookstore owners, which must be as perilous at times as it is rewarding. Books are more than just words on a page; they are bridges to building communities and to developing more compassionate, more aware citizens. Those of you who love books enough to want to share them are truly changing the world.

I'd also like to acknowledge five very special writers: Linda Gerber, Alyson Noël, Allison van Diepen, Emily Wing Smith, and, especially, Wendy Toliver, the writer who brought all six of us together several years ago for the first of what would become an annual writing retreat. We write together only once a year, but that week always means a great deal to me, as does the friendship we've built over the years. I consider the five of you some of my closest friends. Being around you makes me a better writer and a better person. And to Jay Asher: Though you haven't been to the retreat in a few years, you're one of us, too! I can't wait to read the next books from all my Swan Valley friends!

The best writers also tend to be supportive of other writers, and I'm glad to be part of a community of women and men who work to build each other up. A special thank-you to "Mary Alice and the Kristies"—fellow authors Mary Alice Monroe, Kristina McMorris, and Kristy Woodson Harvey—just for being awesome human beings and the best fake bandmates and steam room sisters I could ask for.

A special thank-you to all the book bloggers and reviewers, who do such a wonderful job of building an online community—especially to Melissa Amster and the queen bee, Kristy

Barrett, both of whom went out of their way this year to help a fellow author when I asked! All of you are incredible, and I'm so grateful to you for sharing my books with readers—and for promoting reading in general.

Thanks to my whole family, especially my mom (and favorite Disney World/DVC companion), Carol; my dad, Rick; and my siblings, Karen and David, along with their families. Wanda and Mark, you are amazing in-laws: I'm so lucky. A special shout-out to Aunt Donna, Courtney, Janine, and all the Sullivans and Troubas/Lietzes, too!

To Jason (the best husband in the world) and Noah (my fun, amazing, kind son): I love the two of you more than words can say. I'm sorry that I've had to spend time away from you this year while promoting my books. I miss you every moment that I'm gone! And to Lauren Boulanger as well as Bridget, Kristy, Dayana, Rachel, Dinorah, Debbie, and Cindy: Thanks for being so wonderful with Noah. I couldn't do what I do without you. Thanks, too, to Shari Resnick for your help and generosity this year.

Finally, thanks to you, the reader, for coming on this journey with me (and yikes, for reading to the end of these long-winded acknowledgments!). I know you have a lot of books to pick from, and I am so grateful when you choose to spend some of your time with one of mine. I hope to meet more of you on the road this year.

THE
Book OF
Lost Names

KRISTIN HARMEL

This reading group guide for The Book of Lost Names *includes an introduction, discussion questions, and ideas for enhancing your book club. The suggested questions are intended to help your reading group find new and interesting angles and topics for your discussion. We hope that these ideas will enrich your conversation and increase your enjoyment of the book.*

INTRODUCTION

Eva Traube Abrams, a Florida librarian, is at the returns desk one morning when her eyes lock on to a photograph in a nearby newspaper. She freezes. It's an image of a book she hasn't seen in sixty-five years—a book she recognizes as the Book of Lost Names.

The accompanying article discusses the looting of libraries across Europe by the Nazis during World War II—an experience Eva remembers well—and the search to reunite people with the texts stolen from them so long ago. The book in the photograph, an eighteenth-century religious text thought to have been taken from France in the waning days of the war, is one of the most fascinating cases. Now housed in Berlin's Zentral- und Landesbibliothek library, it appears to contain some sort of code, but researchers don't know where it came from—or what the code means. Only Eva holds the answer—but will she have the strength to revisit old memories and help reunite those lost during the war?

As a graduate student in 1942, Eva was forced to flee Paris after the arrest of her father, a Polish Jew. Finding refuge in a small mountain town in the Free Zone, she begins forging identity documents for Jewish children fleeing to neutral Switzerland. But erasing people comes with a price, and along with a mysterious, handsome forger named Rémy, Eva decides she must find a way to preserve the real names of the children who are too young to remember who they really are. The records they keep in the Book of Lost Names will become even more vital when the Resistance cell they work for is betrayed and Rémy disappears.

TOPICS & QUESTIONS FOR DISCUSSION

1. Mamusia tells Eva, "If we shrink from them, if we lose our goodness, we let them erase us. We cannot do that, Eva. We cannot" (page 16). Compare her stance here with how she behaves in

Aurignon, after Tatuś is taken by the Germans. How does her outlook change? Rereading this and knowing that Mamusia felt this way before tragedy struck, how do your opinions of her and her reaction to Eva's work as a forger change? Do you believe Joseph when he tells Eva that Mamusia said she was proud of the work Eva did to help keep children from being erased?

2. The beginning of Eva's nightmare falls on the night her father is taken away and she is forced to watch it happen in silence. Do you think she did the right thing by keeping quiet, or should she have done more to try to save him? What do you think you would have done in this situation? What did Eva's decision reveal about her character and what she might accomplish later in the novel?

3. Eva has to risk her and her mother's safety on numerous occasions by trusting others. Discuss the many characters Eva and Mamusia trust to keep their secrets. Was any of this trust misplaced? Were there any red flags about those they should not have trusted? What does the selflessness present in so many in Aurignon say about the promise of the human capacity for goodness in times of crisis?

4. Eva watches officers walking around unbothered in Drancy and thinks, "Could they all be that evil? Or had they discovered a switch within themselves that allowed them to turn off their civility? Did they go home to their wives at night and simply flip the switches back on, become human once more?" (page 117). What do you think of her questions? In wartime, do you think those who don't fight for what is right are evil? Do you think they can become immune to atrocities? Discuss.

5. Eva and her mother react very differently to the news that Tatuś had been sent to Auschwitz. What do their reactions reveal about them as characters? Do you think there is a right way or a wrong way to react to such news? Why? Which reaction do you think would be most beneficial in helping someone get through a war?

6. Eva says, "I've always thought that it's those children—the ones who realize that books are magic—who will have the brightest lives" (page 165). How did Eva's love of books help her throughout different points in the story? Discuss with your group your favorite books as children. When did you first realize the power of books? What book made you fall in love with reading? Do you think your life would be different if you hadn't found the joy of reading?

7. Eva thinks, "Parents make all sorts of errors, because our ability to raise our children is always colored by the lives we've lived before they came along" (page 166). How do you think Eva's past has affected the way she raised her son? How do you think children of Jews who survived World War II are affected by their parents' pasts? Do you think it's possible for their parents' trauma and/or resilience to be passed down to them?

8. Mamusia feels as if Eva is abandoning her. She also tells Eva that she is being brainwashed and has forgotten who she is as she erases Jewish children's names and attends Catholic masses. Do you think Mamusia is justified in feeling betrayed by Eva? Did you feel sympathetic toward Mamusia as she is left behind in Madame Barbier's boardinghouse, or did you grow irritated by her inability to understand Eva's drive to help others? Who or what do you believe is responsible for the growing hostility in their relationship?

9. Père Clément says, "The path of life is darkest when we choose to walk it alone" (page 204). Do you agree that this statement is true in all situations? Discuss the moments in the novel when Eva decides to go it alone, and compare them to the moments when she trusts others with her secrets, her wants, and her fears. Do you think the moments she decides to work alone would have been easier if she had a partner, or do you think that would have only increased her stress? What about the moments she opens up to others—would she have been better off keeping to herself?

10. Were you surprised to find out that Joseph is the one who betrays the forgery network? Were there any warning signs? Why do you think the author decided Joseph would be the traitor? What would you have done in Joseph's position?

11. Was moving on and trying to forget Rémy the right decision for Eva, or do you believe she should have waited even longer to make sure that Rémy hadn't survived? Discuss with your group the pros and cons of each choice. Does Tatuś give Eva sound advice in telling her to start living her own life? Would you have moved to the United States with Louis even if you knew you would never love him like you did Rémy?

12. Eva believes that Rémy went to his grave not knowing how she felt about him because she told him she couldn't marry him. Do you think Rémy ever thinks that Eva has given up on him when he waits for her on the library steps and she never shows? If they had ended up finding each other before they both moved on to live separate lives, do you think they would have made it as a couple? Why or why not?

13. Eva says, "We aren't defined by the names we carry or the religion we practice, or the nation whose flag flies over our heads. I know that now. We're defined by who we are in our hearts, who we choose to be on this earth" (page 370). How would you define the main characters in the book? Do their religions or countries play into who they are as people? Do you think they can truly be separate from their backgrounds and judged only by what is in their hearts and what they choose to do?

14. Why do you think Eva keeps her past from her son? Do you think she is embarrassed or still feels guilty about anything? Do you think it is a coping mechanism and a way for her to move on? Discuss with your group.

15. In her author's note, Kristin Harmel says, "You don't need money or weapons or a big platform to change the world. Sometimes, something as simple as a pen and a bit of imagination can alter the course of history" (page 384). Discuss this as a group and share with your book club those people—either famous or not—who you believe best exemplify this sentiment.

ENHANCE YOUR BOOK CLUB

1. Buy special paper and art pens, look up photos of French identity papers from World War II, and try your hand at forgery. See if anyone in your book club would have enough talent to fool the French and German soldiers.

2. Have each member of your book club come to your meeting with books of their own that they are willing to write in. Then send each other messages—or ask each other questions—employing the Fibonacci sequence and code that Eva and Rémy used to record the birth names and fake names of the children for whom they made papers.

3. In the author's note, the author makes mention of the many books she read as research for *The Book of Lost Names*. As a group, choose one of her inspirations as your next book club pick, such as *Adolfo Kaminsky: A Forger's Life* by Sarah Kaminsky, *A Good Place to Hide* by Peter Grose, or *The Book Thieves* by Anders Rydell. Then compare the characters in your book choice with the characters in *The Book of Lost Names*.

DON'T MISS THE NEWEST NOVEL FROM
KRISTIN HARMEL

THE
Forest OF
Vanishing Stars

AVAILABLE SUMMER 2021 FROM GALLERY BOOKS!

KEEP READING FOR A SNEAK PEEK . . .

One

1922

The old woman watched from the shadows outside Behaimstrasse 72, waiting for the lights inside to blink out. The apartment's balcony dripped with crimson roses, and ivy climbed the iron rails, but the young couple who lived there—the power-hungry Siegfried Jüttner and his aloof wife, Alwine—weren't the ones who tended the plants. That was left to their maid, for the nurturing of life was something only those with some goodness could do.

The old woman had been watching the Jüttners for nearly two years now, and she knew things about them, things that were important to the task she was about to undertake.

She knew, for example, that Herr Jüttner had been one of the first men in Berlin to join the National Socialist German Workers' Party, a new political movement that was slowly gaining a foothold in the war-shattered country. She knew he'd been inspired to do so while on holiday in Munich nearly three years earlier, after seeing an angry young man named Adolf Hitler give a rousing speech in the Hofbräukeller. She knew that after hearing that speech, Herr Jüttner had walked twenty minutes back to the elegant Hotel Vier Jahreszeiten, had awoken his sleeping young wife, and had lain with her, though at first she had objected, for she had been dreaming of a young man she had once loved, a man who had died in the Great War.

The old woman knew, too, that the baby conceived on that autumn-scented Bavarian night, a girl the Jüttners had named Inge, had a birthmark in the shape of a dove on the inside of her left wrist.

She also knew that the girl's second birthday was the following day, the sixth of July, 1922. And she knew, as surely as she knew that the bell-shaped buds of lily of the valley and the twilight petals of aconite could kill a man, that the girl must not be allowed to remain with the Jüttners.

That was why she had come.

The old woman, who was called Jerusza, had always known things other people didn't. For example, she had known it the moment Frédéric Chopin had died in 1849, for she had awoken from a deep slumber, the notes of his "Revolutionary Étude" marching through her head in an aggrieved parade. She had felt the earth tremble upon the births of Marie Curie in 1867 and Albert Einstein in 1879. And on a sweltering late June day in 1914, two months after she had turned seventy-four, she had felt it deep in her jugular vein, weeks before the news reached her, that the heir to the Austro-Hungarian throne had been felled by an assassin's bullet, cracking the fragile balance of the world. She had known then that war was brewing, just as she knew it now. She could see it in the dark clouds that hulked on the horizon.

Jerusza's mother, who had killed herself with a brew of poisons in 1860, used to tell her that the knowing of impossible things was a gift from God, passed down through maternal blood of only the most fortunate Jewish women. Jerusza, the last of a bloodline that had stretched for centuries, was certain at times that it was a curse instead, but whatever it was, it had been her burden all her life to follow the voices that echoed through the forests. The leaves whispered in the trees; the flowers told tales old as time; the rivers rushed with news of places far away. If one listened closely enough, nature always spilled her secrets, which were, of course, the secrets of God. And now, it was God who had brought Jerusza here, to a fog-cloaked Berlin street corner, where she would be responsible for changing the fate of a child, and perhaps a piece of the world, too.

Jerusza had been alive for eighty-two years, nearly twice as long as the typical German lived in those days. When people looked at her— if they bothered to look at all—they were visibly startled by her wizened features, her hands gnarled by decades of hard living. Most of the time, though, strangers simply ignored her, just as Siegfried and Alwine Jüttner had done each of the hundreds of times they had passed her on the street. Her age made her particularly invisible to those who cared most about appearance and power; they assumed she was useless to them, a waste of time, a waste of space. After all, surely a woman as old as she would be dead soon. But Jerusza, who had spent her whole life sustained by the plants and herbs in the darkest spots of the deepest forests, knew that she would live nearly twenty years more, to the age of 102, and that she would die on a spring Tuesday just after the last thaw of 1942.

The Jüttners' maid, the timid daughter of a dead sailor, had gone home two hours before, and it was a few minutes past ten o'clock when the Jüttners finally turned off their lights. Jerusza exhaled. Darkness was her shield; it always had been. She squinted at the closed windows and could just make out the shape of the little girl's infant bed in the room to the right, beyond pale custard curtains. She knew exactly where it was, had been into the room many times when the family wasn't there. She had run her fingers along the pine rails, had felt the power splintering from the curves. Wood had memory, of course, and the first time Jerusza had touched the bed where the baby slept, she had been nearly overcome by a warm, white wash of light.

It was the same light that had brought her here from the forest two years earlier. She had first seen it in June 1920, shining above the treetops like a personal aurora borealis, beckoning her north. She hated the city, abhorred being in a place built by man rather than God, but she knew she had no choice. Her feet had carried her straight to Behaimstrasse 72, to bear witness as the raven-haired Frau Jüttner nursed the baby for the first time. Jerusza had seen the baby glowing, even then a light in the darkness no one knew was coming.

She didn't want a child; she never had. Perhaps that was why it had taken her so long to act. But nature makes no mistakes, and now, as the sky filled with a cloud of silent blackbirds over the twinkling city, she knew the time had come.

It was easy to climb up the ladder of the modern building's fire escape, easier still to push open the Jüttners' unlatched window and slip quietly inside. The child was awake, silently watching, her extraordinary eyes—one twilight blue and one forest green—glimmering in the darkness. Her hair was black as night, her lips the startling red of corn poppies.

"*Ikh bin gekimen dikh tsu nemen,*" Jerusza whispered in Yiddish, a language the girl would not yet know. *I have come for you.* She was startled to realize that her heart was racing.

She didn't expect a reply, but the child's lips parted, and she reached out her left hand, palm upturned, the dove-shaped birthmark shimmering in the darkness. She said something soft, something that a lesser person would have dismissed as the meaningless babble of a little girl, but to Jerusza, it was unmistakable. "*Dus zent ir,*" said the girl in Yiddish. *It is you.*

"*Yo, dus bin ikh,*" Jerusza agreed. And with that, she picked up the baby, who didn't cry out, and, tucking her close against the brittle curves of her body, climbed out the window and shimmied down the iron rail, her feet hitting the sidewalk without a sound.

From the folds of Jerusza's cloak, the baby watched soundlessly, her mismatched ocean eyes round, as Berlin vanished behind them and the forest to the north swallowed them whole.

1928

The girl from Berlin was eight years old when Jerusza first taught her how to kill a man.

Of course Jerusza had discarded the child's given name as soon as they'd reached the crisp edge of the woods six years earlier. Inge meant "the daughter of a heroic father," and that was a lie. The child had no parent now but the forest itself.

Furthermore, Jerusza had known, from the moment she first saw the light over Berlin, that the child was to be called Yona, which meant "dove" in Hebrew. She had known it even before she saw the girl's birthmark, which hadn't faded with time but had grown stronger, darker, a sign that this child was special, that she was fated for something great.

The right name was vital, and the old woman couldn't call Yona anything other than what she was. She expected the same in return, of course, a respect for one's true identity. Jerusza meant "owned inheritance"—a reference to the magic she had received from her own bloodline, and a tribute to being owned by the forest itself—and it was the only thing she allowed Yona to call her. "Mother" meant something different, something that Jerusza never would be, never wanted to be.

"There are hundreds of ways to take a life," Jerusza told the girl on a fading July afternoon soon after the child's eighth birthday. "And you must know them all."

Yona looked up from whittling a tiny wren from a piece of wood. She had taken to carving creatures for company, which Jerusza did not understand, for she herself valued solitude above all else, but it seemed a harmless enough pursuit. Yona's hair, the color of the deepest starless night, tumbled down her back, rolling over birdlike shoulders. Her eyes—endless and unsettling—were misty with confusion. The sun was low in the sky, and her shadow stretched behind her all the way to the edge of the clearing, as if trying to escape into the trees.

"But you've always told me that life is precious, that it is God's gift to man, that it must be protected," the girl said.

"Yes. But the most important life to protect is your own." Jerusza flattened her palm and sliced the edge of her hand across her own windpipe. "If someone comes for you, a hard blow here, if delivered correctly, can be fatal."

Yona blinked a few times, her long lashes dusting her cheeks, which were preternaturally pale, always pale, though the sun beat down on them relentlessly. As she set the wooden wren on the ground beside her, her hands shook. "But who would come for me?"

Jerusza stared at the child with disgust. Her head was in the clouds, despite Jerusza's teachings. "You foolish child!" she snapped. The girl shrank away from her. It was good that the girl was afraid; terrible things were coming. "Your question is the wrong one, as usual. There will come a day when you'll be glad I have taught you what I know."

It wasn't an answer, but the girl wouldn't cross her. Jerusza was strong as a mountain chamois, clever as a hooded crow, vindictive as a magpie. She had been on the earth for nearly nine decades now, and she knew the girl was frightened by her age and her wisdom. Jerusza liked it that way; the child should be clear that Jerusza was not a mother. She was a teacher, nothing more.

"But, Jerusza, I don't know if I could take a life," Yona said at last, her voice small. "How would I live with myself?"

Jerusza snorted. It was hard to believe the girl could still be so naive. "I've killed five men and a woman, child. And I live with myself just fine."

Yona's eyes widened, but she didn't speak again until the light had faded from the sky and the day's lessons had ended. "Who did you kill, Jerusza?" she whispered in the darkness as they lay on their backs on the forest floor beneath a roof of spruce bark they'd built themselves just the week before. They moved every month or two, building a new hut from the gifts the forest gave them, always leaving a crack in their hastily hewn bark ceilings to see the stars when there was no threat of rain. Tonight, the heavens were clear, and Jerusza could see the Little Dipper, the Big Dipper, and Draco, the dragon, crawling across the sky. Life changed all the time, but the stars were ever constant.

"A farmer, two soldiers, a blacksmith, and the woman who murdered my father," Jerusza replied without looking at Yona. "All would have killed me themselves if I'd given them a chance. You must never give someone that opportunity, Yona. Forget that lesson, and you will die. Now get some rest."

By the next full moon, Yona knew that a kick just to the right of the base of the spine could puncture a kidney. A horizontal blow with the edge of the hand to the bridge of the nose could crush the facial bones deep into the skull, causing a brain hemorrhage. A hard toe kick to the temple, once a man was down, could swiftly end a life. A quick headlock behind a seated man, combined with a sharp backward jerk, could snap a neck. A knife sliced upward, from wrist to inner elbow along the radial artery, could drain a man of his blood in minutes.

But the universe was about balance, and so for each method of death, Yona taught the girl a way to dispense healing, too. Bilberries could restore circulation to a failing heart or resuscitate a dying kidney. Catswort, when ground into a paste, could stop bleeding. Burdock root could remove poison from the bloodstream. Crushed elderberries could bring down a deadly fever.

Life and death. Death and life. Two things that mattered little, for in the end, souls outlived the body and became one with an infinite God. But Yona didn't understand that, not yet. She didn't yet know that she had been born for the sake of repairing the world, for the sake of *tikkun olam*, and that each *mitzvah* she was called to perform would lift up divine sparks of light.

If only the forest alone could sustain them, but as the girl grew, she needed clothing, milk to strengthen her bones, shoes so her feet weren't shredded by the forest floor in the summer or frozen to death in the winter. When Yona was young, Jerusza sometimes left her alone in the woods for a day and a night, scaring her into staying put with tales of werewolves that ate little girls, while she ventured alone into nearby towns to take the things they needed. But as the girl began to ask more questions, there was no choice but to begin taking her along, to show her the perils of the outside world, to remind her that no one could be trusted.

It was a cold winter's night in 1931, snow drifting down from a black sky, when Jerusza pulled the wide-eyed child into a town called Grajewo in northeastern Poland. And though Jerusza had explicitly told her to remain silent, Yona couldn't seem to keep her words in. As they crept through the darkness toward a farmhouse, the girl peppered her with questions: *What is that roof made of? Why do the horses sleep in a barn and not in a field? How did they make these roads? What is that on the flag?*

Finally, Jerusza whirled on her. "Enough, child! There is nothing here for you, nothing but despair and danger! Yearning for a life you don't understand is like staring at the sun; your foolishness will destroy you."

Yona was startled into silence for a time, but after Jerusza had slipped through the back door of the house and reemerged carrying a pair of boots, trousers, and a wool coat that would see Yona through at least a few winters, Yona refused to follow when Jerusza beckoned.

"What is it now?" Jerusza demanded, irritated.

"What are they doing?" Yona pointed through the window of the farmhouse, to where the family was gathered around a table. It was the first night of Hanukkah, and this family was Jewish; it was why Jerusza had chosen this house, for she knew they would be occupied while she took their things. Now the father of the family stood, his face illuminated by the candle burning on the family's menorah, and though his voice was inaudible, it was clear he was singing, his eyes closed. Jerusza didn't like the look in Yona's expression as she watched; it was one of longing and enchantment, and those types of feelings led only to ill-conceived ideas of flight.

"The practice of dullards," she said finally. "Nothing there for you. Come now."

Yona still wouldn't budge. "But they look happy. They are celebrating Hanukkah?"

Of course the girl already knew they were. Jerusza carved a menorah each year from wood, simply because her mother had commanded it years before. Hanukkah wasn't among the most important Jewish holidays, but it celebrated survival, and that was something anyone who lived in the woods could respect. Still, the girl was being foolish. Jerusza narrowed her eyes. "They are repeating words that have likely lost all meaning for them, Yona. Repetition is for people who don't want to think for themselves, people who have no imagination. How can you find God in moments that have become rote?"

Neither of them said anything for a moment. "But what if in the repetition, they find comfort?" Yona eventually asked, her voice small. "What if they find magic?"

"How on earth would repetition be magic?" They still needed

to procure a few jugs of milk from the barn, and Jerusza was losing patience.

"Well, God makes the same trees come alive each year, doesn't he?" Yona said slowly. "He makes the same seasons come and go, the same flowers bloom, the same birds call. And there's magic in that, isn't there?"

Jerusza was stunned into silence. The girl had not bested her at her own game before. "*Never* question me," she snapped at last. "Now, shut up and come along."

It was inevitable that Yona would begin wondering about the world outside the woods. Jerusza had always known the time would come, and now it was heavy upon her to ensure that when the girl thought of civilization, she regarded it with the proper fear.

Jerusza had been teaching Yona all the languages she knew since she had taken her, and the child could speak fluent Yiddish, Polish, Belarusian, Russian, and German, as well as snippets of French and English. *One must know the words of one's enemies*, Jerusza always told her, and she was gratified by the fear she could see in Yona's eyes.

But she had more to teach, so on their forays into towns, she began to steal books, too. She taught the child to read, to understand science, to work with numbers. She insisted that Yona know the Torah and the Talmud, but she also brought her the Christian Bible and even the Muslim Quran, for God was everywhere, and the search for him was endless. It had consumed Jerusza's whole life, and it had brought her to that dark street corner in Berlin in the summer of 1922, where she'd been compelled to steal this child, who had become such a thorn in her side.

And though Yona irritated her more often than not, even Jerusza had to admit that the girl was bright, sensitive, intuitive. She drank the books down like cool water and listened with rapt attention whenever Jerusza deigned to impart her secrets. By the time Yona was fourteen, she knew more about the world than most men who'd been educated in universities. More important, she knew the mysteries of the forest, all the ways to survive.

As the girl's eyes opened to the world, though, Jerusza insisted upon only two things: One, Yona must always obey her. And two, she must always stay hidden in the forest, away from those who might hurt her.

Sometimes Yona asked why. Who would want to hurt her? What would they try to do?

But Jerusza never answered, for the truth was, she wasn't sure. She knew only that in the early-morning hours of July 6, 1922, as she hurried with a two-year-old child into the forest, she heard a voice from the sky, sharp and clear. *One day,* the voice said, *if she is not careful, her past will return—and it will cost her everything. The only safe place is the forest.*

It was the same voice that had told her to take the girl in the first place, the voice that had always whispered to Jerusza in the trees. Jerusza had spent most of her life thinking the voice belonged to God. But now, in the twilight of her life, she was no longer sure. What if the voice in her head belonged to her alone? What if it was the legacy of her mother's madness, a spark of insanity rather than a higher calling?

But each time those questions bubbled to the surface, Jerusza pushed them away. The voice from above had spoken, and who knew what fate awaited her if she failed to listen.